# Warm praise for THE FANCHER TRAIN:

"A fine first novel. She has combined thorough research with a sturdy narrative."

*The New York Times Book Review*

"It is obvious that the author has looked well and widely into her sources. . . . An excellent fictional account of the appalling Mountain Meadows massacre."

*The Chicago Sunday Tribune*

"Suspenseful . . . vivid . . . A first-rate historical novel of authentic Western life."

*Library Journal*

# THE FANCHER TRAIN

AMELIA
BEAN

ace books
A Division of Charter Communications Inc.
A GROSSET & DUNLAP COMPANY
360 Park Avenue South
New York, New York 10010

THE FANCHER TRAIN



An ACE Book

Published simultaneously in Canada

Printed in U.S.A.

2 4 6 8 0 9 7 5 3 1
Manufactured in the United States of America

To my husband
WILLIAM E. BEAN
with love and thanks—his name, too
should be on the front cover.

## ACKNOWLEDGMENT

I wish to express my deepest gratitude to my husband and son for their patience and continuous affectionate humor; also to my friends for their loyalty during my erratic periods.

My sincerest thanks to friends and neighbors, who asked to remain unnamed, for allowing me to read old family journals. Specifically, I would like to thank my friend, Mrs. Blanche Mace, Kanab Librarian, for her deep interest and unstinting help; also Dr. Phillip G. Fulstowe of Kanab, Utah, and Mr. John Neill Northe of Oklahoma City, Oklahoma.

I would like to acknowledge a definite moment of inspiration which was given me, unknowingly, in a few words voiced by the late Walter S. Campbell of the University of Oklahoma. It was only after I thought them over that I discovered the courage to attempt the writing of a novel.

But in these cases
We still have judgment here; that we but teach
Bloody instructions, which, being taught, return
To plague the inventor: this even handed justice
Commends the ingredients of our poison'd chalice
To our own lips.

—Act I, Scene 7, Shakespeare's MACBETH

# PROLOGUE

It was late afternoon and very hot in the small settlement of Haun's Mill. Women cooked supper in their kitchens and some of the men, their day's work done, had gathered at the blacksmith shop and were engaged in gloomy conversation. There were new arrivals in the settlement—converts headed for the Prophet's headquarters in Far West—and they had camped in tents and their wagons under the trees. Men listened with alarm to the tidings of strife between the Mormons and the Gentile Missourians.

There was trouble in the border state of Missouri that fall of 1838, trouble which had its beginnings in earlier quarrels dating back nearly six years, when the self-styled Latter-Day Saints first showed up in the area. The Missourians came to resent the "Chosen People" assumptions of the Mormons and there had been violence almost from the start. As the followers of the new religion continued to swarm into the state, resentments magnified into hatred and Governor Boggs, alarmed that the balance of voting power was swiftly passing to the Mormon Prophet, Joseph Smith, withheld from the Mormons the protection of such feeble law as there was in the area. Unrestrained and unpunished mobs of hoodlums raided the small settlements and outlying farms of the Saints, flogging, tarring and feathering, raping and killing. There had been savage reprisals from the Mormons, which led to further brutal incidents.

The newcomers listened to these tales with horror. In

these peaceful surroundings such things were almost impossible to believe. The sun sank in a calm red glow toward the hills, the smoke from the cooking fires drifted lazily heavenward; a young man shocked corn in a hillside patch, his movements deliberate and easy; some little girls played hopscotch in a dooryard and a boy romped with his puppy on the bank of the stream which powered the slowly turning mill wheel.

A single gunshot broke the quiet. Suddenly a horde of mounted men, firing guns, burst from the trees across the creek, splashed across its narrow channel and thundered into the village. One minute there had been the everyday quiet of the waning afternoon—the next, out from the trees edging the prairie came violence and death.

The boy with the puppy was the first victim. Even as he faced about, the horsemen were upon him. The blasting roar of a shotgun ripped into his thin body, flung him aside like a red-dyed heap of rags.

People were running wildly. Women desperately herded children before them to the shelter of the wooded hillsides; men scattered like a covey of startled quail—some seeking guns, others trying to reach their families. Those at the blacksmith shop were cut off; they fled inside the building, closed the heavy doors. But the mobbers urged their horses up to the walls and poured round after round of shot between the unchinked logs. The screams of those inside sounded like the cries of trapped and wounded animals.

The young man in the hillside corn patch ran toward his house when the shooting started. His wife came from the back door, running awkwardly, both hands holding her heavy belly; she was with child and her time was near. She saw him coming toward her in leaping strides and called out in terror, "Josh—Josh——"

Then a man on a plunging horse, a big man with a red beard, lifted his heavy revolver. The running woman fell as the flat report sounded, and as she went down Josh saw a red stain like the sudden daub of a paintbrush on her back. The deep roar of a maddened beast rose in his throat, he headed like a charging bull for the redbeard on the horse. There was another shot and a searing blow in his right leg brought the running man down midstride, floundering like a headless chicken in the dust. Half blinded, he rose, fighting to force his leg to bear his weight. He felt rather than saw the approach of the big horse as its rider drove it savagely at him. The animal's shoulder struck him, broke his nose with a blinding crunching blow, hoofs punished his body as the horse plungingly, unwillingly, rode him down. His mouth filled with blood, his eyes were blind as he reared up on his knees, arms outstretched, his big hands were claws fiercely seeking to find his enemy—to find and hold and kill.

For one crazed moment his nearly blinded eyes saw the big form—a red beard, and the beefy hands that reached for him had thick red hair on their backs and there was the gleam of a knife blade. Josh dimly realized the thudding blow of the knife but he felt nothing as his body lay in the dust, nor when the redbeard knelt astride him and cursingly sought to wrench out the deep-driven knife. Even though the wrenching brought the whole limp weight from the ground, the knife remained clutched in the bony vise of the broad chest.

It was black dark before the survivors dared leave their hiding places. The men who crept into the blacksmith shop lit a hooded lantern, and then, of those who looked fully, some went outside to vomit.

The bodies seemed but heaps of limbs and torn parts streaked by dark rivers which flowed to meet in turgid pools on the dirt floor. The smell was like a slaughter yard. A young boy lay with his head blown away and spattered on the anvil behind him. There were twelve dead but some yet lived and they were more terrible than the dead. Two of them died even as they sought a way to help them.

The survivors, knowing they were too few to protect themselves, knew they must flee to the protection of a larger settlement. They dared not take time to dig graves and yet they could not simply walk away from the bodies of their loved ones. Pitifully, they lowered the mangled bodies into a deep, dry well. The wounded were carried into the unlighted houses. Men had gone down fighting at their front gates, on their porches, buying with their lives the brief seconds which enabled their women and children to run to the thick brush on the hillsides.

Grandpa McBride, nearly blind with age, lay dead across his Revolutionary War rifle. The old man had tottered to the roadside, rifle at the ready, straining to see the enemy. They had cut him down with a shotgun blast. Enraged at his show of resistance, a mobber had hacked his body to bloody ribbons with a corn cutter which lay near him. But he'd protected Grandma McBride to his last breath and she yet lived. She lay where she had fallen in a faint inside the door of their home, a long horse pistol in her withered hands. She'd been on her way to help him, as always.

Tall William Leany, man-size but not yet a man in years, sobbed aloud as he gathered up the limp body of his little brother from the creek bank. When they lifted Josh Wade they were horrified to find that he still breathed, horrified because he had lain in a lake of blood and no one could remove the knife from his chest. They put him in the wagon with the wounded but none thought he would live through the night.

The survivors of the massacre fled Haun's Mill as dawn streaked the sky. The small train of wagons with their dreadful burdens plodded the hot weary miles to Far West unmolested. When they reached the doubtful security of that beleaguered town they were met with the news that an enormous mob armed itself to attack the Prophet's stronghold.

People came running to meet them. The Prophet Joseph strode urgently from wagon to wagon, grasping hands, listening to the stumbling terrible words. He gazed piteously on the dead, laid his hands in blessing on the near dead, and prayed for their lives. Tears ran unchecked down his face.

Joseph Smith's hallowed head with its golden aureole of waving hair was bowed low. The broad shoulders bent beneath the burden of his grief and horror. Porter Rockwell, the Prophet's bodyguard, black-bearded face grim, hulked darkly at his heels.

It was Rockwell's strong arms that lifted and carried many of the wounded into the houses. He shook his head in astonishment that the young man with the knife still buried in his chest yet lived, and placed him gently on a kitchen table for the harried doctor's examination. But the doctor could not remove the knife. Rockwell left the house swiftly, returned with the blacksmith's heavy pincers.

The doctor's face settled painfully as he looked at the pincers in Rockwell's huge fist. He looked up into the brooding, bearded face and nodded reluctantly. "He's a goner for sure," he said wearily, 'if that knife don't come out soon—and he's like to bleed to death, once it's out——"

"He made it till Joseph could bless him," Rockwell's deep voice growled insistently, "likely he'll live." He moved to the table, not looking at the corpselike face, and bent his shaggy head to the task. Focusing his gaze on the haft of the knife, he set the pincers firmly below its brass guard. He placed one huge paw spread wide on the bare blood-streaked chest, the other fist clenched the handles of the pincers. With one hand he bore down with all his weight, with the other he wrenched upward, the thick sinews of his wrist knotting with strain. There was a grinding rasp, the knife was dragged free. A fountain of black blood leaped and spread in a torrent. The doctor and the women worked feverishly with pads and bandages.

Rockwell stood back and removed the knife from the pincer claws, wiped the blood from the blade across his broad thigh, and stared at it curiously. It was a handsome knife, double-edged, with a heavy brass guard which now bore small scars from the pincers. The staghorn handle had been carved along the slightly curving grain; small leaves had been fashioned, giving the appearance of a vine which ran the length of the haft. Silver had been poured into the indented leaves and had been kept untarnished and shiny by constant polishing—the owner had taken pride to keep it gleaming. Rockwell slid the knife into his belt and quietly left the house.

The gaping chest wound padded and tightly bandaged, the doctor turned his attention to the leg. It no longer bled, it had clotted; it was a flesh wound, no bones had been splintered. Josh breathed with bubbling faintness. The doctor's eyes were gravely doubtful as he looked at the bruised, misshapen face. "I don't know why he's alive," he said wearily, "only that he's young—and strong as a bull."

Josh Wade lived. Stubbornly his strong young body clung to life, began to heal of its terrible damage. Unwillingly he submitted to existence, for when they told him that his wife lay with the other dead in the well at Haun's Mill he cared little whether he lived or died.

Rockwell had stopped often to see how the boy did and on the day that Josh was able to be propped up in bed he came in to visit with him. The huge bearded man gave him the silver-trimmed knife, in terse words told its savage story. Josh stared at the handsome weapon where it lay across his big palm, the muscles in his bony jaw twitched. "It'll shed no more Mormon blood," he said low, "but likely it'll relish a taste of Gentile meat—"

Rockwell's intent eyes studied the ruined, strangely young-old face with its gaunt cheek planes haggard on either side of the smashed, jutting nose, noted the grim slant of the bitter mouth, and he nodded as at an expected thing. "There's gonna be more trouble," he said softly, "the damned Gentiles are cookin' more devilment. They ain't gonna settle short of runnin' us clean outa Missouri." His eyes studied the knife, raised, and fastened on the bleak face again. "It'd be a proper knife—for a Danite to carry—"

Josh's head lifted, he met the questioning stare of the Prophet's bodyguard. The look that passed between them was long and held much of significance; words were not needed. For Josh knew, as did all the Mormons, of the existence of the Danites, a secretly organized group of fighting men who performed missions of vengeance, reprisals against the enemies of their Church.

"I'd like that right well," Josh said, "to get in a few licks of my own."

Rockwell's shaggy head nodded, well satisfied with this recruit. "I got my eye on a good horse for you—soon's you're able to ride. We'n use ever man that'll stand and fight. Too many of the peoplo ain't—well, they ain't fitted for that kind of thing—"

Rockwell's words were prophetic, for the bloody persecutions continued—as did the fighting back. But among the Mormons there were far too few fitted for the dangerous work of the Danites, most of whom were just such men as Josh Wade—men who had known bitter loss at the hands of the Missourians and had nothing further to lose.

The situation simmered and boiled and Missouri was in a state of almost civil war. Governor Boggs took a firm stand against the Mormon Saints and issued an order: "The Mormons must be treated as enemies and must be exterminated or driven from the state if necessary for public peace."

The Mormon hordes found sanctuary in the neighboring state of Illinois. They had learned many a hard lesson but not the one which would have saved them—for they took the nest eggs of their trouble with them and inevitably disaster hatched once more.

From the day that he could sit a saddle Josh Wade rode with Porter Rockwell, known to many as the Destroying Angel. The legends that were whispered about the silent, terrible figure of Rockwell came to include his constant companion, Josh Wade. Rumor, speculation, and fact laid many savage deeds of reprisal to their credit—or blame. And but for the gentleness of the staying hand of the Prophet, all of them would have been true. For Rockwell loved and revered Joseph Smith and his slightest word was law to the fanatically religious killer. When the Prophet and his brother were murdered by the mob in Carthage, Illinois, while in the supposed safe custody of the law, Rockwell almost lost his mind in grief and then, frenzied by hate and desire for vengeance, he carved a bloody trail of reprisal.

Rockwell and his men learned a grim lesson from the Prophet's death. When the mantle of leadership descended about the sturdy shoulders of Brigham Young they guarded his life with a ring of cold steel that was never penetrated. Never again were they—or any of the persecuted Mormons—to trust the officials of Gentile law. The law, also, had assumed for them the face of the enemy and the label "Gentile" were synonymous and came largely to include anyone not of their faith.

As the situation in Illinois became desperate, Brigham Young turned his thoughts toward a sanctuary in the western wilderness. Joseph Smith had prophesied that his people would found a kingdom in the Rocky Mountains and Brigham Young passionately longed to escape the bondage of an unfriendly government, to be free of all law not his own. They prepared for this monumental trek.

But, even as Brigham led his first caravans west in the spring of 1847, it was already too late—they could not achieve isolation. In July 1846 the American flag had been raised in Monterey, California, and the close of the Mexican War saw further western territory ceded by Mexico.

The Mormons settled in the grim desert valleys of the Great Basin and for a time pursued a way of life unhindered by Gentiles. But, astute though Brigham Young was, he could not guess that his Mormon settlements were to become almost a crossroads for a mighty migration.

Gold was discovered at Sutter's Fort, and by the end of 1849 there were a hundred thousand people in California—over eighty thousand of these were gold-rush arrivals and more than half of this number took the overland trail which passed through the Mormon kingdom.

When the federal government, in 1851, sent representatives into the Territory of Deseret they were powerless to govern, because Brigham Young retained the reins of his kingdom in his strong, square hands and flatly refused to cede even the smallest authority. These officials returned to the nation's capital, frothing over their failures and bitterly spreading stories of lawlessness and immorality among the Mormons.

Rumors of polygamy had existed since the Missouri-Illinois days, but in 1852 the country was shocked and revolted when Brigham Young and his council publicly announced to the world that Joseph Smith's revelation concerning the Doctrine of Celestial Marriage was an integral part of their religion. The ensuing disgust and horror which followed made the very name of "Mormon" an ugly brand—and the feverish detestation intensified the strife which followed.

Brigham Young continued to resist what he considered the intrusions of the federal government until his blunt rejections magnified into an aspect of lawlessness and sedition. In the spring of 1857 President Buchanan decreed that the Mormons were in a state of insurrection and dispatched troops over the emigrant trail from Fort Leavenworth to deal with it.

Tidings of the approaching army—and its purpose—shocked and then angered the Mormons. They could only—in view of the bloody histories of Missouri and Illinois—anticipate extermination at the hands of an army sent by an hostile government. But they had had ten years in which to recover, build their strength. Brigham's sprawling empire now numbered over forty thousand people, and to a man they were dedicated to the decision not to be driven out, they would flee no further. They prepared for war.

# CHAPTER I

Melissa had got a look at the long-legged scout when Captain Fancher and John Barker were making a deal with him at Fort Laramie.

Laramie, so longed for, so beautiful that first glimpse! It was built of dried brick and shining white 'dobe and set in a rich coolness of tall, green trees and deep grass with the cool-looking river winding along beside it. It was a big fort. The walls were maybe fifteen, sixteen feet high, with bastions at each corner. And fitted with enormous, cautious double gates. Small windows peered darkly from high in the walls, really only slits to shoot out of.

So beautiful to look on, so welcome to reach. But as they approached the fort they became conscious of a heavily persistent stink on the afternoon wind. Melissa thought the wagon train had got to smelling something awful but this was thicker somehow. At least they packed up and moved on every day, leaving some of their filth behind for the wind and dust to decently smother.

"My good land alive," exclaimed Annie Fancher, covering her nose with her handkerchief. She and Melissa and Cintha Tackett had walked up to the fort trading post from where they had camped outside. Cintha carried her least one, Jeremy, just two months old and born since they left Arkansas.

"You'd best cover that youngun's face 'fore he chokes, Cinthy," Annie admonished, "I never in all creation smelt such a stink!"

There seemed to be more Indians than whites in and around the crowded fort. Blanketed, most of them, in spite of the stifling heat. Standing, sitting in the shade, sleeping underfoot, or just milling slowly, poker-faced, in the big trading room, their obsidian eyes not missing a thing. You couldn't blame the Injuns for all the stink, thought Melissa disgustedly as they made their way through the crowd. The white ones they passed didn't smell one bit better.

They hadn't come to buy, more to look, and it was a good thing, for prices were sky high. Flour forty-two dollars a weevily barrel and sugar and coffee out of sight. Good thing the Fancher Party was well supplied already. But the Missouri bunch that had joined on with the train at Independence weren't so well off. Some of them were arguing price loudly with the indifferent trader—who told them to go to hell, he didn't give a tinker's damn whether they bought or not. He was getting short anyway.

The women hastily quit the fort and—relief in their noses—strolled back toward camp. They met David, Melissa's brother, leaving a group of men squatting on their heels in the shade of some tall trees.

David told them, pointing, that the big, old guy with the gray-streaked hair was Jim Bridger, the famous scout. Captain Fancher had hoped to hire him on as guide because their scout had up and quit the minute they sighted Laramie. But Bridger wasn't to be had, he had a deal making with the army. They'd heard rumors about that—an army was fixing to set out for the Utah Basin. Trouble with Brigham Young and his Mormons again. The President was getting sick and tired of having his federal officials run out of Utah Territory so he was sending an army to make it stick—and old Squaw-Killer Harney in command. Likely he'd settle their hash fast enough—meanest old bastard that ever wiped out an Indian town, kids and all. General Harney just didn't like live Indians. The word was out he wasn't overly fond of Mormons, either. Seemed that the Mormons had run Jim Bridger out of his fort someplace way out there in the mountains and old Jim was raring to go back with the army. Sounded like the Mormons had bit off more than they could chew, as usual.

So the Fancher Train couldn't get Bridger, but he'd recommended a man and they'd made a deal with him. Looked to be all right and Bridger had vouched for him.

Melissa, for one, was glad they were shut of that other scout. Stinking dirty, he'd been, and so hairy-bearded he looked more like a hulking animal than a man. This one wore old, fringed buckskins, too, and buckskin always looked greasy, but he was not bearded and he looked cleaner. David said you didn't have to stand upwind to talk to him.

They camped near Laramie for three days, resting the live stock and refitting. Kept the blacksmith's forge smoking night and day. They'd been so anxious to get to Laramie and rest that it came as a surprise how relieved they were to get under way again. It had got to be like home, someway, being on the move.

A relief to be wheeling past the bottoms where the tepees were pitched with their swarms of yelling kids and packs of yelping curs—and the constant threat of Injun sneak-thieving that had to be guarded against day and night.

Beyond Laramie the dark slopes of the Black Hills, dotted with pine and cedar, climbed toward rearing Laramie Peak. The train shook itself down and contentedly got in the trail groove again as they passed slowly along the base of the peak.

Melissa saw that David had taken a liking to the new scout right off. Jed Smith, his name was. He didn't hang around the train much. Rode ahead of it daytimes, and slept out and away from it nights. Never talked much except to Captain Charley Fancher and his second-in-command, John Barker. Smith seemed to look away from —past—the women. Not with respect, more like aversion, maybe. Melissa had become very conscious, on the woman-shy frontier, of male stares turning to follow her.

The scout's glance that slid right past a body without taking them in at all sort of riled her a little.

There was a lithe leanness to him, this indifferent Jed Smith. He was tall, his head rose above most of those about him. Wear-darkened buckskins fitted the long frame snugly. His hair was dark, worn long, tied on his brown neck with a narrow strip of doeskin. Under the battered brim of the flat-crowned hat his narrow forehead was high, the jutting, triangle-shaped nose was blade thin. There was that about the slight flaring of the nostrils to put one in mind of a stallion, high-strung and restless—controlled but maybe mean. Neither old nor young was the face with its long-drawn lines running down to the thin-lipped, firm mouth. Dark stubble on the chin did not blur the outline of its stubborn set. It was a watching face; the indifferent eyes, set in deep sun-squint lines, took in much—but offered nothing.

Only once had Melissa seen the withdrawn eyes show any interest. It had been when she was leading Lady Jane to the watering place.

Jane, as usual, was acting the fool. Dancing and sidewinding in high-gaited curvets, deliberately shying at every blowing leaf and barking dog; her delicate nostrils flared with aristocratic disgust at the noise and dust and crowding heavy odors that hung over the train.

Jed's casual glance, as he lounged while his own horse drank, slid, as usual, past Melissa. But his eyes lit with pleasure as he took in the long clean lines of the sorrel mare.

I might as well be a stump, Melissa thought indignantly as she watched his horseman's knowing gaze sweep from Jane's high-plumed tail over her sleek haunches to the deep chest and straight slender legs with their nervous, dainty-stepping hoofs. Great heart and pride, a host of blooded ancestors, all were evident in the perfect, shining lines of the spirited animal. The dark eyes were wide-set, intelligent; the pointed ears ever alertly erect, busy.

Jed's arm, across the shoulder of his dusty roan, absently stroked the rough coat, but in his mind he caressed the proudly arched neck and satin coat of the sorrel. Not that he'd have traded, straight across, for the thoroughbred—nor ten like her. Palouse was something special. A horse that happened to a man once in a lifetime, if he was lucky. Not beautiful by ordinary standards, unless you had the horse sense to see the way he was: built for a purpose, was Palouse, and without the trimmings. He was a roan, red-dust colored, his hindquarters seeming to wear a lighter blanket splotched with rusty brown stains. His faded brown mane and tail were wispily meager. Stockily built, deep-chested with well-sprung legs, plenty of bottom for wind, his straight muscled legs looked especially short below the knees. A man might almost think him deformed, so heavy he was in the forearm. Till he saw him take to a rocky slope like a mountain goat. The muscles in his shoulders, sides, and rump were deep-running curves of tight compactness. The thick neck showed he'd been cut late, and proud, the spirit was still all there, unbroken.

You couldn't rightly evaluate this horse without taking into account the big, straight head with its short, pricked ears and the eyes set deep alongside the wide, bony forehead. They were bold eyes, ringed narrowly with white. Bold, but not wild nor crazy, and uncomfortably cognizant. More than one knucklehead had sheared off from trying to handle Palouse when that big head swung around and there was that personlike awareness in those odd eyes.

Palouse looked mean, and he could be. Injun-trained, he was, to run a man down and tromp him as he passed over. To rear and strike with those hard-grained hoofs that could crush a skull, be it man or beast. Trained, too, in other, gentler ways. Never had Palouse felt the cold steel of a bit in his sensitive mouth. A nose-wrap, soft halter was what he wore and he didn't really need that, for he'd obey knee pressure entirely, leaving a man's hands free for more important things. He was a fast traveler, too. Not to outrun a racer in a short heat, but given a long go in rough country, he'd run that same race horse off its feet and still travel thirty miles before sundown. Injun-wise, he could be mounted from either side—or from behind—which was a saving thing in a pinch.

He could have been a lot less horse and still been prized for his intelligence. A knowing horse, this. And that knowing somehow included most that went on in Jed's mind. And, in spite of his mean look, Palouse was a quiet one, no troublemaker. At night he stayed close to Jed's blanket roll, picketed or not. He paid little attention to other horses, as though he had more important business on hand. It had been one of the worst days of Jed's life, the day old Jim Bridger finally argued him into having the appaloosa gelded. He'd been a tough three-year-old then, an Injun-trained war horse. The redskins never gelded a war horse.

"Jed," Bridger had said, "that there roan stud has fought every horse he's met since you brung him in—and covered most of the mares. He's all horse—but he's gonna get you killed if you use him. You either got to geld him or leave him with the mares. For he's gonna make like a stud any time they's a mare within smell of that long damn nose. He's plenty smart—but he's only your horse when he ain't got stud business to tend to. You'll need him fast sometime—and he'll likely be busy coverin' some Injun broomtail—and he'll lose your hair for you. Now, son, you give me your say-so and I'll cut him myself. Proud, so's he'll have all that meanness and spunk—but he'll be a proper horse for a long trail."

Jed argued mightily with himself. But he wanted to use the sturdy animal and he knew Jim was right. And so it was done.

Palouse sulked, head down and surly, for a while. By the time he healed he seemed to have reached a conclusion. He was no longer a horse, he disdained their society, he was a man in a horse's powerful body. The ringing brass of his challenging neigh was heard no more. But he would trot the length of the pasture to Jed, greeting him with a soft whicker. The strange eyes, wildly rolling before, seemed to focus, respond now, when Jed talked to him, which was continually. Jed didn't just think there was a sharply reasoning personality between those alert ears—he *knew* it.

Melissa was not completely right in thinking Jed had seen only the mare. Not that he'd much interest in the small female, long-skirted and sunbonneted, leading the handsome animal. He figured absently that she must be the little sister David Boller had spoken of. Jed liked David. The stocky, bowlegged little horseman was quiet-spoken, steady-eyed, and they'd found immediate, common ground in David's horses. Jed was gloatingly admiring of these superb thoroughbreds and they were the one passionate love of David Boller's life.

And David had sensed the instant he'd laid eyes on Palouse that here was something special. There'd been deep interest, respect in his manner as he judged the roan's separate qualities. Right away he had seen the sense to him. He told Jed that he and his sister planned a horse ranch in the California Sierras.

"I'd sure like a young stud like that roan of yours," he said. "If a man's going into the business serious he ought to have a breed that fills the bill for rough country—besides thoroughbreds. Know where I can buy one like Palouse?"

Jed's crooked grin was reminiscent. "If you want to pay the price I give." His blue eyes, not at all distant now, were friendly on the smaller man.

David was eager. "I'd pay high—what price?"

Jed chuckled. "Stole him," he said, "out'n a horse herd up in the Nez Percé country. Picked Palouse out to be one I had to have and follered a little war party for nigh onto a week until I seen a chance to take him. He was a trained war horse and they took after me. But Palouse was the best of the bunch and they couldn't catch us—we made it."

David laughed with shared elation in the story so briefly told. "I can sure see why you took him—he's some special. Damn shame he's a gelding—I've got a mare in heat right now."

Jed's face sobered as he nodded agreement. "Tell you," he said, "there's some horse colts of his with a herd back up in Shoshoni country—with some of Bridger's relatives, not too far from Fort Bridger. We'll have a stopover there, refit and all. Likely we'd have time to get up there and bargain you a couple."

David always took night herd, assigned to it or not. He was taking no chances with his horses. Melissa could handle the mule team, so he caught up with his sleep, mornings. And then he'd ride on the wide wagon seat and spell her for a while. And Melissa heard more about the scout.

She was amazed at the warmth of her brother's regard for Jed Smith. David was a deliberate one, sort of standoffish with strangers, not usually given to enthusiasms. He had always been mighty slow to make friends.

David had been father, mother, and big brother to Melissa for most of her growing years. Except for distant kinfolks back in Kentucky, they were all that was left of the Bollers.

Along in the 1830s David Boller, senior, and his wife and son had come out to settle near Crooked Creek, Arkansas. Louisa Melissa Boller had been a delicate, pretty woman, of prosperous family, carefully raised and shielded against hardship. She was vastly unsuited to the life of a pioneering wife on the Arkansas borders. Her nerves and strength had not been equal to the hazards of childbearing in the primitive, doctorless country. She had several miscarriages, each weakening her already frail constitution, breaking her gentle spirit. Gradually the will to live ebbed away. When young David was fifteen Melissa was born. But Louisa sighed tiredly and turned her face to the wall, leaving David Boller a widower.

She left behind her a helpless infant, a confused boy, and a sorrowing, embittered man. David, senior, blamed the country for his troubles, conceived a deep-seated hatred for the conditions that had proved too severe for her frailty. He became itchingly restless. Leaving the children with haphazard menials, and using the horse trading for an excuse, he was more often absent than at home. His son, David, with the ignorant help of a fat Ponca squaw, raised the baby. The squaw, filthy but good-naturedly faithful, stayed with them until Melissa was five years old.

Then came electric word of the gold strike in California. David Boller was among the first of those who went. And never came back.

He wrote a few glowing letters to his son—letters that fairly sang of the beauties of the Pacific Coast, that told of the sweet coolness of the giant Sequoia forests; of the unbroken miles of waving grass, the fat cattle wandering belly-deep in it; of the gracious rancho living of the native Californios.

David Boller had found treasure, but it was not the metal in the granite rocks and cold, rushing streams. He fell in love with the lazily luscious land itself, and wrote that as soon as he made an adequate stake he would return for his children and they would all remove to this heaven on earth. They would raise fat cattle and fine horses, live like kings.

But David Boller was killed by a stray bullet from a shooting fray he had had no part in. He was negligently buried in a drab town high in the Sierra Nevadas by a dutiful sheriff who had more than his hands full. But that tired man did write a short letter notifying his son of his death.

For a time complete blankness settled on young David, who was twenty-two when the travel-stained letter was placed in his hands. He was not staggered by responsibility, he had had it for years. His nature was far more practical than had been his wandering sire's, he had been raised on the rough frontier. He was a better manager and more able to cope with everyday problems of existence. And his heritage was not insignificant. The spreading stock farm was clear of debt, there was a cattle herd, and there was an ever-increasing number of fine, thoroughbred horses, descendants of the animals his father had originally brought out from Kentucky. The property had flourished, proved far more profitable under his sober young stewardship than it had ever been in his father's hands.

So David squelched the echo of the dream his father had inspired and staidly remained on the farm, continued to care for his small, flaxen-haired sister. But as the slow years moved quietly along their unchanging ruts, the near hills seemed to close suffocatingly in on him. Inevitably the dreams began again, colored by the glamour of his father's letters.

And then, suddenly, it seemed that half the folks near about were talking excitedly about California. David's nearest neighbors, George Barker and the Prewetts, talked it day and night. They were for going to California. And his good friends, the Mitchell brothers, Joel and Lawson, were definitely considering the move.

That spring of the year 1857, when Melissa had just turned seventeen, David sold the ranch and most of the horses and stock. He kept only the finest stallions and mares as nucleus for another herd. The brother and his wildly excited young sister, with their friends and neighbors, joined the Fancher Party, which was fitting out for the overland trail to California.

David experienced no qualms about taking his sister on the long, hard trail. She was as eager for change as he, and she was wiry and active, strong as a young boy.

Melissa's upbringing would have been vastly different had Louisa Boller lived. David would have liked to raise his little sister in the pattern of a gracious lady but it was beyond him. His childhood memories of the old gracious way of life in Kentucky were faint. It had not been possible for him to follow any way but the life in which he found himself.

Melissa flatly refused to be a little girl. Even such feeble gestures as he made toward propriety were disregarded by her as being silly. Desperately lonely, without companions of her own age, she trudged after David like a small, stubborn shadow. He became resigned to her tagging underfoot. When she was six he mounted her on a gentle, specially trained pony and she was with him constantly, completely content.

By the time she was thirteen he had to threaten to whip her to force her into skirts. She had learned to ride astride, wearing mostly his hand-me-down clothes and she violently resisted any change. He let it rest for a time but when she was fifteen he had to assert parental authority. She was beginning to look like a female instead of a tow-headed slat of a boy and she attracted far too much attention in men's clothes. Some of it was ugly and downright dangerous on the woman-hungry frontier.

After he'd come home a couple of times bloodied up by fights he'd gotten into on her account, she finally agreed to the necessity of wearing the hampering female garb. They came to an armed agreement: she'd only wear pants when she rode within the boundaries of the farm.

The brother and sister, in spite of the fifteen years difference in their ages, were very much alike. Both were towheaded and hazel-eyed. But Melissa's eyes were flecked with yellow and they slanted slightly at the outer corners, giving her a tawny kitten look. Her wiry, curling hair had to be severely subdued into two thick braids. And even thus restrained it still sprang out into tight rings on her forehead and at the nape of her neck.

David was stockily short, Melissa narrow-boned and tiny. She wasn't exactly a pretty girl; her skin was brown from sun and wind, the loathed sunbonnet rode her braids oftener than her head. Her face was narrow, bony even, her teeth white and large, not perfectly even, at times they seemed too big for the pointed face. But the mouth was happily curved, the upper lip short, and there was a sweet pixyishness to her smile. A small band of freckles wandered across the straight little nose. Always when she smiled her head tipped back, because, being almost child-size, she had to look up to nearly everyone.

She was much too thin for the fashionable, well-padded look, but there were compensations: the sweet curve of high young breast rounding above the narrow waist that had never known corseting; the clean line of swinging, slim legs as she moved like a well-muscled boy with a free and longer stride than a lady would take. But then, few women of the train were concerned about ladylike niceties once they settled down to the trail.

Some of them had started out in style, with notions about this and that. But these had been discarded without argument, without notice, even, by the time the summer was halfway spent and they were out and beyond Fort Laramie. Some adjusted to the trail like fine-mettled mares. And some whined and fussed, complained every step of the way. Some kept track of their kids, kept them busy and working. Others just gave up, let their younguns run wild and untended alongside like the carefree dogs.

Annie Fancher, Cap'n Charley's articulate spouse, did her share of complaining but she kept her seven younguns—and Charley—lined out. Melissa came to like the gaunt, hard-driving woman, once she got past her sourness. There was no fuss nor feathers about Annie, she was hard-bitten, plain-spoken to a fault, but tireless and good-intentioned. Always first to appear with help where sickness was or trouble came. Acidly scolding and laying on blame, but taking hold and seeing to folks and things. Her vociferous opinion was that God's most exasperatingly ineffectual creature was the human male. But then, for a first attempt maybe He shouldn't be blamed too much. Obviously He'd improved the pattern on the second try. Men, particularly those who had run athwart her cutting tongue, prudently avoided her. Most of the women were afraid of her.

But the militant Annie took a liking to the sturdily enjoying girl, whose vitality seemed as tireless as her own. Melissa responded to it, neither fearing the woman nor minding her incessant carping. She only laughed. As a matter of fact Melissa's opinion of many of the men in the train was pretty low. She detested the tobacco-spitting, dirty-talking ones, who nearly all smelled strong.

It was Annie who came to her aid the day Ebony King got out of hand. The King, a black satin stallion, resented it when Melissa attempted to mount him in skirts. He showed his displeasure by promptly upending in both directions. She'd had no chance to get set and slid off over his shoulder, still hanging stubbornly to the reins. There was a breeze and every time she stretched to get her foot in the stirrup—which was very high, the King stood over sixteen hands—her skirt would flip against him and he'd shy away.

The train had rounded into camp early to allow the herders to chase down some stray animals and Melissa had thought to ride the King for a change. She had been riding Jane every day. Skittish though she was, the sorrel mare would put up with skirts, but not so the King. When Annie glimpsed the dusty commotion some yards from her wagon she naturally had to take a hand.

"What in tarnation you up to, Melissa?" she yelled, shielding her eyes against the afternoon sun.

"I'm gonna ride this blankety-blank black mule if it takes me all night!" Melissa's face was red and hot, she was furious.

"Well, my land!" Annie had come up, adding another flapping skirt to the situation, and the King leaped sideways, dragging Melissa with him. Annie looked her instant disapproval of the notional animal. "Ain't that critter broke yet? You got no business foolin' with a wild bronc like that there."

"I've—rode—him"—the words were punctuated by furious jerks on the bridle—"ever since he was a colt." She finally got the big head close-reined. The horse stood warily and Melissa took a quick look around to see if anyone else was within hearing. "He won't put up with skirts"—kicking scornfully at her ankle-length brown calico—"I always wore pants when I rode him at home but David made me promise not to, any more, where anyone could see me."

Annie would have disapproved of a female brazenly wearing pants but on hearing that a man objected she instantly took the opposite view. "Well, my land, leave it to a man to think up ways to hamper a body all he kin!" She thought busily and came up with a solution.

"I'll just hold that beast, Melissa," she announced, "you get on over to your wagon and shed your skirts—put your pants on with just your dress skirt over. Then you'n walk him over to them willer trees"—pointing to a cluster of trees not too distant—"hang up your skirt and get on him. Nobody's gonna notice you, that far off, and you can have your ride and come back and put on your skirt and walk in again!" She finished triumphantly, her long bony face displaying pleasure at the neatness of the circumvention of the male rule.

So, a little later, Melissa rode the King away from the sheltering willow trees, free of the hampering skirt. She had put on her flat-crowned hat, shoving her braids up inside. The brown calico waist was tucked inside the pants, there was not a thing to flap and unsettle His Majesty. She'd ride out a ways, she decided happily, and then turn back, give him his head for a good run. He needed violent exercise to dispel irritation from his system —just as she, herself, did.

Oh, it felt good—riding free in the clean-smelling wind, away from the cluttering, noisy train. Melissa often knew great surges of impatience with so many people constantly around. She noticed few of the hardships the other women whined about, she liked being on the trail. But the constant crowding pressure of people near, the complete lack of privacy and quiet, these things she disliked. She and David had lived almost isolated lives, away from folks, and they had liked it. She wholeheartedly shared the sentiment of the settler who felt pushed, infringed on, when he could see the smoke from his neighbor's chimney.

The King chose to register alarm at the indignant chatter of a prairie dog and suddenly leaped sideways. Melissa, swaying easily with his leap, laughed aloud and loosened the rein, let him play the fool, loving the feel of the powerful animal under her. He shook his great head, fighting even easy restraint on the bit, snorting contemptuously at their slow pace.

Jed had seen the train settled close to water and then headed out as always to scout the next day's drive. It was his practice to avoid the train as much as possible. He detested the shrill voices of the wrangling women and the loud boasting of some of the men bored him.

Palouse loped easily, taking his own pace, the neck rein lay slack. Jed indicated direction occasionally with a knee, but he let the sturdy animal choose his own path. Sure-footed as a cat, he never stumbled or stepped into gopher holes. Some five or six miles ahead of the train Jed halted briefly on a hilltop and surveyed the country beyond. It was smoothly rolling, no hazards; it would be an easy stretch the next day. Satisfied, he turned back, circling into trees, moving slower, quietly, and unslinging his Hawken in case he ran across camp meat. It took a lot to keep their cook pots simmering, fussy as they were, the women not using all the parts the way a sensible squaw would. He didn't get much help from the men with the hunting. There didn't appear to be three of them could bring down a buffler if it was leaning on their sights. David Boller, now, and the Mitchell brothers, they seemed right handy and dependable. But they were taken up with the horse herd, hadn't much time to hunt.

Jed shook his head over the "Missouri Wildcat" bunch that had joined on with the train. And that passel of toughs from Illinois—they were pretty much of a cut. More than likely river boaters—or criminals getting beyond the reach of the law. Bunch of loudmouths, drunken and quarrelsome.

Jed had urged Fancher to hold regular target practice for all the riflemen in the train, but it had been worse than useless. Seemed like all they did was waste powder and argue over the bets they made. Had to gamble over every damn thing they did. He'd been glad if he could get shut of the whole thing already but he'd contracted to scout the train clear to California.

There'd been a rule about liquor in camp, too, but the

Missouri-Illinois bunch flouted that like they did everything else. Pity Charley Fancher was so damn good-natured—he liked everybody. He was a smart man in lots of ways, seemed to have done right well for himself, he was the richest man in the train, they said. But he wasn't the sort to rule strictly, make a stand. Not that he'd be a coward about it likely, and the Arkansas folks would probably back him up, but he just didn't seem to feel the need for discipline. And it wasn't up to Jed to tell the elected captain his business. Nor was he about to mix in on it. Scouting and hunting were what he'd hired on for—advice about the trail, water holes, Indians and such. But not to interfere in running the train, careless though it might be. Unless they did something that endangered the train, he'd keep his mouth shut.

The more he thought of the noisy, wrangling crew of them the more impatient he got. But the pay offered had been high, it had been a chance to set himself up fine. He'd turn that pay into trade goods at a California seaport, get a string of burros off the Mexicans, and come back across the desert in winter. That had been Bridger's advice.

"You won't have no trouble a-tall, boy," he'd said, "you got my maps—your pappy and me made them maps, right after he come back and he knew ever foot of that country. You got enough savvy to use 'em right. You won't likely run into trouble with Injuns—your paw made friends with the Mojaves, like as not they'll remember him. You'n trade them into guiding you to the edge of the Navajo country—they won't go in, they're plumb scared of the Navajos—and Apaches. You stay clear of the 'Paches, too. Stay in Navajo country, they're fighters but they won't shoot first like the 'Paches do. 'Paches is the meanest, orneriest Injuns they is. Don't never wait to powwow with 'em—shoot on sight and git the hell out.

"First Navajo you run onto, ask for Narbona—he's a peace chief amongst 'em and I've done some tradin' with him. Tell him I sent you and be sure you have a special present for him. Maybe you'n get one of them long Mexican rifles, all fancied up with silver inlay on the stock—that'll make his eyes shine. Then trade for Navajo horses.

"Them Navajos got horses to beat anythin'! Bloodlines from the ones they stole off'n the Spaniards, long back. The Navvies are damn smart when it comes to breedin'—they gelded the knot-heads and kept the good mares and studs, good as any white man would. Some of them horses got Arabian heads! And sturdy built, desert-toughened, lots of heart. You'n play 'em out but they'll keep travelin' till they drop!

"You pick the best trade goods and likely you'll be able to come by a couple of studs and some mares—set you up fine in the horse business. Plenty of market for good horses, specially with the army headed this way. And it's past time you quit roustin' around with the Injuns. It's fun—and I know—but you ain't gettin' nowheres—'cept older. It sneaks up on you, boy. I turned trader because I knowed trappin' was done. No need to set on our arses and rot—they's money a-plenty to be made.

"You get you them horses and get a coupla Navajo bucks to trail herd with you. Foller the Colorado up to the forks of the Green—fine grazin' meadows along there. And long about spring I'll send a coupla boys down to meet you—lend a hand bringin' them in!"

Bridger had put in hard money for a share in the trade goods, telling Jed to pick up a piece or two of jewelry for his doe-eyed Snake wife. Pampered her, did Jim, and thought a heap of their younguns. The jewelry he could get in California would be Mexican-made, beaten out of Spanish silver. Some of it was right pretty. Maybe he'd get some for his own use—never could tell when you might happen onto a likely-looking young squaw. Jim had said the Navajo women were uncommonly handsome. The path his thoughts took from there made him grin. The twinkle in his blue eyes made him boyish for a brief moment. Any member of the wagon train seeing him then would have been astonished, so unlike it was to the almost Indian poker face they knew.

Bridger had had his say about squaws, too. "Best not take on a squaw, permanent-like, Jed," he'd said. Times were changing, he brooded, the country was getting crowded with emigrators, unused to the ways of the old mountain men. Jed was young enough to get his craw-ful of fighting without having to down every loudmouth that named him a squaw man. Best look for a white girl, from one of the trains maybe.

Jed didn't know about that, though. He'd have to think on it a pile. From what he'd seen of white women they weren't too damn choice. Settlement-raised women were mighty demanding. Fussy, they were, and shrill-voiced and bossy. Most of them seemed to be either flat-skinny or slobby with fat. Not solid and muscled like a hard-working squaw but lazy fat from sitting around on their big behinds and yelling orders at their kids. Didn't appear to be able to do a day's work without complaining.

Jed's thoughts broke off sharply. His eyes had caught movement a ways over to his left among some trees.

It was a big black horse traveling at an easy canter directly away from the emigrant trail and the wagon train. It sure looked like David Boller's black stud but the rider—a very small figure—could not be David. Jed swore softly. One of those greenhorn herd boys, most likely. Miles from the train in Indian country and riding an animal that any buck would give his whole herd for—with his squaw thrown in.

Sliding his rifle into its sling, Jed lifted Palouse into a hasty gallop. They came out of the trees with a rush.

Ebony King, loafing along under his small rider, was startled. He reared, almost unseating the dreaming Melissa, and bolted away from the approach of the other horse.

Jed swore again, not softly this time, and dropped the rein on Palouse's neck, letting the roan take his own course. Palouse knew he was to overtake the black and flattened into a driving run, his short legs drumming piston-swift. The black could easily have outrun Palouse in the open but here were trees, brush, and small hillocks.

The roan, agile as an antelope at dodging and swerving, closed the distance efficiently.

Jed yelled: "Pull him in, you—" His angry shout was indistinct but Melissa knew she was being sworn at. She was furious, the scout had not only spooked the King but that big brute had the bit in his teeth—all her yanking was of no avail. She was a passenger only, until he chose to slow down or release the bit. Swearing heatedly herself, she just rode.

From behind and slightly to the side of the racing black Jed noted angrily that the stripling swaying so easily in the flat training saddle made no effort to pull in. Maybe the little fool thought they were having a race! A hard rush of exasperated anger rose in him. And as Palouse ranged alongside the black horse, Jed reached a long arm and ungently jerked the rider from the saddle, throwing his light weight across Palouse's shoulders. The King, confused by the suddenly emptied saddle, sheered off, slowing his pace when Palouse stopped.

Melissa struggled frantically against the iron hold pinning her across the roan, the saddle horn bruising her middle. Raising an angry arm, Jed whacked the small rump in front of him twice, openhanded and hard enough to make his calloused palm tingle. Melissa yelped indignantly and then gasped for breath. Jed dropped the kicking small form negligently in the grass alongside and spurred off after the King.

She wasn't hurt when she was so unceremoniously dumped but Melissa was shaking with fury as she scrambled to her feet, rubbing her stinging backside.

Presently Jed hove in sight again, leading the King. Dismounting, he dropped Palouse's rein; the roan would stand. Leading the black, he advanced with a good strong piece of his mind ready to dress down this smart-alecky little squirt.

For the first time the scout's flinty blue eyes looked directly at Melissa. And their expression infuriated her beyond all reason. With a choking little roar she lowered her head and charged, butting like a raging ram right into Jed's flat belly.

Taken completely by surprise Jed staggered, grunting loudly. The King, upset by the melee, reared back, dragging the man down thumpingly hard onto his bony rump. The black continued to jerk backward every time the scout tried to regain his feet.

From the indignity of this untenable position Jed's eyes suddenly focused on the small figure above him, still dancing up and down with fury.

Her hat had slid off the curling blond hair, one braid fell over her shoulder. Jed's suddenly appalled eyes moved from the small booted feet up slender curving legs and hips to the narrow waist beneath the calico swell of rounded breasts. He froze, his jaw dropped blankly. Ludicrous horror was on his face as he cautiously crawled to his feet.

"Look, miss, I didn't know—I sure didn't go to—" He was floundering miserably. "Why didn't you pull him in—when I hollered?" he asked pitifully, "I only—"

"I couldn't pull him in, you big ox!" Melissa snapped. "You jumping out at us that way—he spooked and took the bit in his teeth—nobody could've turned him!"

Jed was completely routed, humiliated by what he had done, defeated by her righteous anger. Confusedly considering the uselessness of apology, he reached unconsciously to explore his bruised rump.

Seeing him wince painfully and still feeling a similarly located soreness, the whole thing suddenly seemed funny to Melissa. The pixy grin appeared and then the big white teeth flashed as she threw back her disheveled head and screamed with laughter.

Jed, a study in stammering misery, was baffled by this unlooked-for glee. Melissa gaspingly paused to stare at him again, pointed to his hand still busily nursing his rump and doubled over hysterically, howling with joy.

Jed's hand stopped abruptly, his sheepishly crooked grin showed, and then his chuckle deepened into hearty laughter.

Palouse lifted his sensible head to gaze at first one and then the other of the hilarious people. His manner as he composedly returned to cropping grass was curiously like the shrug of a human shoulder.

A little later, heading back toward the train camp, Jed looked appreciatively at Melissa riding confidently on the big black. The King elected to dislike the company of Palouse and had to show off about it. Snorting and plunging, he tried to angle close enough to kick at the spotted roan. Palouse evaded him with matter-of-fact ease, disdaining to attach any importance to such coltish antics.

This was a new and heady experience for Jed, riding with a girl who could laugh so riotously, tickled by so earthy a happening. He was relieved to find she didn't appear to be insulted. She chattered, smiling naturally straight into his eyes, put him completely at ease. He hadn't known you could talk to white women easily, like this. Mostly they'd seemed standoffish, prudish and watchful for offense.

"I shouldn't have got so far out, Jed," Melissa acknowledged, using his name naturally, as David did, "but it felt so good, riding alone, all quiet and nice-smelling. I get so sick of the train—people underfoot the livelong day." Jed nodded complete agreement, he felt exactly the same.

Eying him sideways, she explained about wearing pants, told him where her skirt waited. His crooked, appealing grin appeared as he looked deliberately at the slender legs with a wicked twinkle. Melissa's insides gave an exciting lurch. She'd made him look at her, all right, but now she didn't exactly know what to do with it. That slow look was downright male—as knowing as the stare that had covered Lady Jane. She felt deliciously female; tightening her flat little belly, she lifted her rounded breasts. She felt an astonished breathlessness, shc knew Jed was aware of every move she made.

"You better not ride out alone no more, though," Jed was saying. "You got any idea what trouble an Injun would go to, to get a-hold of that stallion?"

"I guess so," she admitted reluctantly, "but it was so

wonderful——" And then as though the idea had just occurred, "*You* ride out every day——" She smiled appealingly.

Jed returned the smile, his look was measuring, he wondered if she knew what she might be getting into. The impishly slanted gaze didn't falter, her half-smile was distinctly challenging. She knew all right. He felt a familiar surging warmth move up his loins. The little devil, that yellow stare was as unashamedly inviting as any squaw's. But more fun—more exciting, somehow.

The gleam that appeared in his eyes almost panicked Melissa. The long look raked her again. "Suits me fine," he said, "let me know when you want to ride out again."

David Boller shaded his eyes against the low, dust-laden rays of the setting sun to stare with surprise at the figures approaching camp. It was Jed and Melissa, walking, leading Palouse and Ebony King. Melissa, now decorously clad in the despised skirt, was chattering animatedly. Jed was grinning down at her, completely absorbed.

David strolled out to meet them. "How about my supper?" he shouted as they neared.

Melissa beamed at him, "Oh, David, listen. Jed says I can ride out with him sometimes—when we camp early like today. It isn't safe alone—but it was so grand——" She looked pleadingly at her brother, hoping for his approval—and permission.

David did not acknowledge the implied question; he was gazing steadily at the scout. Jed, quickly conscious of an almost parental authority in the small man's manner, qualified Melissa's announcement. "Not without your say-so," he said.

David glanced at his sister. Her face was rosy from sun, her eyes were excitedly shining but they became a little puzzled now as she became aware of the quick sobering of the men. David's contemplation of the scout was probing, considering. Then he took the King's rein from Melissa. "Get on in now and rassle us up some supper, it'll be dark in a shake. I'll take care of the King."

Melissa obediently turned toward the wagon but she turned back to call to Jed, "Don't forget you're going to eat with us, Jed. You come back with David, right away!" And meeting his serious eyes, she smiled the pixy-sweet smile. And her brother noticed that the smile was for Jed alone.

The scout felt a sudden surprisingly warm response, quite different from the emotions roused back there on the horses. It had been inexplicably sweet, that smile she had sent back to him. Mischievously female, but confident with something else that he couldn't quite identify. He had not encountered that certain claiming look before. Confused, he glanced at David, caught the man watching him steadily. His odd confusion mounted as he realized that this strange new feeling had been naked in his eyes. Wordlessly the two men turned and led the horses toward the herd ground.

It was David who broke the silence. "Melissa is all I've got," he said soberly.

Jed did not pretend to misunderstand. "I'll sure look after her good," he said, matching the soberness. Both men disdained to underestimate the significance of Melissa's glance. Each was aware, if she was not, of the implications of that smiling look at Jed.

"She's pretty young—" David tried to map out what he wanted to say. He felt the need to go into things a little, lay it on the line.

Jed nodded, met the advance squarely. "I've needed me a woman of my own." His words were slow as he, too, felt an unaccustomed way along. "A white woman," he qualified, his glance sternly admitting. It was deliberate, let there be no covering up, he wanted everything straight and aboveboard with this man he had come to like, respect so much.

David was not shocked at this knowledge of squaws in Jed's past life. It was, after all, only a natural, man-thing. To have said it was enough. He nodded. "Thing is," he said carefully, "Melissa hasn't had a chance to—look around much. I've been mighty choosy about her friends and my own. She'd ought to have time to make a choice. So I'd take it kindly if you'd sort of—maybe go a mite slow. Yet a while, anyway——"

Give her a chance to be sure in her own heart. This was what he anxiously felt but could not put into words. Don't sweep her off her feet, overwhelm and conquer her like you could—being the experienced man you are. You could have her easy, she's no match for you in age or experience. Be gentle, his pleading look urged, cherish her youngness, like I have.

Jed could not have laid tongue to the words either but he heard the tone, answered to the unspoken, deep concern. He had liked this bowlegged little man, respected him. Now he warmed to him still more.

Dark with serious understanding, his eyes met David's squarely. "It'll be however she wants it," he promised. "I won't hurry her." And then, with a half grin, "And I won't let her stampede me, neither!"

David's answering smile was wide, and achingly like Melissa's. He drew a deep sigh of relief. He liked the big scout, had cottoned to him at first sight. And he'd always worried about what sort of man Melissa might set her heart on. There were so damn many trashily showy ones she could be too green to see through. And she was a handful at times, being so bullheaded and willful. Get her mind set in a direction and it took all hell to turn her.

And now, daily moving further into rough, new country, away from even the scant civilization they were accustomed to, it took a special breed of man to have the proper know-how. David felt a surge of relief—Jed Smith would more than fill the bill.

Neither man felt any uneasiness that a matter so serious had been practically settled in the space of minutes. And after only a couple of hours acquaintanceship between a man and a girl. Courtship and the niceties possible of long friendship, the contingent pussyfooting around, these were almost unknown on the frontier. Sparsely settled crossroads never boasted many marriageable women. Time, distance, and the slowness of travel entered into it, and exigency. A man lucked onto an agreeable woman and took her to wife as quickly as possible.

And David had foreseen that Melissa would be courted on the long journey. Already she was beyond the age at which most girls married. Many who were no older traveled with their young husbands in the Fancher Train. Some, in fact, already carried babies in their arms or bulging beneath calico aprons.

David turned now and thrust out his hand to Jed, who quickly gripped it with his own. The strong hold tightened and fell away as they smiled into each other's eyes. Both felt a good relief, satisfaction went along with their understanding. Then David said, "We'd best get these nags unsaddled—Melissa will have supper ready."

Jed ran his hand over his stubbly chin. "Think I'd have time to shave?" he asked seriously.

David threw back his head and laughed; the gesture was very like his sister's. "Sure"—he chuckled—"I reckon Melissa will wait supper till you show up—no matter how long you take!"

## CHAPTER II

Jed felt driven to near murderous rage at the downright viciousness that seemed to crop out so regularly in the Missouri-Illinois faction of the Fancher Train. When they weren't bragging around camp trying to egg someone into a brawl, they thought up some other form of devilment. Like what they were up to now.

Nightly they set up a dice game on a blanket. That was fairly harmless—when they gambled and drunkenly fought among themselves. But this night some Sioux braves wandered in to camp and, having got them drunk on uncut corn liquor, they were gambling for their horses. The Indians were too drunk to realize they'd switched to loaded dice. It was a dirty deal, for a couple of the animals looked to be fine, of good conformation—they weren't just nags.

Jed decided against speaking out, all he'd likely get would be a brawl. But he settled in the shadow, grimly watching. The Sioux were unarmed, but one of them might pack a knife under his shirt and if they caught on, or were pushed too far——

By the time some woman, upset by the drunken squalling of the Indians, had reported it to Cap'n Fancher, they'd won four of the five horses. All except a buckskin pony ridden by a frozen-faced stripling who'd taken no part in the drinking or gambling. Likely he knew the older men were getting cheated, for the black eyes in his thin, proud face were smoldering.

Captain Fancher was a man who hated trouble; it took him a long time to get on the prod. And then, he shared most white men's views on Indians. The emigrators didn't hold a redskin to be hardly more account than an animal—sure not to be considered same as a man. An awful lot of hair had been lifted off just such people.

The gambling blanket had been spread close enough to catch the light from a fire. Now one reeling, slobbering brave was using wide gestures, making some sort of protest. Jed, who knew Sioux talk, made him out to say that he hadn't understood what the stakes were, this last time. This horse was not his to wager—he had not put it up. It was the war horse of Spotted Tail, his brother-in-law, therefore not his to lose. Spotted Tail was in the white man's prison in Leavenworth. It was a family honor trust that the horse be kept safe against his return. A war chief must have his war horse. And his brother-in-law would soon return to his tepee. The whole thing was a mistake. Therefore he would take the horse now and return to his people. He placed an unsteady hand on the animal's bridle, started to untie it.

But the hand was knocked aside and the besotted Indian found himself staring up into the contemptuous gaze of a big red-bearded man. Solomon Ward, heavily booted feet truculently spread, beefy hands on hips, sneeringly dared the Indian to start something. The red-beard's arms and shoulders were immense. His barrel chest wore a mat of thick red hair which protruded through the opening of his dirty shirt. A wide leather belt rode a thick circle just below his bulging belly and supported a sheath which held a knife. It was a fine-looking knife, its elkhorn handle was decorated with silver inlay.

The Indian reeled, stared confusedly up at the man, and reached for the bridle again. Sol Ward grinned mirthlessly. Putting one hamlike hand on the Indian's chest, he shoved straight back, sent him sprawling. Before he could regain his feet Sol kicked him—hard. The other Indians clamored in protest, but the other white gamblers, roaring with brutal mirth, now joined in the fun. Kicking and shoving, they routed the Indians, drove them off. The Indians headed staggeringly for the outskirts of camp.

The quiet, watching youngster wheeled the little buckskin and followed them. But just at the edge of light cast by the fire he halted the pony and sent his gaze back to search out the man, Sol Ward, who stood holding his belly as he laughed.

Jed's eyes narrowed at the expression of the set young face: It was murderous with hate and outrage. Good thing for Sol Ward that the young pup was unarmed, he'd likely been dead before he finished his belly laugh. The glinting black eyes memorized the look of the red-beard and then, kicking the buckskin into easy motion, he rode in the wake of the staggering braves.

Jed, moving in the shadows, followed, wanting to make sure they got on out of camp with no further trouble. No telling what that youngun with the hate-crazed eyes might take on to do. But he saw the boy draw up alongside the reeling group and help two of the braves to mount the pony. Taking the halter rope he led the horse slowly away into the night, his thin shoulders bowed under a weight of humiliation.

When Jed returned to camp he had a short, bluntly put word with Charley Fancher, to the end that the wagon captain dispatched more guards to the horse herd, in case the Indians decided to revenge their loss. And then Captain Fancher expressed his disapproval to the gamblers.

They were parading their winnings, laughing, noisily boasting. Sol had won the war horse and he was having trouble with the plunging brute, finally bringing it to a trembling stand by the use of his full weight on the halter.

It was an unusual and handsome animal—a pinto, or "paint" horse. Satiny black on the thickly muscled neck and shoulders, with a symmetrical white blaze between the wide eyes. The powerfully heavy hindquarters were black, there were white ovals on the belly, the strong, nervous legs were deeply white-stockinged. The arching neck was thick, it was a stallion in the prime of maturity, seven or eight years old, Jed guessed. It was a magnificent animal and probably trained for war. There was nothing an Indian valued higher than a spotted war horse.

Sol Ward noticed the scout eying the horse and turned on him, his heavy face quarrelsome. "Cap'n Fancher, here, says you didn't like our little game, Smith." The tone was belligerent.

Jed shrugged, blue eyes hard in his lean face. "Ain't never very smart to let an Indian think he's been cheated—they can cook up a mess of trouble if they're a mind to."

"Them drunken bastards?" Sol snorted. "Hell, they ain't hardly got enough spine to hold themselves up, let alone start anythin'. Look how they let us kick them outa camp, not a one of 'em would stand and fight!" Clearly he was disgusted to have been done out of a more prolonged brawl.

Jed bit back his anger. "They come into camp peaceful—they was unarmed. They were just visitin' from their camp over the hill a ways—I talked to them myself, 'fore supper. Drunk or not, they knew they were outnumbered here—and that likely they wouldn't get a fair shake."

"Well," said Sol, "they learned not to fool with Sol Ward. They ain't likely to come lookin' for more trouble."

"Half the Sioux nation is camped over there"—Jed waved toward the northern hills—"they're headin' for a big council and these boys probably got a hundred relatives would join up in anything they thought up. They *could* give us a pile of trouble, if they wanted to, once they start thinking this thing over."

"Well, hell"—Sol was still belligerent—"let them! We got enough rifles to take care of any damn thing they try!"

"You ain't likely ever been in a wagon-train attack, Ward, or you'd know it ain't always the men with rifles gets it. You wouldn't be so willin' to start somethin' knowin' sometimes a woman or a kid winds up with an arrow shot clean through 'em."

Among the listeners a woman muffled a scream and Jed went hastily on. "I don't think they're gonna attack the train—but they might try a raid on the horse herd. Like I said, the Sioux nation is headed for a Great Council and they ain't on the warpath—they got their women and kids along. They're mighty leery of exposin' their folks to trouble after what Squaw-Killer Harney done."

Fancher looked relieved. "But, just the same," Jed added, "best we keep a sharp lookout. And no one gettin' out of sight of camp—specially on a horse. They're apt to want to steal a horse or two, to even up, sort of. A Sioux warrior's got a hell of a lot of pride—they get even when they can."

Sol's harsh laugh broke in. "Warriors? Hell, them draggletail punks didn't look like no warriors to me!" He spat contemptuously.

Jed's eyes went bleak. He wanted desperately to smash his fist into the sneering bearded face. The echo of Bridger's advice slowed his twitching muscles. Jed would find emigrators a stupid, pigheaded lot, Jim had warned, seldom willing to take the advice they paid for. "Don't let an emigrator have room to rile you, boy," he'd advised. "They don't any of 'em have what you'd call horse sense, even the best of 'em. Just kinda nurse 'em along like a passel of idiots and pay no mind to what they say."

Jed won the brief fight for control of his temper, his voice was flinty but even. "They're warriors," he repeated. "That biggest brave was Iron Shell, and he's already packin' a grudge agin the whites—his wife and son was killed by a blunderin' bunch of soldiers that'd disobeyed orders. And the kid on the buckskin—I know of him. He's the son of Crazy Horse, the Oglala Holy Man. Ain't nobody got no more influence in the tribes than a Holy Man."

Charley Fancher looked unhappily at the two men who faced each other, hard dislike evident on both faces. Sol's coarse features still wore a sneer. Jed's flat stare was cold, unyielding.

"Well," Fancher said feebly, attempting to break the strained atmosphere, restore peacefulness, "I guess if we just put more guards on the horse herds that'll take care of it. What's done's done—"

Jed spat and turned away. "That's right," he said, "it's done."

The next morning Jed scouted over toward where the Indian encampment had been, some five or six miles from the wagon train. They were all gone. There'd been a big slew of them, lots of women and kids. He returned, following the tracks of the group that had visited the train, halting briefly at the place where the boy had dismounted to let the men ride. From here, where they traveled over a small rise, the tracks of the buckskin were deep from the double load he'd carried. Jed noticed idly that the left hind print was odd: the outline splayed out a little, the hoof must have been split at one time.

Melissa was at first incredulous and then furious when Jed briefly informed her that there would be no riding for her for a spell. David was enormously tickled at the assumption of authority in the scout's tone.

"You mean," Melissa sputtered, "that just because ole Sol Ward cheated an Injun out of a horse *I* can't ride out with you?"

"Yep."

"But *you* can look after me—"

"Not proper, you never know what might come up." He didn't feel the need to explain that he could not have her along to distract his attention at a time like this. He was nettled at her rebellious attitude toward his considered judgment as to what was best. But his gaze softened as he looked down at her. She was mighty pretty.

Melissa had taken to elaborate freshening up, changing her dress for supper each night now that Jed ate with them. The ruby red calico she wore with its rows of little ruffles across the bosom was becoming—flattering. The rich color made her cheeks rosy, her eyes darker. She had fashioned her thick braids into a coronet high on her small head. It made her seem taller, more womanly.

The long sleeves of the demure calico dress were rolled above her elbows, the brown forearms slender above the small square hands that moved so quickly. Efficiently, too, Jed noted with satisfaction. She was a proper one for the trail.

He was so pleased with her, this small child-woman who was to be his, that he softened the strictness of the orders by explaining a little. "The whole Sioux nation is on the move, Melissa," he said gently. "They're travelin' just north of us a few miles—in the same direction we're movin'. They're not likely to attack the train but if they could steal a lone horse or two—to make up some for the paint war horse—they sure would. I just won't have you sky-larkin' around on a horse—even close to the train. You stay off your sorrel mare, too, stay on the wagon."

Melissa's mouth dropped open in outraged protest, her eyes were smolderingly rebellious. Jed's face hardened at her reaction to his attempt at reason. His chin set, he looked his cold indifference to her anger.

Melissa appealed to David, expecting him to qualify the strictness of the orders, but David grinned. He was enjoying the altercation hugely. "Jed's likely right, youngster," he said, "best you don't ride at all for a spell." He got lazily up from his seat on the wagon tongue, stretched and yawned. "Time for me to get on over to the herd," he said, " 'fore I set here and go to sleep." He ambled off across the firelit inner circle of the encampment, stopping to speak to people here and there.

Melissa changed her tactics. Turning the full battery of her teasing, slanted eyes on Jed where he lounged against the wagon, sipping coffee, "Aw, please, Jed—" accompanied by her sweetest, most promising smile.

He cast the coffee grounds into the embers of the cook fire and set the cup on the food box. "Nope."

The inarguable flatness angered her again. "Maybe I will anyway—" she flared.

Jed turned to face her at that, the flint in his eyes again. He looked at her coldly, displeased at this childishness. "Just you do," he said, "and see what you get. I whipped you once for not doin' what you was told—thinkin' you was a boy. I c'n whip you again—if you ask for it!"

It angered Melissa still more because she believed that he actually would. But she was not one to back down. "Like you'd whip a squaw?"

"Like I'd whip a squaw—ceptin' no squaw I ever knowed would act that damn silly!"

"I guess you know a lot of squaws—"

"Yep."

"You lay one dirty paw on me, Jed Smith, and I'll—I'll—I'm not your property—!"

Jed did not answer this. He only looked at her, unsmiling, but a light flared deep back in his eyes at her challenge.

Melissa felt the impact of that look like a blow. Half frightened, she stared at him, wide-eyed, irresistibly held by his flat stare. Jed's long look moved unmercifully from the toes of her small button shoes up her body to her face. She felt the intimacy of that look like a searching hand. Scarlet started in a wave somewhere between her breasts and crowded flushingly to her cheeks. She felt so strong a panic in her stomach she was almost sick. It showed in her eyes and face, that half fear, half fascination. She swallowed painfully, her lips quivered.

A deep knowing was in Jed as he looked down at her. He was remembering all the women he had ever known—at this very instant he knew how sure it was that the woman he wanted to keep stood before him. He felt a surge of joy at how much he wanted her, needed to know she was irrevocably his own. Not with appetite only—that, too, and all the sweeter for how he felt. But not just for the lovely cleanness of the slenderly curved body, untried, shrinking and yet eager. This was a for-life hunger, of a man for his woman. The other, he knew now, had been only to ease a momentary want, brighten an hour. This thing he felt, bound up in this small, strong-spirited one, this was the big thing that a man could search for all his life. And maybe never find.

The change in Jed's face as his thoughts merged from anger to understanding of what was between them wrought a similar change in Melissa. And she knew the answer to her own defiant challenge: She *was* his property, unclaimed as yet, but undeniably his possession. And she was glad to have it so, she felt an exultant warmth in his mastery. She dropped her head, no longer able to meet his gaze.

His hand reached for her chin, raised her face toward him. Her eyes were still half fearful. "You'll do like I say—" he said. It was not command, nor question, but something between the two.

She could not answer, she nodded slightly, her eyes on his. She felt the hardness of the lean hand holding her chin. With the tip of one finger he traced the curve of her cheek, his hand moved behind her neck, he felt wonder that it was so slenderly fragile beneath the pile of heavy braids. Melissa felt the warmth on the nape of her neck; intimately it seemed to burn, brandingly, clear inside of her. When he stooped and gently kissed her parted lips a flame, shockingly strong, swept over her entire body and she trembled slightly.

Jed felt the tremor, tasted the responsiveness of the

soft mouth, and his grin was crookedly tender. He was unaccountably pleased at the stormy nature of her. His big hand pressed her shoulder briefly, hard, and picking up his rifle, he disappeared into the shadows beyond the wagon.

The next few days' scouting left Jed feeling vaguely uneasy. As though he might be missing something. He took to traveling in ever-widening circles. He checked on the night herders constantly to see that they did not relax their vigilance. A quick night raid, spooking the horses, that was about what a party of young braves would be most apt to try. Some of those wild-eyed youngsters itching to make a first coup—and also avenge an insult. But things stayed quiet, normal.

Jed remained watchful for sign, knowing that the Indians' route, so far, still paralleled the emigrant road. Their camps were never far distant from each other but no redskin had so much as been seen near the wagon train since the night of the dice game. As day followed uneventful day, Jed began to breathe a little easier. By now the hordes of Sioux would be turning north, away from the trail, toward Bear Butte where the Great Council was to be held.

And then, days later, when he scouted the first crossing of the Sweetwater he came across sign. Fresh hoofprints of an unshod horse. Not that one set of prints at a drinking place was any cause for alarm. But the minute he spotted them the shape of an odd print leaped at him—the left hind hoof of this horse splayed out a little. These tracks had been made by the little buckskin ridden by the young son of Crazy Horse. More than likely ridden now by one of the relatives of the dishonored lodge of Spotted Tail.

Jed had to grin at how cagey the bugger had been. Traveling along with the train, out of sight completely, waiting till the vigilance relaxed. Probably counted the herders every night, waiting for just the right setup. Being alone, more than likely he had no designs on anything but the recapture of the war horse.

That explained Jed's uneasiness. That itching sensation along his spine. The watched feeling that'd caused him to make like a deer combing the wind with its nose. He'd scoffed at himself for it—and still gone on taking longer, wider swings, watching jumpy-like for sign. And all the time this lone buck had paralleled him, more than likely anticipating his every move, they were damn smart, Injuns, when it came to a deal like this. And leaving him with this prickling uneasiness—he'd been eying every clump of cover like a spooky squaw. Swinging his gaze back and forth constantly, hunting untoward movement near or far. And not finding a thing that didn't belong. The quick startled leap of an antelope maybe, or the peevish flurry of sage hens, sure, but nothing that he hadn't kicked up himself.

He relaxed now, the hair on the back of his neck could stay down, for the buck didn't have designs on Jed himself or he'd have been jumped long before now—there'd been plenty of chance. The only need for care now was extra guarding of the war horse. And that was Sol Ward's lookout.

That night after the cook pots had been emptied Jed sought out Ward. The big man looked at him sourly. He was half a head taller than the scout, who stood just about six foot in his moccasins. Jed motioned him casually aside, he didn't want to spook the womenfolks.

"Where you keepin' that paint horse, nights?" he asked.

Sol looked surprised. "With the horse herd. Why?"

"If I was you—I'd sleep with him wrist-haltered—less'n you wanta take a chance on losin' him."

Sol stared suspiciously at the scout. He had the humorless man's fear of being made ridiculous, being taken in by something. "What makes you think I might lose him?" he asked finally.

"I seen sign at the Sweetwater ford this morning—pony tracks—the buckskin the youngun was ridin' the night you got the paint."

Sol's eyes were first incredulous and then his stare hardened sneeringly. "You seen sign of a pony—and you kin tell by a *track* that it was the buckskin? So you want I should sleep with that big brute trompin' round my head? D'you take me to be a fool, Smith?"

Jed stiffened, his face became masklike. The hell with this stupid, pigheaded bully. He was sorry he'd bothered, he hoped the Indian did take the horse. Serve Ward damn well right—cheating, brawling bastard that he was.

"I don't take to you at all, Ward," he said, the aversion he felt flatly insulting in his voice. "I got a heap a better things to do than worry about a horse—specially one that was got crooked. I've warned you—what you do, or don't do is your own lookout."

Jed turned to walk away. Ward's heavy hand fell on his shoulder, violently swung him back around. He shoved his coarse, bearded face at the scout.

"I don't let no man call me crooked!" he growled, proddingly offensive. "You'll take back the word—or stand and fight!"

Jed, having regained his balance, looked expressionlessly at the big man. He considered briefly and then nodded. Leaning his Hawken against a wagon wheel, he unbuckled his belt with its sheathed knife, hung it carefully beside the rifle. He removed his buckskin shirt, hung that, also, on the wheel. Looking around to where a big fire lighted a dusty clearing, he motioned toward it.

"Over there all right?" he asked.

An expression of almost unbelieving joy had come over Sol's face as he watched these deliberate preparations. True, he'd done his best to pick a fight, but he hadn't thought the scout would dare take him up on it. That slenderly built man looked like a cinch to him—he'd give him a beating he'd remember. There were no rules to the way Sol Ward fought—kicking, gouging, maiming—anything went. He took off his shirt, baring the huge shoulders and arms, the hairy barrel chest. His teeth gleamed through the red beard. Nothing Sol enjoyed more than a fight. Especially when he had an edge on the outcome, like now.

Jed knew what Ward was thinking. And knew, also, the way he would fight. Behind the casual, almost indifferent cast of his lean face Jed was weighing his chances honestly. The red-bearded giant had height and reach on him and possibly thirty or forty pounds of weight. But also at least fifteen years more of age. And he was ponderous-moving as a fat bear. That bulging lard-belly couldn't stand heavy punishment. If Jed could surprise him—hurt him right off—his age and slowness would tell against him. Stay clear of the clinches at first, out of the crushing grip of those big arms—that would have to be the way of it.

Having plotted his course, what could almost pass for a grin flickered briefly on Jed's thin mouth. His boyhood rough-and-tumble days had been spent with the Indians, and he had been well schooled in the peculiarly vicious Indian style of hand-to-hand combat where the single motive was to kill, and quickly. Short of that, the goal was to maim, disable your opponent with no consideration for anything as unrealistic as gallantry. Jed had healed up from several broken bones before the grim lessons were done. The redskins didn't pamper their young, the training was rough and therefore enormously effective.

There was a trick or two Sol Ward might not have met up with as yet. Might have not guessed, either, that the long arms and lean-looking shoulders were solid with hard layers of sinewy muscle. The apparent slightness and habitual easy slouch were very misleading.

Now, slightly crouching, eyes on Sol's big hands, his own forward and loose, Jed waited.

As if by magic a crowd had gathered. Someone rushed off to get Captain Fancher to stop so ill matched a fight.

Melissa and David were among those pushing their way through the circle. "Oh, David," she cried in horror, "don't let Jed—stop them, Divid——"

David turned on her savagely. "Shut up!" he ordered, "and get back to the wagon—you got no business here."

She retreated before the angry order but she didn't leave. Creeping around, away from her brother, she edged up to peer between the shoulders of two intently watching men. She was shaking with sickened fear.

David's face was stern; he, too, was afraid for Jed. But he knew there could be no stopping of it. This sort of thing could be settled in only one way on the frontier. Sol was a mighty man, Jed would just have to do the best he could. At least David could stop it if things got too dirty. And see that it was only a two-man thing, that no one furnished Sol with any advantages he did not already possess.

David looked across the excited circle to where Sol's crony, Les Prichard, watched, his weasel face a-grin with anticipation. Les was a measly sneak, always toadying around Ward, cadging favor with constant bragging on the big redbeard. Sol treated him with contempt but kept him around, bullyingly making use of him, enjoying his fawning.

There was Jake Tibbetts, too, stolidly watching, the usual dead expression on his hoglike face. He was an obscenely fat, dirty man, uncommunicative beyond grunts. His little eyes, buried in mounds of flesh, expressed pleasure only at small cruelties. He'd been in constant trouble in the train because of unnecessary brutality to his animals. Sol Ward never tried to bully Jake; there was a viciousness about the lardlike man for all his boarish lethargy. He seemed somehow capable of monstrosities and not to be scoffed at safely.

Sol Ward laughed aloud now, a great bellow that shook his belly, and with a bull-like rush charged at the scout. One great fist struck at the side of Jed's head—it would have knocked him out had it landed, but Jed had been watching the hands and so it only scraped skin from one cheek. As the redbeard's flailing arms struck, Jed's hands found a hold on Sol's belt. Using an Indian wrestling trick, he exploited all of the rushing weight and momentum of the charge plus his own complete strength into a great, heaving throw. The astounded watchers saw Sol dive over Jed's crouching shoulder and land with terrible force on his belly, his face plowing the dirt. It was a punishing shock to his big body, it hurt Sol Ward. Gasping for the breath that had been knocked out of him, brushing at the dirt that blinded his eyes, he scrambled up, locating the waiting figure of the scout who had not taken advantage of his prone, stunned position.

Slow trickles of blood seeped on Sol's face, he saw that the scout's face wore a half grin and a frenzy of blood lust brought him unsteadily to his feet. He charged again but more cautiously, half crouching, the bearlike arms reaching. Jed backed slightly, waiting until Sol straightened a little before he let the huge grip encircle him. The scout knew a moment of strangling panic as he experienced the powerful savagery of their crushing strength. But his shorter stature helped and he slipped downward, bending his knees. As the brutal vice tightened, sought to bend him, crack his spine, Ward spread his legs to steady his straining stance. Like a steel spring Jed's bony knee came up in Sol's groin, mercilessly hard.

Agony shot upward through the thick body, loosened the terrible grip of the hairy arms. Jed's fists, one after the other, buried themselves piston-hard in the protruding belly. Sol had gone flaccid momentarily and the fists punished deeply again. The redbeard faltered to one knee. His shaking hands sought his tortured crotch, he shook his shaggy head, his gaze dimmed by the pain deep in his vitals. He raised his blurring eyes to see the scout in a crouching stance waiting for him.

"Call it off, Ward?" Jed asked, watching him.

The terse scorn of the question infuriated Sol beyond all reason. He reached and his right hand drew a knife from his boot. The wicked blade glinted in the firelight.

Jed stiffened. A woman screamed, a low murmur growled through the crowd. "Here, now—" It was Captain Fancher's voice as he started forward. David was moving to interfere, also.

Like a swift, leaping cougar the scout came in on Sol. Before the redbeard gained his feet one moccasined toe shot out and connected with the knife hand. A cracking sound was plainly heard, the knife dropped in the dust. Sol bellowed, reaching for his broken wrist as Jed's other foot, toe rigid, swung punishingly deep into his already tortured belly. The huge man went back, his head thudded on the ground. And Jed kicked him again, this time in the thick neck, just below the ear.

Sol shuddered once and lay still, limply mountainous, his eyes rolled whitely under the half-closed lids. A trickle of blood ran from his open mouth, seeped through the dusty beard, dripped onto the ground.

Jed remained in a crouch, his eyes fixed on Sol, waiting. Then he straightened to glare at the watchers. His angry eyes were beadily dangerous.

"Anybody want to take up for Ward?"

No one answered.

Jed reached a long arm, picked up Sol's knife. A woman whimpered. "He's going to scalp him!" That brought a crooked grin to his bloodied face. When he spoke again it was in his usual flat drawl but the words were ugly. He spoke directly to Sol's cronies, Les and Jake.

"Tell Ward—when he comes to—that I stopped fightin' for the fun of it while I was still a kid. Tell him if he tries to start it again, I'll kill him. I c'n use a knife, some, too." Swift as a lashing snake the knife flew from his hand, struck so close to Sol's head that the shaggy hair parted to receive it.

Jed spoke again. "Tell him that when I draw a knife on a man—I use it. And I got no use for crooked gamblers—tell him I called it again: *Crooked!*"

No one moved or spoke as he reached for his shirt, took his rifle and belt, moved deliberately away into the night. There was awe in the eyes of the watchers who hastily moved to allow him passage.

Eyes shining, David watched him go and then turned a suddenly narrowed stare on Les and Jake. They stared at the prone lump that had been their vaunted champion and then with venomously planning hate after the scout.

David stepped forward from the silent circle, his hard gaze knowing on the pair of them. "Anyone takin' it further with Jed Smith has got me to figger on." His eyes were as coldly flat as his voice. The usually genial face of the stocky man was dangerously set.

"Count me in on that." The slow drawl came from lanky Joel Mitchell, who stepped out to stand spraddle-legged alongside David. His cheerful bony face looked eagerly across the circle; his blood was up, he was itching for a fight.

"And me!" Lawson Mitchell stood happily belligerent beside his brother.

The crafty faces turned sullen. "Aw—who's takin' it any further?" whined Les. "Come on, Jake, give me a hand here." They stepped over and, ungently heaving and hauling, they dragged the beaten man off to his wagon.

Sol's wife, Sairy, a thin, tired-looking woman with a bitterly cast face, looked at him unmoved. Malicious satisfaction appeared in her faded eyes as she took in the extent of the damage.

"One of these here days," she said sourly, "he's gonna learn to keep his big mouth shut. He's gettin' too old and fat to fight ever tough youngun that calls his hand." She got a basin of water and with untender thoroughness started to mop him off.

Melissa had squirmed and pushed her way out of the crowd to run after Jed. Catching a glimpse of him moving through the shadows near their wagon, she gathered up her skirts and ran like a boy. Jed heard the running steps following him and turned as she came up with him.

She was breathless. "Oh, Jed!" she gasped, "are you all right?" Her eyes feverishly explored his face, her hands quivered up to his bare chest, there was something about her expression that startled him.

"Were you there?" he asked disapprovingly.

"Oh *yes!* I saw it all—I was so scared—but how you beat him—and—and—oh, *Jed!*"

Now he recognized the look of her. He'd seen this exultation in the faces of Indian women welcoming their men home from battle. Fierce, lusting pride, woman-strong, hungry to passionately reward a strong warrior.

Jed was surprised and shocked. Squaws, now, they enjoyed a brawl, nothing phased or sickened them. But he'd thought white women carried on, fainted, maybe, at brutality. This small one held surprises for him at every turn. Why—she'd not only stood and watched, she'd actually gloried in his ruthless victory! There was shared triumph in every line of her.

Her shaking touch on his bare chest excited him unbearably. She raised a hand, touched his bloody cheek. "It's bleeding, Jed, and dirty. Come over to the wagon and let me wash it—"

The touch of her hands on him triggered all control away. His arms went around her swiftly, lifting her. The rifle, still in his hand, bruised her as she was held crushingly against him, her feet swept off the ground. Savagely his mouth came down on hers, which was still open and surprised, but instantly responded. One arm was pinned down against him but the other wriggled free and went around his neck, the fingers clutching, holding tight. The whole warm length of her answered to his hunger, arching, pressing frantically closer. It was a long, hurting, glorying kiss, taking all of Melissa's breath. A wonder of ecstatic delight ran eagerly shaking through her body and legs.

When Jed set her on her feet she swayed a little. He steadied her with his arm, the while staring down at her with dark astounded eyes. Her face was flushed, lovely with bright adoration. She smiled delightedly up at him and moved to return close into his arms again.

But he held her away, shaking her shoulder a little. "Get off to your wagon"—it was a husky growl, belied by the shine in his eyes, the tenderness of the crooked grin—"before I drag you off into the bushes like the bloody little squaw you are!"

The pixy smile flashed, her head went back, the warm little chuckle was throaty. "I'll go in the bushes with you, Jed," she announced, "you won't have to drag me."

His narrowed gaze twinkled down at her. "I believe you would, you little hussy," he said, "and then I'd have David on my neck. Get off with you now—" His hand turned her, slapped at her calico rear. He hastily took off in the other direction, not willing to test his control further.

Later, making his final round of the camp, Jed noticed that the paint war horse had been picketed with the mounts used by the herders close to the wagons. He grinned mirthlessly. And then, as he considered various things, he had a hunch. Just could be the redskin would make his try for the horse this very night—there'd been no sign this close to the emigrant road before, Jed would have noticed that splayed print right off. The horse being picketed wouldn't likely hinder a horse stealer who'd been so crafty thus far.

Jed moved his bedroll to a place deep in the shadow of some willow bushes. From here he could see the horse herd and also the picket line. Head pillowed on one arm, he figured a little. It was a dark night, moonrise would be well after midnight. If the Indian made his try it would be before the moon cast any light but after the camp settled down. There were still people moving around their fires, so Jed decided to catch a nap. He dropped off instantly into sleep, waking as though at an alarm when all was finally silent.

The night was inky black, thick with quiet. Jed's eyes, as sharp as a cat's in the dark, sought out the picket line. The war horse stood quietly head down among the shadowy shapes of the other horses. His dark rump was higher than the rest, he was a big horse.

Silently Jed sat up, settled himself comfortably cross-legged, facing the herd and the picket line. The only sounds were the slow movement of hoofs, the somnolent crunching of leisurely jaws. He knew he would hear nothing else, but as his eyes swept in slow circles, which began and ended with the war horse, his ears strained for the slightest, unusual whisper of activity.

He sat motionless for well over an hour. Suddenly his gaze riveted on the fringe of the quiet herd. Two animals grazed out a little from the rest. One of them, the furthest out from the herd, seemed to be moving naturally, but gradually it was approaching the picket line. After a long while the lone grazer cropped grass only a few feet from the picketed animals.

An admiring grin appeared on Jed's face. This redskin was truly an accomplished horse stealer. Not once had the scout caught a glimpse of him, there had been no untoward movement nor had he heard a sound. But Jed knew where the Indian now was, as well as if he looked full at him: behind the herd side of the forward grazing horse. His arm would be crooked around its neck, his hand reaching forward under the mane. His head would be flattened against and below the ridge of the animal's shoulder. His moccasined feet moved only in synchronization with the horse's slow, infrequent steps.

This was a master horse stealer. Among the tribes it was an ancient, well-studied science, and a proud skill. For it could only be acquired dangerously. Jed could knowledgeably appreciate this night's proficiency, for he'd learned what he knew of the intricate art from old Red Feather himself, the chief of the Flatheads. The old man had long been considered to be the greatest horse stealer of all time among the tribes.

There was a certain Blackfoot war chief up on the Milk River who was shy a horse answering to the description of Palouse. Jed enjoyed how it had likely been: the Blackfoot probably stole the spotted roan from the Nez Percé up on the Palouse River, and then Jed stole the horse from him. The Blackfoot would be fit to be tied if he knew it had been a white man did the thieving.

Only once did Jed catch a glimpse of the Indian. When the exchange of horses was made he caught the outline of a shadowy figure against the black shoulder of the big war horse, a shadow that imperceptibly blended and was lost as the horse commenced moving slowly, head down and grazing, toward the herd.

Jed stiffened with surprise. The shadow had been so small–slight. He frowned in puzzlement and then it dawned on him. By God, it was that youngster! That proud stripling with the banked embers of hate glowing in his wild black eyes. The half-grown son of Crazy Horse!

Jed sat motionless for long minutes. His mind was racing, marveling. His heart was suddenly full to suffocation with an emotion he dimly understood. That skinny, half-starved-looking kid. Well, by God!

Now, as the time dragged quietly on, the big horse and its invisible guide were on the fringes of the herd. The tall shape became one with the others, mingled, and was presently lost in the dark, indistinguishable from the many shadowy outlines.

Jed was no longer confused, he knew where he stood now. Noiselessly his hand reached for his saddlebags—which he used as a pillow—searched their contents briefly, checked the revolver that he kept there, making sure all five chambers of the heavy Colt were filled.

The dark pool of shadow under the willows seemed unchanged, but Jed no longer lurked in their shelter. Quieter than a drifting hawk, he faded past the sleeping wagon train. Circling the wagons, heading north and east, he made for a high wooded knoll. He had probed the area around the camp before sundown and knew without thinking about it that this was the likeliest place for the waiting buckskin to be tied. He realized with appreciation that the youngster would have patiently waited out his inspection before taking a position on the knoll, from where he could peer down into the wagon camp. He would have watched the picketing of the paint horse.

Jed figured he had plenty of time to find the buckskin. The boy would graze the war horse slowly back through the herd, his eyes and ears alert for the night guards, like a stalking cougar. When he neared that far line of willows by the little creek the horse would be slid through just at the moment when the slow-moving guard was at the opposite side of his circle. The boy would walk the critter slowly, circling away and come up the knoll on the far side, away from the camp. Then, with two sturdy, fresh mounts, he'd be fast running miles beyond pursuit, come sunup. That'd be the plan. And it was good—but the boy wouldn't have counted on Jed.

The buckskin was there on the knoll, tethered under a tree. There was a hunting bow and a quiver of arrows hanging from a near branch. The night was still black but the moon would soon rise. A faintly lighter sky silhouetted rolling hills off to the east. Jed moved off a ways from the patient little buckskin and settled himself to wait.

The rising moon had just modestly bared a narrow curve of her shoulder when Jed heard the first faint sounds. His mouth slitted into his crooked grin, the kid all but had the big brute tiptoeing.

And then they appeared, the slow-moving big horse and the slight boy, at the edge of the small clearing which was ringed about with trees. Jed moved not a muscle as he watched the boy stop the horse and put both arms around its neck. For a long moment his face was hidden by the black mane. Jed could see the deep sigh shudder across the bony young shoulders.

The scout's moccasins made no more than a whisper of sound as he stepped from concealment but the boy whirled like a cat, his hand whipping to the knife he carried. It gleamed wickedly before him as he sank into a half crouch, his slender muscles tight as a coiled steel spring.

Jed had taken only a few steps; he halted in the open, standing easily with both hands extended, palm up, showing he held no weapon. Like statues they were, motionless, each pair of eyes watching for the slightest movement. Then Jed's quiet voice cut into the tension:

"The son of Crazy Horse," he said in the Sioux tongue, "goes lightly armed to make the big coup."

Seen close to, like this, the boy looked very young. His skin was pale for a Sioux, his hair was brown, not black. Jed recalled that his boy-name was "The Light-Haired One"—he'd been mentioned by one of Bridger's cronies, a white man who lived with the Sioux.

Undersized for his fifteen years, he had a frail look which was very deceptive, Jed knew. Those spare muscles would have the swift lash of a whip—he was plenty dangerous. Jed hoped fervently that he wouldn't throw that mean-looking knife. The scout waited, still as a rock. The boy spoke:

"I take back the honor of my uncle, Spotted Tail," it was a challenge, the way he said it. He remained crouched and ready, his eyes beadily narrowed. He'd fight to the death before he'd give up that war horse.

Jed searched for the right words to speak. He tried them out carefully in his mind before he began.

"My younger brother," Jed said softly, "is indeed an accomplished horse stealer. I, who was the pupil of Red Feather himself, have never seen a warrior more skillful than the son of Crazy Horse."

Surprise, confusion, and uncertainty crossed the thin face. The term "younger brother" was a close, familiar greeting. Uttered in the tribal way it had great significance. The boy straightened from his threatening crouch, his eyes were still wary but the frenzied hate was gone.

Jed spoke again, "I have heard of the Light-Haired One from Hotoa-Quaihoois, Tall Bull, who is a great friend to Bridger, my foster uncle."

The boy knew him now. All caution disappeared from his stance, he sheathed the knife. He acknowledged the identification with a compliment gravely delivered and with all the venerable dignity of a patriarch:

"Word has reached my father's tepee of Jed Smith, the pupil who learned his lesson so well—and of the deep-chested roan he now rides. Long have been the praises sung by Bridger and the Bad Hand."

Jed's grin crooked boyishly at that. Sure, Bad Hand Fitzpatrick, old mountain man, now turned government agent to the Indians on the upper Platte, would have had to blow a little, too. He and Bridger took on big and proud over any thing Jed did passably well. These two tough old roosters had raised him from a pup.

The boy spoke again. "And there are still many among the Old Ones who yet speak of Singing Ax. And they say that his son, Little Ax, now walks fittingly in his tracks."

Jed bowed his head with honest pride. Any place he

set foot the deeds of his father, mountain man Jedediah Strong Smith, lived in legend and firelit chant.

The proud name of Singing Ax had been bestowed by his enemies. Old Jed had been a deeply religious man but a mighty fighter. Deadly in a hand-to-hand fight, his usual weapon was the short ax he carried in his belt. And always, as he hewed a mighty havoc, he chanted prayers for the dying—whose demise he himself sought to make certain. The deep bell of his voice ringing out above the clamor of battle had created mighty big medicine around his person. There'd been times when the superstitious redskins would rather shy off than chance a brush with mountain men if Singing Ax was known to be one of the party. The Indians firmly believed that the powerful God of the white man sat on his big arm, breathing invincible power into him, as he fought.

Ceremoniously Jed now returned the compliment. "I knew the son of Crazy Horse that night he visited the wagon train. We have heard many things of his progress with his warrior-teacher, High Back Bone. How the Light-Haired One killed his first buffalo before his head reached as tall as his father's shoulder. We have also heard that when the time arrives for his naming ceremony he will be given the proud name of his holy father, Crazy Horse."

Now the moon had made her final bold leap clear of the eastern hills and the two young men standing face to face in the little clearing saw each other plainly. Their eyes met with mutual respect and friendly confidence. But it grew late and Jed wanted the youngster away from here.

"The moon has risen to make light your path to the Great Council," he said earnestly, "and I would send word to the tepee of your father, if you will carry it."

"The words of my brother, Little Ax, will be carried in my heart and spoken straight on my tongue."

Jed waited a breath, mapping his message carefully. "Say to your father," he said slowly, "the wise and holy Crazy Horse, that there are some men of our race who shame us—the redbeard who took the war horse is one of these. Say to Crazy Horse that I was made glad by the manner of the return of honor to the lodge of Spotted Tail. It is a fitting thing. I would send a token of friendship to Crazy Horse and greetings to all in his lodge."

Jed lifted his saddlebags from where they lay near the tree and held out the big revolver. "It carries five shots," he said, "for the enemies of Crazy Horse. And in the saddlebags there is grain for the horses and some jerky. The Light-Haired One has not overeaten of late but he should not pause to hunt now."

It was clearly evident that the boy could not have eaten much during the many days of stalking vigilance. Above the breechclout and knife belt that were all he wore, his ribs curved gauntly. He accepted the revolver in both hands, his eyes shining boyishly. He examined it with delighted awe before sticking it carefully through his belt.

The boy placed his hand on Jed's tall shoulder and the accompanying smile made the high-boned thin face wildly beautiful. "The lodge of my father, Crazy Horse, is the lodge of my brother, Little Ax. The day will be good when he brightens it with his coming."

He thrust a thin, muscled arm through the slings of his bow and quiver, settling them to ride securely back of his shoulder. Jed untied the buckskin as, with one lithe movement, the boy mounted the war horse and reached for the halter of the other animal. Jed slung the saddlebags across the pinto's satin shoulder in front of the boy.

"Ride fast, younger brother," he said, "and take no thought for your back trail. Little Ax will not be able to discover your trail. And there be none down there"—with a scornful gesture towards the wagon train—"that could track a fat squaw through a snowbank."

A smile flashed white across the dusky, narrow face. "It will be as you say. And as I ride fast toward the rising of the Great One, I will sing a morning song for my brother."

One last long look passed from the dark eyes to the

blue. Then Jed gave the black shoulder of the war horse a farewell slap and stepped back. Wheeling the big animal, with the buckskin moving obediently alongside, the boy rode out of the clearing toward the north.

Jed moved to the high brow of the hill and stood watching for long minutes. The slender rider was dwarfed, tiny on his powerful mount. As they emerged from the shadows at the base of the hill they crossed a long meadow bathed, now, in full moonlight. Jed saw the stride of the horses lengthen, reach swiftly out, flowing into a full run. Faintly as the echo of a drumbeat, the rhythmic rumble of swinging hoofs came drifting back on the night wind. They reached the far side of the meadow, rushed darkly into enveloping trees, and were gone.

A shadow slid down the knoll and drifted toward the wagon train. Jed circled back toward his bedroll, pausing at the picket line. Tethered in place of the war horse was a tall, raw-boned black gelding. Driven into the ground in front of its nose was a Sioux war arrow, its slender shaft ceremoniously dark with the stain of dried blood. The son of Crazy Horse had observed with warrior-like care all of the traditional details of the coup.

Jed thought, not without wistfulness, of the triumphant entry the boy would make into the camp of his people. Riding the great war horse between the lines of the tepees, startling the crowds of people. He'd have given a lot to see it, maybe he'd hear of it one day from Tall Bull. It'd be a story to hear told—holding all the makings of great legend, always so dear to the Indian heart.

He felt a wave of satisfaction over this night's events, his smile was grim pleasure. And as he sank into sleep his heart mounted and rode with fierce pride in the moonlight above the thundering hoofs of the war horse of Spotted Tail.

## CHAPTER III

The circle of tepees was in a wide deep valley, down the center of which rushed a stream of icy water. Beyond, to the north, rose the tall fortress of the Black Hills—and Bear Butte—where the Great Council of the Teton Lakotas was to be held. Some of the people paused and camped for a few days in this valley where the grass was thickly green and there was abundant water for their horses. Here they would refurbish their finest apparel, make ready their toilettes for the meeting of the many tribes of the Sioux nation now gathering for the council.

For the first time many would get glimpses of those whose names were legend around the night fires—the mighty ones who would sit in the huge double council lodge of many painted skins. When the Great Pipe of the Tetons passed, there to partake would be the Hunkpapa, Four Horns and his nephew, Sitting Bull; Crow Feather of the No Bows; the Two-Kettles' war chief, Long Mandan; Lone Horn the Miniconjou and his giant son, Touch the Clouds. Red Cloud, a young warrior already famous in his youth, would sit in council with his elders for the first time. And not least by any means, their own mighty chief, Man Afraid (They Fear Even His Horse), and the most respected Holy Man of all the tribes, Crazy Horse, the Oglala.

The peacefulness of twilight was on the camp, lingering faintly red on the jagged peaks that brooded over the valley. Blue smoke from the fires ascended straight up into the cooling stillness. These were fires purely for sociability, the cooking fires had smoldered out. All had eaten well, for the hunters had brought in much game this day. And so, with full stomachs producing a cheerful atmosphere, there was great coming and going. Friend sought out old friend, people looked about for their relatives, strangers greeted each other in sociable fashion. It had been long since the tribes had thus gathered with peaceful intent and an air of comradeship permeated the bustling camp.

Suddenly a shrill, far-off war cry knifed through the calm evening—a clarion cry of wild triumph. Alarm halted women in their tracks, warriors leaped for weapons; heads swiveled, eyes searched for the source of the cry.

On a high ridge to the west, silhouetted against the liquidly roseate sky was a lone rider on a great horse. He raised his right arm, held high a hunting bow, forming a slender black cross against the sky. The thin, fierce cry sounded again and the horse reared, flung perilously back, pawing savagely at the sky.

Forcing the animal down, the rider kicked him into a thunderingly dangerous run down the hillside and toward the tepees in the valley. As they drew near, a smaller horse was seen to be running free alongside. It was a buckskin, its belly almost to the ground as it ran, bursting with valiant effort to match the headlong speed of the larger horse. The buckskin's black mane and tail flew like sable pennons above the sweating gold of its barrel.

The rider began to saw at the mouth halter of the great horse well before they reached the outskirts of the camp, finally dragging him into another fighting rear. The buckskin nearly collided with the spotted haunch but plunged clear in a dust-raising circle. The big horse was reduced to an unwilling, straining trot and then to a walk. Mouth agape, the heavy, slavering jaws fought the halter; the big head was awry, the eyes wild and bulging as the great hindquarters bunched and knotted with the high lift of each ponderous pace.

The boy astride the spotted stallion—thin arms almost rigid as the long muscles were drawn taut as steel wires with the strain of holding the animal in—faced forward, glancing neither to the left nor the right. His high, thin profile sharp as a young hawk, his eyes somber with pride, he rode slowly between the rows of lodges and the gathering clusters of people.

Palms clapped to mouths to register amazement, voices murmured excitedly. From here and there came welcoming cries from friends and the trilling of female relatives proudly hailed a coup. For they knew him now and the word passed to those who were unacquainted with the fact that the slender rider was the Light-Haired One—the son of Crazy Horse, the great Holy Man of the Oglalas.

Many had known of the loss of the war horse of Spotted Tail. And recalled now that the Light Hair's mother was of the family of the imprisoned war chief. It was most fitting for a relative to have recovered the horse—but almost unbelievable that one so young had accomplished this thing!

The shame and disgrace associated with the manner in which it had been lost had been whispered of throughout the traveling camps. It would not do to speak openly of it, for the brave, who drank of the white man's whisky and so, unwittingly, betrayed an honor trust, was yet a proven warrior in all else. Many there were who became senseless with the poison of the whisky dulling the mind and none felt called on to speak out openly and bring about public dishonor and loss of face. Time would provide this warrior many chances to regain his standing and there were few among them who did not have a shame or two in his past. Sometimes it was good, for, in the proving, the lifting above himself, a man often rose to inspired heights. The great do not become truly great until they have suffered and gone on—remembering humbleness.

The tepee of Crazy Horse stood at the far end of the encampment, the sides rolled up in deference to the warmth of the summer twilight. It was fashioned of creamy white skins and decorated with the images of the Holy Man's visions: the badger, a wildly prancing horse—from which he took his name—and the spotted eagle from which he received much power and holiness.

Crazy Horse stood, now, before his lodge watching his son as he approached, riding the war horse slowly between the clamoring aisles of people. The boy saw his father standing straight and tall, motionlessly waiting, and he fixed his eyes eagerly on the starkly boned, beloved face. The deep-set eagle glance of the man was now shining with pride in his son.

The Holy Man wore only a breechclout of blue cloth and was, as always, without ornamentation. His medicine forbade the taking of trophies for show. His long black braids were wrapped in narrow strips of badger skin which still wore the glossy fur; one braid held a single feather from the spotted eagle. The still face of the man betrayed none of the surprise he felt. He had not known that the boy had undertaken this lone, dangerous expedition. Crazy Horse had supposed his son to still be traveling with his warrior-teacher, High Back Bone, called Hump, with whom he spent most of his time these days. And so he had been, until they had come up with people who paused to hunt where the White Earth River poured past the narrow canyons of the broken-up lands. There had been some of his mother's people among them and they had invited the boy to take part in the hunting. These people had traveled for a few days near the Holy Road of the white man—and had visited the wagon train.

The boy brought the war horse to a halt and slid from its back. His had been a brave show but as he placed the halter in his father's hand it could be seen that the narrow face was drawn, sunken exhaustion was in the feverishly glowing eyes. The clamor of voices drowned the quiet words of welcome the father spoke to his son, but all saw the lifted hand of Crazy Horse and they hushed to hear what he would say.

"My son must have food, now, and rest—but later he will tell us of this thing!" The Holy Man beckoned to his son's friend, young He Dog, to take the horses to the herd. He Dog leaped joyously onto the back of the pinto and rode slowly through the encampment and on to the herd beyond. The people drew near, reached to stroke the sweating, dust-caked shoulders of the war horse. As they returned to their fires many recalled how it had been when Spotted Tail took this war horse from an enemy Crow in the heat of battle. A long-ago coup, before his trouble with the white men, but still good to tell and hear. And the telling brought back memories of other long-stored, proud legends of the people.

The fires were rekindled into leaping, cheerful life. This would be a fine night of story and chanting. The boy's brave triumph was a fine omen to take with them into the Great Council. There had been much shaken faith of late caused by the Lakotas' ordeal with the white men. The banner of tribal honor was tattered, it had been scorned.

Pride had been beaten into the dust too often of late. For they had seen their women and children die under the thundering guns of the whites—in what should have been the sanctuary of undefended camps. Restitution had not been made, nor revenge taken and many felt shame because of this.

The pushing inroads of the countless caravans of wagon trains drove away the wild game from the hunting areas, their very life sustenance was threatened. They were being forced out of land they had roamed since ancient, legendary times. And they saw, with shame and confusion, that their wisest chiefs did not seem able to treat with the whites. The workings of the white mind evaded them—they were betrayed again and again: by broken treaties that the red men had regarded as inviolate; by bad faith, for the forked tongues of the whites promised one thing and did another. There were forked tongues even among those who wore the uniform and said they came with word from the Great White Father—who never came, none had ever seen him. He appeared to have first one name and then another, he, too, changed as often as the incomprehensible white mind. For in each name a different bargain was driven. But not kept; the white soldiers were never seemingly bound to his word. They had seen that honor, where it pertained to the red man, was held a thing for laughter by officers who flourished peace treaties in one domanding hand even as the other secretly beckoned their soldiers and wagon guns to the attack.

It was good, now, to forget the unceasing anxiety of their predicament for a time. To listen to a boy's story of his coup—taken in the very camp of a wagon train of white men. Many crowded close around the leaping fire before the lodge of Crazy Horse. The Light-Haired One stood proudly erect before them but his voice was modestly low as he recounted the days of his vigilant stalk. There was a deep sighing sound as he brought the story to its successful conclusion.

It had been good to hear of the white scout who had shown friendship, sent a properly respectful greeting to the Holy Man. But that might have been expected of that one—who had been raised among the tribes and had learned their ways. Many heads nodded at the indentification of Little Ax, Jed Smith, and all knew of his foster father, Jim Bridger. The Light-Haired One told how he had climbed a tree and watched as Little Ax fought the huge red-bearded one—left him senseless and bleeding in the firelight. Faded eyes gleamed once again among the revered Old Ones, gray heads nodded pleased approbation that the son was as his father had been before him. Some among them had fought against the mighty Singing Ax himself—and felt pride in the fact that they still lived to tell of it. Toothless mouths widened into fiercely reminiscent grins, old heads nodded pleasurably again and again as they paid warm tribute to the memory of an honorable enemy.

On the day following the triumphal return of the son of Crazy Horse the people traveled on to Bear Butte, where the hordes of the Sioux nation gathered for the Great Council. Hearts and hopes were high as to its outcome for the future path of the tribes was to be decided by the leaders.

At its conclusion, the decisions of the Great Council of the Teton Lakotas brought varied emotions to the people. For, as in any council where the few decide for the many, there was dissatisfaction. For some, the decision for peace brought hope, anticipation of better times. But the young warriors, the hot-blooded ones, smoldered, stifled under a barely concealed resentment.

The son of Crazy Horse was bitterly disappointed. He

felt that he was ready, now, to become a member of raiding parties. He was completely appalled by the peaceful future planned for the people. His views were shared by a white trader, one of the few who freely came and went among the tribes, staying to hunt, to join in the raids and occasional fighting whenever the notion took him. The Mormon, Josh Wade, served under Porter Rockwell when he was in Mormon country but at other—and happier, times he traveled among the tribes, at home in the wilderness as he was never at home in the swarming anthill of organized workers that the Mormon kingdom had become. For Brigham Young advocated peace with the red men and the very climate of peacefulness smothored Josh Wade unbearably. For several years he had been known as Takuskanskan among the Sioux tribes—a name that bore mystic significance of his terrible prowess in battle. It was believed by many that the dark night gods invested him with invulnerability, which was not surprising since the dread Medicine Wolf itself was his familiar spirit. Always, it was said, the ghost wolf traveled with him.

Josh Wade was disgusted by the decisions of the Great Council. Were they, then, going to do nothing but sit moaning like old women, licking ancient wounds and figuring how to avoid a fracas? Some of the youngsters had done their best to avert this dull prospect. Young Red Cloud, now, he'd spoken a rousing piece. And that big young rascal, Touch the Clouds, his blood was up, he was more than ready for war paint. The old folks had listened to them indulgently, applauding generously; they had nodded their heads in approval, but only of their spirit, they heeded not at all their words. They had listened closely to Crazy Horse, the Holy Man of the Oglalas, who ceremoniously had chanted and then told of a revelation he had received bearing on their destiny. The people, he said, must cease all intertribal warfare, must unite in brotherhood if they were to survive the invasion of the white man. And he further predicted that it was—and would forever be—useless to fight the white man. They must unite, present a strong front, and deal with the white leaders in peaceable, treaty fashion.

A thoroughly disgusted Josh Wade had decided he might as well get on back to Mormon country if this was the way the stick floated in the tribes. Maybe enough time had passed for Brigham to simmer down—he'd been riled at Josh for sure about the Morris incident. Times were sure changed, even the Mormon leader was getting lily-fingered and fussy—raising all kinds of hell over old Joe Morris and his scraggly band. Brigham had wanted him shut up—stopped in what he was up to—hadn't he? Then why did he get so upset because Josh saw to it they were quieted for all time?

Josh was sullenly packing his plunder. His horse, a long-legged black gelding, stood saddled and waiting when the boy appeared and stood watching him. Josh nodded slightly, acknowledging his presence, and went on with his task. He'd seen the kid before, he was the one they talked so big about having stolen the pinto stallion back from the wagon train. A right likely young one, and spunky. He'd do all right even if his father was a holy man and turning granny-cautious.

The boy spoke. "I would be a warrior." There was a smoldering outrage in the thin, wild face, resentment in the voice. Josh nodded his approval of this ambition, glancing at the boy from under his dark, beetling brows as he tied his few belongings with strips of hide into a compact bundle. The youngun would get around to what he had come to say after a while. It always took the redskins a power of time to get through the preliminaries. Maybe somebody had sent him with a message but he'd have to introduce himself properly and give his views on a sight of things before he got around to his real business. Took time, palavering with Indians. If you tried to get down to business in a hurry, all you did was upset them, confuse them. Sometimes they got mad and refused to talk at all. So he held his peace, waiting. The boy continued.

"I killed my first buffalo, long since, and many more

besides. I have counted coup against the white man, thus returning honor to the lodge of my uncle, Spotted Tail."

Josh's nod this time was ceremoniously deep, commending, but he did not speak his applause, for it was very impolite among the tribes to interrupt a harangue. And this kid deserved the politeness due a warrior, looked like he maybe had more guts than the whole Sioux tribe put together.

"My father, Crazy Horse, speaks only of peace!" It was a bald statement with an undertone of criticism. Josh lifted his brows in some surprise, though there had been no disrespect in his manner, only impatience and rebelliousness. But there was something of scorn in what he added. "And my warrior-teacher, Hump, sits with his women, filling his belly and nursing old wounds!"

Josh's wolf grin spread his beard appreciatively at this. The kid looked about to explode, his whole thin body quivered, he'd wanted excitement and action and his eager, untried ferocity had met with only dampening pacification. Josh had tied his sparse pack behind the saddle, adjusted the saddlebags and gathered up the reins from where they dragged on the ground beneath the nose of the quiet horse. He was ready to mount and ride but he leaned against the saddle now to hear the boy out. His usually ice-gray gaze was almost compassionate on the young rebel. For Josh Wade knew well all the surging depths of exasperation, the impatient boiling of the blood produced by prolonged inaction, peacefulness grown monotonously old and rankling.

This belligerent cockerel had the makings of a prime warrior; he'd give a pile to see him when he'd grown up to his big ambitions. Apparently born without fear—if the stories about him were true, and likely they were. His dark eyes had the intent wildness of a stalking cougar but there was also a passionate intelligence and more than a hint of recklessness.

"My medicine," the boy continued, in his formal, old warrior manner, "is that of a fighting horse. My father read the signs—I am to be a war chief of the Oglalas."

Josh's face was grave, he was listening patiently, although it looked like the boy was going to prolong his palaver like any of the Old Ones would. But his next words came abruptly, in a burst of furious exasperation: "How can I fulfill the prophecies if they but sit, prating of peace? How can I become a warrior if my teacher keeps me coddling my mother's fire?"

Josh shook a commiserating head. He had a point there, all right. Then the boy went on, more quietly. "Takuskanskan is a great warrior, the mightiest of all in battle!" Josh bowed his shaggy head in acknowledgment of the fine compliment.

"I would—" Eager pleading and something of reverence were in the voice. "The Light Hair would become the pupil of Takuskanskan!"

Josh was startled, totally unprepared for this development. His glance held amazement—and it was not without gratification. It was a time-honored custom for the renowned warriors to train the young men but never had he been offered this signal status. It was usually the father who asked it as a boon from a friend, that the son be trained. But at times the young men themselves made such a plea to a warrior high in their esteem. Josh was leaving, it was impossible for him to grant the boy's request. But he did not flatly deny the boy, for he felt oddly warmed. It had been a long time since anyone had courted his sullen company; his gruff voice held an almost unused note of concern.

"I leave now, to travel far," he said, "I go toward the Holy Road of the whites, through enemy country—for one of your people—and then deep into the realm of the white Mormonies"—his look on the youngster was regretful—"I do not know when I will return to this people."

The boy's shoulders straightened valiantly, his head lifted another proud notch, his look burned dedicatingly. "No path is too long, no place too far for the Light Hair to follow in the steps of his teacher."

The bearded man stiffened, straightened out of his lounging position. He was startled, shocked, almost. Pushing back his hat, Josh stared at the boy with astonished conjecture. He thoughtfully scratched a place under his greasy buckskin thigh; restlessly his hand dug out a twist of tobacco and, biting off a sizable hunk, he chewed powerfully, his face thoughtful. He scratched the stubble of hair worn off by his sleeve, and spat. All the time his quizzical eyes considered the boy, who stood rigid, arrow-straight, the importance of this moment of decision freezing every line of his thin body. But his liquid dark eyes beseeched his cause, begged for escape, reminding Josh of a caged and desperate wild thing. Cages were the worst fate to befall a denizen of the wild, he thought, death was infinitely more merciful. God, thought Josh, as the boy's intensity conveyed itself to him with such strength, how long has it been since anything mattered that much to me?

Finally he spoke. "Your father, Crazy Horse, would not look on such a thing with favor."

The boy had an answer ready for this. "My father did not know when I undertook to restore the honor of Spotted Tail—nor did my warrior-teacher, Hump, know. And yet both commended the deed—when it was done."

Josh's grin acknowledged the freeing logic of this reply—this youngun was damn smart as well as spunky. Likely he'd do on any trail, alone or in company. The man gathered up his reins, placed his moccasined toe in the stirrup, and swung easily into the saddle. He settled himself back against the cantle comfortably, checked his rifle in its scabbard and then looked down at the boy, he was frowning thoughtfully. Between them the silence was long and significant. The young lifted face was full of final, desperate entreaty. Josh spoke slowly.

"I'll likely stop to water my horse where the little fork comes around the bluff at the end of the third canyon opening," he said, "likely I'll rest there a while, too." He nodded to the boy. "Should anyone ride up to the water hole while I'm there—likely we could travel on together." He swung the horse's head and rode away into the twilight without looking back.

The night was pitchy dark as the black horse and its tall rider approached the little grove of trees. There was a subdued murmur of flowing water; the moon had not yet risen and stars glimmered faintly through low-hanging shreds of clouds. At the edge of the small stream Josh dismounted and let the horse drink, loosened the saddle girths to ease him. The black drank long and gratefully, the wet sucking noise the only sound in the stillness. When he had drunk his fill he moved to crop the rich grass along the bank of the stream. Josh stretched out under a tree, quietly waiting, listening. There was only a whisper of night wind, the murmur of the stream, and the familiar, crunching sounds from the horse.

It was less than an hour when Josh's ears picked up the faint sounds of hoofs on the trail. At the same time, the black lifted his nose, whickered softly. As a lighter shadow moved out of the night, the buckskin answered his greeting. Light Hair rode into the clearing beside the stream and slid off the little mare. He was dressed for travel in worn hunting leggings and a fringed, wrap-around shirt, the capacious pockets of which now bulged. Around his narrow waist a belt supported a sheathed Green River knife. He carried a short hunting bow and a quiver of arrows was slung over his shoulder. The mare was accoutered for travel, also; tied to strands of her long mane were several small skin bags holding travel fare and she wore a folded blanket belted on her back, which the boy rode, saddle-wise, his legs dangling.

The man spoke calmly. "Rest now—let the mare drink and graze a while 'fore we travel on." The boy obeyed and lowered his slight form onto the grass beside the man. They did not speak further, each listened drowsily to the quiet of the wilderness. For a long time there was nothing but the murmurous background of silence.

Then, from far away to the west where the night still hung a dense, unbroken curtain of clouds came the faint, eerie cry of a lone wolf, and it was like the keening wail of a stricken woman. Again the call sounded, like the ghostly echo of a lost soul. The man's shaggy head turned, his eyes became hauntedly alight. He looked at the boy, waited for his reaction. The head of the black horse swung, lifted as he listened, his wise ears pointing westward. The buckskin raised her sable nose and, listening nervously, moved as though for comfort so that her shoulder brushed that of the big gelding. Side by side the two horses waited motionlessly, their feeding forgotten in the malign warning of that wild call.

It came yet a third time—wailing, drifting brokenly away to be lost in the silence of the shadowy canyons. Josh did not speak, but after a time the frozen boy found his voice and its calmness showed the control he could exert over mortal fear.

"I have heard it said that the Medicine Wolf is a familiar spirit to Takuskanskan."

Josh's grin was hidden by the dark; he approved the almost nonchalant manner of the observation. "I've got used to her," he said. "Heard her off and on for years —she turns up mostly when I'm travelin'."

"I did not know that the Medicine Wolf was female."

"This one is—I got a glimpse of her once, far off. A gray wolf, too small to be a full-growed male—and that call ain't a puppy yippin'. I take it to be female, got my reasons for that. It's been good medicine for me, and bad for my enemies. And then—it was because of a woman that I first set my foot to the warpath."

"Because of a woman?" The boy's excited interest persuaded Josh to elaborate. "I done my first killin' because of a woman," he said slowly, "a little woman with long golden hair. And if any spirit speaks to me from the she-wolf, yonder, it's her."

The boy was silent with awe of the dark depths into which he had been allowed to peer concerning the secret medicine of Takuskanskan. A little woman—with long golden hair. Truly, she must be a god-woman to have set the shaggy giant on his long and bloody path for many had fallen to his hand. The boy had seen a few white women but none with golden hair. It must be a very rare and deadly medicine, for most in the tribe feared this man—who, himself, knew no fear. Truly he had chosen well in his teacher and there would be action. For the old ones said that when Takuskanskan appeared and the Medicine Wolf called, it always foretold bloodshed. Some called it evil but all were glad to number him among the warriors when they rode to seek the enemy, for he was seemingly invincible.

Some days later Josh Wade and his young companion rode into the deep wheel tracks of the Holy Road. As they traveled on toward Fort Bridger they were overtaken by four fast-traveling white men. One of them greeted Josh with surprised cordiality. It was Port Rockwell, gray in his black hair and beard now, but still vigorously riding in the service of the Mormon leader.

Rockwell shook his head musingly as he looked at Josh. "Might have knowed you'd show up," he said, "for there's trouble—bad trouble comin'. Likely Brother Brigham will be willin' to forget he was so riled with you—now. We're gonna need every man——"

Josh's eyes brightened, his wolf grin showed through his beard at the news Rockwell gave him: that an army already marched the emigrant trail, heading for the Mormon kingdom. There might be war. "Guess I'm gettin' back in time for some fun," Josh remarked contentedly.

Port had lifted a quizzical eyebrow at the presence of the Indian youth. Josh was offhand. "Name of Young Crazy Horse," he said briefly, "by way of bein' sort of a foster son." The man had cautioned the boy not to mention his name or Sioux origin while they were in Shoshoni territory—enemy country for the son of Crazy Horse. But, traveling on now in company with the dreaded Port Rockwell and his companions, there would be no risk attached to his identity. Josh had taught the boy a few words of English and also told him to keep his mouth shut in company. No one would question Josh Wade about an Indian boy that he named foster son, for he was light in coloring and hair. He would be taken as the result of some casual breeding of a squaw. Josh did not mind this interpretation in the least, in fact he found it curiously pleasing, the boy would do him proud.

Port accepted the explanation unquestioningly. "He'll have to put out to keep up," he said, "if you allow to travel with us. Brother Brigham don't know about the army yet—we've got to get there, fast!"

Josh nodded, undisturbed. "The buckskin'll do—and the kid, too," he said, "both of 'em got plenty of guts."

There followed hard days of punishing travel for the boy. At Fort Bridger he was sent to the squaw in the kitchen for food after which he collapsed and slept for the few hours of their short pause. They rode out of Bridger on fresh horses, with the black and the buckskin on leading halters. As they traveled at a recklessly fast pace down the rocky canyons, the boy could scarcely contain his excitement. They rode toward a marvel he had never thought to see: the city of the white men.

## CHAPTER IV

Annie Fancher was incurably romantic. Behind the gaunt face and bristling demeanor dwelt a tender, wistful soul. Annie had been an old maid of twenty-two when she had finally captured Charley Fancher and she knew how it was to be alone—how empty a woman's life could be without a man in her bed.

She was vigorously interested in Melissa's romance with Jed Smith. There were a number of single men in the wagon train, but Annie had privately judged the scout to be the most promising specimen of male animal around. However, the man himself was a strange type, almost an unknown quantity. After Jed whipped Sol Ward, Annie's somewhat cautious approval became wholehearted. "That there is all man, Lissy," she said, "but you'd best get a halter on him fast—he's got a sort of wanderin' look to him."

Melissa was willing to accomplish the haltering but uncertain how to proceed. Her record of efforts to manage him was not, so far, impressive. And, opportunities few, their contacts were brief—and public, limited to hand waving and conversations at supper with David present. The ever-present threat of Indians canceled out chances for moonlight strolls. Besides, everyone was so tired. As the trail roughened, Melissa was exhausted when the day was done. It was into the bedrolls at first dark for everyone—for the before-dawn rising.

They had thought the stretch before Fort Laramie wearily hard. And it had been. But they discovered to their dismay that it had been only the mildest of warm-ups for the climb to South Pass.

There had been some discontent in the train—from those who were not stockowners—that the huge herds slowed the rate of travel possible by the strong Missouri mules. But now the herds could easily have outdistanced the straining teams. The grade was up, always up. The trail along the rocky sidehills tilted precariously over chasms, canyons suddenly dropped their floors out of sight as they drove slantingly along their very edge. Great boulders threatened wheels, wagons bogged down in sand. There were frequent delays caused by breakdowns, bad judgment, and just plain cussedness. Tempers grew short, angry quarrels took the place of mild differences. The very country itself was hostile.

The friendly-seeming green hills along the Platte had given way to eroded buttes, monstrous slag formations loomed weirdly. It was late summer and the grass along the upper Platte was a brown, dead color. Very nourishing for the animals, but the sight of it, moving relentlessly under them at the slow rate of their ponderous wheels, was depressing. It had a somber, done-with-life look to it. Daily they passed the pitiful grave markers of those who had died and been buried beside the trail. So very many of them had been women and children.

Silhouetted across the western sky, far enough away so as to seem cloudlike, but still awesomely repelling, loomed the Rocky Mountains—the mighty backbone of the world. Many looked with fear at that rugged outline, knowing that they must be challenged, crossed.

The train toiled on, day after dusty choking day. Following the tediously meandering curves of the Sweetwater; advancing on the fairy-tale splendor of the raggedly snow-capped peaks of the Wind River Range, at the base of which was South Pass—the only way by which wagons could cross the Continental Divide.

Melissa choked on the dust, cursed the heat, the bugs, and snakes, and drove her mules. David took over when the going was hazardous but most of his time must be spent with the horse herd. The sudden violences of the wind in this high altitude had a spooking effect on the horses, they were fractious, had to be herded closely.

The weather had a far from beautifying effect on complexions; Melissa resentfully examined her wind-burned face in a small mirror. There were small dry scales on her nose and forehead, the freckles seemed to have gotten larger and darker. She was dismayed, she just knew that she looked really horrible! For the first time in her life the sunbonnet stayed severely tied and she bewailed her fate to Annie, who commanded her to come over every night for a cup of buttermilk to smear on her face at bedtime. Annie had fresh butter all the time—the churn bouncing along in the wagon produced butter with little further churning.

Melissa, cup in hand, reported at Annie's wagon for her portion of buttermilk. Hildegarde Jones was there seeking help from the authoritative Annie. Her baby—and it was her first—was fretful and feverish, she was worried over what could ail him. Annie looked sharply at the wailing infant and thrust an exploratory finger into his mouth. She exclaimed delightedly when he bit down hard.

"Let's give a look, Hildy," she said, and forced the peevish little mouth open with an experienced finger, bending to peer. "Land alive—he's just teethin', Hildy!" she said comfortingly. "Poor little feller—he'd ought to have something hard and cool to bite on. His gooms is all swole and sore, no wonder he's cross." She thought for a moment. "I got just the thing!" She dove into a chest. "There you are, lovey," she was handing the baby a bone handle that had come off her carving knife a few days back. The baby instantly stuck the smoothly rounded end into his drooly pink mouth. A ridiculous expression of astonished relief appeared on the tiny face, he smiled with toothless gums around the teether. "Hurts good, don't it, honey?" Annie's usually brusque voice was crooning.

Melissa, distracted from her own problem, looked with fascination at the plump baby now contentedly sucking and biting, making little juicy sounds of enjoyment. Tiny babies were outside her experience. He was so cute—suddenly her hands itched to touch, hold him. She looked at Hildy, a pretty, trail-thin girl about her own age. "Could I—maybe hold him a minute?" she asked hesitantly.

Hildy promptly plumped the baby in Melissa's eagerly awkward arms. Her own ached with daylong weariness of toting him. "You sure can! Any ole time you want to—he gets to be an awful load."

It was nearly sundown and Melissa needed to get back to her wagon and get her supper on the fire. But the baby was so sweet. He smelled somewhat sour, he had puked on himself and his diaper was soggy. But there was that wonderful, indescribable baby smell, too. And the soft bumping of the round, downy head against her shoulder, the sweet back of the fat neck to kiss. His round eyes were like a pair of startled blue stars.

Melissa needn't have worried about her roughened skin—it was not even noticed by one who looked at her just then. She was so engrossed in Hildy's baby that she didn't see Jed ride slowly by, taking in with suddenly intent eyes a new picture to add to the kaleidoscope that was Melissa. Sunbonnet pushed back, the fading, rosy rays of light on her bright hair, she was ecstatically absorbed in the baby cradled in her arms. A gurgling cherub of a small baby.

A wonder of startled discovery was in Jed's thoughts

as he took absent-minded care of Palouse. What he had just seen confronted him with an earth-shaking personal significance. It represented a future sequel completely unconsidered before now. He and Melissa—there was very apt to be this sort of development. He edged cautiously around his feelings—did he really want to get tied down, just yet? Get involved in the responsibility for something like that? Babies were such helpless little things—a man couldn't just walk away—life had been pretty damn free, maybe he wouldn't like it——. Sons, perhaps; you'd get all taken up—a man's own flesh and blood, growing up, you'd have to stick around, teach and train them. And daughters—that'd be a chore, always looking after them. Little girls with yellow curls? And small busy hands like their mother's.

His perplexed brow smoothed, the frown became a sheepish grin. Suddenly he felt a ridiculous urge to laugh hilariously, to shout. At least to announce his discovery to someone. He swung away from the horse herd and headed for David's wagon. He'd best not try to tell this to Melissa—she'd think he was crazy. But at least he could look at her all he wanted, all through supper. On the way to her wagon he passed Sol Ward.

The big redbeard went sullenly about his work these days, still carrying his bandaged wrist in a dirty sling. He saw the scout nearing and averted his gaze. Surprisingly, Jed grinned at him and spoke.

"Hiya, Ward," he said easily, "how's the arm?"

Sol squinted at him suspiciously. "All right," he said grudgingly.

Jed's lean brown face was cheerful. "No hard feelin's?"

"Not on my part," Sol admitted heavily. " 'Pears you was right—about the Injun fixin' to steal the horse, I mean."

"Nor on mine," said Jed. He nodded in friendly fashion and as he walked away, exuberance was in every line of his long stride. Sol turned to peer after him, puzzled; the scout's face had been open, the eyes not shuttered in that Indian look he'd habitually held people off with. The redbeard caught the drifting sweetness of a whistled tune. It was—by God, it was a love song!

Sol had to grin. "Well, for Chrissake," he muttered, shaking his head in wonderment. He remembered now. Sairy had said the scout was shining up to that little sister of David Boller's. The slim one with all the yellow hair. Didn't blame him a bit, she was a cute little piece, kind of pert and pretty. And there was something sort of special about a gal with yellow hair. He'd kind of gone for the towheads, himself, when he was young.

His wife, Sairy, had black hair. There was a reason for that, too—him marrying a woman with dark hair. If he'd been willing to think it through. All through the years his thinking had shied clear of the reason. For at a certain point in his life he'd taken to avoiding little, yellow-haired women.

If the memory of it sneaked in on him, there was always pain. Unhealed, in spite of the passage of nearly twenty years. The pain of old shame and a horror of himself. No use, really, to drag it out and fret over it. What's done's done—finished. But a man could argue till doomsday with himself and treacherous memory still haunt sometimes with reminders. Of a small, white-aproned woman—and a snap shot. One that he'd never expected to reach its target. Hell, he hadn't ever been that good a shot with a revolver. Just to scare her a little, it'd been. But she'd run right into it and gone down, blood staining her dress. Even crazy drunk as he'd been, Sol Ward hadn't intended to really shoot down a woman. But with everybody drunk and shooting and yelling—— And then that bull of a man—her husband, more than likely—had come roaring at him and he'd been so frantically scared at what he'd done that he hardly knew how it happened. Even after he'd rode the man down the bugger kept getting up. He'd had to finish him off, when all Sol wanted by then was to get away from there. The terror was chokingly sick in his throat and belly the way the man kept fighting to get at him, kept getting up. Times it came over him in his sleep and he'd wake up shaking and sweating and nothing would help but a big slug of whisky to quiet his nerves.

And he'd lost the beautiful knife his paw had made for him with his own hands. Left it sticking there in the Mormon's chest, couldn't get it out and couldn't stand to stay and try. He'd stopped fighting by then, the big young man—looked to be about Sol's own age—but the knife stayed. Likely was buried with him. The thought was bitter.

Sol had been so horrified at what they'd done—he and that gang of toughs his paw had warned him against—that he went home and told what they'd done. Paw had been good about it, once he got over his first awful anger. He'd made Sol shave off the beard he'd strutted so because it made him look older than he was. And then he'd sent him off to some kinfolks that lived in Kentucky—away from the bad company he'd been keeping. Away from the Mormon war and the consequences of what he'd done.

But—and this was the thing that hurt the most—the Mormons avenged themselves for Haun's Mill. One night, not so long after, two buckskin-clad strangers stopped their horses at Paw's gate and gave friendly hail for Ward to come out and speak with them. It was a neighbor way of passing word in the area of outlying farms. It was after dark, but Paw, not owning an enemy in the world, stepped to the door and opened it wide.

The light from the big fireplace was behind him, the flames making brighter his red hair and beard. Neither of the dark riders uttered a further word, Maw said, after. One of them lifted his rifle and shot Paw down, square through the heart. He was dead when he hit the floor at her feet. And then they rode away, not hurrying, for Maw saw them plainly: two, big, black-bearded men.

After that Sol wasn't welcome around home any more. He didn't blame his maw, for seeing him only put her in mind that his drunken meanness had cost his father's life. And Paw barely forty, strong and hearty as any young buck. She'd given him the other elkhorn knife, the one his grandpap had made for Paw. It was all that he had of his father's.

But he'd evened things up a little. He'd drifted up to Illinois country and took a hand in the Mormon-baiting there. Wolf hunts, they'd called them. They'd had some right rare sport a time or two. A whole pack of them corner a Mormon or two— He'd used Grandpap's knife, more than once; but more careful, he intended to keep this one for always.

But a man can enjoy devilment for just so long and he'd about had his fill of the bloody business when he met Sairy. He and Sairy had been pretty good together for a while. She wasn't a bad old girl—if she'd just give over her nagging and whining. A man had a right to a slug of whisky if he felt like it now and then. Maybe if they'd had kids things would have been better. But it had seemed like Sairy couldn't carry full time. She'd missed on four—or was it five? Seemed to somehow hold that against him, too. Some damfool woman talk about she couldn't go full time because he'd had a dose or two back in his hellraising days. Sure, those waterfront sluts were dirty and none too choice, but how was a drunken youngun to know what misery could follow the laying of them?

Sol's steps slowed as he neared the always dubious welcome of Sairy's cooking fire. More than likely she'd be at it again, like an old bitch dog worrying a worn-out bone. Nagging at him for needing a slug or two to ease the ache in his busted arm. He heard voices, laughter, from the other fires. Pity a woman couldn't have a cheery word for a tired man of a night. Maybe the Mormons had the right idea when it came to women—a passel of wives. Then if the old one got lippy you could just sashay around and sleep with the youngest and prettiest.

Sol's eyes glinted maliciously. He'd just sort of mention that to Sairy, about how it'd be if a man had more than just one old, worn-out wife. Likely it'd rile her so she'd jaw about it the whole night and maybe not notice so sharp how many slugs it took to ease his arm. It ached something fierce.

Sol was not alone with his aches and pains. Many went around stinking of horse liniment put on to ease strained muscles and aching backs. The trail was relentlessly taking a great toll of their strength. Night was so filled with aching exhaustion that the whiners lacked even the gumption to whine.

Up, always up, they toiled. Toward the hot, blue sky boiling with gray-white thunderheads which seldom relieved them with cooling rain. Bombed by thunderclaps which pounded and echoed against the rocky heights, they were also engulfed constantly by dust devils whirling around them, taunting their every effort to breathe. Eyes burned and smarted, ran streams of futile tears. Chests heaved like bellows for air at this altitude. If a man walked with his mouth wide open to gather enough thin air it was only to have it full of dust, which was spat out mud.

No telling which was worse—to walk or ride in the jolting wagons where the canvas top was but a trap to retain the hot dust. Many of the women walked. The kids and dogs thrived, running alongside, yelping like little savages the livelong day. The slow pace of the wagons was no strain on their racing. Gradually the women toughened. The fat ones sloughed layers of weight and the thin ones got skinnier. But miraculously everyone stayed well.

They began to feel as if South Pass would never be reached, the journey was nightmare. And then, suddenly, there it was before them: a wide, grassy mountain valley flowing serenely between snow-capped peaks. It was astonishingly easy of passage; after the torturous climb it was almost a letdown. But they knew they had broken the back of their climb because when they camped at Pacific Springs the water ran due west.

They camped early that day. Jed and the Mitchell brothers brought in game in plenty and spirits revived as the good smell of roasting meat circulated with the wood smoke of their fires. Beauty was here in this high, wild valley. Among the dark columns of pines were trembling, white-barked aspens. They had become used to the bright candle flames of the Indian paintbrush, which grew even on the sage slopes. But here, too, was the heavenly blue of massed lupines and the delicate white stars of the columbine. The very air was sweet, rain-washed and fresh. There had been a shower moving ahead of them all day and the valley around the spring was washed clean for their occupation.

A spriteliness was evident in the women as they moved around their cooking fires. The absence of the usual cussed dusty wind and feeling free to be lavish with water perked them up. After supper Joel Mitchell unlimbered his squeeze box and essayed a toe-tapping tune. A couple of harmonicas and a fiddle promptly appeared and joined in. The people crowded around, singing and clapping hands to the music.

Melissa was distinctly out of sorts. Jed and David had talked all through supper about their plans for going upcountry for horses and the plans did not include her. Both men had brushed her aside as though she was of no more importance than the persistent mosquitoes ambushing just outside the range of camp fire smoke. She flounced off to join the circle around the musicians. A few couples were dancing, the rest clapping and stomping to the beat.

"Wanta give it a whirl, Lissy?" It was Lawson Mitchell grinning down at her, having spat out his tobacco cud in deference to the social occasion. Melissa had known the lanky brothers since childhood, they were both unmarried, being painfully shy with women. But Melissa they regarded fondly as a fractious child.

She returned his grin and stretched on tiptoe to put her hand on his tall shoulder as they joined the couples romping to a polka. Lawson's dancing consisted mainly of violent energy and unexpected lunges. Melissa breathlessly hung on, her feet flying above the ground at times.

She pantingly rearranged her clothing when he released her and tried to tuck back her hair.

Annie Fancher appeared at her elbow. "Look over there, will you!" she hissed in Melissa's ear. The girl stared, with a sense of unpleasant shock. Jed was dancing with Another Woman! And looked to be enjoying himself, too. Melissa's eyes glowed angrily, her mouth set in a severe line.

The other woman was Rosetta Huff—and there were whispers about Rosetta, a tall full-bosomed woman with an untidy wealth of copper-colored hair. They called her the Widow Huff, her two boys went as Huffs, too. But the women talked; if she'd been married, why did she use her brother's name? The pious sniffing with which her sister-in-law greeted any mention of Rosetta left the matter open to speculation. But Sid Huff was fond of his sister so that his wife, Magdalene, dared not speak out openly, for she feared his heavy hand. But what the sluggishly sour Maggie—with five youngsters and resentfully "expecting" again—could not say, she managed to convey by lifted eyebrows and a systematic snubbing of her in-law. The other women understood all too well that Maggie did not consider her husband's sister fit to associate with decent people.

It would have taken more than Maggie's opinions to put anyone outside the pale, for no one liked her either; she was a tiresome woman, forever whining. It was Rosetta herself who accomplished her own isolation from society. For one thing she never sought the company of other women. And then there was the way she looked.

There was something about her white-skinned lushness, the laziness of her heavy-lidded blue eyes that put the women on guard. And made the men itchingly jumpy. Rosetta could walk by at her usual deliberate pace—her eyes modestly lowered—and every head swung, the glances that followed her were wetly loose-lipped and speculative.

Annie's whisper to Melissa was frankly alarmed.

"You'd best get your oar in there fast—if ever I see a bitch in heat——!"

Melissa looked on helplessly. What could she do? Her anger stifled her; well, she needn't just stand here like a ninny and watch, nor lack for partners. She smiled sweetly at young Johnny Dunlap, who came forward eagerly. It was a waltz this time and to Melissa's fury Jed still danced with Rosetta. Her full breasts reached toward his tall chest, her red mouth wore a half-smile, her glance roved archly over his lean, brown face. He was smiling, damn him, that crooked, delighted grin.

Melissa couldn't stand it a minute longer. When Johnny asked for the next dance she shook her head, mumbled about a headache, and, thrusting through the crowd, hurried toward her wagon. Her chest was heaving with suppressed sobs, she felt sick to her stomach with an emotion acutely new and painful. Head down, skirts gathered up, she was almost running when a hand came down on her shoulder, she was swung around.

"Hey—you didn't dance with me yet." It was Jed smiling down at her.

Melissa's eyes flared angrily, "You didn't lack," she snapped, "go on back and dance with that—that old——" Fury choked her, she flounced away from his hand.

Jed's face was astonished, bewildered, and then he grinned. Melissa was peeved because he'd danced with the Widow Huff—she was jealous! He went after her. "Hold on here a minute," he said, "I looked for you, first off, and you were dancing with Lawson—and then the next time there you were with Johnny." His long stride easily kept pace with her quick march. His look was warmly indulgent on the blond crown atop the indignant small head.

"Aw—come on, Lissy," he coaxed, "let's go back and dance."

Her chin rose a notch higher. "I've danced with every one I wanted to, thank you, Jed Smith." Cool, haughty, she did not slacken her pace until she reached her wagon. "I'll just bid you good night——" she snapped.

Jed laughed suddenly. "All right, spitfire," he said, "bid me good night, then." One long arm snaked out, grabbed her around her slim middle. Toting her slung across his hip like a sack of grain, he loped off, out of the circle of wagons.

Melissa gasped in surprised fury, she kicked and fought at him. But Jed only chuckled and paid no attention to her struggles. He carried her deep into a grassy glade where aspen trees stood, their trunks gleaming like old silver, their trembling leaves whispering to the hushed night.

He swung her around, set her feet on the trunk of a fallen pine. His big hands spanned her narrow waist, her blazing eyes were on a level with his own. "Give me a good-night kiss, Lissy," he demanded, his grin making his teeth flash white. "I ain't gonna take you back till you do."

Melissa's bruised feelings had not been healed by the indignity of his manhandling and at this ultimatum her temper exploded. Her head darted forward and she bit him hard on his bony chin. Jed yelped and grabbed at his face; Melissa tried to jump off the log and run. He caught her in mid-air, swung her roughly up against his chest. One hard hand beneath her chin forced her face up. "You little hellcat," he said, "bite me, will you—" His mouth came down, his teeth bruised her mouth. She fought him again, her small fists pounded his shoulders and head, she tried to kick but he held her too close. But she stilled as the angry, punishing kiss became searching, gentled. Her arms went around his neck. When he raised his face the blazing eyes were closed, a tear wandered down her nose. He kissed the damp saltiness of the tear away. "You damned little fool—" His voice was rough with deep tenderness.

Still holding her close he sat down on the log, cuddling her on his lap. She was so light, so little that her feet did not reach the ground. And so damned spunky! How wicked when those kitten claws came unsheathed! Jed's grin crooked, she suited him right down to the ground. He pushed her tousled head against his shoulder and sighed happily. She lifted her face for his kiss again. The aspens discussed them with the moon wheeling through the silence above the looming mountains.

"This here is playin' with fire, Lissy," Jed said after a while. Melissa snuggled against him. "I like fire," she confided, tilting her head to look up at him. "Do you know this is the first time we've been alone together—really alone, I mean—since that first day?"

Jed nodded, his grin remembering that they'd fought that day, too. But he had an uncomfortable feeling that this being alone was risky. He'd better get her on back if he was to keep faith with David. A man could only keep control of things just so long without forgetting all restraint and damning the outcome. For Jed was not a man used to walking away from a woman after promising preliminaries. And Melissa innocently—or wickedly, for the life of him Jed couldn't tell which—abandoned herself with exultance in his arms.

He looked down at her now, the little devil was all but purring like a kitten. He got up suddenly, swung her to her feet. "Come on," he said, "let's get on back to the train before David starts wondering where you are. There'll be plenty more moonlight between here and Fort Bridger."

"Don't we have to worry about Injuns any more?"

"Nope—not near the emigrant road, anyhow. This here is Washaki country—and his Shoshonis are all friendlies."

There were many Indians, mostly Shoshonis—Snakes—when they reached Fort Bridger. They rode, screaming, to meet the train as it approached, their magnificent bronze bodies shining, muscles rippling in long arms, sinewed thighs gripping their horses' barrels. They were superb horsemen, seeming part of the animals they rode.

Fort Bridger was beautifully situated. Jim Bridger had considered long when he gave up his trapping to build himself a trading post and he'd picked the most beautiful spot at a crossroads of the overland trail: the luscious, deep meadows of Black's Fork on the Green River. Noisy, ice-cold water rushed from the Uinta slopes and it teemed with fighting, sweet-meated fish. The surrounding heights were timbered with tall pines and white aspens; game wandered within rifleshot of the fort. This place had been home to Jim Bridger for many years and his hatred for the Mormon usurpers—who drove him from it—was easy to understand.

The Fancher Train pulled into Fort Bridger about midafternoon of a day late in July. The people stared with surprise at this bustling settlement in the high wilderness. Several other wagon trains were camped in the surrounding meadows and hundreds of tepees were scattered among the trees. Parties of wagoners, hunters, and Indians rode recklessly by, shouting jovially, there was a holiday-like atmosphere.

The big gates of the log stockade stood open, streams of people moved constantly in and out. The blacksmith shop was clamorous with rushing business but running a second to the saloon, which was located in one of the log cabins built against the outer wall of the fort.

Noting the arrival of a new train, the four Mormons who now ran the trading post and saloon tapped a couple more kegs of raw frontier whisky. Efficiently they cut the contents with branch water, added red pepper lavishly—to make it too hot to taste—and were thus prepared for the evening's business. It was always rushing when a new train pulled in.

Jed asked around among the Shoshonis and discovered that Dick Washakie, his boyhood friend and son to the old chief, was camped with his horse herds only a day or two's ride away. But the ancient Snake warrior who gave him this information had also delivered another bit of news accompanied by a great deal of ominous headshaking.

"Siksika!" he gobbled, waving dirty hands toward the north, "Siksika—" he elaborated gutturally. Jed was listening intently, his face became irritated and then grim. David watched and listened, mystified by the incomprehensible conversation which seemed to be made up chiefly of grunting. Finally satisfied that he had gotten everything the old man knew, Jed gave him a huge twist of tobacco and turned to David.

"Siksika—Blackfeet," he disclosed angrily. "Been raiding in the neighborhood. They're mean bastards to tangle with——"

David's face showed his instant dismay. "You mean you don't think we'd ought to go?"

"No——" Jed's tone was measuring. "But we'll have to be damn careful—stay off of known trails, it'll be plenty rough goin'. But if we watch ourselves we'll be all right."

Joel Mitchell had begged to be included in the party and just before sundown the three rode out to the north. And so just missed seeing a party of men on gaunted, blowing horses ride wearily into the fort. An Indian boy on a buckskin rode with the five white men. They were all trail-dirty, grim-faced, and there was an urgency in their tired movements that testified to the gravity of their mission. Two of them rode black horses; they were both hulkingly big, these men, black-bearded, and each wore grease-darkened buckskins much the worse for wear. The leaders of this hard-riding party were Port Rockwell and Josh Wade.

The still gaze of the poker-faced Mormon trader sharpened as these men shouldered their way through the crowded saloon. He signaled another man to take his place at the bar and led the way to an inner room, shutting the door and barring it against intrusion. He produced a bottle of good, uncut whisky and the five drank thirstily. The trader studied each grim face in turn with anxious eyes. It was not until after the bottle had made a second round that he spoke.

"What news?" His voice was taut with controlled anxiety.

Rockwell's glance was somber. "Bad," he said flatly, "all bad. They're on their way—we seen 'em—must be all of three thousand troops. And well fitted out, herds of cattle and horses. A whole train of supplies. And wagon guns! Looks like they're bound on extermination this time, for sure."

One of the men spoke forebodingly. "What in God's name can we do agin artillery?"

Josh Wade laughed harshly. "Takes men to fire them cannon, don't it? You just pick 'em off—one by one—"

The lined face of the listening trader had turned pasty white. "Squaw-Killer Harney?" He whispered the question fearfully.

"No," Port answered slowly, "but I don't know if it's better or worse. They made a change, it's a Colonel Albert Johnston in command now. He's no greenhorn, neither, a West Pointer—seen dirty fightin' aplenty in the Mexican War. A rantin' blasphemin' southern cavalryman."

A hasty meal was served to the riders and as they ate, fresh horses were being saddled for them. They must push on with all possible speed. Brother Brigham would not welcome the news they carried, but his quick temper would really flare if there was the least unnecessary delay in its arrival.

Rockwell wiped his mouth on the back of his hand and looked up at the hovering trader. "This train I see—with 'Missouri Wildcats' painted on a couple of the wagons—who are they and when'd they come in?"

"Just today—this afternoon. Big train, well-to-do, big herds of cattle and horses. Noisy bunch, braggy—they're out there now"—he gestured toward the saloon—"drinkin' like hogs." His face was ugly with a smoldering expression as he stooped and whispered hoarsely to the seated men, "It's called the Fancher Train—man name of Charley Fancher is the captain—him and his bunch is from Arkansas—and the others is all from Missouri and Illinois!"

Five pairs of eyes swung to focus sharply on the trader's face. These places named held old bloody memory and significance for any Mormon.

Missouri, where the Gentile mobbers had tortured

and raped and killed—and Governor Boggs himself had signed an extermination order against the Mormon followers of Joseph Smith. They had fled for sanctuary to Illinois; built cities, a temple, prospered—and then it had happened again. Wolf hunts, the obscene members of the gangs that had ruthlessly hunted down Mormons had called them. The Prophet himself and his brother fell before the blazing guns while they were in the supposed custody of the law. And the assassins went free, no one sought to know their names. Just short weeks ago, in Arkansas, the beloved young apostle, Parley Pratt, had been slaughtered at the hands of men who laughed and walked away unprosecuted even though they boasted openly of what they had done.

Rockwell's voice cut into the hot, remembering silence. "The people in this train know the army's comin'?"

"I don't know—I ain't talked to them any more'n I could help"—he leaned forward again, his gaze portentous—"but you know who is scoutin' for 'em? Jed Smith!"

Rockwell's gaze narrowed as he thought about this. "Jed Smith—and Jim Bridger is scoutin' for the army." He pondered this pair of facts for a moment. "Could be they're in cahoots," he offered, "Smith might be spyin' for Bridger. I'll mention it to Brigham. We'd best keep track of this here train. They headed for Salt Lake City?" The trader nodded. "Well, listen," Rockwell went on, "best you don't cut their drinks—give it to 'em strong—straight. Visit with them, get real chummy, get 'em drunk and talkin'! Anythin' you find out—send word of it on—fast!"

The five—and the quiet Indian boy—mounted and rode west under a darkening sky. They would travel long miles before they next offsaddled. When it became too dark they would rest until moonrise and then make their precarious way down the rocky canyons by its pale light. They rested briefly near the forks of the Muddy and then pushed on.

Another small party of riders camped on the chattering run of Ham's Fork, north of Fort Bridger. They doused their cooking fire before dark and turned in early. Jed, David, and Joel each took a turn at guard—they were in the area where the Blackfoot raiders had been reported to be. But the night was quiet, they slept undisturbed.

The next day's travel was rough, they were in the high, narrow, rock-strewn canyons that combed the Uinta slopes. They traveled north, keeping the rushing waters of the Fork to their right. Late in the afternoon they found the Indian camp.

Dick Washakie, the son of the renowned old chief, was not a big man but he was formidably muscled and with the quick litheness of a cougar. His harsh, hawk face lit with joy as he and Jed greeted each other, they shouted and pounded as boisterously as youngsters. Joel and David exchanged grins, it looked as though cronies were alike the world over. David pleasedly anticipated that trading with Jed's good friend would be easy.

He was wrong—the trading was very expensive. At sundown, filled by a vast feastlike meal, young Washakie took them to the horse herd, which was guarded night and day by easy-riding striplings with laughing faces and jet black eyes.

A restless two-year-old, red roan son of Palouse, was driven out. This young stallion was the only remaining one of his immediate offspring. His head was slightly more jugged, he was taller by half a hand, but otherwise he was almost a duplication of that superlative animal.

David wanted him immediately. "How much?" He cocked a quizzical eye at Jed.

Jed grinned. He'd learned horse trading from Jim Bridger, the canniest trader on the frontier. "That there is a fine animal," he offered casually. "Likely I'd ought to keep him, seein' Palouse won't ever stud again."

"All right, all right." David laughed, waving his hand impatiently. "One of his colts goes in the buying price—I know he's valuable—set a price!"

"He's trained, too," Jed reflected. "Dick's boys, here,

have been trainin' him for a war horse. He's all horse, this feller. Tough as a cougar and his legs is longer—likely he can outrun Palouse." He scratched his chin absently, eying the horse fondly. "You know what he'd fetch if I was to trade him to the Snakes? Why, with just a couple of little knickknacks throwed in, he'd be full marriage price for the prettiest squaw in the tribe!"

Joel started to chuckle and then David caught on. Jed was still talking. "You take Melissa, now. On the puny side, not full-growed even, sort of an unbroke filly, you might say. No tellin' at all how she'll turn out, pigheaded and stubborn like she is. She ain't been trained at all to keep her mouth shut and obey like a good squaw, awful inclined to answer back—hard to handle—got a real bad temper——"

They were laughing now and when Jed explained the terms of the trade to young Washakie his bronze face broke into a wide grin. He put a swift question which Jed answered and then laughed in an embarrassed way at the teasing note in the Indian's reply.

"What'd he say?" David asked curiously.

"Well, nothin' decent—if you say it right out. I told him I ain't—— I mean to say, not yet." Jed's face wore an unaccustomed sheepish look.

David's head went back on a roar of laughter in which everyone joined. Washakie, concluding that this trade was happily done, called to one of the young herders. The youngster rode headlong into the herd, swinging a braided halter. He emerged in a cloud of dust, alternately towing and being towed by a gray-blue whirlwind of a colt.

Washakie leaped forward and caught the halter, bringing the animal to a stand. He turned his hawk face toward them, smiling proudly. This was indeed a prize.

It was a long yearling, just beginning to put on heft. This, he explained, was a grandson of Palouse, out of a blue that had been the bell mare of the herd. Which told volumes of the choiceness of the dam. For it was not the stallions who were the guiding intelligence of the horse herds but the wisest and toughest of the old mares.

"My God—look at him!" David's tone was reverent, his horseman's heart was in his eyes as he gloated hungrily over this colt. Washakie nodded, pleased, while the stocky bowlegged man lovingly examined the animal. There were no flaws from the arched neck to the hard hoofs.

He was spotted on the rump like Palouse and the deep chest and sturdy legs of his grandsire were there, but the blood strain of the mare had predominated and his color was dappled blue-gray. The mane and tail were full—they, and the forelock over the dish-face, were shining blue-black. This was no jughead, the skull bones tapered, the eyes were wide, dark with stormy intelligence. He was stocky by thoroughbred standards but longer coupled than Palouse. David's eyes were shining as he walked around the fractious colt, laughing delightedly when the animal kicked at him.

"I've got to have him!" His tone was all excited pleasure. "Ask him what he'll take, Jed!"

Jed's grin was broad as he squatted on his heels before putting the question to Washakie. He knew how long this would likely take. There followed, from the Indian, a rolling flood of sweepingly sonorous speech, much headshaking and sky-high bragging. Washakie wound up his oration with a flourish, shook his head sadly, folded his arms across his broad chest.

"He says he wouldn't think of sellin' such a grand colt," Jed interpreted laconically.

David's face was all agonized patience. "Aw—what'd he bring him out for, if not to trade? Ask him again—what price?"

Jed nodded soberly, but his eyes were twinkling as he put the question again. Came another speech, more emphatic, the dramatic ending much the same.

"Says he'd sooner part with his second wife." Jed's grin was sly. "Don't take her, though, Dave—she's got a hell of a temper. Fat, too. Sets around all day and jaws—"

"Aw—" David miserably shrugged off the unfeeling hoots of Joel and Jed. "Who's tradin' for squaws? Put it to him now—how much, cold cash—gold coin!" He stepped to his horse, dug in a saddlebag, and withdrew a small leather pouch, which sagged heavily, clinking when he shook it. "Gold coin," he insisted, "tell him to set his price!"

Jed reached for the pouch, loosened the string and poured a narrow stream of gold coins into his brown palm. Washakie's face became alert, thoughtful. He launched into another heated tirade; there was much shoulder shrugging, lamenting. Finally, pointing to David's horse, he finished with open palms held out, resigned at last to a trading price.

David was mystified. "Does he want my horse?"

Jed shook his head, flashed a wry congratulatory grin at Washakie. "Nope," he said dryly, "but he'll take—he's tradin' just as a favor to you, mind—he'll take all the gold *and* your rifle gun."

David's face lengthened sorrowfully; he looked helplessly at each intent face. Washakie was no fool, he'd driven a hard bargain knowing well how much David wanted the blue colt. He'd noticed—even encased in the saddle scabbard as it was—that the rifle was a modern, breech-loading Sharps carbine.

David's unhappy gaze lingered on the fine weapon. He'd shopped around, pondered for several days before making a choice, paid an awful price for that carbine. But then his glance swung to the blue colt. He could get another gun but there would never be another horse just like this one. He ached for possession of the colt the way some men ache for a certain desirable woman. Slowly he nodded assent.

The purchase price accepted for the red roan stud was not mentioned to Melissa on their return. Each man cautiously skirted this deal, knowledge of which would surely bring about a real blowup of her temper. David strutted the colts for her instant approval. "And they're Injun war-trained, to charge," said David, "and I know, now, what that can mean in a pinch!"

Melissa listened, wide-eyed, as he told about the brush they had had with Blackfeet on the way back. It had been a near thing for David. Leading the blue and bringing up the rear, he'd been startled by the whistle of an arrow past his ear. He'd taken a snap shot with his revolver at the Indian that had suddenly appeared from behind a bush. But he'd missed and the blue colt had reared, pulling his own mount around so that his back was to the redskin. The Blackfoot was about to let fly another arrow, but Jed, who had been ahead, had whirled Palouse and came plunging back down the narrow defile, seeing that there were now two Indians and unslinging his rifle as he came. The sharp bark of Jed's rifle accounted for one, and Palouse, on command, had hit the other with a deadly charge, trampling him as he went over. The three of them had gotten out of there fast, not knowing how many Indians might be concealed in the canyon. But there had been no pursuit. Probably the Blackfeet had been armed only with bows and had no stomach to tangle further with the long rifles.

Melissa's shining-eyed glance was on Jed; there was gratitude for her brother's life, and joy at having them back. The stay at the fort, she told them, had been something less than pleasant. Some of the men from the train had gotten ugly drunk and there'd been a mess of trouble.

"Sol Ward and that ratty little Les Prichard made an awful row at the trading post," she reported disgustedly. There had been others, too, involved in the fracas.

The heavy drinking had started on the day they arrived. A few of the men had just stayed right in the saloon, drinking and gambling. Two days later Sairy Ward had come to Captain Fancher and asked that he send a party of men to get Sol out of there. The trader had sent word he wouldn't put up with them any longer. Pig-drunk, they all were, fighting and carrying on. It was a wonder how decent the Mormon trader had been about it, he'd put up with them for quite a spell. But the fighting had gotten out of hand, he was afraid someone was going to get hurt, Sol kept pulling his knife. The wagon captain had gotten a bunch of men together and gone over.

Most of the revelers were out cold, sleeping soggily on the floor. The aggravated rescue party had had to carry them out one by one. But Sol's capacity was apparently limitless, he was still on his feet. Quarrelsome and foulmouthed, he was bragging obscenely about how many Mormons he'd personally cut up with his fancy knife. No wonder the trader had got his fill—being a Mormon himself. And the way Sol was talking about Mormons was something awful. He'd wanted to fight the men from the train, too, when they tried to get him away. So there'd been quite a fracas just getting him back to his wagon.

## CHAPTER V

"I thought," said Charley Fancher, "that whisky drinkin' was agin the Mormons' religion."

"Well, and so it is." The man who answered the train captain rode easily, lounging comfortably in spite of his corpulence. Eli Jacobs was a frontier trader and trail-wise, he knew how to take his ease even in the saddle. Jacobs had pulled into Fort Bridger with a small string of freight wagons. They were lighter than the usual prairie schooner but very strongly built, capable of heavy loads. And these obviously carried a valuable cargo, for the genial Jacobs had an armed guard besides the driver on each vehicle. During their short stay at Bridger the wagons had been guarded day and night.

The Shoshonis had seemed to know the man, calling him by name, they had been eager to trade for his goods. But the canvas flaps had remained tied; he had announced to all comers that his cargo was to be delivered intact in Salt Lake City. He had suggested that his wagons travel in company with the Fancher Train, and Captain Fancher, liking the man well, had agreed. The two of them rode ahead, now, of the lurching train, which was making a jouncing, slow progress down the rocky canyons that twisted toward the floor of Deseret, the valley wherein was Salt Lake City, the capital of Mormon country.

They were several days out of Fort Bridger. The weather was hot but not unbearably so at these altitudes. The trail was steep but well broken by the heavy travel of the past several years and each day found them at good and ample water. There were rushing mountain streams pouring from many of the intersecting canyons.

As they neared the Mormon city, curiosity about its settlers made Jacobs a target for questions. He had been trading with the Mormons ever since their migration into the wilderness. And he willingly obliged with all of a lonely traveler's enjoyment of conversation.

"They got a rule—call it the Word of Wisdom," he now amplified his reply to Fancher's question about whisky drinking, "they ain't supposed to drink hot drinks —and I guess that takes in hard liquor—they take it to mean tea and coffee too. And tobacco. Their Prophet allowed that tobacco was only fit to poultice animals with, so they included that in. But you see a lot of them chewin' regular. Guess it's easier to swaller a cud if a man meets up with a bishop unexpected than to ditch a seegar or pipe. Brigham Young, he bore down hard on the coffee and tea and tobacco because he didn't want the people spendin' money on things they couldn't grow here—he hates to pay out hard money out of his kingdom. Brigham's a smart one—he knew damned well his people'd pay more mind to it if the ruling came from the Lord, instead of just making plain common sense."

"Well, if they ain't supposed to drink whisky, neither, how come they're so free with it at Fort Bridger?"

Jacobs chuckled, "Oh hell, man—that's different. The Mormons ain't above makin' money out of other folks' bad habits. Bridger does a big business with all the trains and they sell it just like Old Jim did before they run him out—likely make most of their profit from watered-down whisky. They make their own whisky and you'n make drinkin' liquor outa almost any damn thing. I've even drunk some the Mexicans make out of cactus—and it wasn't so bad after you get the first slug down. Et out your insides a little, but in those parts you're gonna get a bellyache regardless—either on the food or the liquor and the liquor seems to quench down the red peppers a little."

"The Mormons at Bridger didn't seem to drink—do any of them ever break the rule?"

"Oh, sure, but they don't do it open-like, you won't see 'em elbowin' up to a bar in the saloons. They do their backslidin' private-like. But there's a lot of 'em don't see the harm in a little nip now and again. Down in the southern settlements they raise grapes and make a right passable wine. Course, they're supposed to bottle it just for sale and they use a little in their church ceremonies. But I guess a man can't be blamed for sampling his own output to see how she's coming. You don't see any heavy drinkers amongst the leaders, though. I've had a sociable drink with one or two, here and there. Not with old Brigham, though."

"He strict?"

"Strict as hell—about a lot of things. I don't look sidewise at any Mormon women, neither, I watch my step in Salt Lake City. If I was to step outa line and Brigham hear of it, I'd be lucky if all I got was run outa the territory. They don't like outsiders, the Mormons—except to make money out of. To their way of thinkin' ever livin' soul that ain't Mormon is Gentile—and all Gentiles is classed as enemies!"

Charley did not, out of tact, voice the reply that occurred to him. But Jacobs, looking at him shrewdly, chuckled, completely unoffended. "That's right," he said, "this here is the only place in the world where Eli Jacobs is a Gentile!" And his rich laugh rolled out.

"How come," Fancher asked curiously, "that they've let you come and go—makin' money on tradin'—all these years if they don't cotton to outsiders?"

"Because I deal in goods they can't make—and that are hard to get in quantity unless you know the right people. This here cargo I got on right now is goin' to fetch a mighty high price. Higher, maybe, than old Brigham is countin' on—but he'll pay. For he'll want me to keep bringin' my trains in, the way things stand now."

Fancher, until now unconcerned about what the closely guarded wagons carried, looked his curiosity. Eli's liquid brown eyes narrowed, he looked around to see if any rode close enough to overhear.

"Guns," he said, "rifle guns is what I've got on. I deal in guns and bullets and powder. Besides this train I've got three others headed for Mormon country. And I figger Brigham will take ever last gun and ounce of powder at high prices. He won't choke at all over the price—not the way things is shapin' up!"

"You don't think he's fixin' to fight agin the United States Army, do you?" Fancher's voice was incredulous.

"I don't know." Eli's voice and the accompanying look were sober. He had given this question a lot of deep thought. "He might and then again he might not, pretty hard to figger. But he's a forehanded man, Brigham Young, and he'll want the guns handy, just in case. Knowin' him as well as I do, I figger he'll get ready and then watch to see whichaway the cat is goin' to jump. But he'll want the guns. I ain't been in his territory for a year or so but I knew he'd likely take every gun I could lay hand to. I got busy and I was lucky, rounded up a prime lot. Brigham knows I'm comin', I sent word ahead."

Fancher's usually slow rejoinders kept Jacobs well cued, but the enormity of what the trader had said in his opinion now silenced him completely. Eli glanced at the thoughtful face and continued. "I tell you," he said, "I wasn't surprised a bit when I heard about the army headin' for Mormon territory. Brigham overstepped himself when he run them last federal officials out—and burned the court records they were tryin' to get their hands on. He might have known he'd run into trouble. And then he had to go an' make it worse by shoutin' it out in public meeting—knowin' there were Gentiles in the crowd—that he'd kill any soldiers that showed up in *his* territory!" Jacobs shook a disapproving head. "He shouldn'ta said those things, for the eastern papers printed it—and of course, made it sound even worse than it was. He'd ought to have known he wouldn't be let get away with that—defyin' the United States Government."

Both men were silent, contemplating the enormity of the thing. When Jacobs spoke again it was in a musing, remembering tone. "Brigham's a damn smart man, but he's changed a lot in the last few years. I've known him for a long time and now, when I look back, I see how it came on. It's been buildin' up for quite a spell: Brigham's power has gone to his head.

"See—he's been top-*top*-dog in these parts and over all them people—and there's close to forty thousand of them now—and they all think he's right up there next to God. He's got twelve apostles, just like Jesus Christ had, and they allow in all their preachin' that Brigham Young is the only living spokesman for God on this earth! And from some of the things that have happened, I sometimes wonder if he don't believe it himself—or even get a mite mixed and think he *was* God!"

"I've heard it called 'Brigham's kingdom'—all this here country," Fancher offered thoughtfully.

"And it is!" Eli's confirmation was strong. "He rules it—every man, woman and child—he's got, I mean actually, the power of life or death over any body in these parts—be they Mormon or Gentile. He's not so tough on the Gentiles if they mind their own business, but he's almighty tough on any Saint that drops out of his Church. That's the worst sin in their book—apostatizin'. An apostate is likely to find Port Rockwell on his tail—or Bill Hickman or Josh Wade—any one of them get done and an apostate don't talk no more—about nothin'!"

"You don't mean that he'd have a man killed just for leavin' the Church?"

"You're damn right, I do! I've knowed of it to happen. Not that they talk about it, the Mormons, at least not openly. They just clam up, they know better than to talk, believe me. They know damn well what happened to the loose-mouth apostates. Mostly they just use 'em up quiet-like, they don't never leave no trace—they just disappear. But hell, not long ago a whole mess of apostates was shot down, massacreed by the Mormon militia."

"How in God's name could they get away with such as that?"

Eli was enjoying his intent, appalled audience. "Well, first off, you got to remember that the only law in Mormon country is Brigham's law—he's run everthin' else out. And there was this old guy, Joe Morris, his name was, who preached a lot agin Brigham and his bunch of apostles. Joe had got to thinkin' he could do a better job of bein' Prophet than Brigham could and quite a few folks were sort of agreein' with him. This was in a little settlement up north of Salt Lake City a couple days' travel. Brigham sent him several warnings to cut out his talkin' and criticizin' of the church heads, but old Joe just kept right on preachin'. Then when the word got out that there were several hundred folks takin' old Joe quite serious, he sent some of his men up to see. And they heard him goddamning Brigham out loud and regular—and the folks agreein' with every word!

"So Brigham sent a bunch of his militia up there to bring Joe Morris and his leaders in. But the Morrisites—that's the name they went by—barricaded themselves inside of a big building, they wouldn't turn old Joe over to Brigham's militia. There was over two hundred of the militia men *and* Josh Wade. They fired a cannon they had along and slaughtered a whole bunch of women and kids, along with Joe and his bunch. The ones left alive they taken to jail and I guess they're likely there yet."

"I be damned," Charley Fancher said slowly, "if'n I ever heard of such a thing!"

"Oh, Brigham, he said after, that he'd sent the cannon just to scare 'em into not fightin'—but then why'd he send Josh Wade, knowin' like everbody does, that the man is a killer?"

"Who's Josh Wade?"

"You ain't never heard of Josh Wade—or Rockwell and Bill Hickman?"

"Rockwell, yes—and Hickman—the Mormon Prophet's bodyguards or somethin', wasn't they?"

"Somethin' is right! Destroyin' Angels is the name folks whisper—don't none of 'em whisper it loud, though. Rockwell is the one that taken a shot at Governor Boggs, back in the old Missouri days. Damn near killed him, too. But it was at night and the wind blew a curtain just as he took aim. Boggs come close to bleedin' to death."

"Seems like we heard about Boggs and the Mormons —didn't he sign an extermination order against them?"

"That's him—and I bet he wished he'd not been so mouth-almighty brave. He took himself off to California not long after that—thinkin' he'd get away from Mormons —and got right next door, you might say! For there's several Mormon settlements in California. They say Lillburn Boggs don't sleep good, nights, and I don't wonder! He's top of the list for enemies of the Church and Rockwell will get around to him one of these days. And he ain't likely to miss on the second try."

Charley shook his head dubiously at the ex-governor's unenviable position. "This Wade you spoke of—he's a Destroyin' Angel, too? I never heard of him."

"Wade's a bad one—sticks to a trail like a goddamn wolf pack, smellin' out a kill."

"What's he look like?"

"Well, somethin' like Rockwell. Hell of a big man, black-bearded, wears old stinkin' buckskins. He ain't the man Rockwell is—I like Port all right. He takes orders from Brigham and he's dangerous, but he ain't vicious, if you know what I mean. And Rockwell's a good-lookin' man—cleans himself up when he's in the settlements. But Wade's an ugly bastard, got a big crooked nose—somebody done a job of smashin' there. He's bad-tempered and dirty. I bet the most cleanin' up he's ever done is when his squaws pick the lice outa his hair and beard."

"Squaw man, huh?"

"Oh sure, Wade is more Injun than any white man I ever seen. He's blood brother to a Cheyenne war chief and he's spent a lot of time with the Sioux. Wade always seems to show up in time for any fightin'—and the Injuns are glad to see him when they're headed for a fracas. They call him Takuskanskan. I don't know just the words to make the meanin' clear but it's like he was sort of a war god, one of the thunder-beings in their religion. There's a dark night wind mixed up in the meaning of it—and death. Mighty powerful medicine for a warrior."

Fancher was entranced with the strangeness of the fierce legend. "I'd give a heap to see this man, Wade—"

Jacobs looked his warning. "If you're ever that unlucky, steer clear of him. I'd as soon step on a rattler, myself. I've been giving his neighborhood a wide berth ever since I knew how the Medicine Wolf howls when he's around!"

"Medicine Wolf?"

Jacobs hesitated, scratched his jaw. His enjoyment of the other's awed interest in his stories had let that slip. He seldom spoke of such with greenhorns; they misunderstood, were apt to prove scornful. Still, this Captain Fancher didn't appear to be the sort to scoff at a man's honest caution.

"Well, I'll tell you," he continued slowly, "the Medicine Wolf—accordin' to the Injuns—howls only when there's trouble or danger brewin'. Any redskin that hears it howl will get the hell out of the neighborhood. It ain't a real wolf, understand—it's an evil spirit-animal. Sounds more like a dyin' woman than a wolf. I heard it once"—Jacobs shuddered—"and that once was enough!"

Fancher had removed his cold pipe from his mouth and was staring in consternation at the trader. "You mean you really take stock in such a thing." It was not a question, nor was there scorn, only curious wonder. Eli felt called on to try to express his own somewhat mixed feelings. His sober glance on the train captain was almost as puzzled as Fancher's.

"I don't know. To tell the honest-to-God truth, I just don't know. But I've seen a power of queer things come about amongst redskins. They're in touch with—well, there's things—and forces, in nature they seem to sense about that's clear beyond a white man's ken. At least, a settlement-raised man. I've seen sign of such—and many's the peculiar tales I've heard—about the Medicine Wolf, for one thing. And I tell you this—Old Jim Bridger, he hits the grit outa any place, does he hear the Medicine Wolf howl!"

"I met Bridger at Laramie"—Fancher was pleased at this acquaintanceship—"they say he's a squaw man, too."

"That he is, and treats his squaws as good as any woman—white or otherwise—is treated. He's educatin' his kids, half-breed or no. A square man, all the way, is Bridger. He knows more, I guess, about Injuns and their ways than any white man alive. And Bridger believes about the Medicine Wolf—he said as much to me, himself. So—with him believin' it, and all the stories—I wouldn't dare not to give it room. And I'm damned if I'll take chances. I'll keep playin' it safe and get the hell outa there. Any time I hear the Medicine Wolf I'm makin' tracks!" Fancher nodded in complete agreement with this.

Jacobs' fire was circled by a crowd of visitors each night. The women stayed away, judging rightly by the jug passed from hand to hand, and by the tone of the hilarity, that it was purely male conversation.

"Jokin' aside"—it was Lawson Mitchell who spoke, his face cheerfully flushed by the potent contents of the jug Jacobs passed with hospitable regularity—"just how many women has old Brigham got?"

"I don't rightly know, don't guess many folks do know, maybe not Brigham himself, less'n he sets down and counts her up again every day or so," said Eli. "Offhand, I'd guess maybe twenty or twenty-five."

"Holy Christ!" Jared Hardy's voice held amazement; he was a young bull of a man, unmarried and woman-hungry. "You figger he can—take care of that many? Proper take care, I mean?" A roar of laughter greeted the restraint of his query.

"Well, now"—Eli was chuckling—"I'd bet he gets around to all of them sooner or later for there's sure a passel of kids livin' at the Beehive House. That's where the most of Brigham's wives live—in the Beehive House."

"Beehive House! Well, now, that there is a proper name—he's a right busy old bee with his stinger, I betcha! You been in that house, Eli?"

"Hell no—you think they'd let an outsider in there? But I've passed it many's the time, Brigham's office is in the Lion House, on the same block, and I've been there plenty. You can see how many windows there are on the second floor and they tell me the upper hall is lined with bedroom doors—a whole double row of bedrooms and a wife inside each one!"

"My God—how about that, now?" Jared's eyes bulged at the contemplation of this fact. "Just walk down that old hall of a night and take your pick! Now that there would be a proper setup for a man!"

"You figger you could get her done, Jared?" Lawson's tone was teasing. "Twenty-five women sounds like a chore to me——"

"Y'God, I'd sure like to give her a try!" The howls of understanding derision were offensive to John Barker, who had not taken of the drink nor joined in the conversation. He was there because he felt duty-bound to learn as much as possible about the immorality of the Mormons.

Barker, who had been elected Charley Fancher's second-in-command of the wagon train, was a stiff-necked, pious man. He was very unlike his two younger brothers, George and Abel, who were amiable, energetic young men who'd married sisters. John often explained—to himself—that he had made the decision to remove to California because he owed a duty to his easygoing brothers in that he should look after their interests, advise and counsel them. John was not at all close to the four young people, he had only visited them once or twice a year in Arkansas and came away disapproving of them more each time. Himself a bachelor past thirty, John Barker heartily disapproved of both his sisters-in-law, he found them frivolous and light-minded, always laughing and carrying on.

George and Abel Barker looked much alike, they took after their mother's folks, and were of medium but sturdy build, blue-eyed and with light brown hair. But John was the image of their father, Elijah Barker, who had been an itinerant border preacher. And his looks had well suited his hell-and-damnation-dealing profession. Folks used to say in that part of the country that old Preacher Barker looked more like the devil himself than a mortal man had a right to. And seemed scorchingly well acquainted with hell-fire too, seeing as how he seethed about it most of the time. He'd been an abnormally tall thin man, black eyes always glaring accusingly above his sharp nose and black beard. Maybe he was right when he accused the whole world of sin for, to Preacher, sin was in any contact a man had with a woman.

None of the Barker boys remembered their mother well, she had died while the two youngest had been babies. Preacher remained a widower, having conceived somewhere along the line a violent distrust of the opposite sex. The two younger boys, of a happier nature, escaped early, married young, and lived removed from his foreboding presence, but John remained with the old man until he died and was much influenced by his dire views. Like his father he avoided all contact with women, removing himself from their society as far as possible. And so rendered them mysteriously and endlessly fascinating.

He had not admitted to himself the relief he felt when duty pointed out that he should accompany his frivolous brothers to California. The span of years since his father's death had been lonely, drab almost beyond bearing.

Now as he listened to the ribald conversation, the blood coursed urgently through his veins, his whole lank form was tense with the stress of unwilling imagination. A double row of bedroom doors—and a woman waiting behind each one. Just there, waiting, compliant. Somehow his hotly reluctant mind added an odd, personalizing detail to those silently waiting figures. Each became endowed with an oval, white face and masses of red hair. Like the Widow Huff. Furiously embarrassed, John tore his thoughts loose and flung them away from him. Eli was talking.

"Brigham, he's a piker, though, when it comes to wives," he informed his delighted audience. "Heber Kimball, now, he's got about forty, they tell me! And some of the other big buckos in the church have as many——"

"How about forty, Jared?" It was David needling this time. "You think you wanta try her out on forty?"

"I'd die, tryin'," Jared asserted instantly, "but what I wanta know is, how the hell these old birds talk so many women into it—hell, I can't get nowheres, even with one!"

The guffaws hushed to hear Eli's reply. "It's religion, Jared, you just ain't seen the light! It's all—with the Mormons—mixed up in their goin' to heaven and how high they want to stand in with the Almighty. The more women and kids, the more glory they earn. The man who kin get enough descendants on earth gets to be a king in heaven and rule his own kingdom. And they seal it up proper—they get married for all eternity—that's why the important men usually get the choicest women, for if a woman marries some no-account she's stuck for all time. See—they believe you resurrect with your body, none of this spiritual stuff for them, they teach that even God was once a man and has got a physical body. You're gonna have, like they say, 'parts and passions' in heaven."

"By grannies, it sounds like a proper heaven to me,

too." Jared was emphatic in his approval. The gallon jug was empty and Eli was uncorking another.

"There's one thing I might be a mite short on, besides religion," Jared observed into the intent silence while everybody watched Eli work on the stubborn cork, "and you got to hand it to these old Mormons. Hell, I ain't been able to sell what I got for more'n once to any woman, let alone get one interested in keepin' it for herself. And here these old billy goats is convincin' 'em right and left with what they got—divided up in forty pieces! You can't tell me them Mormons don't come special equipped!" Jared's baffled countenance was sweaty red now, as were the howling faces around him.

"Maybe that there religion of theirs is strengthenin'," Lawson offered when it quieted again, "I'm thinkin' serious of tryin' it out myself. How about it, Jared—shall you and me join up with the Mormons?"

"By grannies, I'm with you! I been wastin' a lotta time. What's the use agoin' to Californy to break my back workin' when I can get it done pleasanter in Utah?"

John Barker quietly withdrew from the convivial circle, walked away toward his wagon. Somehow his steps took him past the Widow Huff's wagon. As he drew near he saw her, she stood outside her wagon, the firelight on her, brushing her wealth of red hair. The man paused, irresistibly drawn, looking at her.

Rosetta lifted her head, threw back her hair and, feeling the gaze on her, peered into the half darkness outside the firelight. She was startled at the presence of the tall form and more than startled at the expression she caught on his face. For he immediately nodded and proceeded on his way, leaving her with a peculiar sensation. His eyes had burned across at her somberly, the long, bony nose which ended in wide nostrils had been flaring as though he breathed deeply. He had not been smiling but his mouth had been drawn back in a grimace so that it seemed as though his teeth snarled through the blackness of the beard.

Thinking about the look of him confused her, she tried

to remember where she had encountered such an expression before. It was not until much later, alone in her bed in the wagon that she recalled it—and it had not been a man that had looked so, but an animal. A stallion, powerfully aroused, had been trying to crash through the high fence which separated him from a mare in heat—that stallion had worn such a look.

Rosetta's calm eyes widened in the dark; she thought long about John Barker and the look she had glimpsed as he stared at her. And then she laughed aloud.

## CHAPTER VI

In Salt Lake City most of the houses were dark, but a lamp still burned in Brigham Young's study. The leader worked far into each night. The hours were not long enough for the task he had set for himself—and for his people. On the desk before him was a travel-stained letter, delivered by a special messenger a few days before. It was signed with the familiar signature of Eli Jacobs, which accounted for the satisfied set to Brigham's stern mouth. He might have known he could depend on Eli, the trader was a valuable friend and, more important, infinitely resourceful when it came to foreseeing, gambling on a thing. For Eli had guessed right when he'd gambled heavily that Brigham would want guns—and more guns.

Most of the Saints were already well armed. But Brigham had something else in mind for most of the weapons Eli would deliver. There were other hands that would be eager to grasp these guns. Red hands, the Indian tribes that his Saints had disarmed with friendship, food, and a profession of brotherhood. "Feed them—don't fight them!" had been Brigham's edict concerning the red men, the wisdom of which had never been more apparent. For they were allies now and Brigham had forged himself a mighty tool. Thousands of red hands to fill with guns—just in case he needed to call on them. His missionaries had been teaching the Indians to shape their heathen grasp to the hoe and the plow, but they would be overjoyed with his gift of the guns, take the warpath eagerly. A great battle-ax for the Lord.

It was concerning the disposition of the guns now on their way that Brigham had sent for the man slouching in a chair facing his desk. The whole room stunk of his occupancy, the bearded face was still but his glance on Brigham was sullen. Josh Wade smoldered because he had been detained for a special mission while Port Rockwell and Lot Smith had gone out, leading fighting men, to harass the oncoming army train.

"I'm a-gettin' damn tired a settin' on my ass here whilst Port and the boys is headed for fun," he growled now, "how long 'fore that damned trader will get in?"

Brigham's glance veiled cautiously on Josh. He had come to distrust this man, for the years had proved him to be dangerously unpredictable. He did not always stay within the wording of his orders. Brigham had known for a long time that only an odd, personal loyalty to Port Rockwell held Josh in any check at all. And Rockwell was the only man alive who could give direct orders to Josh Wade—and expect to be obeyed. Brigham had earnestly wished, many times, that the man would get himself killed in one of the Indian wars he was forever messed up in. Or at least stay with the tribes for he had much more in common with the Indians. His kind was not what Brigham needed now. The man was destructive, not a builder or a farmer. Because of his unpredictable temper he could not be depended on in time of trouble either. But, because he did turn up now and again, Brigham used him—as he used every man—in the best interests of his spreading web of plans for empire. But Josh had to be kept occupied or he was apt to get restless and create trouble. And trouble where he lingered almost inevitably ended with bloodshed.

Brigham had directed Port to leave Josh behind when

the picked band of fighting men set out to contact the army. For a very good reason: Rockwell and Lot Smith carried definitely limiting orders and they could be trusted to obey them to the letter. They were to raid, capture wagons, burn them if this was not possible, bring livestock and all possible loot into Mormon territory. But they were not to kill any soldiers. Brigham didn't want a killing war started by his followers. And Josh could not be trusted to refrain from killing. He'd shoot a man down, if he got him under his rifle sights, as any other man would unthinkingly throw down on a wild animal. Look what he'd done in that Joe Morris incident! Brigham hadn't known that Josh was even in the territory, let alone that he'd taken a notion to join in with the militia. The leader had found out only after the slaughter was done that it had been Josh who had fired the first shot, and Josh again who had egged the cannoneer into seeing if he could hit the pitiful fort of the Morrisites. And there had been definite orders against violence issued to the militia, but somehow Josh had led them to think he had special orders in case of emergency from Brigham himself. Sending the cannon had been a mistake. But, at the time, he'd only thought to scare the Morrisites into surrendering by an overwhelming show of strength. Before God, Brigham had had himself a chore justifying that slaughter of women and kids to the people. It wasn't a thing that could be hushed up and folks would whisper if they couldn't talk. Sure, he thought wearily, the whole bunch of Morris's followers were actually apostates, but it still had kicked up a powerful stink. No one was too shocked if a man of that stripe turned up missing or was found with his throat slit. But women and kids cut down—that was different. And it all came of not waiting for Port to return from one of his trips so that he could have headed the mission. It looked, by God, like Port was the only one he could trust. Look at the hornet's nest Bill Hickman had stirred up when he headed the posse that was to bring Jim Bridger in, years ago. Bill hadn't had any orders to confiscate and destroy, much less to shoot down the unarmed ferrymen. And then they didn't catch Bridger, after all of Hickman's drunken violence. So of course old Jim hotfooted it off and saw to it that the government in Washington knew all the particulars. They were still poking and prying around with it.

The most ticklish aspect of the occasional fumbling of his lieutenants was that Brigham couldn't openly chastise or remove them from leadership. A man wouldn't accept responsibility if he knew he'd be cut down if he guessed wrong or went too far. If Brigham didn't appear to respect their decisions he couldn't expect the people to obey the leaders he chose for them. The settlements were scattered, now, far flung, distances were too great for them to run to him for every decision. They had to have leaders and he had to back up what these leaders did, good or bad. But God forbid any further such bloody mistakes, for the people needed to feel safe under the guidance of their immediate leaders, their local church authorities.

Brigham now proceeded to deftly soothe, deal with Josh Wade's discontent. His stern smile sympathized with the man's irritation. "I know how you feel, Josh," he said, "I'd like to have gone along with the boys, myself, but I'm tied to this damned desk eternally. And I needed you here for a special chore"—his tone was warm, significant of speciality—"one that nobody else could do up just right." His quick ascertaining glance assured him that Josh was listening intently, his interest aroused.

"I think Eli Jacobs will show up any day now," he went on, "and I want you to take the guns he brings with him to the Injuns down south. You get along with them better than anybody—unless it's Jacob Hamblin. And I'd like it if you could see your way clear to stay in that territory for a spell." Anything to get the man out of this dangerously touchy area. "There aren't too many what you'd rightly call fighting men down that way. Colonel Dame has got his militia, of course, but they're mostly farmers. I'd feel a lot better, knowing one of Port's top men was around to give them a hand."

Josh's yellowed teeth showed in a wolfish grin at the designation. "Why don't old Jake Hamblin hand out the guns? I only been in those parts a coupla times—he's better known amongst them tribes than me."

"Jake could do it," Brigham agreed quickly, "but"—and here he demonstrated his famous talent at handling difficult people—"Jake can't do exactly what I've got in mind as well as you could, Josh—he just isn't the sort of man for this deal." He leaned forward over his desk, taking his listener into his confidence with an important lowering of his tone of voice.

"See, here's how it is, Josh: Jake Hamblin is my apostle to the Injuns. He's been converting them, feeding them, preaching peace. We're trying to make farmers out of them—make them forget the warpath. And Jake's done a damn good job, they've had little trouble in those parts outside of the usual thieving mischief. The lazy scoundrels don't even bother to hunt any more—just set around on their red behinds and scrounge food from the people. It's a nuisance, but it's better than to have them hostile. But now, we want to sort of direct them a little different. And that means a different sort of leader——

"Now, you, Josh, know better than anybody how Injuns think, what their customs are. They always have a whole raft of chiefs and each one has a special chore: peace chief, war chief, holy men—somebody for everything. Now, to the southern tribes, Jake Hamblin is a sort of combination peace chief and holy man. John D. Lee is the same—he's teaching them how to farm and he preaches to them, too. But here it is, Josh—I want those redskins in a fighting frame of mind! And so I got to send them a man they know is a real war chief! That's you!" Brigham pointed his finger at Josh and smiled confidently into the man's damaged face. "Because if it turns out that we have to tackle that army, I'm going to turn the Injuns loose! And I want them ready and boiling for a scrap—and well led!"

Josh's eyes flared in fierce agreement, his wolf grin spread his tangled beard. Brigham continued, "Port tells me you're the most famous white warrior amongst the tribes—that they've even got a name for you—what is it, now?"

Josh was immensely gratified at how his notoriety had reached Brigham's ears. "Takuskanskan," he said, "means —sort of thunder god of battle."

Brigham's strong, square hand came down hard on his desk, emphasizing his point. "That's exactly what I mean, Josh! You're exactly the man to get those lazy rascals in a fighting frame of mind—lead them if we get in a shooting war!"

His deliberate elation took an abrupt tangent into his old brisk, planning tone. "Now, here's what I want you to do: The minute Jacobs gets in, you're to take this whole load of guns and ammunition and head for the southern settlements. He's got several trains on the way but this first one is the biggest and it will all go to the Pahvants and Paiutes in the south. There's a hundred redskins for every white man down there and I want to make sure they fight on our side if we need them. And if—like we've heard—another army lands at San Diego and comes across the desert to attack the Dixie settlements, we'll need every Injun in those parts. I don't want my people to panic, run away from the settlements and forts, I want them to stay put. It's been too hard getting them settled. I want to hang on to what we've got there —if we have to fight for it!"

Josh sat silent, but his eyes glittered; this was talk to his liking. He nodded his complete agreement and understanding. Brigham looked at him sharply and went on.

"Now, I've sent word to Jacob Hamblin that he's to come here, picking up the local chiefs from the tribes as he comes, bring them here for a powwow with me. By the time I get done with our red brothers they'll be primed and ready to start daubing on the war paint—and willing to throw in with us if we tackle the army. And the way things are shaping up I might have to do just that!" His measuring glance stayed on Josh, and he was satisfied with what he had wrought.

Josh had no way of knowing that Brigham was absolutely certain of the fact that no army approached—or would approach—from the south, via the port at San Diego. But the Mormon leader was astute, he knew the word would be passed and shrewdly calculated the prompt effect it would produce. He wanted the people in the southern settlements to become alarmed. Sometimes a man didn't feel called on to obey an edict to the letter if he himself was not endangered by heedlessness. Those in the south were basking in the notion that they were far removed from the danger area, he wanted to stir them up a little. A frightened man, worried as to the safety of his women and children, would hew strictly to the line of obedience if the danger was revealed as not remote but possibly imminent. The people would take with greater seriousness his edicts about conserving, storing the crops they would soon be harvesting. And also there would be more diligence in the performance of the militia drills and minute-men preparations. Let them get a little spooked, Brigham thought, it was all to the good, for he was trying, with desperate haste, to create a hair-trigger frame of mind in every last member of his scattered hordes. He might trigger it and he might not. But he damn well didn't want the embarrassment of an empty gun if he needed to fire.

Brigham rose now and, moving briskly around his desk, shook hands vigorously with Josh. "When you get down to New Harmony," he said, "you tell John Doyle Lee why I've sent you, special and tell him how things stand. He'll help you, for he's likely in charge of the Injuns' affairs while Jacob Hamblin is away. And say, Josh" —his eyes twinkled at an afterthought—"you be sure to sample some of that good brandy Brother John is making these days. Just sample it, mind!" His chuckle brought an answering grin from Josh. "And you might just mention it to John that he'd just as well send me a flask or two—for medicinal use, of course!" And having put the conversation to a jovial finish—and on Josh's level of humor—Brigham slapped the big man's buckskin shoulder and saw him take his leave, chuckling at the leader's joke. It was with relief that Brigham realized the success of his maneuvering. Josh Wade would shortly be headed off, not only on a useful errand, but away from the powder keg that the Mormon capital might well prove to be.

Brigham closed the door on his visitor and, moving at once to a window, opened it to stand breathing deeply, sucking the clean night air into his abused lungs with relief. His barrel chest exhaled cleansingly, explosively. Before God, Josh had smelled worse than an old he-goat!

He returned presently to his desk, trimmed the smoking wick of his lamp, and considered the pile of paper work yet to be finished. The clock on the wall, near the handsome portrait of the Prophet Joseph Smith, pointed its hands close to midnight but it would be hours yet before Brigham sought the hard bed that he shared with no woman. For all that he kept strict track—by means of a checked list—of his methodical visits to each wife in her turn he always returned to sleep in his own room alone. It had always been thus, even in the days when his nightly visits to his numerous wives had been activated by more than his present only dutiful fervor. Brigham Young was an amazingly sturdy and vital man, but he was now, in the summer of 1857, past his fifty-sixth birthday.

The hands of the clock had moved past two when he straightened, rubbed at his inflamed eyes, and flexed the cramp from his powerfully thick shoulders. It was an endless task, the business of empire building. And now, faced with a crisis, there seemed so little time in which to prepare, so little room in which to maneuver. Time was of the essence—and yet, he couldn't complain, for he'd had just what he'd demanded: ten years.

"Ten years!" Brigham had said angrily, that long-ago day in the year 1847, "just give me ten years free of our cursed Gentile enemies and I'll ask no odds! We'll never run again!"

Well, he'd had his ten years. And, aghast, brooded that he hadn't held himself to be blessed—or cursed?—with so accurate a gift for prophecy. Was the Almighty calling his hand? Smiling, maybe, grimly—challengingly? Was He testing Brigham's mettle, and that of His Chosen People?

Brigham pondered the strangeness of the timing. He'd best be a little more careful about making public predictions. It was unsettling to have the people drag out some remark he'd made years ago and repeat it word for word! It was gratifying to have them thus treasure his every utterance, but he'd been new at leadership then, and he'd watch himself in the future so that complications wouldn't arise from unguarded remarks. He was stuck with it now, ten years later, for they were saying to each other, wonder in their tones: "Remember? Just exactly the way Brother Brigham prophesied: he asked God to give us ten years—and it's been ten years to the day!"

It was one thing for him to be taken at his word by his people, and not so unexpected, because he had seen to it that he had delivered most of what he promised them. But to be taken so literally by the Almighty, Himself—that was a little more than he'd bargained for.

Ten years he'd had in which to mold his wilderness kingdom toward self-sufficiency and the goal still far from secured. Ten years of relentlessly driving his slaving, praying, weeping, cursing hordes on to accomplish the well-nigh impossible. For sometimes his demands had been met with dumfounded unbelief—it couldn't be done, they'd argue. But under his impatient prodding they'd gone ahead and accomplished what he asked of them. And then shook baffled heads—how had Brother Brigham known they could, when they themselves knew they could not? How could he know, unless God did, indeed, speak through Brigham's stentorian voice? Their growing faith in his infallibility gave it a savor of omnipotence that was at once gratifying and alarming. Challenging.

It had been on the twenty-fourth of July 1847 that he'd struggled weakly up from his sickbed on the floor of a wagon; staggered, with the aid of helping arms, to a view point. There, from the boulder-strewn edge of a mighty shoulder of the Rocky Mountain fortress, he'd gazed long and silently down onto the desert floor of a wide valley.

It was no garden spot, sagebrush barrens—shattered, tumbling rocks. And the haunted, dreaming stillness of desolate, forbidding wilderness. No life, nothing moved in the unbroken, limitless quiet. The still valley moved starkly south to lose itself in hazy blue distance between the grim bastions of interminable mountain ranges, whose snow-capped peaks were repellingly aloof, remote. The faraway glitter of the great inland sea was mocking, for its waters were salt, it promised nothing, it was dead—its waters killed any living growth.

Brigham Young had been warned that this valley would not sustain life—he had been assured that no one in his right mind would want it. No one wanted his people either——

Brigham's spine stiffened, he shrugged himself free of the supporting arms, lifting his eyes to inspect the merciless blue glare of the heavens. Impatiently he waved back those who attempted to sustain him. Their drawn faces betrayed their worried concern, for he had been sick near to death and they'd known a terrible, clutching fear at the thought of losing him. But now his mighty lungs filled deeply with the thin, sweet dryness of the mountain air, which carried a pungent tang of pine and cedar and sage.

Brigham was a practical man, he expected no heavenly sign, but something stirred within his great intelligence and he envisioned a plan which he was confident he could bring to pass.

Here was a mighty land—unwanted by men—an unconquered, vicious, virgin land. And his was a horde of people thrust out, rejected. But not conquered! They were strong in their faith, determined, praying, contentious, fighting. His people—and they were a match for this land.

His exultant gaze roamed claimingly. There was water for the taking from those surrounding heights—and timber, metals, game. They'd channel the water down. It needed only labor—sweating, backbreaking labor—the supply of which was endless. They'd bring the life-giving water down, impregnate that barren soil. Force it, rape it into fertility. They'd drag, cursing, an endless stream of logs from the timbered slopes. They'd build temples from the granite rocks. By God, they'd even make use of that dead sea—a man had to have salt on his meat, didn't he? And there would be meat for his workers; there was game, wild meat was vastly nourishing!

A cooling breeze ruffled his mane of shaggy hair, his eyes were gloating over the untamed majesty of the panorama, his busy mind had already encompassed the miracle he would accomplish. And Brigham Young laughed, joyously, welcomingly, for here was a proper homeland for his people. Peculiarly right for their peculiar tenacity. Theirs to have and to hold—all they had to do was go forth and take it with their toil-hardened, obedient hands. Their roughened hands were strong—and so were their battered, belligerent souls.

Brigham swung his leonine head; his deeply significant glance brought his companions forward to stand at his side. He lifted his arms and gestured, sweepingly, offered the kingdom to them: "This is the place!" he said.

They looked and their faces paled with fear, they cringed before the forbidding countenance of the wilderness, for it had not been given to their workaday minds to share his confident vision. But, at his command, they obediently swarmed down the terrible canyons. Laboriously they reached the floor of the desert valley. And before the sun had set on the day of their arrival a field had been cleared of sagebrush and planted with seed potatoes brought along for that purpose. Another group of perspiring men labored at digging ditches to bring water from the hills to irrigate and ensure a crop.

Ten years later, on July 24, 1857, the Mormon Saints joyfully observed the tenth anniversary of "This is the place" day. And on that day of celebration Port Rockwell and his companions flogged their foundering horses the last miles to deliver ominous news. The United States Army—three thousand strong—was on the overland trail, heading west. Their destination was Brigham Young's Mormon empire. Orders from the President were that the army was to deal with the reported rebellion against federal authority in Utah Territory. It was also reported that a federal marshal accompanied the troops with warrants for the arrest of Brigham Young and thirty of his leaders. The charge was said to be treason.

## CHAPTER VII

When the Fanchers packed and sorted their gear and household possessions to take the trail to California, Annie spoke up with her usual vigor, demanding that her buggy be included. It was an elegant vehicle with excellent springs, bright red wheels and tasseled fringes on its canvas top. It signified, to Annie, an elevated social rank. Few women possessed husbands so tolerant of their wishes or the money to indulge them. Charley Fancher was, and had. And, although he had never said as much, he enjoyed seeing his wife, in her Sunday-best taffeta and beflowered bonnet, setting forth on a round of calls on her envious neighbors.

Charley had never considered leaving the buggy behind, he knew full well the value his wife placed on it. But he let her have her say, which included her favorite carriage horse, Deacon.

"I don't care if he is on the old side," she insisted, "I just won't have no other horse. Deacon knows my ways and I won't have no frisky, addlepated colt to upset me!" Deacon was a middle-aged bay gelding whose pompous composure had been the reason for his assignment to Annie's somewhat mercurial tooling. Almost anything could set Annie off, but nothing had ever been known to intrude on Deacon's monumental calm.

Charley, after waiting to see if she had presented her complete case, nodded indulgently, giving the appearance of having been won over. So Annie, from time to time, pointed out to her husband how right she had been in convincing him that the buggy not be left behind. There were many days when the trail was such that Deacon could be hitched up and Annie could spend a restful day traveling in high-springed comfort out of the continuous trail of dust. And it had immediately set the captain's wife up as a person of social importance.

It rapidly became a matter of desirable distinction for a woman to be singled out with an invitation to spend the day in the buggy. Regardless of who else might be thus favored, there was always another small passenger, Annie's youngest, Tryphena.

Annie was an efficient, if somewhat dictatorial, mother to all her brood but this small daughter was clearly her crowning jewel, the lovely fulfillment of romantic longings. Tryphena, the last-born of Annie's seven children, was like a tiny doll; there were reddish glints in her curling brown hair and she was pretty and sweet-natured. The older children did not appear to resent her partiality, they accepted their mother's delight in Tryphena's prettiness and shared it, the whole family adored and petted the tiny girl.

The most regular guest in the buggy was Melissa, when she could relinquish her team to David or one of the older boys. And on the day after they reached the Salt Lake Valley Annie invited the girl to go along in the buggy for a tour of the Mormon city. The emigrant road bypassed the city proper and led to an area of pasturage to the south by the Jordan River.

Everyone who wanted to visit the city departed in

one fashion or another but none was turned out nor conveyed quite as elegantly as the three in the Fancher buggy.

Annie had resurrected her black taffeta and floral bonnet. Tryphena's curls bounced above a yellow dimity and she wore ribboned slippers below the crocheted edge of ruffled pantaloons. Melissa's red-sprigged challis, with its snug basque and small white collar, was infinitely becoming and she fairly quivered with pleasure. The color of the day was heightened because alongside rode Jed. Having offered to squire the ladies and point out the sights, he had felt considerably at a loss as to wardrobe. He had only one shirt, a faded butternut brown, with which to replace his trail buckskins. But, in lieu of a string tie, he had knotted a red kerchief around his throat. Having scrubbed down furiously, shaved, and spruced as much as possible he felt equal to the occasion, for Melissa's dancing eyes looked on him with complete approval. And even Annie Fancher had nodded with grim approbation at his appearance.

Deacon, brushed and shining, paced gravely along, drawing the buggy decorously. Palouse high-stepped with equal composure, conforming, as always, to whatever demands were made on him, traveling quite unalarmed close beside the turning wheel of the buggy.

The city was surmounted by a pleasant sea of waving green, for the first settlers had transplanted young trees, fast-growing willows and poplars. Many of the houses were hut-small and of log or adobe construction but there were also quite a number of respectably ample two-story structures. And most of the houses, large or small, had lawns and flower gardens, boasted neat fences. Surprised to find that scrupulously clean boardwalks lined the wide streets on either side of the business center, Annie nodded a dour head in reluctant approval.

"Well, they might be immoral as alley cats, jumping in and out of bed with six or eight women, but it appears they got the strength left to do a day's work now and again," she observed acidly. "This here is a proper built town." Annie's seldom bridled tongue had forgotten that she was accompanied by a young man as well as an unmarried female. She cleared her throat brusquely and glared at the passers-by to hide her chagrin.

Jed smothered his chuckle and Melissa kept her eyes demurely down, but he saw the deepening of the errant dimple at the corner of her quivering mouth.

"My lands!" Annie exclaimed disgustedly, "that man Ward don't waste no time about gettin' his big gut full—" Jed and Melissa looked where she pointed in time to see Sol and his cronies, Les and Jake, disappear urgently through a doorway which bore a sign reading "Oasis Saloon."

"What that poor soul, Sairy, don't have to put up with!" Annie complained. "I swear I'd taken an ax to him long 'fore this. She sent along some money and asked me to fetch her a dress length of calico. First cash money she's seen in years, she said—and earnt every penny herself, helpin' Cintha Tackett with her younguns and gear."

Annie pulled in the placid Deacon in front of a sign which read "Millinery and Dry Goods" and was lavishly embellished with fanciful flowers. "Right here is where we'll shop," she said.

When the ladies returned, laden with bundles and an air of satisfaction over their purchases, they proceeded up the street slowly. Annie's stare darted suspiciously from person to person. "I wonder how a body would know if they're plural wives or decent people," she whispered, avidly scanning the women for evidences of sinfulness. She settled back, clucking at Deacon discontentedly. "My land, they all look just like anybody else," she complained. "Appear to be just ordinary folks—musta just fell into nasty habits." Thus disposing of the futility of pigeonholing the people on the street, Annie looked with interest at an imposing structure that Jed pointed out as they approached.

"That there is the Lion House," he said, "Brigham Young's headquarters." It was a large building with a wide veranda and topped by a row of gables and many towering chimneys.

"*Lion* House!" Annie snorted. "Ain't what I'd be of a mind to name that man's house!" She had remembered to censor the more apt term she had obviously thought and Jed laughed aloud. "Well," he said, "there's those stone lions at the door and then the Saints call Brigham the 'Lion of the Lord.'" Annie sniffed at the puny inadequacy of their naming and then craned like a curious bird as Jed pointed to the next big building. It was, he said, the Beehive House, where Brigham's plural wives lived, all together.

Annie and Melissa came erectly alert and stared with unabashed curiosity at this abode of Brigham's "harem." It was a large, dignified structure, several stories high and topped with a square tower. The wide veranda was two-storied and Jed explained that the many windows on the second floor each denoted a wife's separate quarters. Annie almost fell out of the buggy in her excitement as a double line of children filed out of one side door, shepherded by two young women. The decorous little procession marched to a small, rock-constructed building and trooped inside.

"School kids," said Jed, "Brigham has got so many kids that he built that schoolhouse just for them." He added then, "Them two young women would both be wives."

Annie had been leaning out to stare backward as they proceeded and hung there, precariously balanced, until the young women disappeared inside. "My good land alive!" she exclaimed, "if they didn't both look like nice girls! Neat-dressed and lady-like-walking and teaching school and all! How on earth do you suppose that old booger could get nice girls like that all mixed up in such a thing?"

Annie was not short of subjects on which to enlighten her husband that night. Charley sat contentedly drawing on his pipe, his eyes twinkling, as she indignantly told of Brigham's immoral success in luring nice young girls into his harem. The train captain had had a busy, if not so entertaining, day. There had been a prolonged conference among the male members of the train. For here, in Salt Lake City, the train was splitting up. Some of the freighters were taking the northern route into California, the Hastings Cutoff. This trail led across the alkali wastes of the Great Salt Lake Desert, the balance of the journey lay through the high, snow-capped Sierra Nevadas. Echoes of the horrors experienced by the Donner Party some years before deterred family men from favoring this route late in the summer.

There had been argument among the train members, some wanted the train to stick together, all go by the Hastings Cutoff.

Charley, pipe in mouth, let them wrangle. He placidly enjoyed the view of the mountain horizon below the still blue vault of the late-summer sky. When there was a long silence he looked up, found them staring at him insistently, waiting for his official opinion. He removed his pipe and spoke mildly.

"Everybody go the way they want—that's how I see it. We're outa hostile Injun country—any size train is safe enough. The north route is likely fine for the ones without livestock to slow them up. But I'm goin' south. I ain't in a hurry, I wanta take all my stock through. There'll be no chance of gettin' snowed in and the south way is through settlements for three hundred mile—good, easy road. Everybody do as he pleases, but regardless, I'm pointin' south." It was a long speech for the captain and he replaced the stem of his pipe between his teeth and settled back with relief.

"That's right," Joel Mitchell agreed, "and Jed says we can likely buy garden truck and fresh food at the Mormon settlements. And not have to guard much—the Injuns is friendly."

John Barker felt called on to probe a little. "What about that other desert—the Mojave? I've heard it's bigger'n the Salt Desert—and that there's that place called

'Death Valley' that did for a party ever bit as bad as the Donners!"

"Ain't no place this side a'hell worse than the Salt Desert," one of the freighters spoke up. "And I know, for I've crossed it and I'd turn around and go all the way back to Missouri 'fore I'd tackle it right now! This here is August—the hottest time of the year. That desert is a graveyard of wagons. The water holes is seventy-five miles between and the water ain't hardly fit to drink when you get there! And hot! It's so goddamned hot you raise blisters on your ass right through your clothes if you set down on it. Our stock went crazy—run around in circles till they dropped down dead. The sun glares on that alkali like it was snow and some of the men damn near went blind. You get near loony watchin' a lake with trees around it movin' always ahead of you—you never get to it—it ain't there, really. We only pulled through because we taken to stayin' under the wagons while the sun was up, and travelin' at night." The man's rough voice dwindled, he shook his head marveling at the horror of it. A respectful silence followed the veteran's account.

Lawson Mitchell added his bit. "Anyways," he offered, "we don't go through that 'Death Valley.' Jed says there's a big desert, all right enough, but the Mormons has got a freight and immigrant road right across to San Bernardino in Californy. This road travels plain from water hole to water hole. He says there's a couple of dry runs but not further than we can tote water in barrels. We pass right by the mouth of Death Valley but we don't get into it—we stay off to the side and go on down through a place called the Cajon Pass. Why, Jed says on the southern route we foller along streams a lot of the time. One of them is named the Virgen River—and his own pappy named it. Not virgin, like"—he searched for a proper term for there were women listening and with some relief brought up a suitable definition—"not like the Virgin Mary, but named for a feller name of Tom Virgen that got killed by Injuns there."

"Thought there wasn't supposed to be no hostiles?" There was alarm in this query.

"Oh hell"—Lawson waved his hand—"that was more'n thirty years back. The Injuns is all tame now—the Mormons has made farmers outa them, Jed says."

"He been down that way?" John Barker was still insistently checking details.

"Not all the way," Lawson said, "but his pappy explored all that country clean to the Pacific Ocean and back again! And him and Jim Bridger got together on maps and Jed has got copies of them maps. He says Bridger allowed a ten-year-old couldn't lose himself on the south trail these days."

Captain Fancher nodded. "Just so," he said and walked placidly away. All of the undecided group were convinced of taking the southern route.

But there was one member of the freighters' group—which had decided on the shorter, northern route—who had not heard the discussion but nevertheless was determined to accompany the Fancher Train. Sairy Ward was packing her clothes, muttering as she worked. She was "done with that drunken, no-good lout" at long last.

Annie had delivered the dress length—bright red calico sprigged with little white flowers. The unaccustomed loveliness that she had provided for herself with her earnings went to Sairy's head. Plus the fact that there was a place where she was not only needed but warmly appreciated—and loved.

The bony woman had taken the calico over to Cintha Tackett's wagon to show it off. Cintha's husband had died of inflammation of the bowel at Independence while she, herself, was still weakened by childbirth. But she had decided to go on to California anyway when Captain Fancher had promised to see to her needs and had found Sairy Ward to help her out. Sairy's thin arms had hungrily gathered the three small children to her lonely heart, especially the new baby. Little Jeremy spent the first weeks of his life in her arms while she drove the wagon, for his mother was slow in regaining her strength.

Sairy only parted with him at night when she returned to her own wagon to look after Sol's meals.

Cintha's eyes filled with tears now as she looked at Sairy; the two women had grown close. "I don't know what I'm gonna do without you, Sairy," she said, her voice shaky, "and the baby—he bawls for you ever time you set foot away. Seems awful hard that you ain't goin' with us the rest of the way. I don't know when I've felt worse about a thing."

Sairy's eyes watered also, she looked down at small Jeremy, who was blowing contented bubbles against her shoulder. "That old Sol could just as easy of gone along with the Fanchers," she complained, "I wouldn't put it apast him to be goin' the other way jist to spite me." Bitterness turned down the corners of her mouth. "I just ought to let him go on—and me go along with you." Her eyes showed her surprise at the suddenly conceived and tempting thought.

Cintha's mouth opened with astonishment and then she smiled eagerly, reached out to touch Sairy. "Oh, if you only would—I'd pay you just the same, Sairy." The offer tumbled out. "And we could have a nice home together in Californy—Jason left me well fixed—you and me and the kids—it'd be awful nice!" Her look was soberly level now. "I mean it, Sairy, I couldn't think more of you if you was my own sister. You come with us and what I've got is your'n, too." Both women were sobbing happily and presently Sairy went back to her wagon to pack her meager belongings.

When Sol arrived, drunk and staggering, she informed him of her decision.

Shrill screams rang through the camp. Annie Fancher, investigating, saw Sairy trying to dodge her husband's slapping big hands as he pursued her unsteadily around the wagon. He was roaring and cursing. There were men who stared in angry disgust but they hesitated, reluctant to interfere with a man's disciplining of his woman.

Not so Cintha Tackett, who arrived at the scene, broom in hand, having immediately guessed the cause of the fracas. She was accompanied by Annie, and several other women hurried in their wake. Sairy was backed against the wagon with upraised, shielding arms, her terrified eyes on Sol. But she was defiant.

"You'n beat me to a pulp, Sol Ward," she declared shrilly, "but I'm done. I ain't agonna drag along of you another day. I got a chance to do for folks that care about me and I'm goin'—I ain't gonna put up with your carryin' on no more!"

Sol bellowed his wrath and moved in. But he was caught across the back of his thick neck by Cintha's broom, swung with all the strength of her not inconsiderable weight. Dazed, he lumbered around to face this unexpected attack from the rear. His hand lowered, his mouth dropped open in surprise.

Cintha stood her ground, broom threateningly uplifted. Annie Fancher capably carried a pitchfork and her face did not encourage heroics from the redbeard. Melissa ranged beside Annie and she carried her long mule whip. Rosetta Huff and the torpid Magdalene, unarmed, but for once united in common cause, both looked their angry disgust.

Sol stared uncomprehendingly from face to face of this pause-giving crew. Cintha spoke, feeling confidence in the sturdiness of her reinforcements.

"You lay one dirty paw on Sairy again, Sol Ward, and you'll have all of us on your back! They's been just enough of your bullyin' and sousin' and brawlin'! Sairy's got a right to get shut of it and make a decent life for herself if she so wants to!"

Her cohorts, until now in the dark as to the reason for their crusade, nodded stanchly. Annie made a threatening gesture with her pitchfork. Sol jumped and staggered back. "Just look at you!" Annie said loathingly, "so sodden drunk you'n hardly keep your big feet!"

A few men had come up and were listening, vastly entertained by the spectacle of the bully brought to bay by the petticoat squad. Sol, furious with embarrassment, sought help from the male contingent.

"Ain't a man got a right to a little family ruckus without gettin' into a hen fight?" he complained.

Charley Fancher removed his pipe from his mouth as he considered, trying unsuccessfully to quell the twinkle in his mild eyes. While he tried to frame a fair answer, John Barker replied somewhat heatedly, having become inspired by the disturbing presence of the Widow Huff.

"Arguin' is one thing, but it appears to me it's gone some further! The train rules don't allow for drunkenness and you've made trouble time and again, Ward. And we won't stand for a man abusing the weaker sex!" Rosetta's slanted gaze approved his verbal heroics and John felt his righteous manhood swell; he realized that he was quite willing to rush into action, teach Sol a badly needed lesson.

Jed had lounged up and was grinning broadly at Melissa. When she noticed him he winked at her. Melissa flushed but held her ground. Sol also saw the scout and realized by his expression that he would likely back the women in their stand. He wavered, having no wish to tangle with Jed again.

"But, looka here, now," Sol floundered, "Sairy's fixin' to take up with Miz Tackett and leave me without my own woman to do for me!"

Annie snorted loudly. "And why would any woman care two hoots if *you* starve or no?" She looked him over scathingly. "Ain't a one of us but knows the misery you've drug Sairy through. And if she don't wanta put up with you no more then what I say is: good riddance!" She finished with an emphatic nod. The other women nodded with equal firmness and moved a step closer. Sol retreated nervously.

The starch had gone out of the man entirely, he looked flabbily helpless. "You gonna let 'em get away with this?" he whined to Charley Fancher. The captain looked with distaste at the sodden big man and then at the thin, toil-worn woman whose eyes met his with sick beseeching. He nodded decisively. "Looks like it's done settled, Sol," he said, "for Miz Ward can sure go along with us if she wants to."

Insane fury blazed up in the bleary eyes resting on the stocky figure of the train captain. He took a threatening step toward the smaller man. The tall figure of the scout was suddenly at Fancher's elbow. "What Cap'n Fancher says goes for me, too," he said warningly. Sol halted in his tracks, weaving a little, staring at the brown face suddenly devoid of humor, gone hard. The redbeard began to curse under his breath, then he turned away and lurched off into the darkness.

Cintha Tackett called after him, "You come anywheres near my wagon, Sol Ward, and you'll get a load of buckshot! I'm gonna load Jason's shotgun and if you come skulkin' around I'll fill your hind end so full you'll have to walk all the way to Californy!"

The armed guard waited while Sairy scrambled into the wagon for her bundle and then they escorted her triumphantly off to Cintha's wagon. All but Melissa. Jed put out a hand and took the arm from which the black whip trailed. "If you're done bullyin' poor old Sol," he said, "maybe we could walk in the moonlight a little—only I'm scared you might start on me."

She tossed her head, wrinkling her nose up at him. "You didn't appear to be too scared, just now," she said.

"Oh, I figgered you'd help me," Jed said solemnly. He looked at the whip she was looping into one hand. "You gonna use that on me, if'n I don't toe the mark?"

"Maybe—if you need it—"

They strolled in silence, his arm was pleasantly heavy across her shoulders. "It's nice, bein' able to just walk anywhere and not be thinkin' is it safe or not," Melissa said presently.

They were in shadow now and he swung her around close to him. "Safe from Injuns," he said, "but not from me—" He lifted her up and her ready mouth met his. There was a long silence, he was still holding her so that her feet were clear of the ground when she said, "I'm not one bit afraid of *you*—"

"Maybe you should be."

Melissa's arms were around his neck, she gave him swift little kisses on his hard chin. "It's you that's afraid of me," she taunted, "in just a minute now you'll start to worry is David looking for me." Her teasing eyes challenged him.

He looked down at her taunting smile, exasperation was in every limb of his hungry male body. His arms tightened until she gasped and he kissed her again. "We'll not go back, yet a while," he said and she smiled with satisfaction. Still carrying her, he walked further into the friendly shadows.

Charley Fancher's face wore a troubled expression as he turned back toward his wagon. He had not enjoyed the final act of the domestic drama he'd been called on to judge. The goaded humiliation of Sol Ward had not been pleasant to watch. He'd be downright glad when the freighters pulled out and took the troublesome red-beard with them.

An anxious-faced thin young man waited in the shadow of the Fancher wagon. "You Cap'n Fancher?" he inquired cautiously. His voice had an accent that Charley presently identified as English. The captain nodded, staring curiously at the man, for he kept glancing furtively around as though someone might be watching or following him.

"I am William Aden," the nervous man said, "I would like to arrange—purchase transportation with your train to California."

Fancher's deliberate regard was speculative, this was surely a queer-acting man. "You a Mormon?" he asked.

Aden hesitated and then nodded reluctantly, "That is —I—we were—— But we've decided to go to California— if we can find a train that will take us." The man kept peering nervously at shadows and passers-by. Charley removed his pipe and scratched the side of his nose with the stem, his puzzled stare contemplated the frightened man. Suddenly he remembered his conversation with Eli Jacobs and he spoke abruptly. "You'd be an apostate, maybe?"

Aden started violently, his stance became frantic, he peered around in all directions before he answered. "That's what they call us," he said bitterly, "any of us who speak out. I guess it's no use tryin' to get away—" He turned hopelessly away. Charley put a detaining hand on his arm.

"Now, don't get het up, man," he said soothingly, "I just made a guess—I ain't got a thing *agin'* apostates, nor Mormons, either, for that matter. Maybe we can fix you up. I'll listen to what you've got to say, anyhow." He took the thin arm and guided Aden to a seat on a small keg well in the shadow of the wagon. "They ain't nobody can hear you," he said reassuringly, "let's see if the wife has got a drop of coffee left in the pot." He poured two tin cups full of the potently re-boiled brew and added sugar lavishly. He seated himself on another keg and said, "Now—let's hear it."

Aden sipped at his coffee gratefully. "First coffee I've had in a long time." The scalding brew seemed to give his thin voice strength. "My wife and I were converts, in England," he said, "and when she came into a little money from her mother's side of the family we decided to come to Zion. They'd made it sound like heaven on earth where everybody lived in brotherhood and was building up a great kingdom. But when we got here we found that they'd—exaggerated everything—worst of all, they'd lied about polygamy. We'd heard rumors, of course, in England about it but Brother Richards—that was the missionary that converted us—just laughed and said the whole thing was made up by enemies of the Church." His face worked convulsively, he had trouble with his shaking hands. "We just couldn't stay in a Church where—and they know how we feel about it, that's why we have to get away. It isn't safe here for people who want to leave the Church!"

Charley drew meditatively on his pipe. "I ain't had much truck with Mormons—but I have heard that they ain't above bein' rough on apostates."

"Oh, Captain Fancher, you don't know—you just

wouldn't believe what those people——" The strangling fear in the man's face and voice gave Charley sober pause. He reflected that if he had not heard of such things from Eli Jacobs he would have taken Aden's talk for hysterical imagination. Fancher's first impulse was to accede to Aden's plea—help him and his wife to leave. But he hesitated, reflecting that he could not make the decision alone, he had no right to involve the whole train in what might turn out to be ruckus with the Mormons.

"You sure you ain't imaginin' a lot of things?" he inquired mildly.

"Imagining!" Aden's voice was slightly indignant. "You *can't* imagine how it was here last winter! They started a reformation in the Church and the bishops and their councilors called on every member, snooping for backsliders. They were already suspicious of me—the bishop had been at me and at me to enter Celestial Marriage—*celestial*—that's what *they* call polygamy!"

"Well, I don't see how they could make a man take another wife if he didn't want to——" Charley was grateful that Annie was apparently spending the evening at Cintha Tackett's wagon. He could imagine the comments she would have intruded into this conversation.

"Oh, they've got lots of ways to put pressure on you," Aden said bitterly, "with everything—business, law, and all controlled by the Church. The mistake I made was in telling Birdie that they were at me to take another wife. Birdie—my wife, her name is Victoria, for the Queen, God bless her, but her mother always called her Birdie—she just went all to pieces over it. And when the bishop and his councilor came around to the house she—Birdie, spoke right up and said we'd been lied to, right down the line! That Brother Richards had lied to us about how things were in Zion, but especially about polygamy. And she said that if she'd known that the Prophet himself was an adulterer she wouldn't have joined his Church for anything in the world!" Aden shook his head at the memory of Birdie's declaration. "She really told them," he went on, "she talked for ten solid minutes, at least. And when they got up and left—without saying another word to us—Birdie followed them right to the door and before she slammed it she said, 'Good riddance to bad rubbish!' "

Captain Fancher smothered a grin. Looked like Birdie—named Victoria—had enough starch for the both of them. He sympathized with the timid Aden, for Charley knew well what it was to be married to a woman who "spoke up." But the younger man hadn't apparently been blessed with anything like his own well-cushioned nerves.

"It went from bad to worse, after that," Aden continued resignedly. "They began to look into our tithing—the per cent of our income we're supposed to give the Church. We hadn't paid it for a while and Birdie had her back up about that, too. So when the elder called on us she up and told him we weren't going to pay it because she'd heard it was to go into the immigration fund—to help more converts to come to Zion. And she said we weren't going to help them lie to trusting, innocent people so that they packed up and left their homes to come to this place of—of obscenity. That's what she said, right to his face! Place of obscenity! Well, that elder didn't come to the house any more but he stopped me on the street one day and said he'd had to report us to higher authorities and he came right out and warned me that I'd better rule my household better or I could expect any amount of trouble! He warned me about the fate waiting for apostates in hell—but I knew he didn't mean just in the hereafter. And he told me that we'd both better be in meeting the next Sunday because the leaders were going to talk about apostates. We decided we'd better go, and it was horrible—the things they said.

"Brigham Young stood up there and shook his finger, seemed like he was pointing right at me, and he said the worst of sins was committed by the apostate. He said the only atonement possible was to atone *by the blood!* He said a man was better off dead than headed for hell! And then he said that rather than apostates should flourish in God's kingdom, he'd draw his own knife and see to it himself! And the people"—Aden shuddered—"the people cheered him!"

Charley silently refilled their cups from the capacious pot and Aden gulped with a sort of desperation, beads of sweat had broken out on his brow. He resumed his shaky monologue.

"The day we got home from that meeting Birdie just went all to pieces and said we had to get out of Zion. I agreed with her—we just couldn't stay with people like these. We didn't go to any more meetings and no one came near us. But the pressure started. I got pushed out of my business. I was in partnership in a nice little business. But my partner told me he'd been ordered to lock me out. I had to *get out* and we were *partners!* He said they would contrive some way to get it in court—he was a good Mormon, but he knew of cases where they'd done just that—and he advised me to let him buy me out or I wouldn't come out with a cent! He didn't dare, on account of his family to associate with me. He blamed it all on Birdie, of course, he never did like her way of speaking out, and even after I told him I agreed with her, he still thought—— Well, so anyway, I guess we were lucky to get the money so that we have enough to pay our way to California." Aden sighed wearily. "But I've had trouble finding a way for us. I tell you, Captain Fancher, they've been watching us." Fancher's face must have reflected a dubious acceptance of this, for Aden, after glancing at him, nodded emphatically. "They have, Captain, we know that for sure. They don't want people leaving here that might talk against the Church. Birdie's good friends with a woman that lives next door to us and she's a plural wife of the bishop of our ward. What he'd likely do to her if he knew she was friendly to us! But she told Birdie they were keeping close track and they'd stop us if we tried to leave! Why, *she's* supposed to watch us herself! But she'd get away, too, if she could. She's only a girl, really, but she's got three babies already—and the bishop is nearly sixty!"

Aden was encouraged to see that there was no doubt

on the captain's sober face. "We *have* to get away from here, and soon, Captain Fancher," he said earnestly, "for with the army coming it will be twice as dangerous—they've started calling the backsliders 'traitors' and God knows what they couldn't make out of it. They're going to secede from the United States!"

Fancher's face did not show as much surprise as Aden might have expected. He nodded slowly. "I heard that they might," he said slowly, "a trader who deals with them all the time figgered Brigham Young just might fight to keep the army out. But I didn't know they'd bring it right out in the open——"

Aden nodded vigorously, encouraged by Fancher's comprehension. "They did—right out in meeting. It wasn't a regular church meeting—it was called special—and we went. We thought we ought to know what was going to happen. It was downright treason, Captain Fancher, what Brigham Young said! First Heber Kimball talked, and then John Taylor——"

Captain Fancher's pipe smoldered out, untended, as he listened to Aden's account of that portentous gathering of the Mormon people.

They came, all within traveling distance, to hear the word from their leader, Brigham Young. The tabernacle would seat two thousand but the restlessly whispering crowd numbered many times that. They stood in the aisles, solidly packed the back area, and milled about the entrance. The doors were open to the bright summer day and they stood on tiptoe to glimpse the speakers as they filed to the platform.

Heber Kimball, the strong right arm of the leader, spoke to them first. Handsome, laughing, irresistible Heber—of the forty handsome wives. But his usual geniality was absent, his voice swelled with anger. "Great God in Heaven helping me!" he stormed, "I will fight this thing until there is not a drop of blood in my veins!" The congregation roared instant approval, and he showed them a little, then, of the old, humorous Heber. He smiled widely as he said, "Why, Good God, I have enough wives to wipe out the United States!" and they joined him in a gale of laughter when he added, "and, by golly, some of 'em are so fond of fightin' they'd just as leave tackle an army themselves!"

The tension was relieved, they were at home with this Heber. But he did not leave them comfortable. Shaking his head sorrowfully he spoke of the deluded rascals who now administered the government of their beloved country.

"Poor, rotten curses," he grieved, "the President of the United States, and all those around him who are howling for the destruction of this people." His melodious voice deepened with ominous intensity. "For they have cast me out and they will cast you out! And for this I curse him." Heber Kimball was shaking with emotion now, he lifted a threatening finger, shook it wrathfully. "And all those around him who have aided in this foulness—*I curse him in the name of Jesus Christ and the authority of the holy priesthood!*"

There was a breathless, stricken silence. Then a woman sobbed aloud, and another. But the sobs were drowned by a flooding, rumbling tide of "Amens." The congregation had sustained Heber's curse on the President. He stood still, looking out over the sea of bowed heads, lifted his hands in silent blessing, and sank into his chair. Brigham Young's gaze, full of somber approval, followed him. The leader nodded to the apostle John Taylor. The firebrand had flung the torch—the beloved apostle would sanctify the flames.

There was a quiet dignity about the frail man who now moved to the front of the platform. His gentle gaze embraced the people. They were still, returning his gaze and his affection, and with something else that ventured near reverence. John Taylor had been the constant companion of the Prophet. He had been imprisoned with Joseph Smith, had heard him speak his last words on earth. And carried scars on his body from wounds received at the time the Prophet was assassinated.

He stood for a long moment regarding them. When he began to speak his voice was slow, the words were painfully uttered. "Who would not rather die"—the question dropped shatteringly into the quivering pool of silent listening—"than bow down to the yoke of the enemy?" His words hung suspended, it seemed, over their tense minds for an interminable time and then he answered it himself.

"I thank God," John Taylor said simply, "and I rejoice that His people are determined to be free and have peace—*if they have to fight for it!*"

There was no sobbing this time, only a sweeping sigh of benediction, like the faint throbbing of faraway thunder before a summer storm. They looked at Brigham Young now as he rose and made ready to speak.

He planted his feet firmly, the heavy shoulders squared up to their burden, his leonine head was high, that determined chin thrust out as his glance displayed stern pride in this, his people. As he began to speak there was the old, beloved gesture, that raised forefinger emphasizing his words, expressing his feeling of paternal domination.

"The time must come." Brigham Young's voice was clear as a deep bell, he spaced his words deliberately, made no demands on emotion. "The time must come when this kingdom must be free—and independent of all other kingdoms!" He leaned forward over them and his significant, roving gaze held the very breathing suspended in their throats.

"Are you"—the stark question descended on them like a swift blade—"*are you prepared to have the thread cut today?*"

Their silence was like that of the perilously quiet center of the hurricane and then they surged to their feet, their tumultuous answer shook the foundations of the building as they thundered their approval.

Brigham's square face worked strongly as he heard their reply, his eyes gleamed with fierce exultation. Deafened by the mightiness of the accolade, he let them roar, savoring to the full the omnipotence they accepted—nay, demanded! Then he lifted his hands for quiet and the turbulence ceased as a stream which is suddenly dammed.

The lifted faces waited, each head thrust forward to hear his next words.

"I take it," ringing with triumph, solemn with weighty conclusion, "as a witness: that God Almighty desires to cut the thread between us and the world when an army undertakes to make their appearance in this territory to chastise me, or to destroy my life from this earth!"

"That was what he—Brigham Young—said." Aden's voice trailed away. He had done his best to tell how things were, now, in Mormon country, to make the train captain realize the danger in which he and Birdie stood. Fancher had not uttered a word in a long time; Aden had no way of knowing his reaction.

The captain's thoughts held consternation and yet he doubted none of the apostate's story. This was no harder to believe than the things Eli Jacobs had told.

"I believe you," he said suddenly and Aden's eyes lit with quick hope. "If it was up to me, alone," Fancher added, "I'd say right now—come ahead, the hell with the consequences. But I got a train council that has to be consulted on anything that concerns the whole train. We don't want trouble with the Mormons, and I can't give you a 'yes' or 'no' without their say-so. Do you want to wait while I call them together?"

Aden's expression was much more cheerful but he shook his head. "I'd better get on home. I've left Birdie alone so long she'll be half frantic, wondering if anything has happened to me. Could I come tomorrow night?"

Fancher nodded. "I'll have a definite answer for you then—but it'll crowd you a little—we plan to pull out the next morning, early." Aden waved that aside as immaterial, "We'll have to sneak off, anyhow," he said, "we can't take much with us."

Aden wrung the captain's hand fervently. "Now," Fancher said soothingly, "don't you worry none, likely the others will see it the way I do—you tell Birdie not to fret." The apostate peered around suspiciously and then slipped off into the darkness.

But it was not William Aden who came into camp

to hear the verdict the next night. A small, veiled woman crept up to the Fancher wagon, careful to keep out of the light from the fire. From shadowy concealment she hissed and beckoned with a small, black-gloved hand.

Annie moved curiously near in answer to the odd summons. Charley had told her about the previous night's visitor, and his business. He had also taken the matter up with John Barker and the council. Barker had been completely in favor of helping the Adens escape from their "place of obscenity." And the others were willing. Sid Huff had offered to let Aden earn their passage by driving Rosetta's wagon. Sid, although fond of his handsome sister, regarded her with constant, uneasy suspicion. He would sleep more soundly if he knew another woman shared her wagon bed.

Annie hurried back to the fire, having conferred in agitated whispers with Birdie Aden. "My good land alive, Charley," she exclaimed in a flustered whisper, "they—the Mormons set on that poor young man last night and like to beat him to death! Miz Aden says they guess he was seen leavin' here—"

A hasty conclave was held, including John Barker, Jed, and Sid and Rosetta, the latter, because her wagon was involved. Annie was clucking over the tiny Birdie Aden. "Now, don't you carry on, Miz Aden," she comforted. "We're gonna see to things."

But Birdie Aden wasn't carrying on—her small spine was stiffly straight, she was as mad as a little wet hen. "I think they would have killed Willum, there were three of the ruffians and right before my eyes! I screamed for help but, of course, the neighbors wouldn't—didn't dare to interfere." She spoke in a clipped, disdainful English way. "But I had loaded Willum's pistol to protect myself when he had to leave me alone—"

Captain Fancher hid a grin behind his hand, Birdie was about as helpless as a rattlesnake. He wondered if she'd really used the gun. She had.

"I fired over their heads, of course," she went on briskly, "but I called out and informed them that I had four shots left and they wouldn't be fired in the air. I was afraid of hitting Willum or I would have shot the lot of them!" She tossed her pointed chin, her brightly indignant glance challenged, what were they going to do about this outrage?

"Didn't anybody—the law—come, after the shooting?" It was John Barker.

Birdie sniffed, "What law? The Church is the only law here, and likely it was the Church sent them to do Willum in! But they weren't so brave they'd walk into a pointed gun—nobody's come near the house all day!"

"My land, Miz Aden," said Annie, "why on earth didn't you both come tonight? You coulda just stayed, then."

Birdie stared at her, "Didn't I make it clear, Mrs. Fancher? They beat Willum—*really* beat him. He's so bruised and sick he can't take a deep breath without moaning! He must have some broken ribs, or cracked anyway. I had an awful time getting him into the house. I had to drag him most of the way. And it wasn't until this afternoon that he was able to tell me how to find you, Captain Fancher."

"Do you think they're watching the house?" Captain Fancher's voice was troubled.

"Of course they are!" Birdie was vehement. "I sneaked out the back way."

"Well, I don't see how—without gettin' into a mess—" It was Sid Huff unhappily observing.

Birdie glared at him. "Well, he'll just have to be fetched," she said tartly. "Somebody's got to help me. You wouldn't be able to face your own conscience if you leave us here to be murdered! If my poor Willum ain't laying dead in his own blood this minute! I left the lamps lit, like I was there—but if somebody got to snooping around, and him as helpless as a babe—" There were smothered gasps of horror from the women.

Fancher reminded them that the whole train might get involved in trouble if they rescued the Adens. And so—as he had counted on—inspired John Barker to an indignant stand that they must remove these good people from the clutches of immorality and danger. All were agreed.

Various plans were suggested and rejected. It was finally Rosetta's softly voiced solution that was dubiously accepted. The men opposed it as being too dangerous for womenfolks but Annie and Birdie both approved. Rosetta smiled meltingly at John, his had been the loudest voice against the ladies taking risks. Jed had agreed with the womenfolks first.

"I don't think even Mormons will bother us, the way we'll do it," Rosetta said. "I think I can talk my way past any we might meet." She looked at Birdie Aden. "You won't be able to take anything but the clothes you stand up in."

"My goodness!" the pert little woman replied, "all I care is to get Willum out of there before we get our throats cut from ear to ear!"

Jed paused and spoke to Rosetta. "Remember," he said, "we're going into town by another way—but we'll be there ahead of you. So if you get in a fix, fire that pistol and we'll be there—*fast!*"

John Barker fidgeted as he watched Rosetta listen intently to the scout, her wide eyes soberly on his face. "I shall be there, too," he informed her sternly. Rosetta smiled then and completely upset the man. "I knew you would be, Mr. Barker," she said.

It was Rosetta handling Deacon's reins as the buggy pulled sedately away from the wagon train. Birdie Aden sat beside her, a small bundle on the seat between them. A short time later three figures, all, apparently, long-skirted females, crept from the back door of the Aden house and crossed the yard to the alley, carefully staying in the shadows. Two of them supported the other, who stumbled weakly between them. They reached the buggy and hoisted the staggerer in to sit between them. Rosetta urged Deacon into a fast walk as they headed for the outskirts of the city. William Aden, dressed in women's clothes, head covered by a shawl, slumped half conscious against his wife's shoulder. Birdie supported him with one arm about his thin shoulders, in her other hand she clutched the pistol concealed by a fold in her skirt.

Rosetta drew in her breath sharply, warning. A small party of mounted men were coming toward them down the quietly dark street. "Don't say a word or do anything," Rosetta whispered sharply, "unless it gets outa hand. If it does, *you shoot right at the nearest one* and then hang on to Willum, for we'll have to make a run for it!"

Rosetta pushed her bonnet back on her neck, touched her hair to be sure it was smooth, and composedly reined Deacon in as one of the mounted men rode near the buggy and stooped to peer in at its occupants.

He was a big, bearded man. "You sisters are out kinda late, ain't you?" His voice was rough but courteous.

Rosetta smiled up at him. "Yes, we are." Her mellow voice was pleased at the encounter. "But Sister Lewis, here"—her nod indicated the crumpled heap that was William—"well—I'm a midwife and she——" Her smile deprecated further unseemly explanation. "I'm taking her to my place," Rosetta explained. "There are so many children and she has only two rooms, where she lives. It came on her, sudden-like, so we thought best to get her right to bed." Her smile was somehow intimate, asking for indulgence of female indispositions.

The bearded man removed his hat, bowed gallantly; he was staring at the lovely face raised to him. "I'd be glad to ride along," he offered, "see you get home safe."

"Oh, thank you, sir"—the smile deepened—"but it's just around the corner now." Her head tilted to one side, she widened her eyes slightly. "Why don't you—call around tomorrow night—just to see how Sister Lewis is doing?" She lowered her gaze as though embarrassed by her own forwardness, but quickly raised it again, meeting his suddenly intent stare. "Just ask for the Widow Huff's place—I'm a widow, you see."

Teeth flashed whitely in the bearded face, the man was smiling broadly as he replaced his hat with a flourish.

"I'll just do that, ma'am," he said, seeming almost to strut as he sat his horse. "Expect me early tomorrow evening, Sister Huff."

Rosetta nodded gaily, she was still smiling as she clucked gently, starting the plodding Deacon on his way. She looked back as they turned the corner, waved to him. The man had held his horse, watching the buggy, now he waved vigorously and moved to rejoin his companions.

The buggy moved quietly along for a few moments before Birdie released her strangled breath in a deep sigh of relief. "My word"—her voice was admiring—"you should have been in the theater! I never in all my life—the way you handled him—why, the big fool was eating out of your hand!"

Rosetta chuckled. "Men are all alike," she said, indulgently cynical, "and I doubt there's any difference in Mormon men."

"Well, I'd just like to see his face when he tries to find you tomorrow night!" Birdie giggled. "Will he be furious!" They were nearing the edge of town now and she smothered a little scream. "Look, there's some more riders!"

Rosetta stared into the gloom ahead. "It's all right. That would be Mr. Barker and the others." The riders ranged cautiously nearer, Barker rode up to the buggy. "Are you all right?" His deep voice was urgent. "All right, thank you, Mr. Barker." Rosetta's voice was warm. The three riders, Jed, Sid Huff, and John, fell in behind the buggy and escorted them the rest of the distance to the wagon train.

When the Fancher Train wheeled into dusty formation at the cry of "Stretch out!" the following morning, they headed south. The freighters who had chosen to take the shorter Hastings Cutoff pulled out earlier. But one of their number remained. Sol Ward's mules were hitched, standing in harness, but the redbeard sat motionless on the driver's seat, his big hands slack on the reins. He was miserably sober, his stomach sour, but no more so than his frame of mind.

He had watched the Fancher Train pull out, had glimpsed Sairy where she sat, holding the baby, beside Cintha Tackett, who capably handled her mules. Sairy had not even turned her head, not even so much as a glance did she spare Sol.

He glowered at the tail of dust diminishing southward. Go off and leave him, after all these years, just like that! Not even a nod, or word, go to hell, or anything else! Well, by God, he didn't know if he was going to stand still for it or not. He looked around; even the dust had settled back on the empty camp ground, everything was quiet. Away off in the field somewhere a meadow lark broke the silence with a prattle of melodic observation. Then it was still again and the man felt somehow smothered by his aloneness. Suddenly his chin thrust out, let Sairy do what she damn well pleased, he guessed he could travel, too, in any direction he took a mind to.

Sol whipped up his mules so suddenly he startled the animals and they bolted into a curving circle as he sawed at the lines. They stayed in a headlong gallop until he pulled them in. The lone wagon continued, then, at a steady gait throughout the hot day. Late in the afternoon he caught sight of a hovering dust cloud far down the valley ahead of him and knew it was made by the Fancher Train.

## CHAPTER VIII

There just weren't any rules when it came to trying to figure womenfolks. Charley Fancher's mild gaze above his pipe rested speculatively on his wife. Annie bustled around her cook fire with the same half-irritable air with which she'd rushed about her own kitchen, back home in Arkansas. She tore into a day like it was an enemy that had to be throttled down anew every morning. It wore you out just to watch her. And her mind busier yet! The things that woman could bring up to confuse a man with!

How long did a man have to live with a woman, he wondered, before he gained even the faintest notion of that alien territory, the female mind. He'd never been away from her a day since they were wed, they'd begat seven kids together, he knew every inch of her vigorous body like the palm of his hand. And yet she could still surprise him, take him unawares by the way she thought things out.

Take this latest, now, an abrupt about-face in her attitude toward another woman. For, seated on the small keg that served as a "company" chair, was Rosetta Huff. The same Widow Huff that, not long since, had been scrupulously shunned by every wife in the wagon train. The fact that she'd had a hand in rescuing the Adens and, then, a few days later, helped Annie with a birthing, hadn't changed what made the woman sort of an outcast, like. She still had the same suspiciously seductive look that kept the women constantly bristling. As a matter of fact it had been that effortless attraction she possessed that had ransomed the apostate and his wife. Birdie Aden had endlessly told and retold the thing. Only confirming the dark suspicions of the women that Rosetta Huff wasn't to be trusted and they kept a closer surveillance of their men.

Charley grinned as he saw Annie pause in her bustling and draw a keg close to Rosetta's. The conversation must be getting interesting, the way they were whispering. The captain was well aware that the tone of female talk, even from this distance, could clue you as to the topic. This type of guarded murmuring informed him that Rosetta and his wife were surely talking about men. In relation to women, which, of course, involved bedding.

Birthings, and the variety of complications involving female organs, were accorded the dignity of a lowered tone and a superior air toward men, who could not possibly be expected to comprehend. But this pleasurably shocked intentness always indicated some one getting laid. Charley speculated idly as to who it was.

Rosetta, he thought, would likely prove to be quite a one in bed. She had a bedroom look about her. Caused no end of talk among the men, both married and single. Fancher wondered if any of the men had gotten anyplace, bound to have been more than one to have tried. Natural that they would, for the woman put you in mind of a sleepy cat, just waiting, expecting to be fondled. Not that she was open about it but you knew. A man just knew—the way an old dog lifting his nose to a breeze will suddenly up off his lazy haunches and take off spry and businesslike for an old bitch he'd passed the day before with hardly a sniff. A male could tell from the very air around her when a female was in season.

Seemed like the dumb animals had an edge on humans when it came to knowing how things stood. There was a cycle to it and no confusing taboos like the rules men had contrived for themselves. Animals simply inclined toward their instincts in the business of life itself, freely and unhindered by moral reservations—unless, of course, some man decided against it and penned them in, frustrated and confused. Odd, too, how often people seemed penned in, themselves. And grew to seem queer because of it. And then there were the ones who had been dealt with so as to make them top-heavy in one way or another. Like this Widow Huff, now. Few women exuded that intriguing fascination all the time, like a female always in heat instead of just now and again. There were men like that, too, but they were more open in their habits and not secretive, usually, like a woman nearly had to be. The men of this stamp seemed to be eternally bent on proving something, always hunting, brutally mounting any woman they could procure. And in continual trouble because of the urgent hunger they were born having.

And then others lopsided, nearly shy of any urges at all.

These plodded dutifully through life, passively ox-dull, taking smug pride in respectability and full of superior scorn for the lusty ones.

Captain Fancher grinned at himself for thinking off into such deep and muddy waters. He hadn't any answers and doubted if anyone had. He emptied his cold pipe against his palm and strolled off to see what the kids were up to. Annie had chased them off to play so she could have her visit out. And from the looks of the two heads so absorbedly bent together it was going to be a while, yet, till supper.

Charley would have been shocked to the depths of his mild soul had he known the actual subject of conversation between Annie and the Widow Huff. Annie was hearing about a place that she—or any respectable wife—had never visited, but had had a lively curiosity about—Rosetta was telling about living in a whorehouse.

For Rosetta's guard was down, the cloak of calm indifference with which she shielded herself against the usual snubs of the womenfolks. Annie's attitude toward the intriguing Widow Huff had undergone a drastic change in the past few days. Rosetta had evolved a plan for rescuing the Adens and then had coolly accomplished it. And then she had taken a hand in a difficult birthing when Annie, herself, had been completely at a loss.

Above all things Annie Fancher respected competence and a cool head in a crisis and she had come to respect Rosetta Huff for these very reasons. Her abrupt but wholehearted friendliness had disarmed Rosetta completely. The ostracism she had endured in the wagon train had been lonely and she confided in Annie now with eager relief.

"And you not fourteen yet?" It was Annie's shocked question.

Rosetta nodded. "But I looked older—I was—full formed when I was twelve."

Annie looked her understanding, taking in, too, the full swelling curves beneath Rosetta's gray linsey. It was fashioned no differently from any of the women's workday garb—high-buttoned neck, long sleeves pushed elbow high for work, yards of skirt, not as full as Sunday best but ample enough not to outline the "limbs." The dress might be similar but the effect, on the Widow Huff, was not. There was just something about the very lines of her, the full breasts, the rich spread of ample hips, that brought, unbidden, to the mind an impression of white, luxuriant warmth of thigh.

"And your baby was born there? In that—that kind of a house?"

Rosetta nodded, a shadow darkening the blue gaze. "Ain't many places anxious to take in a lone girl fixin' to birth a woods-colt," she explained.

"But, my land," Annie wondered, "seems like your folks would have stood by you——"

Rosetta's glance dropped to her hands, which plucked at the coarse weave of her skirt. "It was my paw that drove me out," she said, "called me a Jezebel and a whore out of Babylon." She paused, remembering without bitterness. "Paw was awful religious." This was added as a perfectly logical explanation. "I ain't never told a living soul the whole thing, before, Mrs. Fancher, but you been so—nice to me." Her gaze was grateful for the comfort of sharing an old burden.

"I'd never breathe it to a livin' soul, Rosetta," Annie Fancher assured her.

"I was just past thirteen that summer," she said. "My maw had been sick for a long time—couldn't get out of bed no more and there was this neighbor man—not a young man, either—that wouldn't leave me be. I was afraid to tell Paw and usual I could fight him off, but this once——. Anyway, when I commenced to show, there wasn't no use namin' him because he had a wife and younguns. So when I had to leave I went to a cousin of mine, a girl who worked in a near city. That is, her folks thought she worked, but she was one—of them. She was good to me, though, a sight better than my folks was."

Annie sat silent for a little, digesting the misery of it, horrified but not blaming. Then she asked, "What happened to that baby? You was just a little girl—you couldn't—"

"He come 'fore his time; he was born dead."

Annie sighed with relief. "Blessing the good Lord took him, the way it was," she said, mentally congratulating Him on the wisdom of His decision. You sure couldn't always count on things to be resolved so properly. Times, you just knew the Almighty was a male creature, the way He allowed messes to happen, and the fumbling till they got all out of hand. Just let a man get to trying to figure a way to bring something about and you wound up, like as not, with everybody stumbling around in circles.

"And this old woman," Annie inquired, "the one who ran the—house. She was the midwife you talked about?"

"Yes. She was a mean old bitch, most ways, and ugly about a lot of things. But I never seen her beat when it came to birthing babies. She knew more about what to do when things wasn't right than you'd think a body'd live long enough to learn. You learn lots, though—in a hurry—in a place like that."

"Had she been—one? The old woman?"

"Oh sure, till she got too ugly and crippled up even for the drunkest ones. Her joints stiffened up on her, she couldn't make out to walk around, some days. But she made a lot of money, running that house. Set a great store by money. All there was for her, I guess, when you get right down to it. I don't think she had any folks—she wouldn't let us have anything to do with families or relatives. She wouldn't let any of the girls keep their babies. She was awful strict about that."

"What happened to the babies?"

"Well, there wasn't as many as you might think, and some of them didn't live. There was something wrong with quite a few of them. Natural, I guess, seein' as how— Anyway, that's how I come to leave there."

"How do you mean?"

"Well, like I say, she wouldn't let anybody keep their baby. Told us to our face we wasn't fit to bring up younguns. Guess she was right, at that. She'd find homes for 'em—sold some that I know of. I felt bad, even the mess I was in, when that first one—died. So when Juddy, my oldest came, I started right away thinking about getting away. He was a beautiful baby, healthy and all. I knew she'd take him away and I didn't want to give him up." Annie sat silent, hurting somehow along with her. The husky tones were almost absently monotone, the wide eyes were remote, had wandered off back down the years.

"There was a man, an older man, who thought a lot of me and he helped, gave me some money, and I ran away. I'd never been able to save much because the old woman claimed I owed her for taking care of me, at the first. And then, about the time I was in the clear, there was another baby. So, you see—— I got away, though, this man took care of me for quite a while and when he died I took up with—— I couldn't have supported the three of us, the other boy had come along by then—so I was sort of caught. Maybe the old woman was right about us not deservin' to keep our babies. But I couldn't give Juddy up, seemed like. He was so sweet—and clean." The slanting eyes came back to the present, were fixed with urgent question on Annie.

That gaunt woman nodded, met the gaze squarely. "You done right, Rosetta," she said vigorously. "My land, you wasn't to blame, gettin' off on the wrong foot so young!"

"Seemed so good to have something of my own." Rosetta sounded the memory of her feelings. "But I want to be honest with you, Miz Fancher—it wasn't 'cause I thought I was too good for—the house, I didn't mind it. I really ain't no good, nor fit to be a mother, I guess. I—like men. And there always seems to be some around who——" Her glance was troubled. "But I ain't—no matter what they say, them finger-pointin' old biddies—I ain't let not one man in this train as much as lay a finger on me, since we started!"

Annie's face showed her belief, there was respect in her reply. "And that ain't been easy." It was not a question, for of her own experience she knew the urgency and the blessed relief and, knowing, marveled at the woman, her history and her present strength.

"No, it ain't been easy," Rosetta admitted. "But I've got to be—different, on account of Sid. I can't shame him and he's been so good. I happened to meet up with Sid again last year. He told me Paw was dead, and Maw long ago, too. I had these two boys and went as a widow. Sid don't know it all, but he knows I ain't a widow. He offered to help me, take me and the kids along for a new start in Californy, if I'd change my ways—stay away from men. He didn't tell Magdalene everything but she suspicions, she ain't a bit sold on me. But Sid's a good brother, he does what he can and he mostly makes her keep her mouth shut, too."

"Well, now"—this was the brisk planning tone of Annie Fancher—"what we need is for you to have a man of your own! A strong, well, a good husky sort of man—you'd best get yourself married!" Rosetta's smile was weary. "The things they whisper to me ain't none of 'em about gettin' married," she said, "and mostly, it's been the married ones come smellin' around."

Annie nodded. "We'll put a stop to that. Men is dumb brutes, some ways, but they've seen how the women—— Oh, I know, I was offish, too. Natural, the men took notice that you was different and the women—— Well, anyway, now things is goin' to be different. Ain't none of the women but will fall in line after you've rode in the buggy with me a few days. And Maggie—I'n handle Maggie with one hand tied behind my back!" Her joyously belligerent smile warmed Rosetta and she smiled back at the captain's wife, her face beautiful in its red-lipped softness.

Annie shook her head, looking at her. "I don't know as I ever seen a prettier woman than you," she said generously. "It'll be easy. You wait, one of these times when a man whispers to you he'll be wantin' to have it all legal and proper!"

Annie's thoughtful gaze followed Rosetta's swaying

walk as she went back toward her own wagon. You sure could never tell who could stand up to things when the going was rough and who gave out on you. No one could have been more surprised than she'd been herself when the red-haired woman came into that tent and took over.

They'd circled into camp early that day near a small stream with the heathenish name of Peteteneet Creek. The youngest Barker boy's wife, Clara, had gone into labor.

Clara was a pretty little thing, had seemed to be carrying her first baby just fine. She'd been frisky, feeling good —and then the pains had come on her all of a sudden.

The crowded wagon was no good for delivering a baby and the men had pitched a tent out and away from the wagons, under some trees. Annie and Magdalene Huff, the two women who'd had the most experience with birthings, were in charge. The men had built them a fire, toted water for boiling, and then taken themselves off, as was seemly. This was women's business. Young Abel Barker had hung around miserably, traveling uncertainly between the kindly joshing of the experienced fathers at the wagons and the impatient dismissals of the women when he intruded on the business in the tent.

Sundown had come and the hours moved on toward midnight and Annie was getting worried. Clara's pains had been hard and close together for a long time, one right on top of the other, now. Her grunting groans ended in shrill, tortured screams. Things were not progressing normally, something was wrong. The baby had dropped, but its position must not be right, it was not coming. The girl's agonized cries had brought her husband storming hysterically into the tent to see what they were doing to her.

Annie had summoned Charley then and ordered him to get out that bottle of brandy he had cached away—take the boy away and keep him away. They couldn't have him storming in and out, he was upsetting Clara more.

The wagon train hushed uneasily. The men stood

around in uncertain groups, feeling guilty in their helplessness. The lantern that hung inside the tent cast grotesquely humped shadows as the two women moved about the laboring girl. They were misshapen, ominous, those slow-moving shadows.

John Barker stood with the silent men. His long, bony face wore a look of stern alarm. He had never experienced this particular concern. Clara and Abel—they had seemed to be but heedless children, laughing, romping together like carefree young animals. The sight of his brother's face working as he sobbed, the tears running down through the sparse stubble on his young chin, these things stayed in John's mind. He had not been aware of these unplumbed depths of the youthful husband's love for his wife. John had undertaken this expedition partly because he felt a protective duty toward his much younger brothers; this included their wives, who seemed like little girls to the austere man. Yet here he stood, helpless and of no use. It had been Captain Fancher who comforted and sustained Abel. George and Libby, the other brother and wife, were in their wagon. Libby, who was also expecting—somehow the girls seemed to do everything in unison—had become hysterical and George had been told to keep her away. There remained, now, no member of the Barker family standing by Clara.

John's mouth set firmly. He lifted his chin and strode deliberately toward the tent. The quiet men watched him go, none stayed him. He set to work building the fire to an unnecessary height, moved the kettles about restlessly. Then he just stood, hands twitching, facing the tent with its hidden crisis. It seemed to him, after a while, that the humped shadows moved with more agitation as Clara's groans grew weaker.

Suddenly the tent flaps parted. Magdalene emerged. Her doughy face was convulsed, her eyes wild and staring; her breathing was a labored wheeze. "I can't stand it no longer," she gasped, "there ain't a thing kin be done for her. It's caught, that's all, and she'll die if it don't soon—" She threw her apron over her head and sobbed violently before she stumbled away toward the wagons, moaning under her breath with each step.

John stared in horror at the tent. The shadow that was Annie Fancher was humped unmoving over the mound of the girl on the mattress. There was absolute, deathly quiet from within. John strode to the tent, lifted the flap, stepped inside.

Annie looked up at him. Her hair hung in sweat-soaked strings around her face. Her eyes, not wild like Magdalene's, yet were disturbed and fearful. She did not seem surprised at John's entry, she invited his glance toward the girl who lay motionless on the mat. Her eyes were closed, she breathed heavily through her open mouth.

Annie's voice was a hoarse whisper. "I'm afraid for her, John. Everything's stopped. There ain't a thing I know to do for this here."

John tore his glance from the strangely deformed figure that had been pretty Clara. His voice was hushed. "What's—wrong?"

"It's caught someway," said Annie, looking at the pasty whiteness of the girl's sweating face. "Don't hardly seem possible, little and thin as she is, but I think it's crosswise. And don't seem likely it'll turn now." She looked up at him despairingly, her eyes deep in dark circles. "She can't stand much more—she's got awful weak."

The tent flap raised, someone stepped inside. John turned to see Rosetta Huff, her slanted eyes soberly intent, her mouth set in a firm line. She glanced at him without seeing him, spoke to Annie. "Maggie was all upset—said something was wrong——"

Annie's hand brushed wearily at her dank hair, she nodded. "I think it's crosswise," she repeated, "I don't know how to do for her." She looked accusingly at her strong hands as though they failed her.

Rosetta spoke to John. "Go outside," she said, "and wait"—her voice was peremptory, but calm and even—"stay close, within call, we might need you." He obeyed, somewhat bewildered but also reassured by her air of authority. As he left the tent she was already kneeling beside Clara, throwing back the sheet that covered her.

Annie's look sharply probed the intent face of the Widow Huff and then moved to Rosetta's hands, which were moving exploringly over the distended body. There was a knowingness in those hands. They were long and narrow, small-boned with delicately formed joints; the nails were beautifully oval. Rosetta sat back on her heels, looked up at Annie. "You got some small scissors?" she asked. "And where's the grease you were goin' to use for the baby—"

Annie nodded, supplied these things. The grease was carefully rendered white lard. Rosetta trimmed her fingernails down to the quick, ran a finger tip over each one, searching for roughness. Satisfied, she handed the scissors back and rolled up her sleeves above her elbows. She carefully greased her right hand and forearm.

"You'll have to hold her," she directed, "like this": she bent the knees so that the sole of each small foot was flat on the mattress. Annie kneeled, facing away from Clara's head. Rosetta took a crouching position between the widely spread feet. "I might can turn it," she said, "get the head around and away—bring it feet first. But we're likely to need help. You got brandy?" Annie nodded. "Call Mr. Barker, then," Rosetta said, "he's going to have to help."

John came hastily into the tent, his eyes alarmed, but he took the brandy bottle as directed. He did not speak, and kept his gaze carefully averted from the business at hand. He obeyed promptly and implicitly.

Annie's expression of dubious anxiety changed to one of awed surprise as she watched Rosetta's hands. The right as it began its slow groping passage to the trapped infant. The left, on the distorted bulge of the abdomen, pressing, exploring, manipulating.

"Hold her now!" the order was sharp. There was a long silence broken only by the moaning gasps of the unconscious girl and the labored breathing of Rosetta, whose bent body tensed with its terrible, slow effort. Her eyes were wide and blank, had a removed expression. It was as though the sight from them had transferred to the working, skillful hands.

"Mr. Barker." John started at the commanding tone. "Give her some brandy now—hold her head up a little so she can swallow. When she starts to come to, get a-hold of her shoulders, hold fast, don't let her twist. Miz Fancher, don't let her hips turn—hold her still."

Annie nodded her understanding, got in position. John was not surprised to find his hands shaking as he obeyed. Clara swallowed the brandy convulsively, a long shuddering moan broke from her. The man held her slender shoulders and prevented the convulsive writhing. Clara's eyes rolled, opened wildly, she cried out sobbingly.

Rosetta was working strongly, the muscles in her arms taut with effort. Suddenly she gave a triumphant sounding grunt. "Mr. Barker!" she called, "speak to her—make her hear you—she's got to help us now——"

"Clara!" John's voice thundered, frightening himself with its betrayal of urgency. "Clara, listen—*Clara, hear me!*" It reached through the mist of tormented delirium, her eyes focused on the bearded face above her. John Barker smiled down at her. "It's all right, Clara." His voice was deep but the tender tone was reassuring. "It's going to be all right—but you've got to help us." The girl moaned, tried to answer him, she was fully conscious now.

Rosetta's voice, insistent, clear, reached Clara. "Now, Clara," she called, "you've got to bear down, honey, push——"

The girl attempted weakly to obey, and groaned. "That's it, Clara, like you was going to the toilet—that's it, honey—only harder!" The grunting became violent, animal-like. Rosetta's voice again, "*Now,* Clara—*now,* hard—*hard!*"

There was pain, indignant fury in the sounds she made as the muscles convulsed and ejected strongly. Annie saw Rosetta's arm move back slightly, the forearm was drenched in spreading red, she held the feet of the baby and now the body was emerging.

"Once more, Clara," she called excitedly, "just once more—*now!*" Her hands were together now, manipulating the tiny body and suddenly the head burst free. Clara shuddered, her straining body collapsed and she lay still, only her eyelids fluttered weakly.

Rosetta's voice was bell-like. "It's all right, Clara." Her tone was lovely. "It's all over, honey, and the baby's moving already!" Clara heard her, the pallid lips made a feeble effort to smile. The eyelids fluttered down and she was all at once deeply asleep.

Annie, feeling almost paralyzed in her position, sat back and saw with wonder that the tiny crimson form was, indeed, squirming. Her sudden laugh was more like a sob. "My land!" she gasped, "look how active the little scamp is—" Both women laughed shakily.

John, realizing that the emergency was over, went outside the tent to stand staring vacantly, his mind a blind whirling, he felt a little sick. Presently, from within, he heard a tiny, furious cry, followed by a burst of infantile wailing. Then there were chuckling crooning sounds from the women, rich with relief and tenderness. John marveled at their swift adjustment from perilous urgency to female joyousness. He himself still shook uncontrollably and he felt almost offended when he heard them laugh heartily. Annie stuck her untidy head through the tent flap and commanded him cheerfully: "You can go tell your brother he's got a strappin' boy, John!" she said, "and tell everbody—Clara's fine!"

When Abel appeared, reeking of brandy, the tearstains still blurred his face; he was sobered by the impact of the good news and sobbed anew, but this time with relief. Clara slept deeply, one hand under her cheek. She looked like a frail child, her long lashes making little shadowy fans on her cheeks.

Abel was permitted only a glance at his wife and it was Rosetta who brought the baby for his father's inspection. Washed and greased, wrapped in a clean blanket, his puckered little monkey face was ridiculously set in a ferocious scowl. Rosetta held him against her breast, looking down at him tenderly and with a peculiarly sweet indulgence for all the trouble he'd caused.

John Barker looked at the wizened, purplish infant and then raised his eyes—to become trapped by the pale oval beauty of the woman's face. His stare focused so intently and was so disturbed that Rosetta sensed it, lifted her eyes. She felt a distinct and disturbing shock.

John Barker had stared at her before, with all the great penetrating force of his peculiar personality. She had not forgotten that violent, lusting look. The difference, now, in this regard, almost equally violent, caused her to drop her eyes with confusion.

"Mrs. Huff"—the deep voice was intense—"I want to——" He stopped, cleared his throat, realizing with horror that he had been about to reveal his earlier opinion of her. He had barely stopped in time—having been about to apologize for having thought her the essence of all evil.

Rosetta had removed the bloodstained apron, but her hair was in disarray, her sleeves were still rolled above her elbows, her face shone with perspiration for the evening, though cool, had been exhausting. But to the slightly delirious man she seemed madonna-like, with the baby in her arms. He tried again.

"Mrs. Huff"—the tone was reverent—"I have just witnessed—a miracle. I—I want to thank you for——" Here again he could not finish. He did not mean the miracle of birth; that, too, but his mixed feelings leaned strongly to the miraculous view he felt he had had of the woman herself. He stared at her again with all that peculiar intensity.

Rosetta looked up at him uncertainly. She flushed slightly and murmured something, abruptly re-entered the tent. There had been an oddness in John Barker just now that had alarmed her. This look, even more than the other. She could deal with lusting—that was old familiar ground. But this completely unknown quality she had just encountered left her confused.

It was several days later that John Barker passed the Widow Huff's wagon after they had circled into camp. He paused, ostensibly to inquire for the health of William Aden, sitting, palely acquiescent, attended by Birdie, who fluttered around him like an insistent hen with a score of chicks. She even clucked, John noticed disapprovingly. He deplored fussiness in women almost as much as frivolity.

Rosetta was just heading toward the creek, water bucket in hand. John touched his hat ceremoniously. "Please let me fetch your water, Mrs. Huff." His tone was severe, unctuous. She nodded and surrendered the bucket almost helplessly. As she did so, their hands touched and both started perceptibly. The man's eyes flared at her for an instant and were quickly averted. When he returned with the water he set the bucket down and hurried away; there was the impression that he escaped. Rosetta looked after his hurrying, tall figure. He was a queer mixture of a man, for sure, she thought. Awfully pious-acting and proper. But still—— She shook her head, gave up trying to figure him out.

John Barker was puzzled with himself. The days found him unbearably restless, his mind abstracted and full of unbidden thoughts. He had difficulty sleeping, even when bone tired. Now he kept thinking of the moment his hand had touched hers. He was alarmed to discover that the place tingled, burned a little. He stared accusingly at the hand.

After the evening meal John roamed the camp restlessly, stopping here and there to visit with unwonted geniality. He desperately sought company, anything to distract his obsession. To no avail, for as though led, or driven, his steps took him finally toward Rosetta's wagon. And it was with a feeling of fatalism that he found the tall woman alone, leaning quietly against the back of her wagon, her eyes dreaming away toward the looming, shadowy mountains.

He paused a short distance away, staring at the oval-face, white-limned in the dusk. The stillness of her was healing, peacefulness flowed through him. And a feeling that for all his life he had but walked toward this moment, which seemed stopped in time, the essence of it shiningly clear—unutterably simple.

Her slow gaze moved, she saw him there but neither spoke, there was no need for words. He held out his hand and she met it with her own. They moved unhurriedly together toward a shadowy grove of trees. In the enveloping shadow he paused and put his hands on her shoulders, turned her, looked down into her lifted face. As she came close into his arms, her full, woman's body pressed against him with a sure knowingness of his need. He groaned as his mouth met hers and then bruised her with sudden violence.

Time had seemed to pause for John Barker, and yet had moved effortlessly over seemingly insurmountable barriers as a while later, he looked down at the woman in his arms. The lush, female smell of her was in his flaring nostrils, her body was warm against him. And his was at peace, satiated. And yet he knew an urgent hunger, deeper for having known fulfillment.

"Rosetta"—his voice was a hoarse whisper—"we must be married—at once!"

Rosetta's mouth opened with astonishment. "Oh no, I—we can't——"

He clutched her close to him, buried his mouth in her hair. "We *must* be——" The words were muffled. "We have committed mortal sin. I take responsibility, but we must be married at once."

She stared up at him, searching frantically for words to tell him she was not the kind a man had to marry, regretting the need for the telling. This man was too good to realize—— But he was planning swiftly.

"We have no minister, of course, but we can have a frontier marriage—where a man and woman stand before witnesses and say the words. Until we get to California and find a minister. Rosetta?" The last was an urgent plea and she realized, with accompanying panic, that the man only thought he proposed marriage because of the sin. He wanted her desperately. He caught her shoulders roughly, then crushed her to him, his mouth sobbingly roved over her face. She was a limp weight in his arms, too alarmed and confused to think or speak. He rose, pulled her to her feet with excited vigor.

"Go to your wagon," he commanded, "make yourself ready. I'll fetch you after I speak to your brother and Captain Fancher." He actually pushed her, impatiently, for she stood uncertainly, hesitating. But despairingly she obeyed and walked mechanically toward the wagons. He strode off toward a high fire where a group of men were gathered.

Rosetta did not go to her own wagon. She sought out Annie Fancher, drew her aside, and hysterically confided what John Barker was about. "Well, for the good Lord's sake!" Annie gasped, "John Barker, of all people!" She examined this surprising development, found it much to her liking. "What'd I tell you? That the men would commence thinking different about you? Sure, frontier weddings is legal enough. I know more'n one couple didn't have the words said over 'em—some of 'em not 'fore there was two-three younguns. Some folks lived so far out the preacher only showed up ever two-three years. But everbody figgered it was respectable enough, before witnesses and all."

Rosetta was shaking her head, "You don't understand, Miz Fancher." She was almost sobbing. "I can't—do it—not to *him*—he's a decent man—he don't know what I've—— He thinks he has to make an honest woman outa me. I couldn't seem to tell him. Somebody's *got to*—tell him what I am—was." She put her face in her hands and sobbed with quiet bitterness.

"Make an honest woman? O-ho, so that's the way it come about." Annie comprehended now. "Well, my land." She grinned hugely and then, looking at the bowed head, sobered and put an arm around the shaking shoulders. "Listen, Rosetta, if things was different, would you want to marry John?" The tousled head nodded. "Oh yes, Miz

Fancher." The whispering voice was wistful. "He's—wonderful, good, different from any man I ever knew."

"Well, then!" Annie took Rosetta firmly by the shoulders and shook her slightly. "Raise your face—look at me!"

Wonderingly the despairing face lifted. "Now you listen to me, Rosetta Huff, for I'm gonna give you an honest piece of my mind, hear?"

The slanting eyes, frightened, were childlike with intensity as she stared into the vigorous compassion of Annie's bony face. "We're all of us headed for new country, and a sort of new start. Ain't that exactly what Sid brung you along for? Well, this here is it! Your new start! There ain't a living soul here that knows about you but me, and I'd die 'fore I'd breathe a word. You ain't got one thing to stop you! Why, there's no man in the world but keeps a thing or two from his wife, and likely a lot of women ain't told everythin' to their men, neither. John Barker's no pink-faced kid you're puttin' something over on—he's a growed man. And you're not to ever tell him a thing, understand? He's a peculiar man, some ways, and likely all it'd do is drive him crazy. So you keep your mouth shut and take him if you want him! That's what I say, and I'll stand by it. All that you oughta be thinkin' about is do you want him or not?"

Like a quenching drink of cold water, Rosetta was relieved by the vigor of Annie's persuasion. "I'd give anything in the world to be John Barker's wife," she admitted.

Annie nodded briskly. "So there! Now, you and me best get on over to your wagon and spruce you up! Wipe your face on your apron. Come on, hurry up! We don't want to keep the dear man waitin'."

John's abruptly announced intention silenced a suddenly gaping-mouthed group at the fire. Before anyone could find his tongue the man had rushed off to find Rob Fancher, his friend—the captain's sourly bachelor cousin. John wanted Rob to stand up with him. But Rob had the bad judgment to object to the whole thing.

"My God, John," he said disgustedly, "you outa your mind? You don't have to marry her kind—why, she ain't——" and surprisingly found himself hitting the hard ground most painfully. John Barker had struck him in the face with all of his righteous indignation. And then, more surprising, was instantly helping him to his feet, agitatedly brushing him off.

"Rob," his deep voice rumbled eagerly, "you must never say such things—you couldn't be more wrong! I thought the same—I admit that—but it is only her beauty! If you could have seen her, as I did, saving Clara's life and with the baby in her arms! Rob, she was like a picture of a madonna and child. She saved Clara and the baby. There is a sort of—a healing good in her. I know—I am a new man!"

Rob Fancher stared at him aghast, he had never seen the dignified man thus. John sounded about like his father, old Preacher Barker, he thought. He felt gingerly of his jaw, it would more than likely swell. He cursed under his breath, John was clearly out of his mind. Rob wasn't going to argue, invite more blows—let the stupid fool marry the slut. He'd live to regret this day and then maybe remember that Rob, his best friend, tried to prevent it. And got knocked down for his trouble.

The wedding party assembled at the fire; the witnesses, with an uncertain manner, stood looking at each other blankly. But there was no uncertainty in John Barker. His face shone above his beard as he possessed himself of Rosetta's limp hand and drew her forward.

With Annie's flustered help Rosetta had donned a light blue dress, her hair had been severely drawn back into a big knot on her neck. Her face was dead white, she moved like a sleepwalker, her eyes were fixed on John like a drowning person reaching for a raft.

Annie ranged herself alongside Charley, giving him a swift nudge and a triumphant nod, taking full credit for her matchmaking accomplishment. He grinned and got to his feet, took his pipe from his mouth, and assumed an official stance of sponsorship. Sid Huff, his rough features an odd mixture of approving but absolute astonishment, stood beside Magdalene, whose doughy face did not conceal her sour begrudging of Rosetta's good fortune. Rob Fancher, disgruntled and fidgeting, nursed his jaw with exploring fingers, wincing as he did so. He appeared to be suffering an attack of acute indigestion.

John, looking around at the assemblage, began to speak. "We are gathered together"—the somewhat embarrassed audience noticed that he sounded just like a preacher—"in the sight of God and these witnesses, to declare our intention of Holy Matrimony." He paused and cleared his throat, obviously seeking the exact wording of the ritual. But then his eyes turned on Rosetta's exquisite paleness and in a quiet, tender voice he spoke the words directly to her:

"I, John Barker take thee, Rosetta, to be my lawful wedded wife, to have and to hold from this day forward, for better or for worse, in sickness and in health—till death us do part."

Rosetta returned his gaze, her face trancelike, her trembling lips parted. She knew, vaguely, that she was supposed to say the words now but she could not find her voice, helplessly she stood, she could not remember what they were. She stared at the bearded face tenderly looming over her. There was a long, hushed pause. John seemed completely unaware of the delay, he was so absorbed in looking at her that he had quite forgotten the spectators.

"Well, my land." Annie Fancher's exasperated whisper was audible. She stepped purposefully forward, took a grip on Rosetta's arm. "I, Rosetta," she coached insistently.

"I, Rosetta," her voice obeyed faintly, "take thee, John, to be my lawful wedded husband." The echo waited, but Annie, flustered and embarrassed, could not remember the rest of it and so finished hastily, "till death us do part." The husky whisper confirmed, "Till death us do part."

Annie stepped back, her eyes on them bright with curiosity as John bent and reverently laid his bearded mouth on Rosetta's. He turned and faced the intent audience. "We are now man and wife." There was exultation in his face and in the tone. "I thank you, one and all, my friends!" Firmly placing his arm around Rosetta's shoulder, he led her away.

The assembled wedding guests stared blankly after them. "Well, for Chrissake!" a man said in surprised but approving understanding of the groom's apparently immediate plans. There was a general chuckle of comprehension and then hearty laughter all around.

Annie was bustling about getting wagon boxes packed for loading the next morning when she looked up and saw Rosetta approaching. Her eyes narrowed, there was something different about the erstwhile Widow Huff. Annie grinned when she spotted what it was: Rosetta walked differently. With the same long, beautifully flowing stride, but her shoulders were back, the head was up, her face bared to the sun—no longer hidden by the deep bonnet. The wide eyes were lifted, not secretively glancing sidelong. Annie chuckled.

"Good mornin' to you, Miz Barker!" she called.

Rosetta smiled shiningly. "I just wanted to say thanks for—last night. Helpin' me with the words to say, I mean. And for—everything else, too."

Annie's friendly, prying eyes took her in: the violet shadows under the slanting eyes, the swollen redness of the lush mouth. "Musta been quite a night," she hazarded approvingly. To her great pleasure Rosetta did not dodge the inference. She flushed slightly but she nodded, clearly joyous. She glanced around to see if anyone could overhear and, in a low tone, she confided.

"I used to wonder, Miz Fancher," she said, "if I'd be satisfied, to be married—if I ever got a chance, that is. After, well, after knowin' so many—well, anyways, I wondered if there was any one man who could—— Well." She looked with frank female knowingness into Annie's entranced face and that redoubtable woman answered promptly, "I know just what you mean."

"I got nothin' to worry about." Rosetta was quietly

jubilant. "Last night—well— I guess I've found me a man that can look down as long as I can look up!" There was prideful possessiveness and a host of other things in the brightly beautiful face.

Rosetta and Annie looked long at each other and with satisfaction. Annie nodded knowingly, her underlip pushed out, her eyes twinkling. Then they both laughed.

## CHAPTER IX

The woman was tall and her bosom was like a thrusting shelf. She was not fat, but big-boned, powerfully built, her face was like a man's with its set square jaw and grimly thin mouth. Irrigating her vegetable garden was an easy chore compared with her usual work in the fields.

She looked up from under the brim of her straw hat to see three riders making dust down the lane toward her place. Two men and a girl who rode a fractious sorrel mare. They pulled up at her fence and one of them, a tall man on a spotted horse, called to her. He wore fringed buckskins and his hair was tied Indian-fashion on his neck. The big woman blinked against the lowering afternoon sun, she could not make out who they were. Shovel in hand, she walked to the fence, peered up at them. They were strangers, she could see that now.

"You Sister Wyatt?" the buckskin-clad man asked. She nodded. "They told us you had goats—milk goats," he said.

The woman nodded. "I got goats."

The smaller man spoke. "We'd—I'd like to buy a milk goat." He was scarcely more than a boy, a fresh-faced, nice-looking youngster. He smiled down into her grim face.

The woman stared at them. "I don't place you," she said, "you ain't from around here?"

"No, ma'am," the boy said, "we're from the wagon train camped yonder on the creek." He waved toward the south.

As the woman considered this, a mask seemed to settle over her face. "Where you from?"

"Arkansas and Missouri, most of us, goin' to Californy."

The big woman stiffened, an odd expression slid across her face and disappeared. Her gaze rested for a moment on the girl, who smiled at her, but Sister Wyatt did not acknowledge it. Her tone was noncommittal. "Arkansas, huh?" then with elaborate casualness, "anybody by the name of McLean in your party?"

"McLean? Yeah, there is—one of Cap'n Fancher's herders is a McLean, ain't he, Jed?" Abel Barker turned to Jed, who nodded, but it was a reluctant nod and his glance suddenly prodded at the woman.

Sister Wyatt's eyes had narrowed slightly. "What's his first name?"

"Well, the boys call him Mack," Abel offered. "Don't know if I ever heard his first name, you know, Lissy?" Melissa shook her head.

"You got kinfolks, maybe, named McLean, back in Arkansas?" Abel was trying to be neighborly, thaw out the forbidding woman. She said, "No, not exactly," and lifted her shovel as though putting an end to a useless conversation. Abel spoke hurriedly. "About the goat, ma'am, I'll pay a good price for a milk goat—hard money."

Sister Wyatt shook her head. "I got no goats to spare."

Abel grew anxious. "Look, ma'am—we've—my wife had a baby a few days back and he can't keep nothin' down. The women said goat's milk was the best thing. See, I've just *got* to get a goat. The folks back in the town said you had a big herd of milk goats."

The woman ignored the pleading explanation. "I got a herd of goats," she said shortly, "but none to sell."

"Sister Wyatt!" Jed's voice was compelling, she paused, turned to face him. "Well?" He looked at her for a considering moment and then he asked, "Was you related, maybe, to Parley Pratt?"

Sister Wyatt was plainly startled by the question. She considered it—and Jed—for a moment and then decided to answer. "One of my girls was married to him." Jed nodded seriously, his look was compassionate. "The McLean in the wagon train, Sister Wyatt," he said, "is right young, not more'n twenty. I ain't sure what his first name is, but I know it ain't Hector."

She received this stolidly, thought about it. "You'd say that, a'course," she said, and lifted the shovel with finality.

"Mrs. Wyatt!" it was Abel, "if you won't sell a goat, could I buy some milk?"

"No."

"Listen, Mrs. Wyatt, I'll pay anythin' you ask!"

"I got nothin' to sell."

"But my baby boy is like to die if he don't soon get somethin' he can keep down!" Abel's face and voice begged her.

She looked long at him. Her face had been grim but now there was something terrible in the pitiless twist of the bitter mouth, the stare of the cold eyes.

"Likely you'll learn how it feels, then," she said, "I lost two babies for lack of food—in Missouri." Sister Wyatt looked them over with open hostility and then turned to walk away without further word. They sat in uncomfortable silence as she crossed her garden, began to shovel out a sod dam to allow the trickling stream of water to enter another furrow.

"What in hell ails that woman?" Abel was furious. "By God, I ain't a'gonna leave here without a goat!" he started to dismount.

"Stay on your horse"—Jed's voice was sharp—"we ain't messin' with her—I know her kind. Push her and you'll wind up starin' into a loaded rifle barrel. Ain't a damn thing you can do with *her*. We'll have to try somewheres else."

As they rode away, the grim figure turned and watched

them. "What was that all about?" Melissa was curious. "McLean and who she was related to?"

"Oh, it's just"—Jed considered and then decided against the lengthy telling—"old trouble. Some of these folks pack a grudge a long time." Melissa sensed there was more to it and was about to pry further but Jed suddenly lifted Palouse into a gallop. "Come on!" he shouted, "get that jughead movin'—race you to the top of the hill."

Palouse had plunged swiftly ahead and Lady Jane indignantly thundered to catch him. Abel's sturdy bay broke into a pounding gallop and the three raced headlong toward the wagon train, which had circled in to camp several miles down the valley.

Twilight lingered long after the sun had set, bathing the snow-capped peaks of the towering mountains in liquid flame. Jed sauntered up to the wagon, to find David dreamily nursing a cold pipe as he watched the blending colors change and fade.

"Where's Lissy?"

David showed mild surprise. "Thought she was with you," he said, "said somethin' about goin' for a ride."

"Alone?"

"Well, I thought she meant with you. She headed off to the herd a bit ago, had her pants on under her skirt——" He started to get up.

"Set still," Jed said, "I'll find her, she's more than likely right around——"

David was disturbed. "Maybe I'd better see."

Jed grinned down at him. "You ain't invited," he said, "who in hell wants a chaperone?" David chuckled and sat back down, lit his pipe and waved a teasing hand.

Melissa was not at the horse herd but the herder had seen her. "Saddled her mare and took off up the valley," he said, "just a little while back." He waved to the north. Jed nodded and whistled shrilly, twice. His eyes, searching the shadowy twilight, came to focus presently on a rider disappearing into some willows far up the valley.

In the horse herd Palouse's head lifted at the whistling, his eyes quickly located Jed. The stocky gelding broke into a plunging gallop, slowed to a trot as he neared Jed. He paused for just an instant as the man grasped a handful of mane and leaped on to his bare back. Palouse had wheeled and was off at a lope by the time Jed's long legs tightened on his barrel.

The herder shook his head, pleasurably entertained. "Smartest damn horse I ever seen," he mentioned aloud to himself. "Like a tame kitten with him—nary even a bridle. But mean!" Palouse's lashing hoofs and swift teeth had taught the herder to keep his distance. That self-sufficient animal had no liking for strangers handling him.

Jed leaned forward, touched his heel against a flank and the spotted horse poured into a driving run. Very shortly they entered the willows that lined the banks of the creek. Hoofprints crossed, continuing north on the further bank. Jed's lean face set in a disapproving frown as he realized that Melissa was heading straight for Sister Wyatt's place.

He should have figured the little hothead would try something like this. And she'd likely get involved in all kinds of hell if she let fly that temper at the tough old Mormon woman.

Melissa had muttered and scolded all through supper at their failure to get a goat. The Barker baby's thin wailing provided dismal accompaniment to her scorn at their weak-kneed submission to Sister Wyatt.

Jed caught a flicker of movement in the trees ahead. He found the sorrel mare tied to a tree, it had been the switching of her bright tail that he'd noticed. Melissa was not there. He slid off Palouse and gave him a directing swat. The gelding moved near Lady Jane and dropped his head to crop at the clumps of grass. Jed's eyes covered the area, he was puzzled to find Jane tethered here, there was yet a large pasture to be crossed between the Wyatt house and these trees. Then he saw her.

Melissa was cautiously peeking toward the pasture

from behind the trunk of a big cottonwood tree. She'd taken off her skirt, held it wadded up in one arm. Intently watching something, she didn't hear Jed's silent approach. He stopped, grinning, to survey her. Wasn't as big as a ten-year-old boy but there was nothing boyish about the tiny waist and the neat curve of slender hips. Her hair was in one thick braid hanging between her shoulder blades. He reached a long arm, tweaked the braid.

"Lookin' for somethin'?" he drawled.

Melissa gave a smothered shriek as she whirled. Her face set in angry exasperation at the sight of him. "Damn you, anyway, Jed Smith," she sputtered, "sneakin' up like an Injun, scarin' me to death!" She glanced quickly around the tree, "Sh—be quiet—she's just goin' into the house. She's been milkin' the goats."

Jed peered over her head. The slow-moving form of Sister Wyatt could be made out nearing the house, she carried a milking pail in each hand.

"Look, Lissy," Jed said earnestly, "this here ain't gonna do one damn bit of good—you could argue till doomsday —she ain't gonna sell you a goat."

Melissa shook her head stubbornly. "I'm not fixin' to buy a goat off the mean old thing," she announced, "I'm goin' to wait till it's dark and then *get* one!"

Jed stared down at her in shocked astonishment, then his grin crooked delightedly. "You mean you're aimin' to *steal* a goat, Melissa Ann Boller?" She heard the amusement in his voice. "Yes," she snapped furiously, "I'm gonna steal a goat! Maybe you big brave men can set peaceful and feed your stupid faces while the little baby cries and cries——" She was near to angry tears.

Jed's grin softened as he took in the quivering mouth. "How was you plannin' to go about it?"

She gestured with the skirt. "I'm gonna wrap its head in my skirt and I've got two pieces of rope to tie its feet."

"You got any idea how much fight a full-growed goat

can put up? Or how heavy it'll be? Just think you can sling it over your arm and run off, huh?"

Melissa glared at him. "Go on, laugh," she stormed, "you can just get on back to the train. I'm gonna stay here and get a goat if I have to rassle it and drag it every step of the way! I ain't goin' back without a goat!"

He suddenly reached and pulled her roughly against him. As he set his mouth down hard on hers he marveled at how disturbed he got when she let fly that temper of hers. She struggled at first but then her arms went around his neck, tangling them both in the skirt and rope. Her body arched against him and her response to his rough kiss was as furiously passionate as had been her temper. She was gasping unevenly when he set her back on her feet. The man's eyes were glintingly alight as his grin crooked down at her.

"Damn," he said softly, "didn't know I was gettin' me a goat thief into the bargain." She opened her mouth to protest but he stooped and kissed her quiet. "Give me your rope," he said with resignation, taking it from her hand, "and get on back to the horses—I'll steal your goat for you." Melissa's smile flashed white, delightedly up at him. She scuttled obediently off toward the horses.

She stood tensely listening for many minutes, hearing nothing but the prattling of the little creek and the crunching sounds from the grazing horses. Then Jed's tall figure loomed up, only a darker shadow in the now full dark. He carried a goat, its feet tied, muzzled by his neckerchief. Palouse calmly accepted the animal's weight across his shoulders and Jed mounted behind. The goat had ceased to struggle, seemed resigned to its odd fate.

They rode at a quiet walk back toward the south end of the valley. Melissa presently reached over to stroke the goat. Jed chuckled under his breath. "You feelin' to see if I got a nanny or a billy?" he asked. Melissa smothered a giggle. "I felt over damn near every goat in that field," he bragged, "this here goat has got the finest set in the herd!"

They had come quite a distance when Jed suddenly halted Palouse. "Hold up." His sharp whisper caused Melissa to pull Jane in. Jed turned Palouse off the road, motioning her to follow him into shadow behind some tall bushes. He slid off, lowered the goat to the ground. "Stay here," he whispered and slid noiselessly away. Melissa, peering excitedly from behind the bushes presently made out the figure of a man walking toward them. Jed stayed silent until the man was almost abreast.

"Just out for a little walk, Abel?" Jed's tone was calmly conversational.

Abel Barker started convulsively, his hand went to the revolver tucked in his belt. "Jed Smith," the tall shadow identified. Abel let out a relieved breath, "Oh–I thought—" He did not finish, stared sullenly at Jed. He could not see the grin twitching at the scout's mouth. "Well," Jed drawled, "if you was plannin' to make a call on a goat herd, likely you'd best change your mind–jist happens that Melissa's got herself a nanny goat over yonder—"

The next evening Jed was at the horse herd when he spotted riders approaching the wagon camp. Four–no, five riders. One was a woman, a big woman mounted on a heavy horse, looked to be a draft animal. Their ordered, pounding approach was somehow ominous. As they drew near Jed could see that the men all carried rifles across their saddle horns. The man in the lead wore a black frock coat and a tall beaver hat. His beard was dark and long on his chest, his belly crowded the saddle horn. He sat his horse with conscious authority.

Jed went swiftly to his bedroll, caught up his rifle, checked the double loads, and headed fast for Cap'n Fancher's wagon. No one went armed in camp except the guards. And if Sister Wyatt was in the frame of mind he figured she was, this could get out of hand. None in the train would be prepared to deal with the particular brand of highhanded hell an irate Mormon bishop could supply. That black coat and beaver had the look of a bishop, for sure. Jed loped past the Mitchell brothers lounging around their wagon. They came bolt upright at his flung words. "Get your guns and come on—fetch the McLean boy with you." He was on his way as they leaped to obey.

The bearded man introduced himself to Captain Fancher. "I am Bishop McKenzie," his harsh voice was important, "also sheriff, in these parts."

"Get down, get down, Bishop—uh, Sheriff." Fancher was smiling cordially, pipe in hand, "come on over and have a seat by the fire. What can we do for you?"

None of the visitors dismounted. People were beginning to gather, curiously. The bishop peered around suspiciously. The three other riders, also bearded, did not speak, their eyes darted here and there with shuttered watchfulness. Sister Wyatt, riding astride, her full skirts tucked decently around her legs, sat her horse in silence.

The bishop spoke. "You've got a man name of McLean in your party." It was a statement rather than a question.

Fancher nodded, puzzled by the manner of the visitors. "One of my herders," he confirmed.

"Where is he?"

The Mitchells had come up to stand behind Jed where he had paused in the shadow of the nearest wagon. He glanced around at them swiftly. Each carried a rifle, their eyes were alight with anticipation. The lanky brothers were good-natured but joyously quick to join in on a fracas. Young McLean, his face blankly puzzled, was with them. The Mitchells had come by the Boller wagon and David, also carrying a rifle, now appeared at Jed's elbow. Jed nodded with satisfaction. "Don't do nothin'," he said, "just back my play." He motioned McLean forward and stepped into the firelight with the young man beside him. The eyes of the mounted party swung on them instantly.

"Good evenin', Sister Wyatt." Jed's fingers briefly touched his hatbrim. His voice was flat, his eyes gray slits. He spoke, then, to the bearded leader. "This here is McLean."

Bishop McKenzie's hooded gaze settled on Jed, itemizing the buckskins, the leather-brown, poker face, dropped to the easy carriage of the heavy, double-barreled rifle. "Who might you be?" he inquired testily.

Jed pushed back his hat, revealing the flinty gaze clearly in the firelight. His tone was equally flinty. "Name's Jed Smith," he said, "scout for the train." He let that lie for a moment and then added significantly, "*Used* to live at Fort Bridger—old Jim is my foster father."

McKenzie's brows met frowningly above his strong nose. An almost imperceptible narrowing of the eyes, the slight jutting of his arrogant beard betrayed recognition of the warning gauntlet of grudge. He made no answer, turning his wrathful gaze on McLean, a medium-sized, stocky man whose scraggly beard hid the youthfulness of his face. McKenzie seemed about to speak—Jed spoke first.

"Give out your full name, Mack," he said. The young man looked puzzled. "John Quincy McLean."

"Where you from?"

"Around Springfield, Missouri."

"Where's your folks, your paw and maw? What's your paw's name?"

"Dead—both of them—I was named for my paw."

"How old are you?"

"I don't rightly know—my folks died when I was a youngun—about nineteen or a little more, I guess."

"You ever been in Arkansas?"

This question made little sense to McLean, he looked anxiously around at the intent audience and then back at Jed. "Nope," he said positively.

"There you are, McKenzie," Jed finished. The Mormon's eyes registered the deliberate ignoring of both titles announced so importantly. There was silence as the bishop and his party discontentedly viewed the situation. Jed stood waiting for them to make the next move.

The Mitchells, rifles at ease in their long arms, angular jaws moving with rhythmic vigor on tobacco cuds, set a bright, unwinking gaze on the bishop, nor shifted the stare as each spat, deliberately, in turn. David's stocky person, bowed legs spraddled, was alert, his rifle slanted from his square hands. Captain Fancher stood somewhat to one side of the belligerent four, his face troubled, mystified at the proceedings. Into the fraught silence a goat suddenly gave voice, plaintively, carrying.

Sister Wyatt's shawled head swung. She kicked her horse into ambling motion and rode toward the sound. Abel Barker and Clara, the baby in her arms, were there by the wagon. Alarmed by the sudden appearance of the forbidding figure on the heavy horse, the girl got weakly to her feet.

Sister Wyatt stepped her horse to the edge of the light cast by Abel's fire. She sat, immovably large and fateful in the saddle, taking in the girl and baby. She did not speak as the girl came falteringly across toward her, the firelight limning her light hair, the thin, pale face. Clara stopped at the woman's stirrup, lifted the baby a little, pushing back the blanket from the tiny, mottled face. Her eyes were wide, seriously confiding on Sister Wyatt.

"He's sleepin' good"—her soft voice was hesitant—"first time he could hold somethin' on his little stomach. He ain't puked once all day."

Sister Wyatt's face remained stolid but her eyes became angrily offended, exasperation in her voice. "How old are you?" The tone was accusing but Clara did not seem to find the question odd. "Goin' on seventeen," she answered simply in her gentle way.

The angry gaze impatiently took in the girl and baby. The evidences of Clara's recent travail were there: the violet shadows deep under her eyes, the pallor of the almost transparent skin, and the frailty of the thin, drooping shoulders. "You had a bad time," the prodding voice stated.

"Yes, ma'am," Clara answered, "they had to finally take him—feet first."

The shawled head nodded knowledgeably—commiserating. "And then your milk didn't come in?"

"No, ma'am, only a tiny bit and it didn't agree with him. He puked up cow's milk, too."

Sister Wyatt's attention transferred to Abel who hovered protectively behind his wife, his face a mixture of pleading and defiance. She glared at him accusingly and then dismissed him as she turned back to the girl. "You got no earthly business up on your feet so soon, and totin' him around!" The tone was harsh but Clara smiled suddenly and with heart-catching sweetness, for she had recognized—with a sudden pang of homesickness—the quality of concerned maternal scolding.

"He ain't heavy," she said affectionately to the big woman, "poor little mite, he's been near starved, he's only ten days old tomorrow."

Sister Wyatt's heavy shoulders shrugged impatiently, she was helplessly annoyed with herself at what she knew she was about to do. The goat called plaintively again and her glance darted toward where the animal was tethered to a wheel of the wagon. The woman's head lifted jerkily, her hands tightened on the reins, the docile horse raised his head. She leaned from the saddle and spoke in a lowered tone to Clara.

"You'd best drink the goat's milk, too," she advised roughly, "it's right strengthenin'." She rode without a backward glance back toward the other fire. Clara's head went down, relieved tears fell on the sleeping baby's head. Abel put his arms around her, gently helped her to a seat. The single long glance he sent after Sister Wyatt was shining with the unshed tears in his own eyes.

The bishop's peremptory glance challenged the woman. "Well?" he barked.

Her gaze was stonily dismissing. "It ain't my goat."

"Ain't your goat——!" Incredulous anger erupted in his face. He eyed her with significant hotness, his manner commanding a different response. Her returning stare was strong and unabashed, she did not shy from facing him; indeed, Sister Wyatt seemed to be finding a certain enjoyment in the situation she had created. "Guess I know one of my own goats when I see it, Isaiah." She pronounced it "Isayer." "I taken a look at that goat, over there, and I say it ain't my goat."

Jed tried to hide the grin he felt coming at Sister Wyatt's truculent calm baiting of the bishop. That dignitary's face turned a dark, mottled red at the indignity of the familiarity with which she addressed him and at the finality which had disregarded his unvoiced but definitely understood will concerning the goat.

The bishop glimpsed Jed's swift grin and his fury threatened to choke him. He seemed to swell as he sat in the saddle. His baleful gaze turned on McLean. "We'll have to take this man in," he announced.

The startled McLean started to protest but a long arm swept him back as Jed stepped a pace forward, bringing his rifle waist high, at the ready. The Mitchells and David moved promptly in unison, formed a challenging line with him. The firelight emphasized the blackness of four heavy rifle barrels.

"You ain't takin' nobody in, *Bishop!*" Jed's grinding voice contemptuously underlined the title. "You ain't ridin' outa here with nothin' you didn't bring in!"

McKenzie was no coward, he stared unwinkingly at the rifles. "I'm the law hereabouts," he reminded evenly, "these men are sworn deputies. You figger to hinder the law, Smith?"

"I'll hinder *you!*" Jed snapped, "one barrel's loaded with buckshot,"—he patted the rifle—"that one is all yours." His gaze darted to the woman. "You'd best ride, Sister Wyatt," he advised, "we ain't Mormons, we don't fire on women!"

At this goading, intentional insult McKenzie's hand jerked his rifle, half raised it. But froze, for hammers clicked back in chorus, four long, black barrels raised, pointing, ready. There were smothered gasps and a moving back of the spectators. Then a long, heavily breathing silence.

Sister Wyatt abruptly laughed into the silence. "Come on, Isayer," she said scornfully, " 'fore you make a bigger fool of yourself." She kicked her horse into a ponderous trot and turned, rode away. McKenzie's head turned balefully after her and swung back to lay a fanatically glittering gaze on Jed. Then the bishop brutally jerked his horse's head and rode after the woman. The three silent deputies followed him.

Watchful relieved silence held until the riders cleared the circled wagons and the thudding hoofs diminished in the distance.

"Jed, what in hell was that all about?" Captain Fancher didn't know whether to be angry or not. "Wasn't you a little hasty, throwin' down on a bishop thataway? What did they want of Mack?"

Jed looked at the puzzled, mild face and thought, how can you make a man like this understand how the Mormons have got? He tried. "Cap'n Fancher," he said, "don't never make the mistake of figgerin' a Mormon like you would other folks, for they're peculiar—and they're always on the prod for Gentiles. And don't *never* knuckle under to an armed Mormon bishop! They been rulin' this roost of theirs so long they think they're the law and God Almighty to boot! I had to get rough. If'n we'd let them take Mack, here, he'd been dead 'fore sunup!"

McLean's jaw dropped in horror, Fancher's pipe jerked in his hand. "Dead! What the hell——?" He stared at the young man. "What's he done—they know somethin' about him we don't?"

Jed shook his head. How to explain so they would understand? "His name happens to be McLean," he said doggedly, "and some of you hail from Arkansas. This figgers for them evidence enough to hang him—for murder!" He cut in again on the chorus of horrified exclamations, "Oh hell," he said disgustedly, "Mack's as innocent as you or me—he had nothin' to do with what they're frothin' about——"

The apostate, William Aden, who had remained discreetly in the shadow while the visitors were in camp, came forward now, nodding his head, his thin face solemn. "They would have hanged him, Captain Fancher," he confirmed gravely, "this Pratt-McLean business, it's very ugly. The Mormons aren't scrupulous when it comes to taking vengeance. Why, they preach right out in meeting about avenging on their enemies right down to the second and third generation!"

"Pratt-McLean? I still don't know what—"

"Well"—Jed drew a deep breath—"likely you didn't hear it—it happened about the time you'd have been just headin' outa Arkansas." The spectators drew nearer, everyone was tense with curiosity. "The way I heard it," Jed began, "was that a man named Hector McLean killed Parley Pratt. Pratt was one of Brigham's favorite apostles—real high-up man in their Church. And he was well known in these here parts, he headed up the explorin' and settlin' of the southern forts. I knew Pratt. He came and went through Fort Bridger several times while old Jim still had it. He was a handsome cuss, friendly and sociable—had a big, hearty laugh. He sure liked the women, too, had a lot of wives and they tell that every one of them is good-lookin'. He used to carry on a lot about how he'd like a Shoshoni wife if Jim would find him a pretty one. Well, just last winter, Pratt and a man named McBride was off on a proselytin' mission for the Church and they converted Hector McLean's wife. McLean himself wouldn't have any part of the Mormon beliefs but his wife went whole hog for it—or Parley Pratt. She got herself secretly baptized and then she up and run off with Pratt—became one of his plural wives."

"But she was already married, how could—?"

"Oh hell, the Mormons don't count a marriage bindin' unless it's done in their Church! They wouldn't have figgered McLean counted at all, him bein' a Gentile. Pratt wasn't the first proselyter to talk a man's wife right outa his house. But McLean, he didn't take it settin' down, he got on their trail. And, a while later, he caught up with Pratt in Arkansas. Him and some of his friends. Whilst his friends throwed down on Parley Pratt with guns, McLean tackled him with a Bowie knife. But Pratt was unarmed. I guess McLean cut him up good and proper, they left him bleed to death in the road. And they bragged, after, in the town, what they'd done with the Mormon proselyter. The law in Arkansas never lifted a finger, guess they figgered Pratt got what was comin' to him. McLean went scot-free. And a'course the Mormons figger Pratt was the innocent victim of blood-thirsty murderers."

Captain Fancher—and the intent listeners—heard the history of sordid violence with appalled faces. The captain turned to look at McLean. "You aren't——"

McLean shook his head vigorously, his face was as alarmed as anyone's. "Knew he couldn't be," Jed supplied. "Hector McLean would be lots older than Mack, here. There was some kids—the woman deserted her kids, too, the whole kit and caboodle, when she run off with Parley Pratt. Yesterday, when Sister Wyatt asked if there was anyone named McLean in the train, I had a hunch we hadn't heard the last of it."

"How's the old woman mixed up in this? I thought she came about the goat."

"Well, that, too, sure. But she said, yesterday, that her daughter was one of Parley's wives, so, natural, she'd feel strong about what happened. They coulda figgered Mack, here, to maybe be Hector McLean or a relative. Lackin' the man himself, they'd feel obliged to take vengeance on kinfolks."

Fancher unwillingly considered this alien attitude. He shook his head in bafflement. Then he said, "How come you suppose she lied, then, about the goat? She knew damn well that there was her goat!"

Jed grinned at the memory of Sister Wyatt's about-face. "Damned if I know—looked like she done it mostly to spite the bishop. These old Mormon women ain't lackin' in guts. They don't knuckle under to the menfolks near as often as you might think, not the old ones, anyhow. And their opinion of men ain't got too much respect in it, seein' their old husbands prancin' and ruttin' after the young girls all the time. They get mean, sometimes, and get even in their own way, when they kin."

Sister Wyatt, homeward-bound with Bishop McKenzie's sullen party, surprisedly pondered her own actions. Ruefully she admitted being a softhearted old fool. Her lined face softened as she thought of the pale girl, so young, and the tiny new baby. But it hardened again as McKenzie ranted on and on. He had now singled out her disobedience and went on to her lack of respect. He was taking out his frustration on her.

"You can just hush your mouth, Isayer McKenzie," she interrupted tartly, "and don't try to come over me with that bishop-sheriff pose! You're still only my brother-in-law as far as I'm concerned. Though, goodness knows, with all them young girls keepin' you excited, it appears you forget my sister Mariah is your wife, too!" McKenzie let out an angry gust of breath but she gave him no chance to speak. "And I don't want to hear no more about any goat. I said it wasn't my goat and that's that! It wasn't my notion to spend the day chasin' down country about the McLean man–anybody but a fool could see plain that man was too young to be— And then you have to go and try to pull church authority on a pack of Gentiles. I never in all my life seen anythin' so silly!"

McKenzie fixed a revolted stare on her. "Sister Wyatt," sternly pontificating, "I suspend you from the privilege of attending meeting until such time as you show a proper respect toward your bishop!"

"Oh, pshaw, Isayer," not at all discomfited, "you're always gettin' so mighty-mouthed. Far as that goes, I could use me a good excuse to skip meetin' these days. I'm that sick and tired of all the rantin' and ravin' about blood avengin' and hearin' that this here is a holy war we've got on our hands. And all you men rushin' off to drill and play soldier, leavin' the harvest work to us women. I declare, if men ain't the limit! If you ain't off smellin' around for a new young wife, you're gettin' into some row so's you can make out to fight somebody! And I'll just have my say"—she raised her voice shrilly to drown out his rumble of denunciation—"I say right here and now that I think even Brother Brigham has up and took leave of his senses, sendin' word that we're to get ready to fight the United States Army! I swear, I never heard of such downright tomfoolishness in all my born days!"

They had come to the lane that branched off toward Sister Wyatt's place and, before she herded the old horse away from the party, she fired a parting shot that did nothing to ease the bishop's choler.

"Isayer"—definite malice was enjoyed in her advice—"better stop by and have Mariah brew you up some herb tea. Less'n I miss my guess, you're gonna have one of your dyspeptic spells tonight. Mariah and me might be gettin' old, but her tea will likely do you better than anythin' them girls a'yourn can dish up!"

The enraged man did not deign to answer although he was further incensed by the accuracy of her prediction. Already there was a grinding sourness in his ample middle. It always seemed to follow, that knotting up of his innards when he got really riled. But before he sought relief in his first wife's kitchen he paid a call on the express rider who was scheduled to travel south with the mail at dawn.

"You pass this word, at every stop," he ordered, "that this Fancher Train—headin' south—is a pack of stock thieves, and worse! There's a man named McLean in it and they're from Arkansas and Missouri and Illinois! And Bridger's bastard, Jed Smith, is scoutin' the train, just itchin' for trouble, ready to throw down on anybody! Tell them to pass the word, and warn them aginst the people in this train!"

Sister Wyatt did not sleep immediately when she laid her weary body down. Her small cabin was quiet, forlorn quiet, for she lived alone. Her children were grown and gone. Her husband divided his time between six wives. Since she had passed the age of childbearing her status as first wife had gained her little but loneliness and her thoughts were accustomed to bitterness.

A sound intruded on her exhausted half sleep. She lifted herself heavily to one elbow, listening intently. There was the faraway sound of a running horse drumming faintly through the stillness of the night. It was coming nearer, sounded like it was pounding down her lane. Sister Wyatt resumed old acquaintance with sickened dread, foreboding, combined with resentful anger that she was alone to meet whatever drew near on the pounding hoofs. For a dark, urgent rider in the night usually spelled danger, trouble, disaster.

She rose instantly from the corn-shuck mattress, moved with ponderous speed across the room, taking a loaded rifle from where it rested on pegs driven between the logs, checked it efficiently. That rifle gun was as familiar to Sister Wyatt's strong hands as were her kitchen utensils.

The horse had been stopped at her front gate, just a few feet from the doorstep. She listened for the hail that would identify friend or neighbor. There was only the quiet night. Then there was a small thud, something had been flung against her door and dropped to the stone stoop with an odd sound.

There was the sound of the horse moving again, breaking into a run. She crept to the small window and peered out of a corner of the wavery glass pane. She could faintly make out the shadowy figure of a tall rider on a stocky horse moving swiftly down the lane, vanish into the night. And then all was quiet again.

Sister Wyatt knew from the sounds that there had been but one horse, but she waited for long moments, listening, her rifle at the ready. Finally she cautiously unbarred the heavy door to peer out. The lowering moon cast a faint light on the white stone doorstep. A small leather bag lay there. She picked it up wonderingly; as she hefted it there was a significant clinking sound. Re-barring the door, she pulled the calico curtain across the window and lit her lamp. She sat down at her table and, loosening the bag's drawstring, poured a little heap of silver coins into her calloused palm. And sat rigidly staring, unbelieving the evidence of her own eyes.

Sister Wyatt had not seen this much money at one time in more weary years than she cared to count. Then she noticed a crackling sound within the little bag. There was a wadded piece of paper, scrawled with writing. She moved the lamp nearer and spread the paper in its light. "The nanny rides in the wagon. We treat her like a queen. God Bless You."

The big woman sat immovable for a long time, her heavy, lined face was puckered painfully. Then she shook her head from side to side vigorously and commenced to count the money. When she had finished her face wore a grimly delighted smile. And then she sobered, considering. Her expression became belligerent, she nodded decidingly. She'd just not happen to mention this to a living soul, for she'd be expected to share and damned if she was going to split with her husband's younger wives! And, did he hear of it, Isayer McKenzie would be right on her doorstep, with his hand out, all mealy-mouthed and grabbing for what he'd call the Church's rightful share. If he'd had his way, this night, likely it'd wound up with no goat and no money, either. So she'd just keep it hid away. A little private hoard would be a great comfort to think about. Just the knowing she had it would make a lot of things a sight easier to put up with.

She refolded the note and tucked it back in the bag and then, pleasure in the doing, replaced the coins, one at a time. New-minted, they were, shining silver, and she handled them lovingly, like jewels. She stood up briskly, blew out the lamp, and crossed to crawl back in to bed. She placed the pouch under her pillow and lay thinking, her fingers reaching to touch it from time to time. There was satisfaction in the set of the grim mouth. Take it all in all, it had turned out fine. It had been a long, miserable day, jolting painfully on the plodding old work horse, trying to make him keep up. But she was glad, now, that she'd let Isayer make her "do her duty." And it pleased her that he'd got the short end of the stick. Served him good and right! She hadn't wanted to chase after the wagon train and start trouble, one goat wasn't worth it. All she wanted, now, in the world was to get done with trouble—and killing. Peacefulness, undisturbed, that was what they'd been promised when they reached Zion. Looked to be way off the mark, sometimes. It tried a person's patience, having it dinned in all the time that all Gentiles were to be hated and feared as enemies. Look at those folks in that train, now, just ordinary folks. Mighty well-to-do, though. For this was a handsome price for one milk goat. Course, they likely figured they were paying for more than the goat. It was right nice of them. Likely those folks weren't anywheres near so bad as Isayer McKenzie made them out.

## CHAPTER X

Jake Tibbetts did not like mules. He regretted, now, that he had traded his ox bulls for the faster team. He'd been a bullwhacker for many years and changing had been a mistake. For the mules were tempery, they got skittish, took more driving. And they resented his use of a bull whip. Jake was proud of his skill with that fifteen-foot lash, he could nip a fly from the ear of his lead animal without touching flesh. It was a weapon that had proved out handy on men, too. He'd taken an eye from that young fool that had kept prodding at him, feeling brave because of the gun in his belt. He'd not used it, he couldn't see to use it after Jake flipped the whip just once. Since then he kept it always with him, liking the feel of its handle in his hand. The heavy man had no wife nor family. His fat ugliness had deprived him of much that most men took for granted. That—and his sullen temper. It was a constantly seething thing beneath the boarish lethargy, fed by dull contempt for all that was denied him.

He had been able to relieve some of his universal hatred by taking it out on his oxen, and these patient beasts had tolerated this burden as they accepted the heavy yokes under which they toiled out their days. But mules were different-natured. These were big, sure-footed beasts and they were intelligent. At times their eyes held a disturbing cognizance. The big near-wheeler, now. Jake had cut his rump right smart a time or two for not throwing his weight into a pull quick enough. The animal had turned its head and eyed him deliberately. With a sort of remembering look. And then, a day or two later, when he was harnessing, the wheeler had seen his chance and kicked. Jake still walked with a painful limp because of it. At the time, he'd got up and done his best to beat its brains out with a singletree.

Captain Fancher and John Barker had interfered and threatened him furiously against further abuse of his animals. It was a hell of a note if a man couldn't do as he saw fit with his own property. If they hadn't been way out on the trail, he'd have left the train, but a lone wagon in Injun country wasn't too good a proposition. And after that everybody in the train had avoided him like the plague. He damned them all, muttering obscenely to himself under his breath. He had remained on what might be called friendly terms with only two men, Sol Ward and Les Prichard.

Jake had missed Sol when the big redbeard had elected to travel apart from the train, following Sairy's rebellion. The fat man wondered if anyone, other than himself, knew that Sol was trailing them, traveling just a few miles back but keeping pace each day. Likely Jed Smith was aware of it, for the scout didn't miss anything, but he was probably pleased to have Sol stay away from the train.

Jake customarily brought up the rear—by choice. He

preferred this position for a reason. Jed Smith usually traveled ahead of the train and the fat man knew the scout would jump him fast if he caught him using his whip as he was doing. Just keeping his hand in, Jake said to himself, getting a little practice now and then.

The porcine face was derisive as he thought of the riled Mormons he left behind when he practiced his skill on a chicken or a dog as his wagon wheeled through the outskirts of a town or passed a farm. A dog was an eminently satisfactory target. Just let a noisy cur run out to bark alongside the wheels and Jake could wrap half the length around its belly. Just the right twist could nearly disembowel the animal. Chickens were the most fun, though. You could snap their silly, squawking heads right off, leave them spouting a fountain of blood as they flapped around in the dust.

This last episode had been the most entertaining of all. Jake wanted to share it with someone. Sol was the only one he could depend on to see the humor of it, so he slowed his team, gradually letting the train move away from him. He'd decided to wait for the redbeard.

Just out of Fillmore, the last town they'd passed through, Jake had let fly at a big red rooster. Took his high-combed head off as neat as if he'd had him on a chopping block. Then a kid had run out and a long-legged hound-dog, barking furiously. He'd taken them deftly, in turn. The dog had landed off in the weeds, yelping with pain. Jake had only just dusted the seat of the kid's pants a little when the woman ran out, yelling and carrying on. Quite a good-looker, he remembered. He'd not hurt her any, just flicked her skirts up a little. Got a look at a fine pair of legs. The women hereabouts didn't wear pantalets apparently, she'd been bare-legged, underneath. It made him chuckle as he thought how damn near bare-assed, she'd been, too, time he got through. She'd done some nimble dancing around to get out of range. He'd ought to be more careful, though, he admonished himself. He'd been so interested that if a man had showed up at that place he could have gotten his head blown off. But after he'd driven on, the woman and kid were bending over the dog, which was still screaming in the tall weeds. The woman had straightened up and sent a long, hating look after him. Done his heart good, Jake told himself, all women were whores and he figured Mormon women were likely the worst.

Sol was glad to see him. And wonder of wonders, he had a bottle of whisky to share. They hitched the red-beard's team behind Jake's wagon and rode together, swapping long slugs from the bottle as they went slowly along. Sol had got two bottles in the last town.

"How in hell you manage that?" Jake queried, "the goddamn Mormons wouldn't sell a grain of corn to anyone in the train."

Sol's grin was crafty. "Well, I offered to pay for it," he said magnanimously, "had my hard money right out in my hand. But this here runty little bastard got uppity—said he wasn't sellin' nothing in his shop to Gentiles. He'd oughta knowed better'n to get uppity with Sol Ward. I ain't takin' no crap offa no pipsqueakin' Mormon. The little puke couldn't a'had much sense, mouthin' so free what he'd do and wouldn't do—and him alone there. I just sort of slapped him around a little and helped myself." Sol chuckled fondly at the memory of it. "I bet he ain't come to yet!"

At nooning time they pulled the wagons into a grove of trees edging a small creek, hobbled the mules, and turned them out to graze. With their food and bottles, Sol and Jake found a shady spot in which to take their ease. They sprawled comfortably enjoying the coolness. The nights and mornings were cool but the middle of the late-August days still were very hot.

Sol, propped on one elbow, peered interestedly off through the trees. "Hey," he said in a low tone, "look over yonder." Jake's eyes followed his pointing finger and saw a woman and a boy moving slowly along by some bushes fringing the base of a hill. They watched intently for a while and then Jake said, "Looks like it's just the two of 'em alone, gatherin' berries offa them bushes." They exchanged stares of sly amusement; this offered possibilities. "Maybe we'd ought to just check up a little," Sol suggested, "it ain't safe for a woman to be wanderin' around alone with just a kid, like that."

The boy noticed their approach and spoke to the woman. She wore a red calico dress and her hair was black, shining black, she was plump and still young. She turned to stare at the approaching men and then, speaking to the boy, she picked up the pail from the grass beside her and started away. But she paused and turned when Sol hailed them in friendly fashion. The men could see now that they were Indian, the woman very handsome in a savage, black-eyed way. The boy looked very much like her although he was small and thin, probably six or seven. He wore faded jeans and a calico shirt.

"What's your big hurry?" Sol's coarse voice was bantering. The woman's eyes showed slight alarm as she realized that these were not local settlers that she knew and trusted. She did not like Sol's tone nor his look and she did not answer. Reaching for the boy's hand, she turned and started away.

Jake's whip flicked out, perked the pail from her hand. It flew in a wide arc, scattering red berries into the dry grass. Sol's laugh bellowed out. "Damn nice shot, Jake!"

Her eyes blazing, the woman spat Indian words at them and hurried away, the boy looking back over his shoulder with bewilderment in his dark eyes. The men were following them in long purposeful strides. "Sounded like she swore at us," Sol said disapprovingly, "maybe she needs a lesson in how to treat white folks."

Jake grunted. "Never did like a mouthy woman," he rumbled sourly. "Specially not a goddamn dirty squaw." He lifted his arm, the whip flicked back over his shoulder and then forward. The lash curled around the woman's ankle and he jerked sideways. She was yanked from her feet to roll helplessly sideways, her skirts raking up to display shapely bare brown legs and thighs. The boy halted, stared at his mother and then at the men in consternation. The woman tore the whip from her ankle and swiftly regained her feet. Her body was tense, anger and humiliation were in her face. She glared at them for a moment and then she spoke, "I am Sally," she said tautly, "wife of Kanosh, war chief of the Pahvants, this is his son!"

"Well, for Chrissake!" Sol's tone was surprised, "Listen to her spout white man's talk, would you!"

The woman's eyes moved from face to face and found no reassurance. She knew, from their flushed faces and thick-tongued words, that they were drunken. She did her best to warn them away. "It would be best," she advised in an even tone, "for you to go your way, now. Kanosh will not take it lightly that you insult his wife."

Sol seemed to find something immensely funny about this, he grinned widely. "He won't, huh?" His bloodshot eyes were interestedly disrobing the woman, discovering the opulent breasts, the full curve of plump hips. Sol had been without a woman for quite a while. At what grew now in his face the woman instinctively retreated a step, her arms went across her bosom in a covering gesture. Her full red mouth opened, she was panting slightly with deep alarm.

Sol's eyes narrowed, his mouth sloped in ugly derision as he enjoyed the beginning of horror in her face. "Watch the youngun," he said thickly, "whilst I tame this wildcat."

Jake grunted and shook out the whip, letting it lie in front of him like the gracefully vicious curves of a moving snake.

Sol stepped slowly toward the woman. She backed away until she came up against a tree, her eyes never leaving the man, like an animal in a trap. She froze for an instant as one huge paw gripped her shoulder, the other, hooking into the neck of her dress, jerked roughly, ripping her waist.

The tawny satin of her shoulders and bosom had a warm richness, the dark nipples were firmly erect on the full roundness. She had begun to fight him, silently, as vicious as a wirily strong cat. Sol had trouble holding her, he tried to drag her close, but she bit his forearm so that her teeth met through his flesh. He howled in painful rage, relaxing his hold. She leaped away but he was after her, caught her in two lumbering strides. With his open hand he hit her twice, on either side of the head, the blows cracking like pistol shots. She collapsed and he dragged her behind the bushes.

The boy had cried out shrilly when she began to fight, and started to run to her. Jake, pig eyes glinting, sent the whip flicking, caught the boy around his thin waist and rolled him. The boy sprang to his feet like an infuriated bobcat, only to meet the flicking lash. One brown cheek was slashed in a long line that was wetly red, it had been sliced to the thin bone.

"I coulda taken your eyes just as easy, bub," Jake rumbled warningly, "just move one inch and I'll take 'em—one at a time."

The boy was motionless, half crouching, one hand to his bleeding cheek, his dilated eyes fixed on the whip. From time to time the fat man's hand twitched and the tip end of the vicious lash quivered like a cat's tail just before the leap. Threshing, grunting sounds came from the bushes, and then a sharply agonized cry, but the boy moved not a muscle.

Presently Sol reappeared, a smirking grin spreading his beard. "Pretty good for dark meat, Jake," he reported jovially, "she don't stink hardly at all—like most squaws. You gonna try her?"

As Jake lumbered around the bushes the boy's eyes met Sol's. There was nothing childish in the malignant stare of the black eyes, and no abjectness or fear in the set of the wild young face. Sol was dissatisfied with the look of him, he expected shrinking and terror. There was nothing of these in this cougarlike watchfulness. He reached a hand and caught him by one thin shoulder, shook him hard till his head whipped, his body hung limp, dangling from the big hand. "Mind your manners, you filthy Injun puppy," he growled, " 'fore I slap some sense into your skull!"

The limp form stiffened, the boy uttered one scathing Indian word, insulting in tone and spat defiantly on Sol, staining his shirt front, there was blood in his mouth.

Sol roared with rage and cuffed the boy's head, first one side and then the other. He flung the small form from him, looking disgustedly at his fouled shirt. The boy had fallen in a small, seemingly boneless heap. Sol nudged him with the toe of his boot but he did not stir. That'd ought to teach him, he thought irritably, likely wouldn't come to 'fore sundown.

Later, riding together somewhat silently on the seat of Jake's wagon, the two men finished off the last of the whisky. The late afternoon was hot, both sat in a sort of satiated torpor.

And then off to the west, at the foot of a wooded hill, they saw a large Indian camp. There were many tepees under the cedar trees, a good-sized horse herd grazed in the wild meadow grass beyond and quite a number of people moved around. Uneasily they estimated the size of the camp, the probable number of Indians it would contain.

"Think her and the kid come from there?" Sol's voice showed that he was disturbed.

Jake took a while to reply, his voice was equally concerned. "Likely did," he said.

"Hell of a lot of 'em." Sol's torpor was gone, he was definitely alarmed.

Jake pondered sluggishly. "Likely nobody'll miss 'em before dark. It'll take them two that long to get back—the shape we left them in." His pig eyes surveyed the position of the lowering sun. "Just to be on the safe side, though," he suggested, "we'd best get the hell outa here, join up with the train. They'll likely circle in an hour or so—we'd best catch up, quick."

Sol returned to his own wagon, completely sobered by the sight of the many Indians and a sudden awareness of their vulnerable isolation. The two whipped their mules into as fast a pace as the loaded wagons permitted. They joined the train just as it pulled into a circle in a wide green valley. It was a pleasant place, enclosed by rounded foothills that stepped upward toward the tall western range. A stream rushed noisily across the valley. Jed Smith had named the place to be Corn Creek.

Just before full dark Jed had reported to Captain Fancher that a small train had pulled in from the south and was encamped at the base of a hill a mile or so from the Fancher Train. They looked, Jed said, to be Mormons and there were women and also some Indians in the party.

Captain Fancher issued orders that no one from the train was to visit the other camp. He felt that it would be best to avoid all unnecessary contacts with the Mormons. Every encounter lately had been unpleasant, created problems. The Saints seemed to be extremely touchy, some of them openly hostile.

The captain hadn't expected anyone from the smaller train to show themselves and he was surprised at the appearance of three visitors, a dignified, soberly dressed man and two Indians. The man gravely introduced himself as Jacob Hamblin.

Fancher's somewhat wary reception gave way to a pleased smile, he extended his hand warmly. "Mr. Hamblin, I've heard a lot of fine things about you"–his enthusiasm was genuine–"wouldn't you be the famous peacemaker to the Injuns?"

Hamblin, a tall, almost cadaverous man, with well-trimmed chin whiskers, was dressed in rusty black clothes, a white plait-front shirt and black string tie. His dark hair was cut just below his ears, piercing eyes were sober beneath a high, bony forehead. He nodded in answer to Charley's query, unsmiling but not unfriendly. Somewhat ceremoniously he introduced his colorful companions: Tutsegavitt, chief of the Paiutes, and Kanosh, chief of the Pahvants–through whose territory they now traveled.

The Indians were immensely stolid of face but they were gratified by the unhesitating cordiality of Captain Fancher's extended hand, the vigor with which he shook their strong brown paws. He ushered them genially to seats around his fire and sent a boy running to find Jed Smith.

"Jed'll have some questions he'd like to put to you, Mr. Hamblin," he said, "I hear you've traveled this country a lot. Jed's got maps and he was sayin' he'd like right well to get them up to date on water holes and such."

"I will be glad to help," Hamblin answered seriously. "Not long ago I traveled to Las Vegas Springs, which is on the California trail. I can help with information about the trail right on to San Bernardino—we have a settlement there."

Fancher was agreeably impressed by the dignified Mormon, and cheered by his sober friendliness.

Jacob Hamblin had been reluctant to visit the Gentile camp but the two chiefs had been insistent on going. Knowing how violent Kanosh's temper could be if aroused by real or fancied insult, he had agreed to accompany them, mostly to avert unpleasantness. Hamblin had been an apostle to the red men for several years and had been eminently successful, they would heed his word always.

The sober Mormon had heard the warnings, the bad reputation of the Fancher Train traveled ahead of it. But he was well acquainted with Bishop McKenzie, who had instigated the rumors. Jacob had never found much in common with the dictatorial bishop and he was unwilling to accept the man's judgment unreservedly. Now he had been pleasantly impressed by the obviously sincere welcome of Captain Fancher. The wagon captain did not have the look of a troublemaker, nor one who would condone stock thieving.

When Jed's buckskin-clad form loomed in the firelight Hamblin's gaze explored him closely. McKenzie had labeled the scout as a proddingly vicious killer. But Jed's bright blue eyes met his steadily, with openness, and the two men stared searchingly, their glance on a tall level. And each recognized, with the beginning of warmth, that there was much common ground between them. The handshake, which had begun automatically, finished with vigor.

Jed managed—in properly respectful Paiute—a few words which brought glinting gratification into the obsidian eyes of the chiefs. Both wore broadcloth pants, rusty green with age and much the worse for wear. Each sported a bright calico shirt. Many bone and bead necklaces adorned the broad chests and their greased, black hair was braided, lavishly decorated. Tutsegavitt was old and very fat but, withal, of a ponderous, unshakable dignity of carriage.

Kanosh, the Pahvant, was not young, but still in the vigorous prime of heavily muscled strength. He was impressively handsome in a hawklike way. His eyes were set somewhat close to the high bridge of a fierce, hooked nose. The mouth was thin and wide, the underlip jutted, giving the immediate impression of proud disdain. This was a real war chief, Jed thought, and a right proper one. He'd just as soon not ever have to tangle with this one. For there was fierce pride and intelligence and a feeling of primitive ferocity. He'd be utterly fearless, proudly reckless. It was evident in the stiff-necked, almost flaunting carriage of the eagle head. Kanosh returned their greetings in excellent English, his voice deep, sonorous.

Hamblin gravely explained that the chief's favorite wife, Sally, had been reared in Brigham Young's own household and educated with the leader's daughters. She had been given in marriage to Kanosh as evidence of Brigham's great love and esteem for the war chief of the Pahvants. Kanosh had had a brick house built for this wife, who had borne him a son, now six years old. Sally had taught her husband to read and write as well as speak English. Hamblin's sidelong glance saw that Jed was listening with appreciative understanding of the diplomacy of the expansive harangue. Hamblin added a final, flowery item—respectfully he described Sally as being the possessor of a gentle, soft voice as well as great beauty.

Kanosh listened with dignified interest to every word of the eulogy, admitting the truth of the words with a restrained nod from time to time. His black eyes glittered with pride at the finish. Obviously the fierce war hawk did set great store by this beautiful and gifted wife.

While Captain Fancher, having presented the chiefs with huge twists of tobacco, visited with them genially, Jed and Hamblin discussed the California trail. Jed produced his map and Jacob's long bony finger pointed to this and that place designating water, grazing, and much else of value.

"What about the Injuns, south of here?" Jed inquired.

"You won't have to give it a thought till you get in Mojave country," Hamblin answered, "except for the usual stock thievery. We've been able to talk them into keeping the peace, but we've never been able to stop them from stealing."

Jacob's face was troubled at his own mention of stock thieving. This term had been used about these people, the Fancher Train stood accused of thievery in all the southern settlements. But, in view of his own judgment of these men, Hamblin was inclined to the feeling that there must have been misunderstanding; at the least, gross exaggeration. He had seen the size of their spreading herds—that they would bother to steal seemed ridiculous.

"You had any trouble, back up the line?" the Mormon asked. "Not with Injuns—I mean with our people."

Jed's glance was quickly understanding. The word had been passed ahead, then, like he'd figured it would be. He decided to tell Hamblin the whole story, he liked and trusted the sober man. He recounted the entire goat incident, freely acknowledging his own part in it.

"But young Barker wanted to pay Sister Wyatt," he added, "they felt mighty grateful. I rode over and left her a bag of hard money—more'n the goat was worth but the Barkers wanted it that way."

Jacob nodded, he could see how the thing had come about and regretted the exaggeration. "And the other thing—the man McKenzie tried to arrest?"

"McLean." Jed shook his head, feeling a surge of the

same graveling anger as he thought of the highhanded Bishop McKenzie. "Hell, Hamblin," he said, "this McLean is too young to be Hector McLean and too old to be his son—and McKenzie could see that with his own eyes. Cap'n Fancher hired McLean on at Springfield, Missouri, and Parley Pratt was done in about the middle of May in Arkansas—near Fort Smith. By the middle of May the train was beyond Independence. Any way you take it, this kid couldn't a had nothin' to do with it."

Hamblin's gaze had been steady on the scout's face. He nodded. "I believe you," he said simply, "although the report we had was very different."

"Shouldn't have been—we give McKenzie the straight of it—but the bishop was already riled when he rode into camp, and with an armed posse. He didn't want to hear reason, he just wanted to shove these folks around. If I hadn't throwed down on him first he'd a took McLean and God knows what would have come of it for we'd a had to gone after him. Gunplay and killin', most likely."

Hamblin agreed soberly. "I know McKenzie. He's, well, apt to judge hastily at times." Jed's grin crooked at this mercifully temperate description of the ornery bishop.

"Cap'n Fancher has made a ruling since then," Jed said, "for all in the train to leave the settlers alone. We haven't been able to buy grain, though, and it's playin' hell with the mules. The teams are gonna have a bad time on the desert—just grazin'."

Jacob's expression was seriously concerned. "I don't believe you will be able to buy grain at all," he admitted, "the people have been counseled to store what they harvest. They have usually sold their surplus to the wagon trains, the money has been welcome. But you won't be able to buy now—they will obey counsel."

"Well, lackin' grain," Jed said, "we've got to find a place to lay over—pasture place. Get the teams and stock fed and rested up before we tackle the Mojave. You know of a likely place?"

Jacob felt strongly that a duty lay here, this wagon

train had been victimized by conditions that were not of their making and also had been unjustly maligned in reputation. "Yes," he said, "give me your map." He stretched the rough map on his knee and traced with a pointing finger. "Here is a big valley between the mountains," he said, "fine pasture, and near the trail. Up here, at the north end, I have built a rock house. My wife, Rachel, and children are there now. The meadow stretches south for several miles. Good deep grass, plenty of grazing for all your stock. There is water, a big spring. This is my property, Smith, and no one will contest your right to be there—camp as long as you like."

Jed was smiling broadly. "Well, say now, Hamblin, that's fine—we can pay well."

Jacob brushed this aside. "The grass is there, I have no use for it this season, you are welcome. I only ask that you stop at the house and tell Rachel that I gave permission for you to camp in the south part of the pasture near the spring. Give her my greetings, say that I am well and in good spirits."

When Hamblin and the chiefs left, it was with a feeling of good will on both sides. The Mormon's solid friendliness was gratefully accepted, appreciated.

Jacob's thoughts, too, were cheerful. His steps quickened as he thought of Priscilla waiting for him at his fire. They traveled now to Salt Lake City so that they might make their covenants in the temple, she was to be his wife. She waited for him by the fire and she had changed into a white dress. She seemed to the man like a pale, swaying lily, the eyes raised to his were shy and yet warm and glad. Inarticulate with his joy in her, the sober man could only look into the girl's delicate face. Then he took her small hand in his and led her to sit beside him in the firelight.

There was also one who waited for Kanosh. But in deep shadow, and this one did not see fit to make his presence known to Jacob, the peacemaker.

Kasota, brother-in-law to the chief, Kanosh, had ridden hard to bring evil news. Long after dark Sally and her son had managed to drag themselves into the Indian camp. They were in pitiable condition. The boy would wear a ragged scar from his brow to his jawbone as long as he lived. The woman would not speak, Kasota reported. It had been her son who had sobbed out the terrible story of how the two white men had come, calling out as friends, and then of how they had dealt with the woman and child. Used the whip on them both. And then dragged Sally, the wife of Kanosh, into the bushes, where each had used her so brutally that she lay unconscious for many hours.

A stillness was on Kanosh as he listened. His eyes were sightlessly fixed, staring. When Kasota had finished, the chief turned his head and looked at him and his eyes were tortured and sick. Then fury possessed his strong body, his big hands tore at the shirt as though he strangled for air. He ripped the cloth, tore it from him, and flung the shreds away. The deep chest swelled, his whole body distending with the passion of his anger. Lips drawn back from his strong teeth, he snarled like a vicious animal, his eyes had narrowed into glinting, fanatical slits. He strode back and forth as though he could not bear to stay still, his heavy hands clenching and unclenching.

When he halted at last before the grimly silent messenger there remained no shred of the white man's peaceful influence in the Pahvant's swift reversion to primitive savagery. The storm had passed through him and it was the controlled stern voice of the chief which spoke. "I send greeting to my wife, Sally," he said, "I shall not visit her and witness her shame. Have purification ceremonies done for her at once. Take my son to the Mormonie doctor in the town of Fillmore." He paused for a moment and put his hand heavily on Kasota's broad shoulder. "I will go on to this council with Brother Brigham," he said, "but you, Kasota, take a few picked warriors and follow this train. Do not lose them for one hour. Do what you will to annoy them, but do not give battle—that I will lead myself. I will return soon and ride out at the head of my warriors. It may be that we must wait until the wagon train has traveled out of Mormonie country. But, if need be, I will follow them to the very sands of the great western sea!" Kanosh gestured strongly, his body was restless with inaction, but when he spoke again his voice was gentler, the pain in it was evident. "Place your hand on my son's shoulder and give him his father's message: That I, Kanosh, take pride in his wound—for it is on his face as he defended his mother. Tell him of his father's many scars and how the wounds were taken, and that there are none on his back." His eagle face hardened, as did his deep voice. "And this message to my wife, Sally—that I have said it—there will be much blood shed of the white men in this train, because of this day, and many scalps!"

Kanosh did not sleep; he sought the solitude of a hilltop where he remained until dawn. His brooding, ominous gaze never leaving the Fancher Train. He had not divulged his evil tidings to Jacob Hamblin, for he did not want to hear the soothing palliatives which would flow from the facile tongue of the peacemaker. This was a tribal thing and he wanted no interference from the Mormons. It would be settled Pahvant-fashion and not in the new, Mormonie way.

Near the dying fire that night, Jed had spread his map for Captain Fancher. "Jacob Hamblin showed me a place where we can lay over for that rest and feed the animals need," he said. His finger traced the wavering line that marked the trail.

"Here, just off the trail a little, he's got a mountain ranch—south of that is a long valley, plenty of good meadow grass and a big spring. Hamblin says it's a right pleasant place to rest, cool, it's high in the mountains. We can rest and refit there, stay as long as we like. Jacob Hamblin named the place Mountain Meadows."

# CHAPTER XI

The horse herd could be hard to handle at times. Ever since the addition of the red roan stallion, which David had named Washakie, there had been contention. Ebony King resented the presence of the young stud and lost no opportunity to challenge him. The usual cause of uproar was Melissa's sorrel mare, who was not above flaunting her attractions beneath the flaring nostrils of either or both her swains.

After several violent clashes between the jealous studs David had put the King on a lead line behind the wagon. The big black traveled balkily along, smoldering with resentment over his banishment from the herd.

The train neared the small Mormon settlement of Beaver, winding tortuously between the steep foothills of the stupendous Wasatch Range, encircled by craggy heights of forbiddingly dark volcanic rock. The lower slopes were sparsely dotted with cedars and sage, tall pines dark-penciled the ascending heights. It was desolately wild country and they were presently surprised to find themselves passing cultivated fenced fields, the chief crop of which appeared to be corn.

With the King absent, young Washakie grew bolder, ventured to nip the mare's haunch. Jane would shriek like an insulted old maid, lash out at him with her heels, and gallop away, exciting the other horses to run. This type of commotion happened frequently and David's temper had grown short; he wore out his most lurid vocabulary on the skittish mare.

Ebony King, whose black velvet ears were ever pointed toward the herd, became rearingly obstreperous every time he heard her whistling shriek.

The train had just passed between two cornfields, the road trailing dustily betwixt roughly zigzagging fences fashioned from trimmed saplings stacked at angles. The herders closed in to funnel the horse herd through the narrow pass between the fields. The young stallion crowded the mare, nipping at her. Jane's offended shriek was instant and loud. She reared and pawed, took off, romping and kicking through the startled herd.

Up ahead, in the wagon train, the King heard her and reared back suddenly on his haunches, all the strength of his thick neck tugging against the lead rope. The rope held but the halter strap beneath the bony jaw gave. With a despising shake of his head the King was free and galloping furiously toward the herd, which was plunging toward him.

He breasted it like a swimmer diving through high breakers. The horses veered before his charge, opening a path. Jane and Washakie were in the center of the bobbing mass and Jane swerved away from the approaching juggernaut. Washakie did not see the King until the furious black was almost upon him. He dodged vainly, the heavy shoulder caught him and the smaller horse rolled. He was back on his feet swiftly, cat haunches knotted with curving muscle, teeth bared, ears laid back, ready to give battle. But he was crowded against the fence and the King's cleaverlike hoofs slashed at him repeatedly. The black suddenly whirled, presented his huge hindquarters, the back hoofs struck together with thudding force. The roan was caught broadside, he rolled into and over the sapling fence, which collapsed under his weight. The black followed him into the cornfield, screaming and striking.

Jane fled through the wide gap that opened in the fence and the herd swept after her, pouring into the cornfield, flattening the tall stalks as they spread. The corn was tall, heavy with brown-fringed ears, the crop had been about ready to harvest.

David managed to drive his mount between Washakie and the murderously intent King. The smaller stallion got somewhat shakily to his feet and sped for refuge in the plunging herd.

David's furious bellow carried to the scattered herders. "Damn it—hurry up, get these nags out of this corn!" The herders had trouble, for the horses felt like romping and whenever they paused, it was to strip a mouthful of the succulent green corn. The field, which had recently been irrigated, was soft and muddy. Some of the horses slipped, floundered around, breaking and flattening the corn.

David took the halter from his horse and was letting out notches to fit it onto the King, who plunged around him in snorting circles, held in by a short rope. The stallion was still blustering, his nostrils flared, his big head kept turning, his eyes seeking the mare. David worked fretfully at the halter, hindered by his antics, and was cursing futilely as Jed trotted up on Palouse. Melissa was astride behind him, the King's halter in her hand. The two grinned coldheartedly at David's appearance of near apoplexy.

Melissa slid off Palouse's haunches; she wore her pants. "Where's Jane?" she asked hastily, to forestall David's reproof. He had frowned at her skirtless state. His face was tired and smeared with dirt. "That damned little slut! She started the ruckus with her silly screeching and then took off across the cornfield like a grizzly was on her tail. She jumped the fence yonder, and went off up that hill."

Melissa's grin faded at this. She stared worriedly at the cedar-dotted hill to the west. "If she's decided to run," she fretted, "it'll take the King to catch her." She turned to her brother. "Put your saddle on him—"

"I can't chase off after the mare till we get this damn mess cleared."

"I'm going after her."

"You can't ride the King out in open country," David snapped irritably, "not riled up like he is."

"Oh, pooh, David"—Melissa shrugged—"don't be an old granny—"

Jed chuckled. "I was sort of figgerin' to tag along," he said. David's glare at his sister was mollified; he considered. "Well, but hold him in," he said. "He'll be fisty as hell."

Jed nodded. "I'll see she does," he said, "and likely the

mare has stopped just over the hill, anyhow. It's pretty steep; she's likely had her run and is grazing on the far slope."

David cinched his saddle on the King, shortened the stirrups for Melissa, and turned back to the business at hand. The crop was all but ruined, he could see they were going to have to hunt up the owner and make it good. Some Mormon was going to be right put out when he saw what had happened.

The King was still snorting, traveling sideways, throwing his hoofs high, his silken tail an arching plume over his sable haunches. He flung his big head constantly, fighting the restraint on the bit.

Jed eyed him with amusement. "Don't let the big brute take the bit in his teeth," he warned, "he's just liable to run off with you—like that other time——"

"You mean after you spooked him, Mr. Smith?" Melissa glanced affectionately at Jed. "And don't you worry about me—I can handle the King or any other horse!"

Jed's grin agreed. The slenderly strong arms controlled the mighty stallion, she swayed easily in the saddle but her legs gripped his barrel strongly, she was like a small, unshakable burr on his back. They ascended the hill to its crest. Beyond, at the bottom of a narrow canyon, a small stream wound between tall willows. "She's likely down there in the willers," Jed said, "had herself a drink and croppin' grass."

Jane's trail approached the stream. But here Jed uttered a startled grunt, pointing. Moccasin tracks came from the willows, were interposed with the hoofprints, which became deep as though the mare had plunged in fright. A few steps on, she had been halted and when the tracks continued there were no further moccasin tracks. Their owner had mounted and she was ridden away, fast.

As Jed read the story told by the tracks, Melissa's face paled, the small bridge of freckles stood out across her nose. "An Injun! But, Jed, we haven't seen any Injuns around for days and days——"

"That don't ever mean there ain't some around," Jed

said, "you only see Injuns when they wanta be seen. And a redskin is ridin' Jane this minute." His eyes ranged thoughtfully. The narrow valley wound off between foothills toward the south and west. He glanced at the sky; the sun was lowering toward the craggy horizon, it was late afternoon. "He can't have got too far, yet," he said, "and he's got to be caught up with before dark or it's no go."

Melissa fidgeted angrily. Was he just going to sit there muttering? Why didn't they get started? Just as she was about to explode at him he spoke. "Can the King outrun Jane?"

"Oh yes—he's the fastest of all the horses—he's never been beaten——"

Jed was dismounting, pulling his rifle from its saddle scabbard. "You take Palouse," he ordered, "and get on back to the train. Tell David. I'll take the King and get on after the mare."

Melissa was sputtering protestingly. "Now, listen, Lissy," Jed said, "you can't go. I don't know how long this'll take or how it'll be. That Injun might have already met up with more of his people. Now do like I told you."

Melissa's eyes were resentful as she watched him lengthen the stirrups on the King, shorten them on Palouse. She mounted the roan and Jed swatted his rump, watched them head back up the hill.

The big black shied, his body gathered and trembled as the scout's weight settled flat in the saddle. The feel of this man was different. David and Melissa had a lighter, balanced seat and the King shook his head disapprovingly, fighting the bit. But there was no mistaking the strong grip of the long legs about his barrel, the sure mastery with which the man swung the stallion's head around. The big horse shot obediently forward, aware at once of who was in charge.

On the hilltop Melissa pulled Palouse in and faced around. Her lower lip jutted angrily, her face was rebelliously set. She was just sick and tired, she thought, of being sent off like a small child when anything exciting was about to happen. Men were so disgustingly cautious. And always hogging the fun so they could strut back and brag about it.

Jed and the King were nearing the end of the first canyon which angled at the mouth of a narrow cut off to the west. They passed out of sight as she watched. Palouse stood lazily hipshot, his ears cocked slightly back toward his rider, waiting for an indication as to what she wanted. It was as if the stocky gelding, gauging her indecision, was agreeable to accommodate, regardless.

Melissa tossed her head defiantly. If she followed, Jed wouldn't send her back alone, he'd *have* to let her go along. She lifted the rein and Palouse went briskly back down the hill, crossed the stream and settled into a mile-eating lope along the tracks. She rode to the mouth of the branching canyon and paused irresolutely. It was very still and wild-looking, as though no man had come this way since the world began. But the tracks wound on through the high sagebrush and she followed them. The canyon turned and twisted as it headed west; weird-looking rock formations stood intently listening on the steep hillsides. She nudged Palouse with her heels and they traveled faster. She began to glance around, back over her shoulder and to each side, peering nervously at the dark shadows cast by the hulking black rocks. She felt very much alone, and the enveloping ridges covered the floor of the canyon with gray shadow. It was so quiet that she was startled when the faint wind murmured through the sage.

Jed had emerged from the second canyon onto the slightly rising floor of a wide, sagebrush-strewn mesa which extended far toward the west and south. Gnarled cedars stood forlornly at intervals, there was cactus here, too—the symmetrical burst of the Spanish dagger yucca and a Joshua tree now and again.

There was movement far out on the mesa—it was the bright sorrel and her Indian rider. Jed settled his hat firmly, his eyes, on his quarry ahead, were calculating.

"All right, now, you big black devil," he muttered to the King, "let's see what you've got!"

He lifted and loosened the rein as his moccasined heels dug sharply into the black's flanks. The startled stallion, realizing the sudden freeing of his head, hurtled into an instant pounding run.

Jed had—quite matter-of-factly—chosen to ride the black for the reason that he could overhaul the mare in less time. He had not anticipated the deep thrill which shot through him now at the powerful response from the great horse. He became conscious of the gathering and releasing of the enormous muscles as the long legs thrust out in tremendous strides. He marveled at the flowing ease of action, the flawless, almost gliding recovery. No guidance seemed necessary, the big hoofs swiftly threaded their own way between sage and cactus. The horse ran as though he had a private purpose and Jed figured that the stallion had scented the mare and was furiously bent on overtaking her.

The heady excitement of the chase was an old story to the scout. But never had he ridden such a horse as this—who flew like the desert wind, blurring the objects they passed. Never had he encountered this peculiarly headlong yet controlled fantastically long stride. For it was controlled, the black still ran smoothly; for all his speed there was something yet retained, the final mighty effort had not been released.

Jed felt a rush of joyous exultancy that only horsemen can know, coupled with confidence in the outcome of the race. For no horse that he had ever seen could equal this black stallion when he ran free on a nearly flat course, as now. King he was, and well named.

The mesa was sandy and dry. For a little while the great hoofs made small sound, but as the slope lifted, the ground became harder and the Indian heard the rapid drumming thunder of pursuit. He turned and with startled eyes took in the horse and rider coming swiftly across the mesa after him.

It was Kasota astride the bare back of the bright sorrel mare. Obedient to his chief, he had kept the wagon train under close surveillance, waiting his chance to make mischief. The mare had walked right into his eager hands. But he had not counted on this immediate pursuit. That she had been missed promptly he well understood, for now that he had ridden her, he knew that she was a prize. She was beautiful, strong and fiery, as fine an animal as Kasota had ever seen. He had every intention of keeping her.

But he did not wish an encounter with the one who rode so hotly in pursuit, for the man was surely carrying a gun. Kasota had only a hunting bow slung across one bronze shoulder. He was confident, however, that with their present lead, the mare could run away from the other horse. He lifted her into a driving run. She answered to his heels and hand with a quick burst of speed. Sleek belly flattening near the ground, her beautiful tapered nose stretched, her mane flew back in his face like tongues of bright flame. She gave him all she had.

And Kasota, wild desert horseman, knew—like Jed—the marveling joyousness in the feel of the fine, gallant horseflesh beneath him. He knew—as if he watched—the look of the flowing, surging muscles which co-ordinated in a perfection of symmetrical rhythm.

But his confidence was short-lived. He realized that the mare, fine as she was, could not outrun the black, whose thunderous hoofs pounded ever louder. He glanced back over his shoulder. The black loomed nearer and he could now discern the rider hunched forward over the big neck, swaying with the momentum of the enormous strides. He rode like a growth, was one with the horse. An ominous growth, for the dark line of a long rifle extended on one side. And Kasota knew that the distance between them would shortly lessen to shooting range.

The mesa stretched out on all sides in unbroken flatness. There were no gullies or canyons near—no way to dodge, hide from the relentless pursuer. The sage was high, haunch-high to the mare, but there was no possible concealment for her. Kasota dug his heels desperately into her flanks, forcing the last effort of speed from her. Valiantly she answered, surged yet more swiftly. But before many strides he knew it was hopeless, she could not maintain this gait. Her breathing had roughened, foam flew from the gaping mouth, soon her legs would falter under the prolonged strain. He could ride her till she dropped and then hide himself in the sage, ambush the man who followed. It would kill the mare, but the white man would not have her, either.

But Kasota, knowing bitterly that he was losing the race, felt an odd reluctance to destroy the gallantly beautiful animal who still ran with all her great heart. For it was heart alone, now, that sustained her stride. The race had already been too long.

Melissa had reached the edge of the mesa and saw the faraway moving dot that was Jane. And the larger blur that was Jed and the King. The stocky roan loped along, following the deep, running tracks of the two horses ahead, swerving from brush and cactus spines, needing no guidance from his rider's hands. Melissa dropped the reins on his neck, gave her rapt attention to the swiftly moving drama far down the mesa.

Jed had advanced to within shooting range of the flying sorrel but he held his fire, for the crouching Indian was almost indistinguishable from the copper-hued horse; he was afraid of hitting the mare. He rode on, undecided, the King's mighty strides inexorably shortened the distance, neared the straining sorrel.

Jed saw the mare swerve and falter, for a moment he thought she would go down. His glance was hindered as they swerved past a cedar tree and when he looked again the mare ran alone, her rider had thrown himself off into the sage. Her stride broken, she pounded bewilderedly on, slowing, her gait rough and unsteady. She was spent but she could not stop. She ran on staggeringly, finally slowed to a grunting, whimpering halt. Her head was down, her breathing came hoarsely flecked with foam, her sweat-caked barrel beat in and out like frantic bellows. Her forefeet were widely spread, propped, but she barely stood, so deep were the convulsive shudders that shook her frame.

Jane did not raise her head as Ebony King plunged to a dust-raising stop beside her. Nor did she answer the stormy whicker that burst from him. His great head lowered, he inspected her, his flaring nostrils inhaled her sweat-strong odor, he smelled her over thoroughly, possessively. A deep, rumbling whinny broke from him, he lifted a big hoof and pawed restively at her lack of response. Jed felt a great relief as Jane lifted her head slightly, a weary whisper of a whicker answered the stallion. He had been afraid that she would collapse, but the shudders were lessening in violence, she would likely be all right.

The scout had dismounted hastily, so as not to provide a tall target and peered cautiously in all directions, his eyes combing the sage for the whereabouts of the horse thief. He did not expect, however, to see either the Indian or signs of movement. What he needed to guard against now was ambush. Jed had seen that he carried a bow, not a rifle, but a well-aimed arrow was as deadly as a rifle bullet. The Indian would have to show himself clear of the sage for the fraction of a second he let fly an arrow and if Jed kept his rifle cocked, he had an even chance of dropping him first. The scout calculated that the return, leading the exhausted mare, would be the risky time, for the redskin would circle and wait for him, more than likely. But Jed would veer away from the trail, make the varmint show himself.

Jed noticed that there was little sweat on the King. He placed his hand beneath the stallion's proud crest. The horse was warm but not hot. The wide nostrils flared redly, the agitated muscles flexed, rippled with every restless shift of his hoofs; he was still excited but the great horse was only just warmed up—he had not been near having out his run.

"You big, iron-jawed brute." There was deep affection in Jed's tone, to which the stallion responded, shoving his hard head against the man's shoulder for an instant and then swinging it back to regard his ladylove with unwinking obsessiveness. There was disapproval in the King's intent regard of her, and Jed's grin crooked at the stallion's indignation. He reflected that it was similar to his own feeling for Melissa—concern, chronic disapproval, complete infatuation. The girl and her fractious mare had much in common.

Keeping a wary eye out, Jed pulled off his neckerchief and began to rub the salty white sweat caking on the sorrel's flanks and shoulders. He had gone around to the other side of her when a flicker of movement caught his eyes at the same time that he heard the faint drumming of hoofs. He stared down the slope of the mesa, squinting his eyes against the harsh rays of the lowering sun, and began to curse softly, vehemently. Melissa and Palouse were approaching at a gallop far down through the high sage. He marveled that he had not seen them before—she was nearly halfway across—but realized that they could have been shielded from his view by intermittent clumps of cedar and Joshua trees. And his gaze had been directed nearer, watching for the Indian.

Jed's face set angrily. Wouldn't the headstrong little spitfire ever learn to do as she was told? But his anger gave way to leaping, convulsive fear.

Down the mesa, off to the side, he had caught a glimpse of movement in the sage. He groaned aloud, for a dark figure was swiftly nearing the path of the girl and the horse. The Indian was running, crouchingly, head down, angling to intercept them. And Jed was too far away for a rifleshot to be effective.

He waved both arms, frantically signaling for her to turn back—and realized immediately his mistake in waving. Her eyes had found him, she was waving gaily, she wouldn't be keeping a lookout—she would not see the Indian's approach.

Melissa smiled, seeing Jed wave. He wasn't going to be mad then, she thought with satisfaction, for he had waved to direct her straight to him.

And then her heart plunged sickeningly. The Indian

sprang from the sage directly in Palouse's path, his arms reaching to catch the bridle. He came out of cover with the swiftness of a leaping cougar, his bronze hide rippling with muscle, his teeth bared and white like the fangs of a snarling beast.

Melissa screamed, every muscle jerking with sudden horror. Palouse felt the convulsive clutch of her thighs as she shrieked and, to the well-trained horse, this composed a signal. It was the way in which Jed had hurled the sturdy gelding into many a charge.

His ears flattened viciously, he snatched the bit between his teeth and hurtled forward, not swerving or dodging as Kasota had expected. The hard, square chest struck the Indian with terrific impact and the man went down beneath the cleaving hoofs. He had caught hold of the rein with one hand but he went limp and was flung aside to roll over and over in the dust.

Palouse did not slacken pace after his vicious onslaught, but continued on at a pounding, headlong run. Melissa, sobbing, swayed in the saddle. The reins still lay on the gelding's neck, she rode hanging on to the saddle horn as he flashed through the sage.

Jed had mounted the King in a flying leap that startled the black forward like a projectile. But even as they tore down the trail, he saw with a surge of relief that the gelding, with the girl still in the saddle, was coming unhindered toward him. Jed had seen Palouse rear slightly as he plunged into the charge and now he grimly surmised what had happened. Jed's suddenly released breath was a deep sob.

When the two horses met in the sage Jed was down and had Melissa's shaking little form in his arms in one lunging sweep. She clung to him, her nose buried against his chest. "You all right, Lissy?" His voice was shaken, he held her out, stopped to peer anxiously into her face, which was covered with dust and smeared with tears. She was still trembling violently but she managed a nod, tried for a weak grin. "I was just scared," she admitted.

Seeing that she was, indeed, unharmed, Jed's sickened

fear gave way to exasperation. But it was not the time for a reckoning, he had a matter to attend to. "Stay here," he said, "I'll finish off that Injun you run down."

Melissa had gotten to Jed safely, she felt supremely brave now. "I'll go with you," she said instantly and turned, put her foot in Palouse's stirrup.

This absolute disregard of his orders a second time kindled Jed's smoldering wrath, his control snapped. His long arm shot out, caught Melissa's shoulder, spun her around. She looked up at him, surprised and questioning. He slapped her hard, open-handed, across one cheek. He leaned down to glare right in her shocked and unbelieving face.

"Goddamn it!" he hissed, "*will* you do as you're told, just once—or do I have to break every bone in your stupid head?" He shoved her from him so hard that she reeled against Palouse. "Now, damn you, you *stay right here!*"

He flung himself on the King and galloped off. Melissa stared after him, stunned and motionless. Her mouth quivered, her hand sought her cheek, tears left new rivulets down her face. Her jaw felt as though he'd nearly knocked it off. She swallowed sobbingly and took off her neckerchief, mopped at her face. Her mouth steadied at the pain in her face, began to set angrily. Resentment of his brutality rose chokingly, grew with every passing moment. She mounted Palouse, thinking to ride to where Jane stood, head down, quiet as a dusty bronze statue. But even in the act of turning the gelding Melissa pulled him up again. The damn, big bully, she thought furiously, he'd said to stay here, and he'd likely enjoy the excuse to hit her again. Her chin tilted defiantly. He'd pay for this, she promised herself, she'd show him! Nevertheless, she obediently waited, watching with concern as Jed and the King slowed down to approach cautiously the fallen Indian.

Jed dismounted, rifle at the ready, warily watching the motionless form. Kasota lay in an abandoned-looking dusty heap on his face. There was blood on him in several places—under his head, likely from a crushed nose. It was hard to tell if he was badly hurt, his skull didn't look to be cracked and his limbs lay naturally. He was breathing, but unconscious; he did not stir.

Jed stared at him, undecided. He felt he ought to put a bullet through his head and be done with it. But in the shape he was in now he certainly offered no further threat. Jed's trigger finger held, too, because he was aware that many redskins would callously have ridden the mare to her death rather than give her up. This warrior had shown himself to be a horseman with whom Jed felt much in common—he had valued the life of the mare even though he could not keep her.

Abruptly the scout decided to spare the man to the extent of leaving him where he lay, to take his chances of getting back to his people. He put foot in the stirrup and swung up, rode deliberately away from the quiet form of Kasota.

With the sorrel wearily plodding on a lead line, they set out back across the mesa. Melissa's eyes were cold and averted, she would not speak to Jed. He made no attempt to appease her, for he was still angry and he had no intentions of apologizing. So the two rode in self-conscious silence through a splendor of sunset bathing the western range with a tapestried scarlet and gold. The air was suddenly cool, sweet with the aromatic sage and piñon.

Jed turned his head and surveyed Melissa's disdainful profile. She felt his stare but she did not meet it, her chin lifted a further notch. The cheek he had slapped was still a smarting red. Jed's irritation boiled again. "You can just set there," he blurted, "and nurse your damned temper all you're a mind to!" and added, threateningly, "Any time you get so damn fool notional you're gonna get slapped around like any other smart-aleck youngun!"

She did not deign to answer, her mouth curved willfully downward. "You little fool." Jed's voice held anger in direct proportion to the recollection of his sickened fear for her. "*You* could be laying off there in the sage instead of that Injun, you know that? He had a knife on him, he could easy have stuck it in you—or drug you offa Palouse—and maybe you'd been tromped to death! And all because you won't mind, ever! I won't have it, Melissa!"

At his peremptory, possessive tone she turned her head and glared at him, shocked at what he had said, but still angry. "I won't take you with me no more," he said, "until you learn to mind your betters!"

Now she did speak. "My *betters!*" she flared, eying him up and down with furious scorn. "Who do you think you are, anyway, Jed Smith?" She tossed her head, her laughter was brittle, shrill. "My betters—huh!" Jed realized hastily that the term had been unfortunate, he'd meant "elders" but he was given no chance to change it. Once unleashed, Melissa's tongue spat venomously. "I'll tell you just what I think of *you*, Mr. Jed Smith—you're part Injun, that's what—and you can just get on back to your greasy squaws that'll take your beatings and still kiss your feet every day and twice on Sunday!"

Jed could not control the grin that twitched at this and her eyes shot flame at his amusement. "I've had me a bellyful," she announced, "of your bossin' and bullyin'. I don't want anything to do with you—at all, ever, any more." She all but flounced, sitting on her horse. She spoke once more when they neared the encampment, before she rode away toward the wagons.

"And you don't need to come crawlin' around for supper, tonight, or any other night! You can fix your own vittles, till you can get a squaw to do for you!" She rode off without looking back.

Jed's face was a study. He'd seen her mad before, but not this mad. She'd always left the way a little open, come halfway in the making up. He re-examined the cause of her anger, the course of the day's events, studying seriously to see if he had been in the wrong. He was forced to shake his head ruefully, knowing he'd do the same again. You just couldn't let a woman go on running around all featherbrained and silly, taking risks and asking for trouble. It was dangerous, you couldn't seem to make the greenhorns appreciate the need for constant caution when it came to dealing with redskins.

Jed's jaw set stubbornly; let her boil! Be damned if he was going to back down one inch, let her just see how she liked it without him coming around.

## CHAPTER XII

When David remarked Jed's absence at supper Melissa reluctantly told him the story. David was furious at her. "By God, Lissy!" he exploded, "Jed was right—you'd oughta been tanned till you couldn't set down! I've a good mind to finish it, myself!" He stormed around the fire, threw his plate down, glared at her. "And you don't need to set and sulk either—you've got only yourself to thank—and likely lost the most man you'll ever have a chance at. I can't see Jed Smith wantin' to bother none with a silly kid that plays the fool ever chance she gets! As if we'd not already had enough trouble this day——"

David's temper had been stretched to the breaking point before Melissa had added to it. The owner of the ruined field had shown up before they'd rounded up the horses. There'd been two other men with him and they'd all been armed. For a while there it had looked like they were mad enough to start shooting.

The owner's name was William Leany, a gaunt, overworked-looking man. "Money ain't gonna make up for that there corn," he said bitterly in answer to David's offer to reimburse him. "That there crop was my winter store. I can't buy none—nobody's got any to spare."

David had offered cattle, horses, but the man had refused each with the same hostility. It was apparent that he preferred a grudge over an unpaid debt. Some of the men from the train had come up and were listening to the odd debate. Sol Ward and Jake Tibbetts stood whispering together, smirkingly enjoying the Mormon's predicament. They seemed to think David had pulled a clever trick.

David noticed the odd expression that slid over Leany's thin face. It had been bitterly angry, suddenly it seemed drawn and horrified. He broke into what David was saying. "You people are the Fancher Train?"

"Yes." David stared at Leany curiously; the man looked actually sick.

"Some of you from Missouri?"

"Some of us."

"Those men——?" A nod of his head indicated the group in which Sol and Jake stood, now with their heads together. Sol was obviously telling them a joke, they were chortling. David glanced toward them.

"Yeah, Sol is, anyway, the one with the red beard. I think Jake, the fat one, is from Illinois." He regarded the man, Leany, puzzledly. "You know Sol, maybe?" he asked into the uneasy silence.

Leany's haunted gaze jerked back to David. He stared blankly for a moment as if trying to recall what his business with him had been. "No," he said and pulled his horse around. With no further word or glance the three rode away toward the town. Leany beat his horse into a jolting gallop. Bouncing up and down in the saddle, coattails flapping, he rode as if the devil was after him.

David pushed back his hat, wiped the dirty sweat from his face. "I'll be damned," he said wearily, "if these Mormons ain't peculiar! Me trying to pay him more than his whole patch was worth—acreage thrown in—and he ups and looks like he's seen a spook and rides off with nary a word!"

William Leany did, indeed, feel specter-driven. A thing out of the pain-ridden past had reared suddenly and was like a nightmare. The gaunt farmer headed straight for his bishop's house.

That sturdy man had just finished his supper and greeted him affably. But at the strained urgency exhibited by his visitor the bishop ushered Leany into his office and closed the door. "What is it, William?" His sober look was concerned.

"Bishop." Leany's haggard face worked, he had trouble with his words, saliva appeared at the corners of his mouth. "That wagon train that ruined my corn—they're the Fanchers!"

The bishop nodded, the word had reached him in advance of the train's approach. "Did they settle for your corn?" he asked.

Leany's words crowded feverishly from his shaking mouth, "My corn don't matter, Bishop, compared to what—just wait till I tell you what——" He was almost gibbering.

The bishop's face tightened. What, he thought, has this train of renegade trash pulled now? "Bishop," Leany went on, "what we've heard has been a passel of little stuff—stock thievin'—tormentin' Injuns—givin' them an excuse to steal—as if *they* ever needed an excuse——"

"William!" The bishop's voice was sharp. "Pull yourself together, you're not making sense."

"That man"—Leany obeyed—"this man—I seen him with my own two eyes and he's the same one. I'd a known him if it was a thousand years a'back, so help me God!"

The bishop took Leany's thin arm in a firm grip. "William," he said sternly, "*who* did you see?"

"In the Fancher Train, a man with a red beard, a big man—they said he's from Missouri, too——" At the mystification, showing the beginnings of impatience, in his listener's face, Leany made an effort to clarify himself. "Listen, I saw that man—*twice* I saw him—the first time *in the mob at Haun's Mill and again in the mob at the jail in Carthage!*"

The bishop's rotund figure stiffened, his eyes showed his shock. "You sure, William?"

"Sure as I'm standing here. I'd swear on a stack of Bibles to it!"

"Haun's Mill was nigh twenty years back, William—a man would change a lot——"

"He has changed, aged, some." Leany's voice held certainty. "He's fat in the belly and his beard ain't so bright red, but he's still hulkin' and sneerin', just like then. Oh, he's changed some, Bishop, but I swear by the blood of the Prophet that this is the same man—for a knife don't change!"

"Knife?"

Leany nodded. "A knife that he's wearin' this minute, and like—exactly like one I seen, at Haun's Mill." He wiped his mouth with the back of a grimy, shaking hand. "That day at Haun's Mill . . ." His words slowed, his eyes became haunted. Far back in his mind he saw once more that time of ultimate horror.

"When the mobbers rode down on us, that day, I jumped behind a picket fence, across the street from Brother Joseph Young's house"—the strange voice was halting, remembered terror convulsed his face—"I see this red-bearded man shoot down Sister Wade—Josh Wade's wife—and her expectin' a baby any minute. And then Wade come tearin' down the hill and I seen the redbeard gun him down and when he tried to get up he rode his horse over him. And then he got off and drove that knife into Wade. I was caught without my gun or I'd have—— I crawled back into the bushes and laid still, I knew I was a goner if they saw me. I had to lay there and listen to the screamin' and moanin'——" Leany's mouth hung open, he had fallen silent, paralyzed with remembered horror. When the voice continued it was with a sleepwalker's dulled slowness.

"They left when the sun went down and it was quiet and there was the smell of blood, rivers of blood in the dust. It made me sick and I vomited when I seen what was in the blacksmith shop. And my little brother Ben —he was ripped across the middle—a shotgun on him, they'd used. He was cut in half. I never knowed there was that much blood in the whole world——" The grieving voice paused to remember the pitiful boy's body, drained and still. "And we put him, my little brother, in that well with the others. No better than stinking carrion—the way we had to do—like carcasses of animals. And there they lay to this day——" Tired sobbing shook the voice. "And Isaac—the Leanys sealed their faith in blood that day, for Isaac had twenty-seven bullet holes in his clothes and four bullets left in his body—they just shot and shot—— Why he didn't die—— In pain, he's been, all these years, from the lead too deep to dig out. He near bled to death, but he lived, Isaac did, to tell it."

Leany's eyes had sunk back in his head, he tottered, seemed about to collapse. The bishop reached a comforting hand, was about to lead him to a couch, but Leany steadied, began to speak again.

"About that knife, Bishop"—his tone was clearer—"I helped carry Josh Wade in from the road where he fell. And that knife that the redbeard drove into him was still there, buried so deep we couldn't get it out, not then. A knife with a horn handle, silver leaves set in it. We all saw it—for all of us tried to get it out of him." He paused and his eyes were glitteringly cognizant, he had returned from the past. "I seen that knife when the redbeard put it in Josh Wade and today I seen a knife just like it on that big redbeard yonder in the Fancher Train, not an hour back! Not twenty feet from me, and when he turned I seen the knife on his hip. And I'd swear to God and by the blood of the Prophet that the same man made both knives!"

The bishop's face mirrored Leany's emotion. He, too, had endured unspeakable persecutions. He understood only too well and it was with difficulty that he controlled himself. For control this situation he must. His was the responsibility for every soul in the tiny wilderness settlement. He must calm this furious man, soothe him some way, avert violence.

"I believe you, William," he said, "but there's nothing we can do. There's no proof, except your word against his and he'd lie, deny it, of course."

"*I* don't need more proof," he said viciously, "I know what I seen and it's enough for me. I'm goin' to—"

The bishop interrupted him. "You are going to do nothing!" he said sharply, "you must stay clear of the Fancher Train!"

"The hell you say!" Leany's face was snarling. The bishop overlooked his disrespect, knowing how Leany felt, he felt scarcely less vengeful himself. But he could not allow this to get out of hand.

"William," he said soberly, "*think* a minute of how many rifles—armed men—we have here in Beaver? Not half as many as there would be in the wagon train! We know they're well armed and troublesome. They threw down on Bishop McKenzie when he was trying to do his duty as a peace officer. You want to start a shooting that could wind up like Haun's Mill *here?* No, William, our duty is to the women and children entrusted to us."

Leany was listening but his face was mutinous, protesting.

"I know," the bishop continued, "believe me, I know how you feel, but we can't risk it. I'll deal with this in the only way we can—tell the people at the train to stay out of our town. I'll do that, but further we can not go, weak as we are!"

Leany was breathing hard, his anger had transferred to the person of the bishop. His mouth was set determinedly. The bishop sighed, he hated to use his church position to enforce obedience. "Brother William." Leany was startled by the sudden pontifical authority in his voice. "This is an order from your bishop." He set a stern gaze on the gaunt, unwilling face, his tone underlined the words. "You stay clear away from this train, hear? I will not have you fomenting bloodshed for us all. I want to hear you say that you will not go near any member of the Fancher Train!"

Leany seemed unable to comprehend this attitude. "Bishop," he said, "catchin' up with the murderers in the train oughta be *church business*. I seen that man in the mob *at the Carthage jail!*" His fanatical eyes glowed with pain at the memory of that day. "He could have been the one that shot down the Prophet!" His voice became hushed. "I was there in Carthage with a letter for Brother Joseph—and I seen it all—I seen the Prophet come to the window and then there was this shot—and then they all commenced to shoot—why, this man—he's still got a knife like—he could still have the gun that shot the Prophet, too!"

The bishop nodded, confirming the possibility. "I know, William," he said gravely, "but it changes nothing. We cannot avenge his dear blood at the possible price of the women and children here. We are helpless to do it, now. I want your word that you will obey my counsel."

Leany stared in outraged, unyielding silence. Wordlessly he turned to the door. "William!" Peremptory authority stopped him, he turned. "Your word?" The Bishop's glance was strong, direly expectant. Leany stood still, his face worked, the silence grew taut with the straining of their two wills. Leany's gave way, his voice was low, almost strangled. "My word on it, Bishop."

A short time later the bishop and a group of his men, mounted on horses, approached the Fancher camp. Leany was not among them. Captain Fancher came to meet them, John Barker at his elbow. Noting their rifles, the captain somewhat dubiously invited them to get down. They paid no attention to the invitation.

In a flatly hostile manner the bishop warned that none from the train must approach the town. An armed guard ringed the settlement, he informed tersely, they had orders to shoot to kill.

Fancher was shocked and bewildered at this brutally put edict. "But, look here, we offered to pay for the corn —much more than it was worth. The owner just rode off. He wouldn't set a price. We'll pay, *now*—"

The bishop's eyes flared with scorn. "We don't want your dirty money, we don't want anything to do with any of you. It's not only the corn, as you well know. There are many other things"—his voice accused—"the latest report from the Indians, for one."

"Well, say, now, look here," Fancher was indignant, "that redskin stole a valuable mare—all we did was get her back!"

The bishop was puzzled, he'd had no word from Kasota's Pahvants about any trouble over horses. He shook his head. "Horses had nothing to do with the other thing," he said.

"What other thing?" Charley asked. "We ain't seen hide nor hair of Injuns till today, not since we camped at Corn Creek."

"Corn Creek! You had truck with Injuns—Pahvants—there at Corn Creek, you admit that?"

"Admit? How do you mean, admit? Sure, Kanosh and some of his people were at Corn Creek when we were!"

The bishop's nod was significant, judging, he stared with open hostility at the wagon captain. "Fancher"—he was ponderously bitter—"we're friends—brothers—to the red men and we want to keep it that way. We are surrounded by Indians—a hundred to one—but *we* treat them right and they're friendly to us. The Pahvants are a warrior tribe, and I won't have Kanosh and Kasota think we're friendly to the likes of you! So you'd best heed my warning: stay away from my town. My men will shoot on sight!"

The bishop stared at the listening group with loathing and lifted his eyes to encompass the whole of the wagon train in his scathing survey. He raised an arm, turned his horse. The mounted troop wheeled behind him, rode away into the night. The pounding of their horses' hoofs was the only sound in the fraught silence they left behind them.

Captain Fancher stared after them in furious indignation. "Well, for Chrissake," he said finally, "I do believe all of these Mormons is just plain crazy. Damned if I can make head nor tail of 'em—always accusin' about some damn thing that don't make sense—forever het up and mouthin' threats. I'll be damned glad to be out of their goddamned, Godforsaken country!" The peaceable man had been pushed to a degree of anger vastly unusual to him. This had proved to be just too much.

"I've took about all the pushin' around I'm goin' to," he announced, "the next goddamn bishop pokes his high nose into my camp is goin' to find me ready and waitin'. They want a fight, by God, we'll give it to 'em! I've had me a big bellyful of Mormons!"

Still engulfed in fury, Captain Fancher called his train council together and issued blunt orders. Orders that brought approving nods and respectful glances from Jed Smith and many others.

"From right this here minute," Fancher announced grimly, "every man and boy goes armed, night and day! The women and kids are to stay close by the train—no wanderin' around at all. And *no one* is to have any truck with any Mormon! I don't know what the hell it's all about, but I don't like the look of things. I want the guards doubled at night on the train and on the herds."

After giving his grudging word to the bishop William Leany had gone home but he had not stayed. He saddled his horse, put trail provender in the saddlebags, and rode out of town alone. He headed south on the emigrant road. The next settlement was Parowan, a small village completely enclosed in a high wall, with fortlike gates only to the east and the west. The emigrant road passed through the center of the fort.

Leany rode steadily throughout the night, stopping only to rest and water his horse. His mind dark with morbid thoughts, he brooded through the long hours of starlit stillness. The moon wheeled across the frosted heavens, her peaceful beauty completely disregarded by the seething, sullen man.

Off to the west a coyote sat back on his haunches, lifted a lonely nose to the moon. His mourning, yelping cry fled through the vast quiet. The plodding rider did not lift his head. But now there came another call in the night, a thin, sobbing wail that echoed and re-echoed eerily, to finally blend with the faint moaning of the night wind in the piñons. Leany's eyes raised watchfully at this call.

From under his hatbrim he uneasily surveyed the dark mountain wall. The shadowy heights seemed to hover, to wait threateningly.

"Funny"—his mutter was disturbed—"sounded like a timber wolf. And then, again, it didn't. Wasn't a coyote, that's for sure, but I never knowed the wolves to come down out of the heights this early in the season." He took his rifle from its saddle scabbard, checked the loading, and rode on with it balanced across the saddle horn.

It was near to noon when the weary horse and rider passed through the open gates of the fort town, Parowan. Leany rode directly to the cabin that housed Bishop Tarleton Lewis and his family. They were old friends, these two men.

Tarleton heard Leany's story out in shocked silence, which progressed to violent agitation.

"Haun's Mill!" His rumbling voice was a boiling pitch of memory. "They left me for dead—the mobbers—at Haun's Mill! And dead I would have been but for the blessed laying on of hands from the Prophet himself!" The two had retired to a separate room for privacy and now the man rose from his chair, walked restlessly back and forth, his hands clenched and unclenched.

"God knows how I have prayed"—his voice was like muted thunder, this man was a power in the pulpit—"we have all prayed for vengeance! We were driven, raped, murdered in Missouri! How many countless times have we not cried aloud to heaven for the dawning of the day of vengeance? Has God, at long last, seen fit to answer our prayers, to deliver our enemies into our hands?" The man's passion seemed about to overwhelm him.

Leany listened, drinking in the quenching concurrence with his own turmoil. For this relief he had come to Tarleton Lewis; he knew well the man's passionate personality.

"Did you"—Lewis calmed to direct a tense question—"did you see any others that you recognized besides the red-bearded murderer?"

Leany shook his head. "No," he said, "but after that I

didn't need to look for more! Not after McKenzie sent word about McLean himself bein' in the Fancher Train—Brother Parley's murderer! And Jed Smith, Bridger's bastard, throwin' down on McKenzie and bringin' up that Fort Bridger lie again! There's a lot more to this than meets the eye: looks like a whole slew of murderin' mobocrats, and right at the time the whole government is persecutin' us again!"

The bishop's eyes had narrowed, he nodded at this interpretation. Suddenly a thing occurred to him. There was a shocked glazing of the eyes he turned on Leany, his face took on an awed expression. The gaunt man waited breathlessly, something momentous had revealed itself to him.

"Brother William." Lewis's tone was hushed, wondering. "The hand of the Lord is clearly in evidence here—it is exceedingly plain to see!" His eyes were glowing, his face had become exalted as though he had seen a vision.

"A few days ago," he went on in the same trembling significant voice, "a man traveled through here with freight wagons, bound for Brother John D. Lee's place in New Harmony, a man that you and I knew well, twenty years ago at Haun's Mill! Do you know—can you guess?—what man is, even now, only a few miles from here? And he comes from Brother Brigham—he has a curious mission to perform——"

Leany was caught in the spell of the mysticism, his hypnotized gaze hung on the other's illumined face. The bishop flung his head high, eyes triumphantly gleaming.

"That man was—*Josh Wade!*"

Leany's bony jaw dropped. "Wade! *Josh Wade?* Down here, *now?*" The eyes of the two men met, shared the significance of it. "And Wade is one of Rockwell's men."

Lewis nodded. "He is. I've heard from many sources that he is Port's most invincible Destroying Angel. They swear that no enemy, no apostate, has ever escaped Josh Wade, once he took their trail!" The two men fell silent, each engrossed with tumultuous thoughts. "His mission," Lewis continued, "is the final evidence of Divine Plan!

He comes with arms for the red men, and to lead them against the enemy that Brother Brigham predicted would appear in our midst!"

Leany's face convulsed with sudden comprehension of the precise dovetailing of the evidence. "And the very man that killed Wade's wife," he stammered, "is in the Fancher Train!"

Lewis's nod was portentous. "Wade must be acquainted with this information, at once"—his whole big form energized—"we have a clear duty here, William, we must take the word to Brother Isaac Haight and see that it also reaches Josh Wade!"

Bishop Lewis immediately called a meeting of his councilors, revealed his information to them, and announced he was leaving immediately for Cedar City, and Stake President Isaac Haight. Haight was the highest religious official in the southern territory.

Lewis charged his council with safeguarding the town. His final orders were blunt: "Put a lookout on the emigrant road—when the Fancher Train is sighted, close the gates—mount armed guards on the walls—keep the enemy out of Parowan!"

One of the councilors had the bad judgment to inquire, "Well, how are they gonna get a-past? The road goes right through——"

Lewis's baleful glance withered the man. "Let the damned, thieving, murdering mobocrats make their own road, let them break their wagons on the hillsides, and be damned to them!"

At Cedar City, Tarleton Lewis and William Leany had a long conference with Isaac Haight. After a short rest and food Leany mounted a fresh horse and headed for New Harmony and Josh Wade. As he rode he marveled, gloried in the evidence of the Almighty's guiding hand, and the prophetical power of Brigham Young's accurate foresight. It fitted into place like the separate parts of a puzzle. Leany did not spare his horse, he was anxious to tell his tidings to John Doyle Lee as well as to Josh Wade. For Lee had been at Far West when the pitiful remnants of the Haun's Mill massacre were brought there. His hand had been one with the Prophet's in the ceremony that had saved many a life. He had endured the Missouri and Illinois persecutions—Lee was a kindred soul to Tarleton Lewis and William Leany—they had all suffered.

But most of all, Leany wanted to impart the word of the redbeard's presence to Josh Wade. He wanted to see the fury of righteous anger and thirst for vengeance rise in the dread visage of Port Rockwell's most dangerous Destroying Angel.

## CHAPTER XIII

President Isaac Haight never allowed emotion to interfere with his judgments. Nor personal likes or dislikes to sway his plans. Like Brigham Young, he shrewdly used whatever tools came into his capable hands. He did not, for instance, get on well with Colonel William Dame. There was constant rivalry between them. The colonel outranked Haight in the Mormon militia but Haight was Dame's superior in the Church—and in Zion, church authority was the supreme ultimate.

Colonel Dame had never quite put the question of authority to a test but he appeared to enjoy being uncooperative. Haight was too practiced a diplomat to bring it to a showdown. Instead, he found a way to circumvent the obstacle. It had proved simple, for Colonel Dame lived in Parowan, miles from Cedar City, and Haight himself held the rank of lieutenant colonel. The next in authority in the militia was Major John Higbee, a vigorously devoted young man who was ambitious and therefore vulnerable. Higbee never questioned whether his orders came from Colonel Dame or originated with Isaac Haight.

Just before noon on Friday, September 4, Higbee brought word to Haight that the Fancher Train had just pulled in to camp below Cedar City. Haight thought over the jumbled reports he had had of these people and decided to visit the train himself. His only companion was Phillip Klingensmith, Bishop of Cedar City.

Captain Fancher, flanked by John Barker and Jed Smith, advanced to meet the mounted men, noting with surprise that the visitors appeared to be unarmed.

The tall bearded man dismounted. "I am Isaac Haight," he announced, removing his black stovepipe hat and mopping at a noble expanse of brow. The day was sultry hot, thunderheads reared above the eastern mountains. His companion, a stocky, dull-eyed man, also dismounted but he did not speak. He appeared to have been fat at one time but now his clothes hung on him loosely, his jowls were pendulous. He nodded as Haight made him known as Bishop Klingensmith.

Fancher was astonished at the lack of hostility evidenced in these two. Haight was a lean, handsome man, his blue-black hair and spade beard were stylishly trimmed, glossy from grooming. He wore a well-fitting black frock coat, his white shirt was immaculate. Klingensmith was a slovenly figure. He was attired in baggy barn-door pants, his vest hung open over a soiled calico shirt and an accumulation of grizzled stubble adorned his heavy face. He was a blacksmith by trade and his heavy rounded shoulders and long, hanging arms gave him an almost simian appearance.

In spite of their unarmed state, Fancher was wary. They had added reason to avoid the Mormons since Parowan. They had closed the gates of the walled town, forced the train to make their own trail precariously over a rocky hill. Several wagons suffered broken wheels and two mules had been destroyed because of broken legs.

"I've given strict orders," Captain Fancher anticipated bluntly, "no one from the train will go near your town—you don't need to fret on that score."

Haight's black brows rose in surprise; he and Klingensmith exchanged glances. Then Haight spoke. "That wasn't entirely necessary, Captain Fancher—I presume you are the captain?"

Fancher nodded. Haight continued, now with a slight smile. "Whether your people come in or not," he said, "is entirely up to you."

Fancher showed his surprise. "It's been different back up the line," he observed caustically.

Haight nodded, his smile begging indulgence. "The small settlements get alarmed easily about the presence of strangers," he said. "We've had—difficulties—with some trains. The gold-rush trash, for instance, we had continual trouble with them." He paused and then continued. "We have had, I'll admit, some rather unflattering reports on you people, you seem to have had quite a to-do with Bishop McKenzie over a goat!" Isaac Haight laughed, revealing fine white teeth through his beard. They joined him, somewhat uncertainly, completely baffled—a Mormon official with a sense of humor! "And then, of course," Haight went on genially, "the Indian reports, but if we took stock in every fairy tale the Indians bring us, we'd be in an uproar all the time!"

Jed had been eying Haight sharply and he felt relief at the man's reasonable intelligence. "The folks back yonder," he said, "made out that the Injuns might jump us any time, but none showed themselves. How are they, hereabouts?"

Haight smiled with gentle scorn. "The Paiutes? You must not be well acquainted with them."

"Peaceful, are they?"

"Oh, they squabble among themselves, but they're too lazy to be warlike. The Pahvants, now, further north, and the Utes, they're dangerous when they're roused. But you are out of their territory now. You need guard against only thieving in Paiute country—they'll steal anything that isn't nailed down!" Haight smiled reminiscently. "It was their fondness for mule meat that made trouble with the gold seekers. We were blamed, of course, when their mules were missing."

Jed nodded, his grin returning Haight's pleasantness.

This view had been advanced by Jacob Hamblin, also. Hamblin and this man, Haight, were of a different stamp than the other Mormon zealots they had encountered. It was a relief to be able to talk sense, get reliable information.

Captain Fancher spoke. "There's a power of things the folks are needin'," he said. "You think there won't be trouble if we come into your town?"

Haight took a moment to answer. "I can guarantee that my people will not *make* trouble," he said gravely, "but neither will they tolerate abuse. It will depend, of course, on the attitude your people take with them. You will find little to buy, though, we have had orders to store our supplies and harvests."

"How about powder and lead?"

Haight shook his head. "We have none to spare. Are you dangerously short?"

"No," Fancher said, "but we ain't too long on it. Some of the boys got shoot-happy, burned up a lot when there was game. Some are short, some aren't. We're all right if we don't run into trouble, and likely we won't, if the Injuns are peaceable, like you say." He paused and thought, then asked, "How about greens and such—fresh garden truck? And gettin' a little work done at a blacksmith shop—that's needed bad."

Haight nodded promptly. "We have two blacksmith shops to serve you," he said, "and I think I can arrange for you to get some greens and melons. They do not store well. Inquire in town for Jesse Smith—I know he has a surplus of melons—he may have other things he can spare."

Captain Fancher nodded, smiling his thanks. Jed put a question, "How far—how many days to Hamblin's place, Mountain Meadows?"

"Two days—two and a half at the most," Haight answered readily. "You plan to stop there?"

"We saw Hamblin at Corn Creek. He gave us leave to stop over, rest and refit there."

"It's a good place," Haight commended, "fine grazing,

plenty of water; several trains have stopped there in the past." His gaze wandered to the herds spreading over the nearby pastures. "You have brought a large herd," he observed, "have you had trouble finding feed?"

"That we have!" Fancher declared. "That's why we need a layover—figger to stop a week at Mountain Meadows. David Boller's fretting over his horses, he's run out of grain. He coddles them thoroughbreds like babies!"

Haight approved this attitude. "A fine horse deserves the best," he said, "I'm very sorry we can't spare grain, but we have our orders."

Bishop Klingensmith had remained stolidly quiet during the whole of the conversation. When Isaac Haight mounted and touched the brim of his tall hat in leaving, Klingensmith nodded briefly. The two men halted their horses at the crest of a small hill and faced about. Haight's eyes, resting on the train with its spreading herds beyond, were oddly intent, calculating.

Klingensmith spoke. "You were uncommon friendly to the Gentiles." There was no criticism in the comment, uttered in a flat tone, his voice had a dragging quality. He was an able, if somewhat heavy-handed and uninspired, bishop. Haight deplored the man's humorless phlegm at times but he had a peculiarly priceless value: he could be depended upon to obey implicitly. And since Haight had made it clear to Klingensmith that the privileges of plural marriage did not include physical abuse of his wives, the man had maintained a spotless record, risen in the Church.

Haight concealed his impatience; he would have to frame it simply, paint a picture. Klingensmith had absolutely no intuition in spite of the fact that he was aware of the whole situation regarding the Fancher Train.

"Phillip," he said patiently, "we have had many reports on the Fancher Train and there are many who are clamoring that we take certain action. But there were things that we needed to know. How much would we have learned had we ridden to their camp armed and hostile? Now, we know many things: They plan to lay over at

Mountain Meadows for a week—so we have ample time to perfect a plan; they have only a small supply of ammunition, which is all to the good; we have viewed their herd unhindered and seen its immense size."

Klingensmith understood Haight's subtleness now and his face brightened. Before he could divulge a comment Haight was speaking again. "Look, Phillip"—his arm waved sweepingly—"we have nothing like those herds in our barren, hard land."

Klingensmith looked long, nodded discontentedly, a slow grudging anger in his face.

"Only a few days ago," Haight continued, "Apostle George A. Smith told us how Brother Brigham had sent men to raid the army's herds and supplies! They will bring the loot into Zion—fine provisions and badly needed, but"—his voice lowered significantly—"we'll see none of it, this far south." He brought the full brilliance of his gaze to rest on the bishop.

"You were there, Phillip," he said, "and heard the tidings brought to us by Brother Leany and Bishop Lewis. The clamoring for vengeance against these enemies has grown." He allowed these facts to simmer with Klingensmith for a moment and then continued. "Brother Brigham has set us an example. It is very plain that he considers it justified in this present crisis to seize the enemy's supplies. I agree with him entirely and I see no reason"—his voice had become vigorously strong—"why these intruders in Zion should not also be relieved of their herds. They have manifested themselves as enemies, time and time again!" He looked with satisfaction at Klingensmith, whose gross features showed unwonted animation.

They turned now and began their ride back to town. Haight gave orders as they traveled. "I'll see Jesse Smith, myself," he said, "I want you to see every shopkeeper. Tell them they may sell such items as they can well spare, but no grain or foods that will store. But—this is important, Phillip—I want the word passed to all that *they are to be friendly*. I want them to visit with the people from the Fancher Train—find out all they can about them. And I want reports from those who get information. Tell them to report directly to me as soon as the train pulls out. Go, also, to Brother Aaron's stillhouse, tell him to sell them all the whisky they want. God knows we don't need the sort of swill he's been turning out lately—and tell him that's my direct order: sell them all they want. If there are hard drinkers in that crowd, I want them drunk!"

Klingensmith's grizzled head was nodding in response to each command. Though a painfully slow thinker, his memory was prodigious. Once assimilated, each duty would remain in a pigeon-hole of his mind until accomplished. He would, moreover, carry out the numerous orders in the exact sequence in which they had been given. Haight knew from long experience that the slow, choleric voice would repeat the very wording verbatim.

"And, after you have done these things," Haight continued, "ride to Pinto, stop at the Indian camps on the way. Send Moquetas and Big Bill to me, but tell them to wait until after dark to come in. At Pinto, get hold of that young hothead, Tesanto, but warn him to come straight to me. I don't want him jumping the gun. Send one of the bucks from Pinto over to Toquer's town. I know old Toquer himself went north with Brother Jacob, but the war chief, that big ugly one, is likely there. Tell him to gather up some of his boys and get on over to John D. Lee's place, report to Josh Wade, and wait there for word from me." He paused, thinking swiftly. "On second thought, Phillip," he said planningly, "I think it would be better if all the redskins went directly to Wade. I'll send word for Brother John Lee to come to me, instead. I'll tell you—you pass the word that Josh Wade has got guns to give out to the Indians. That'll send them on the run! And then I won't be bothered with them." Haight peered searchingly at Klingensmith to see if he had confused him, was going too fast. But the bishop was nodding, smiling, he looked unusually alert. "Send all the Indians to Josh Wade," he repeated approvingly.

A relevant item occurred to Haight. "What about Kasota? Have you seen what shape he's in?"

Klingensmith nodded. "He's at Brother Amran's. Sister Martha patched him up some. But he's a mess—and madder'n a hornet!"

Haight frowned. "Is he disabled?"

"Not bad. Oh, he's cut up, bruised, but hell, Kasota's tough—you can't kill them red bastards. His face is smashed, nose smeared way over to one side, and his teeth are splintered. But it's his pride that's hurt the most, over who done it."

"He knows who rode him down?"

Klingensmith's short laugh was gruffly like a bark. "Seems it was a woman, a young girl."

"A *girl rode Kasota down?*" Haight was incredulous.

"That's right!" Sardonic amusement was in Klingensmith's heavy voice. "He got a glimpse of her—not too big, yellow hair. Charged him like a war chief—said she was up on a stocky, heavy-built roan. You'd think he'd be glad to be alive, but not Kasota! He's boilin' mad because they must not have figgered he was dangerous enough to kill when he was layin' helpless!"

Haight shook his head, smiling at the inexplicable thing that was Indian pride. "Kasota, war chief of the Pahvants, ridden down by a girl!"

Klingensmith's grin agreed, but he warned, "You'd best not grin, or say any such thing about Kasota to his face, he's ready to jump his weight in wildcats—mutterin' about takin' himself a blond scalp if it costs his life! He ain't so sore about the man, for he said he was mounted on a big black horse that run like the wind! Kasota said that the sorrel he stole was fast—a race horse—but this here black stud caught her like she was standin' still! He says he never in all his life seen a horse run like that one, says it had a stride twice as long as the fastest animal he's ever seen!"

Isaac Haight's eyes shone. He loved fine horses, and even mediocre mounts were scarce. Should the raid be a success, he could own that black race horse! Because of his position he was entitled to first choice of the loot from the raid. All he need do to ensure its delivery into his hands was to give the orders to Klingensmith. Haight suddenly felt he must have this king among horses, he had long desired a mount in keeping with his position, his personality. He allowed himself to dream for a moment—a fine, already legendary, black horse, ridden by himself, meticulously clad in his usual black and white. His dream stepped further. Perhaps, he thought, the sorrel mare for Caroline! The proud, beautiful Caroline, his favorite wife, how she would love the spirited sorrel. What a picture they would make, mounted, riding side by side! He loved to see the light in her brilliant eyes when he made her a fine gift. She was a rare treasure—Caroline. Isaac Haight smiled, sighed with pleasure at this confident view of the future.

Captain Fancher was pleased to be able to announce that the people from the train could visit Cedar City, that there would even be a few items for sale. "But," he warned emphatically, "you all keep a civil tongue in your heads. I won't have no trouble. These folks are of a mind to act decent with us and the least we can do is behave ourselves! Just to make sure, though, Jed and a few of the boys are goin' to patrol and anybody gets outa line will wind up with a busted skull! Now I mean that!"

There were few people to be seen on the streets in Cedar City, the settlers prudently stayed within doors. The shopkeepers, if not overwhelmingly cordial, seemed inclined to visit a little in a stilted way.

Sol Ward, Jake Tibbetts, and their cronies smelled out Brother Aaron's stillhouse immediately. Having been able to purchase a number of gallon jugs of whisky, they returned peacefully to camp and stayed there. Sol and Jake were unusually inconspicuous these days, having guessed accurately what the "Indian trouble" amounted to that the Mormons had become incensed about, but had not revealed to any in the Fancher Train.

William Aden, the apostate, prodded by Birdie, went reluctantly into the town to buy a few articles of clothing. It had been a great trial to Birdie that they must borrow clothing in order to keep clean. Aden finally agreed to the expedition but only on the condition that Birdie—and her unruly tongue—would stay in camp. He was unusually firm about this and his wife finally conceded and supplied him with a long, meticulously annotated list.

Aden accompanied a group which drove into town in a wagon. The rest of the people in the party were intent on locating the blacksmith shop, so Aden, alone, entered a small shop whose sign indicated that dry goods were for sale. There was no other customer in the shop, which boasted a rough plank counter and shelves fashioned of unfinished pine slabs, from which gum still oozed stickily. The clerk, a thin, shabbily dressed young man, advanced soberly, somewhat hesitantly, to meet his customer. And then he stopped short, his gaze became blank with astonishment.

"Why, it's William!"—his voice was joyous—"Brother William Aden!" he came from behind the counter, embraced the stupefied Aden warmly.

Aden gulped frantically, his Adam's apple bouncing with painful agitation. Three hundred miles from Salt Lake City, and the first Mormon he allowed to face him was an old friend! Benjamin Aldrich—this was the clerk's name—and his wife, Millicent, had traveled in the same group of converts with the Adens from England. On the long voyage the four young people had become fast friends. In New York they had been assigned to different emigrant companies, had lost track of each other.

Aldrich's eyes were moist with joy in the reunion. "Where is Birdie? Wait till Millie knows you are here! We speak of you so often. Are you going to settle here? You must stay with us——" He broke off, noting for the first time the misery of Aden's face, realizing, too, that his friend had not appeared happy at the meeting. "What's wrong, William?" he asked. "If I was distant at first it was because I thought you were one of the Gentiles from that train—the Fanchers——"

Aden peered nervously about, his face fear-ridden. His

pale eyes besought Aldrich, who regarded him with alarm.

"Benjamin," Aden began hesitantly, "if we—hadn't been like brothers—I'd never dare tell you——" He glanced suspiciously around again. "Is there anyone to hear us?"

"No," Aldrich said, "I'm alone here. Whatever is it, William? Don't tell me something has happened to dear Birdie?"

Aden shook his head, "Oh no, it isn't that—Birdie's all right—we're both all right, now——" He swallowed painfully. "We are going to California, Benjamin. We're—with the Fancher Train."

Aldrich's face stiffened with shock. "William! No wonder you hate to speak out! Oh, you must leave them at once—surely we can find another way for you to travel. Have you been called to the San Bernardino mission?"

Aden's shaking head interrupted. "Benjamin," he said, so low as to be scarce heard, "we've—Birdie and I—we've left the Church. We got into awful trouble in Salt Lake City, and we were threatened, Benjamin—*my life was threatened!* Why, we barely escaped! The Fanchers befriended us, helped us, or I wouldn't be alive to tell it!"

Aldrich withdrew his hand, recoiling as from a hideous reptile. There was a long, miserable silence. Aden tried haltingly to explain. "We just couldn't seem to—get on with them, Benjamin," he said. "Birdie was like a crazy thing whenever they brought up plural marriage—and you know they lied about that, Benjamin!"

Aldrich had not spoken, he did not answer this. Aden went on. "And when we wouldn't obey council about Celestial Marriage things just went from bad to worse! And Birdie just wouldn't bridle her tongue. She tongue-lashed everybody from the bishop to all his councilors! She just wouldn't keep her views to herself. You know how she is——"

Aldrich nodded. His face had lost its first horrified expression and Aden felt encouraged, but he failed to note that his friend's eyes were now oddly veiled—watchful.

"We were in hot water almost from the first," the apostate hurried on, "we *had* to leave, but we weren't to blame. We could have put up with the rest of it if they'd just left off harping about plural marriage to Birdie!"

"You should have been more firm with her." Aldrich's tone was unctuous.

Aden snorted. "With Birdie? How would you go about telling Birdie she *had* to share my bed with another wife? Tell me, just how would you convince Birdie?" Remembering the determined, articulate little woman, Aldrich shook his head.

"How about you?" Aden demanded defensively. "Has Millicent let you take another wife?"

Aldrich did not meet his glance. "It hasn't come up," he said, "there aren't many extra women here. The leaders are mostly plural but nobody's suggested that I—that we——"

"Well, you just wait till they start on Millicent and then you'll know how it was!"

Aldrich was nettled by the prophecy. It was a thing that disturbed him, for he had given a great deal of thought to plural marriage. And he wasn't at all sure he could handle Millicent. He devoutly longed to emulate the leaders, practice the beautiful doctrine of Celestial Marriage. But it had been a touchy subject with his wife, it was becoming a sore one, and now he bristled at Aden's thrusts.

"I am sure"—his tone was stiff—"that if the occasion arises, Millicent will see her duty clearly." Aden sniffed with open scepticism. Aldrich cleared his throat importantly. "I am on the bishop's council now. We have done well here." He waited for the congratulations he felt were due and was offended when none was offered. Obviously William Aden attached small importance to church position these days. Aldrich's peevish glance hardened. It occurred to him that it was foolish to stand thus, overlong, in intimate talk with an apostate.

"William," he said, "we've been told we can sell things we can spare. But you shouldn't linger in town.

The Brookses and the Enderbys—you remember them—they settled here, too. If you should happen to meet them, and they knew you were with that Gentile train, it could be—awkward."

Aden agreed, dug out the list Birdie had provided. The clerk shook his head. "We haven't much of this, but I'll do the best I can." He began to take various items from the shelves, pile them together in a hurried heap on the counter. He wanted to be rid of Aden, see the last of him.

Aldrich slowed his filling of the order, remembering that he was supposed to get information about the Fancher Train. For a moment he was inclined not to question an old friend. But the moment of indecision was brief. Hadn't William, he thought, thrown away the right to be called friend? He was now no better than a Gentile. He was worse, for those who embraced the True Gospel and then cast it aside had committed the greatest sin of all!

"This train you're traveling with, William," he observed, "doesn't have a very good reputation."

Aden showed his surprise. "Why, Benjamin," he said quickly, "they're wonderful people! They've been good to us—very generous. But then, they're well-to-do people, a lot of them. Believe me, they aren't poor trash trying to do better. They're going to California with enough to start out in fine style! Why, about half of that cattle herd belongs to Captain Fancher, and David Boller has a whole herd of thoroughbred horses. And the Barkers—why, young Abel Barker paid a whole bag of silver coins for a nanny goat, just to pamper his wife and baby!"

"William," Aldrich said when Aden paused, "we buy cattle in California and bring them here. Why are they driving such herds to California when they could much easier buy them there?"

Aden's brow furrowed. "I don't know," he said. "Mr. Rob Fancher—he's related to the captain—sold his herd someplace on the way. He wears a money belt around his waist. It seems to me they spoke of it that he sold cattle to an army buyer."

A sudden suspicion appalled Aldrich but he controlled his voice, kept his face turned away. "Maybe they're going to sell these to the army, too," he said.

"But the army is on the plains——"

"I know, but we've heard that there was an army in California that might come up. Maybe these herds are for them." His casual tone did not match his eyes; he waited intently for an answer.

Aden had become alarmed. "Benjamin!"—he was agitated—"I'll bet that's it." He placed an urgent hand on the clerk's arm. "Benjamin, you'd better get yourself and Millicent out of here—you're in terrible danger! There's sure to be an awful war and the Mormons can't win, not against two armies. You'll all be slaughtered! Why, with an army coming across the plains and another coming from California——! Benjamin, you'll be caught like rats in a trap!"

The two men stared at each other, their faces alike set in consternation.

Aden paid for his purchases and fled to the safety of the wagon train. He did not tell Birdie about the meeting with Benjamin, for he knew she would insist on seeing Millicent and he wanted no further entanglements.

The next morning, following the dusty departure of the Fancher Train, the people filed slowly in to report to Isaac Haight. As one meager and useless detail after another straggled across his desk, Haight became increasingly impatient. Then Benjamin Aldrich was ushered in, took a hesitant perch on the edge of the chair facing the desk. His sober face exhibited how impressed he was to be in the presence of the Stake President. Aldrich's regard for the elegant Haight amounted to worshipful awe.

Haight sensed his insecurity and smiled, knowing well the effect that brilliantly contagious smile had on the members of his flock. He was never stern or prodding with the timid ones. It would be, Haight thought wearily, another useless mess of trivia. And then Aldrich found his voice and began to tell about his visit from William Aden, apostate.

Isaac Haight came bolt upright, his eyes were startled. Aldrich faltered, slowed under the strange expression. "Go on, Brother Aldrich," Haight urged, "don't leave out the smallest thing—this is the most important information I have received! Tell me every single word, carefully, I want you to remember the smallest item."

Isaac Haight did not interrupt again, he folded his long hands on the desk and, leaning slightly forward, his fine eyes never leaving the other's flushed face, he listened with flattering intentness. His swift mind leaped ahead, measuringly. The balance of the scales against the Fancher Train had become very heavy.

Aldrich's words, at the last, were uttered in a voice which shook with very real terror. "And he—William," he stammered, "he said that we—Millicent and I—should get out of here as fast as we could! He said the army coming across the plains had bought cattle from someone in the Fancher Train, and he was sure they were going to sell these cattle to the army that's in California right now!" His face twisted, naked fear was in the pale eyes. These words had lodged relentlessly in his mind, kept him tossing, sleepless, all of the preceding night. "William Aden said, President Haight, that if we didn't get out of here we'd all be caught—like—like rats in a trap! Those were his very words: 'like rats in a trap'!"

## CHAPTER XIV

A number of men, their clothes still soiled from work in the fields, filed into Isaac Haight's office immediately after noon dinner on Saturday. There was some low-voiced grumbling among them. For if their hay, lying cut in the fields, got wetted down by the threatening thundershower, they'd rue this lost afternoon's work. They muttered, but none had considered noncompliance with the summons delivered by Major Higbee.

Benjamin Aldrich sat stiffly silent among them, full of misgivings as to why he had been included in this select gathering. His immediate superior, Bishop Klingensmith, was not there. These men were all elders, mostly older men, the stanch backbone of the Church and the Mormon militia. Colonel William Dame alone was absent of the militia officers.

President Isaac Haight sat at his desk. There were not chairs enough for all and some squatted on their booted heels against the wall. Each man had sensed, as he arrived, a turbulence under the composed manner of Haight's greetings. There appeared to be a matter of importance to bring before the council to have called it thus—during working hours in harvest time.

Haight did not keep them waiting; without preamble he announced that theirs was the duty to decide what action must be taken concerning the Gentile enemy in their midst: the Fancher Train.

Surprise registered on some of the faces. Not at his terminology, for all Gentiles were classed as enemies of the Mormon Saints, but at the disclosure that action was indicated. There was a restless, considering silence.

"Ain't that a mite different than yesterday's orders, Brother Haight?" It was rugged Laban Morrill. His plain strong face was puzzled. "We was told to be friendly to them people—"

"I'm glad that you mentioned that, Brother Morrill," Haight said, "I had a reason for it, as I will explain presently."

Morrill nodded, clearly not convinced, but subsiding to wait. Some of the older men resented Haight's rapid ascendancy in the Church, resented still more his prosperity, not earned by horny-handed toil in the fields. These elders were a hard-working, stolid set. They reflected deliberately, were slow to anger, and complied undeviatingly with the policies set by Brigham Young. Their cooperation was not so wholehearted with those who moved brilliantly, swiftly—as had Haight—into positions of authority.

Isaac Haight presented facts concerning the Fancher Train. His voice was neutral, he did not presume to interpret, the whole implication was that he asked the council to function as a judge.

Reports, he said, had reached them some time ago from as far north as Fort Bridger. Men calling themselves the "Missouri Wildcats" had openly told of having taken part in the Missouri persecutions. Port Rockwell himself had seen the Fancher Train there and sent on the word. That Jed Smith, Bridger's bastard, was scouting for the train. And Jim Bridger was a sworn enemy of the Church. Smith, Port had reminded them, was known to be a renegade killer, and was possibly spying for Bridger, who was scouting the army on the plains.

But, Haight continued, they had not needed these warnings to convince them that the people in the Fancher Train were dangerous. The stories had preceded them every foot of the way—reports of outlawry, thieving, brutality, and violence. As they had passed through the settlements they had insulted women, wantonly killed chickens and dogs; had stolen whisky, leaving a man bleeding and senseless on the floor of his shop. Bishop McKenzie reported that the Fanchers had stolen livestock from a lone woman on an outlying farm. And further, that a man named McLean—believed to be the murderer of Apostle Parley Pratt—was a member of the train. McKenzie, who was also sheriff, had not been allowed to question the man himself. The renegade Jed Smith and his crew—Captain Fancher approving—had resisted the officials of the law with cocked rifles. Bishop McKenzie reported that he had desisted only because there were women and children present.

The ugly trail of violence had continued. At Corn Creek, where Jacob Hamblin had befriended them, they had committed unspeakable atrocities on the favorite wife of the powerful chief, Kanosh, and injured his small son. Kasota, the young brother-in-law of Kanosh, had been ruthlessly ridden down by a member of the train—left for dead. The Pahvants, with so much difficulty rendered peaceful by the Mormons, were ready to take the warpath, and justifiably so.

At Beaver the train had broken a fence and let their herds in on a field of corn. It was completely ruined and no payment had been made to the owner. Only an armed guard had kept the enemy out of the town. At Parowan they were driven to closing the gates, placing armed guards on the walls to force the Fanchers to pass around the town, not enter it.

These things, Haight continued, were public knowledge. But there were certain facts concerning individual members of the train that all should now know. Brother William Leany, well known to them all, had ridden hurriedly from Beaver to deliver to Haight a shocking piece of information. Leany had recognized a man in the Fancher Train to have been one of the band of mobsters involved in the massacre at Haun's Mill!

Haight paused, every man present had stirred, had drawn a sharp breath.

Brother Leany, Haight resumed, could positively identify this man: he was a big man with a red beard, wore a distinctively styled horn-handled knife—the knife had been in evidence at Haun's Mill, also. Leany had *twice* seen this man taking part in bloody violence against the Mormons; the second time had been at the jail in Carthage! This red-bearded man had been among those who assassinated, *martyred their beloved Prophet, Joseph Smith!* For Leany said that this man had been with those who fired the deadly volley! The redbeard still carried a knife like the one he had used at Haun's Mill. It was possible he had the gun that had killed the Prophet!

Haight rose from his chair as though he could not bear to remain still, moved to the window to stare unseeingly at the bright September day. He appeared to be making a tremendous effort to control his emotion. He returned to stand at his desk, his long fingers drummed nervously on its surface.

"Brother Leany's statement is supported," he went on. "He was accompanied by Bishop Tarleton Lewis of Parowan. You have all heard Bishop Lewis tell how he himself was shot down and left for dead at Haun's Mill." Haight sat down, his black brows drawn into a knot on the high bridge of his nose. "But this is not all." Haight sighed as though the burden of horror grew heavy. "Some of you know Josh Wade—all of you know of him." There were nods, some undecided, some faces tinged with alarm, for Wade was never a subject for public discussion. All had heard whispered accounts of his activities. Isaac Haight knew well what passed through the mind of each man at the name alone. As he looked at them now his glance was weighted with significance.

"Brother Josh Wade is at New Harmony, now, as we are gathered together here. Brother Leany rode from here to tell Josh Wade a thing of importance—this man, the red-bearded man, whom William can positively identify, is the man who shot down Wade's young wife and left Wade for dead when he tried to protect her, for *Leany saw the very act!*" A cold chill slid the length of each man's spine as he estimated Josh Wade's reaction to this news.

Haight's glance burned from face to face, his mouth set downward bitterly. "I am responsible here," he said, "by the power vested in me by the priesthood and the holy authority of Brigham Young. I could stay the hand of Josh Wade!" he drew a deep breath, his bearded chin raised. "But"—his glance moved restlessly over them—"*I sent Leany to Wade!* If Josh Wade takes his vengeance, by the Almighty God, brethren, I will bow my head and say 'Amen'!"

There were whispered echoes of benediction, a fraught silence waited for him to resume.

"I knew all of this," he said, "when I sent the word to be friendly to the people from the Fancher Train." His glance flickered toward Laban Morrill, whose heavy features sharpened. "There were two reasons for that order: first, there was no time to acquaint everyone with the situation; second, I wanted information. And this we now have. I know the size of their herds, and they are immensely valuable thoroughbred horses, fine cattle. I know that they plan to be at Hamblin's Mountain Meadows for a week or more. There are about one hundred and sixty people in the train. Approximately seventy-five are armed men, the rest women and children. And I know that they are not too well supplied with ammunition." The significance of this last was not lost on his listeners.

Laban Morrill spoke. "Sounds like you're maybe of a mind to test out their supply of shot, Brother Haight." Haight met the man's level gaze steadily. "That is why I called the council together," he said. "Any action taken must be decided on by all. I think I should mention, though, that we are powerless to prevent an Indian attack on the train. Kasota had definite orders from Kanosh, and the other chiefs are gathering. If Josh Wade takes the vengeance trail, the Indians will follow him to a man. He is a war god to them, he will not lack for warriors!"

Morrill's heavy fist smote his knee. "Let 'em," his voice rumbled angrily, "let the Injuns go right ahead. I hope they kill every damn murderin' Gentile in the lot!" There was a murmurous roar of agreement.

"The question is," Haight said, "should we let the Indians do as they will—or should we support them?"

There was a brief silence of shock and then a tangle of voices. Haight held up his hand for silence and elaborated. "If we leave it to the Indians, what happens to the herds—the fine horses and cattle?" he asked. "Brother Brigham sent men to raid cattle and supplies from the army—shall we not follow his example here? Or do we want the Indians to do our work for us?" he flung it at them. "We can use—we *need* those herds! We know the Indians are irresponsible; they will amuse themselves by shooting arrows into the animals, there will be a useless slaughter, much will be wasted if we do not take a hand!"

This put a different light entirely on the problem. There were some ready agreements, some were reluctant, all were disturbed.

Young James Haslam, the express rider, spoke up for the first time. "If we help the Injuns, what kind of story won't those people tell the minute they hit Californy? They'll tell for sure that Mormons attacked them—"

Haight had apparently thought of everything; he nodded. "Our men must dress like Indians and stay in the background, direct more than act. See to conserving the herds."

There were still those who objected—innocent people might be killed, there were many women and children in the train. Raiding the army was different, they insisted, that was an actual fighting enemy.

Haight listened with growing anger. It showed in the growl of his voice. "These people, the Fanchers"—his voice despisingly spat the name—"*are enemies*—Gentile spies, rapists, assassins, thieves! Are we to be tender of *such*? And did *they* ever—in Missouri and Illinois—stay their hands because *our* women and children were present?" He laughed with cold scorn. "Our women were shot down, knifed, raped, and abused! They had no mercy when they drove us out in midwinter. Remember how it was? On the riverbanks? Your first wife, Pierce, died giving birth to her baby, and your old mother, Andrew, of lung congestion. They were not shot, no, but were they any the less murdered?"

The two men thus named nodded, their faces sickening at the memory. All looked sympathy and then the faces hardened as they listened.

"I want to remind you," Haight's voice went on, "of what Apostle George A. Smith counseled us, just a few days ago, in meeting. Do you remember his very words, as I do? He said that perhaps the fruit crop in Dixie would bear more abundantly if our trees were *dampened by the blood and fertilized by the bones of our enemies!* You heard those words uttered by the blessed apostle sent to us by Brigham Young! Who also counseled us to prepare to fight to save ourselves from extermination! Arm yourselves, he said, look to your supply of bullets and powder, store your crops, drill the militia, prepare for the final battle! Make ready for the Gentile hordes, for they will spare no one!"

Some cringed under the lash of his tongue, all were silenced, most were in agreement. He continued on.

"You think we—and our wives and children—can feel safe here? Because we are three hundred miles from the battle front? Let me tell you, brethren, we are in a far more precarious situation than the people in the capital! We, too—few as we are—we face a battle front! Will you be willing to take up arms only *after* the enemy has shot down your children, raped your wives?" Their horrified eyes told of mystification at his words.

"There is more, more than I have yet divulged! There is a thing that you must know," and his gaze rested on Benjamin Aldrich, who had sat, shrinking with dismay, and wordless throughout.

Benjamin felt that he could more easily die than speak but he had no choice. Under the compelling gaze of Isaac Haight he rose to his feet and, like a schoolboy, haltingly spoke his piece.

Benjamin's whispering voice was so low that the circle of listeners leaned forward, eyes and ears focused on him with an intensity he could feel like the strangling loops of a rope around his shivering body. No orator could have had the effect this frightened man created as he told them of the apostate, William Aden. Of how his flight had been engineered by the Fanchers, how his vision was now clouded by Gentile wealth. The things that Aden had unwittingly revealed were recited in the same nervous murmur: that the Fanchers had sold cattle to the army that moved toward the battlements of Zion; that this herd, now moving toward Mountain Meadows, was destined for sale to a regiment which advanced across the desert from California. It must be cavalry—the terrible, saber-slashing cavalry—else why did they also deliver a horse herd, if not for cavalry mounts?

The sharp indrawing of breath almost drowned his hesitant whisper, but they stilled to hear him again. He had trouble with his voice, it was caught strangling in his throat, and, to a man, their breathing stilled as he repeated the apostate's warning: that they must save themselves, get out, else they would be caught between two armies, like rats in a trap.

When Benjamin Aldrich, drained and exhausted, sank into his chair they sat wordless. Each man glanced at his neighbor, only to meet the same haunted stare. Isaac Haight watched them. There was compassion for them and urgency was in him but when he spoke it was in a quiet, judicial tone, as though he concluded a summation, released a case to its jury.

"Now you know all," he said simply, "and it is up to you, here and now, brethren. Shall we act—seize the herds? Or shall we withhold our hand and allow them to deliver their herds to fill the bellies of the cavalry now spurring on to slaughter us?" He glanced at his hands, which restlessly played with a pen on his desk. "We cannot," he went on, "depend on the Indians to do a thorough job. We know the Paiutes to be lazy and not warlike. They will take some cattle and mules, have a feast and gorge themselves, and then be quite content to go home. Kanosh and Kasota will be intent only on revenge. The cattle will be immaterial to them."

All were now agreed that some action must be taken. But now voices raised the question that, since the situation seemed so serious, should they not send, ask counsel from Brigham Young? Was it right to deal with it themselves?

Haight managed to conceal his impatience. What, he demanded, did they propose to do when the cavalry arrived? Sit waiting, perhaps, for the week it would take to get permission to defend their lives? Haight mentioned that he had discussed this very possible contingency with Apostle Smith, only a few days ago, and the apostle had agreed—before many witnesses—that the leaders in Dixie must determine their own courses. The Apostle had reaffirmed that they were too distant for any other solution. For their own safety they must use the combined judgment of the council to the best interests of all.

The stolid Morrill was the spokesman for a small faction who hankered after more divine authority than was present. "We ain't had orders to figger the emigrant trains as enemies," he offered, "leastways, not to jump them like that there. They're gonna be at Mountain Meadows a week—they can't move fast, we can catch 'em any time we want—and that gives us time to get proper word." His narrowed eyes reminded Isaac Haight that there were those held in much higher esteem and authority than the suave Stake President—for all his manners and airs, and his handsome, well-dressed wives.

Haight, accurately interpreting the belittling expression, still refrained from taking it as a challenge. "I am willing," he said evenly, "to abide entirely by any decision this council sees fit to make." He stared levelly at Morrill. "That is exactly why I asked you all to come. It is far too serious when the lives of all of us and our loved ones are threatened!" This last registered strongly and Morrill looked his discomfiture.

The result was a compromise: They would seek counsel of Brigham Young, but at the same time they would prepare, move to support the Indians, but hold them from actual attack until word from the capital could be brought.

Young Haslam offered to ride to Salt Lake City. "I can make it in three days," he said confidently, "use the express stops for a change of horses, and be back in three more." Before the hour was out, Haslam was in the saddle, spurring a fast sturdy mount north to the capital.

In response to Isaac Haight's message, John Doyle Lee rode to Cedar City from New Harmony, arriving on Sunday evening. Haight wanted privacy for his conference with Lee and the two men sought the quiet of a building at the ironworks at a late hour. Since Lee had not been present at the meeting of the council, there was much with which to acquaint him.

They kindled a small fire for light and sat near it,

their tones low and tense. The black shadows seemed to dwarf the feeble flames, crowding in on them somberly. A chilled foreboding was born in the impressionable Lee as he looked at the man opposite him, for Haight's burning eyes and black spade beard on his sallow face seemed to have an almost ominous caste. Lee's pulse became irregular, he could feel that a thing of terrible significance was about to be revealed. He realized, too, a culmination of sensations he had been experiencing for several nights. He nodded, acknowledging that he had been warned. He had been wakened the last three nights by the call of a lone wolf. A terrible call, like an animal and yet like a woman in agony. Again and again it had mourned, somewhere off to the west, through the darkest hours of the still night. It had been an omen, of course, Lee thought, and mopped his brow, something tragic was going to happen.

John D. Lee, having just reached the age of forty-five, looked younger. He was a sturdily vigorous, smooth-faced man with clear, steady eyes that were almost childlike in their intense expression. Lee was an impetuous man, forever embroiling himself in sudden quarrels. His gusty tempers subsided as quickly as they rose and he was equally quick to forgive and forget for he was a generous man and kindly. He was dedicatedly zealous in his religion. He had known the Prophet Joseph personally and had come to believe with joyous fervor in the significance of dreams and signs—as had the prophet. He felt that a man thus visited was also gifted with interpretation and he enjoyed the conviction of his own ability to do so. He often told of his dreams and visions in public meeting, interpreting and expounding on them. He also believed that happenings in nature frequently prophesied, if one had insight as to their significance. Lee's mission in the southern settlements was to teach farming to the Indians and he was successful, they loved him. But they also imposed on his generosity and had a name—"Yawguts"—for him, which meant, roughly, the softhearted.

At Haight's question, Lee affirmed that Josh Wade and

his Indian boy were now at New Harmony. "And I've wished he'd take himself off," Lee said ruefully. "Josh has changed, you wouldn't know he was the same man. He's in a bad temper, too, my womenfolks are scared to death of him. That boy waits on him hand and foot and then just squats in a corner, fixin' those beady eyes of his, starin' till the women get all jumpy. He's an odd one, you can't get a word out of him." Lee shook his head doubtfully and then added, "Josh was sore because he missed out on going with the others to tackle the army—always itching for a row, Josh."

Haight hitched himself closer to the other man and in a low tone began to speak. John D. Lee did not interrupt the swift voice. His eyes dilated from time to time, his breathing became deep, he groaned as the crimes of the Fancher Train mounted. When Haight unfolded the plan for the raid on the herds, Lee approved, assuming an attitude of dedication as to a holy crusade. He was surprised when he learned that he had been chosen to accompany the Indians to the vicinity of Mountain Meadows.

"They will listen to you, Brother Lee," Haight said, "they love and respect you. Josh Wade, of course, will actually lead them but you will be present to advise their councils." Haight glanced at the worried expression on Lee's face. "Be of stout heart, brother," he admonished soberly. "This is the bidding of the council—and oddly enough, of Brother Brigham, himself. For how do we know what premonition—revelation—caused him to send Josh Wade among us just in the hour of our great need? Brother Brigham told Josh he sent him to lead the red men in case of trouble. It is only another evidence that he is divinely ordained to watch over us!"

Lee's eyes were bright with emotional tears; he nodded reverently. Haight went on to promise him immediate support at Mountain Meadows. He would be met there by Phillip Klingensmith and several others, all men who spoke Paiute—Jacob Hamblin's brother, Oscar, young Nephi Johnson and Dudley Leavitt. Lee was to bring his son-in-law, Carl Shirts, who also worked among the Indians. "Use Dudley Leavitt and Nephi Johnson for messengers," Haight advised, "I will want you to send word of any developments. Keep in close touch with me at all times."

When Lee spurred off into the night he urged his horse to a fast gallop. He rode, dedicated to fulfillment of the duties assigned by the council—and the awesome omniscience of Brigham Young. John Doyle Lee, adopted son of Brigham Young, bowed his head as his horse carried him through the night, and prayed for strength to accomplish his mission in a manner pleasing to Brigham Young and God.

## CHAPTER XV

Just at sundown the Fancher Train struggled to the rim of the Great Basin, down the slope of which, to the south and west, lay Mountain Meadows. Jed and Lawson Mitchell, scouting in advance of the train, stopped at the little rock house at the north end of the valley to deliver Jacob Hamblin's message to his wife. There had been another woman with her, young Sister Knight, who had a small baby in her arms, and there was a flock of small children.

Mountain Meadows was all that Jacob Hamblin had claimed it to be. To the east and the west were the towering snow-capped bastions of the Wasatch Range. In this long valley the floor of the meadows was not flat but a continual rolling, hilly expanse. A valley only in that it was lower than the abrupt ascent of the foothills edging it about. It was fine, natural pasturage. The cattle would require little herding for the circling hills were almost barren except for rocks and cedar and juniper trees, thick clusters of scrub oak bordered and filled gulleys. The animals would be inclined to remain in the green bottoms near the course of the winding stream.

Mountain Meadows was beautiful: deeply green on its rolling floor, splashed around with color on the ascending heights. The frosty September nights at this mile-high altitude had touched the leaves, the clusters of scrub oak bore flaming scarlet crests. Here and there on the rock-strewn slants were startling bursts of the golden candles of aspen, white-shafted and delicate, their trembling leaves never still. Higher was the somber green of piñon and juniper mounting to the tall stateliness of pitch pine. Tall cottonwoods shook their leaves in the coolness around the bubbling, rocked-in spring, which released a good flow of water to the west. The meadows were still richly green in spite of the lateness of the season. Grass and wild hay, richly nourishing, grew deep in the bottoms between the moundlike hills.

Lawson exclaimed with startled pleasure as a doe and fawn sprang away from the stream and bounced fleetly up a hillside. "Looks like we'll have fresh meat a-plenty," he said.

Jed looked around appreciatively, "Scrub oaks and water—this will be fine deer country. Be a good idea," he said, "if everybody jerked a supply of venison. It's right handy, you don't have to cook it."

Lawson grinned. "Handy for them as just got fired by their cook?" Jed's admitting grin was rueful. He'd come in for unmerciful joshing from the Mitchells since Melissa had banished him from her cooking fire.

They found the ground near the spring to be spongily soft, and so, as the wagons rumbled down the slope, Jed waved them beyond to more solid ground. The wagons circled, but not so close together as usual. In this well-recommended, peaceful spot it was a relief to feel they could relax their accustomed strict guard. The cool quiet, the liquid glow of the crimson sunset, the tall trees and luxury of spring water—these were like a benediction to their trail-tired, aching bodies.

There was a festive air around the cook fires that

night. Laughter rang out often, children ran freely, shrieking and gleeful, gamboling in the grass like frisking lambs. In the shadowy meadows the horses rolled luxuriously, lunged to their feet to shake and flex, dropped their heads to crop the deep grass. The cattle grazed, drank their fill from the rushing stream and grazed again, only to return and suck greedily of the cool water. Their parched bodies quenched and glutted, the animals became content to stand or lie still in the unending grass, their jaws moving in drowsy rhythm.

The herders ceased to circle the herds, rested in their saddles. None of the livestock would stray this night, none so much as moved. Their content was so deep that none even turned an inquiring head at the yapping of coyotes on the hills, nor showed alarm at the faraway moaning howl of a timber wolf.

Melissa was not in a happy frame of mind. She scrambled into her wagon immediately after supper and sat resentfully in the shadow, listening to the sounds of merriment.

Jed had not ventured near her since the day she ordered him off. The few times she had encountered him it had been irritating, for his glance slid past her exactly as in the days when he first joined the train. If it happened that, unavoidably, they met face to face, he wordlessly touched the brim of his hat, let his indifferent gaze move away.

She had expected little sympathy from David but she resented his "I-told-you-so" indifference to her discontent. He reminded her often that she had gotten exactly what she'd asked for—she told Jed to stay away and he was staying away. He refused to keep her company when she moped, left her alone on the wagon during the day and at night deserted her for more cheerful company. Melissa did not seek company at the other wagons, this would only advertise her embarrassing loneliness, so she would creep off to bed to lay fretting bewilderedly. Then usually cry a little before she slept.

It helped not at all that Jed appeared to be enjoying

life. He rode out each day accompanied by Joel or Lawson, took his meals with the bachelor Mitchells. At night the brothers' fire became the gathering place for the unattached men and they were a rowdily jovial crew. She could often distinguish Jed's deep chuckle among the others.

But, although he had concealed it well, Jed was miserable. He had somewhat haltingly sought David's advice. David had ruthlessly advised him against making the first move.

"Let her sweat it out a spell," he said. "You give in to her now and you've got it all to do over again! I know Lissy—if she gets the notion that she can wind you around her finger, man, you're done for! Hell, I been so busy fightin' with her all these years I ain't had time to look up a woman of my own to fight with! And I still wouldn't gamble on it which of us is boss. You'd best take a firm stand—do her good to worry a while longer, anyway, she's still sorta mad."

Jed conceded that his reasoning was probably sound but he felt foot-loose, aimless. His heart constricted painfully whenever he caught a glimpse of her small figure. He ached to gather her up close, push her towhead against his shoulder again.

That first morning in the meadow was cloudless and bright, promising a hot day. Most of the women turned to early and got out big washings. Trail garb was scrubbed and spread to dry on nearby bushes. Having finished her laundry, Melissa enjoyed a leisurely all-over bath in a wooden tub in the wagon, donned clean clothes from the skin out, and then washed her long mop of hair.

It was past noon now, and many of the women and children were napping. It was very hot; a sultry wind moved across the meadow and from below the mountain rim was a continuous belching of dirty-white thunderheads, rolling and mounting till they covered half of the brilliantly blue sky. The men had set up a forge and there was the continuous musical clang of a hammer providing accompaniment for their distance-softened voices. By the walled spring another group were engaged in cleaning and soaking water barrels for the long desert haul.

"You look mighty pretty." A soft voice penetrated the drowsy silence at Melissa's wagon. The girl's head was bent, she was brushing her hair to speed its drying. She threw its damp weight back and looked up to see Rosetta Barker eying her appreciatively. Rosetta wore fresh clothing and her glistening copper hair showed that she, too, had groomed herself from head to foot.

Melissa did look pretty with her curling yellow mop unconfined, framing her small face. She had donned a white shirtwaist, its full sleeves were rolled above her elbows, its high, banded neck was unbuttoned for coolness. Under her brown calico skirt she had left off all but one petticoat and her slenderly curving lines were delicately evident. Her bare feet felt delightfully light in soft strapped slippers. She had resisted, not without a struggle, the inclination to run barefoot in the grass with the children. Melissa smiled wan thanks for the compliment and invited Rosetta to sit down on a packing case. In spite of the lift from freshening up, her tone was listless and the older woman noted the unhappy droop of the red lips, the melancholy of the hazel eyes. Melissa was finding life draggingly dull these days.

Rosetta watched the girl test the dampness of her hair and begin to comb, separating it, preparatory to braiding it up. "Oh, no, don't do it up," she protested. "It's so pretty hanging loose in those deep waves. Why don't you just tie it back with a ribbon? Have you got a blue ribbon, or a pink one?"

Melissa nodded, went to her bureau in the wagon, and returned with a length of blue ribbon, which Rosetta took firmly out of her hands. Brushing back the thick blond mop, the woman brought the ribbon from the nape of Melissa's slender neck forward and back of her ears to tie in a flat bow on the top of her head. Tiny, curling wisps were coaxed forward to make a soft frame for the pointed face. Rosetta finished and, head to one side, nodded and smiled. "You're as pretty as the first yellow rosebud in the spring," she said, "and men like hair ribbons—especially blue or pink ones."

Melissa's face became indignant. "Men!" she said witheringly.

Rosetta laughed aloud. "I know, honey," she agreed, "but it's not much fun to get along without them, is it?" Melissa looked down at her hands and sighed, soberly shook her head.

"Well, he's not enjoying it, either," Rosetta consoled, "I've seen the way he looks at you—"

Melissa raised a surprised face. "Why—he hasn't looked at me for a week—"

Rosetta chuckled. "Oh yes, he has!" she contradicted gaily, "not when *you'd* catch him at it, but I've seen him skulking around in the shadows, peeking at you and looking woebegone as a sick calf. He's just hoping for some sign from you, is all. Men are funny, Lissy, and touchy; a man's pride is a sore spot. They're mighty slow to say they're sorry, even if they are, and I expect Jed is afraid you'll snub him."

Melissa dropped her pose of unconcern. "What shall I do, Rosetta?" Her voice was wistful. "I don't know what to do—"

Rosetta's face was mischievous, "I'll tell you," she said, "Jed and Lawson rode out early to hunt. They weren't back at dinner time so they'll likely be along soon. I'll bet they'll be back any time, now." Melissa's eyes were puzzled. "Why don't you," Rosetta continued, "go for a ride? Don't change into pants—go just the way you are. Off over that way." She waved toward the hills to the east. Melissa looked uncomprehendingly. "Don't worry," Rosetta said, "wait just over the first hill till someone comes looking for you."

"Jed?" Melissa brightened.

"Jed."

"But, what if—" She had misgivings. "He'll just scold me for riding off alone—"

"I don't think Jed Smith will scold this time!" Rosetta's wide eyes were knowing. "And listen, Lissy, I'll tell you how to handle him—it's easy. Just keep in mind this one thing." She touched the sweet-smelling hair, caressed the pale curls. As she smiled down into the lifted, anxious face, her own was tenderly all-wise.

"Lissy," she said softly, "don't ever waste your breath arguing with a man that wants—loves—you. You don't need to ever say a word! No matter how Jed greets you, no matter *what* he says, just you walk straight up to him and right into his arms! I promise you, if you'll do that—not say a word, just get close, hold up your face to be kissed—he'll forget how mad he was at you!" Melissa's eyes were wide, her nod was solemn as she absorbed this gospel.

A little later Rosetta watched the girl ride out on her sorrel mare, pause on the crest of the first hill, look back to wave, and disappear over its ridge. The woman then watched until Jed and Lawson hove into view and moved to intercept them. She smiled up at the two men. "Jed," she said, "can I talk to you a minute?" Jed's face was puzzled at the request but he swung down from Palouse. Lawson rode away. Bet a dollar, the lanky man thought, that Rosetta and Melissa are ganging up on Jed. He grinned and started to whistle.

The scout's expression was somewhat wary, but Rosetta smiled reassuringly. "Melissa rode off, over that way, a little bit ago," she said, waving toward the direction the girl had taken.

"Alone?" Jed frowned disapprovingly.

"Don't scold her, Jed," Rosetta said softly, "she feels pretty bad about things."

The man's face was suddenly eager. "You think maybe she—that I should——"

Rosetta nodded, smiling warmly. "I think you should go find her, right now."

Jed was on Palouse and galloping away; he turned to wave exuberantly at Rosetta, his teeth flashing white, he looked suddenly very young. The tall red-haired woman watched him speed away and there was a knowing, almost tender smile curving her full lips.

Melissa had knotted Jane's rein to a branch back of the hilltop and returned afoot to crouch behind a cedar tree and peer down toward the camp. Her pulses raced as she watched Rosetta talk to Jed. And then, when he swung up on Palouse and was nearing the hill so fast, she suddenly panicked. She ran to Jane and mounted quickly, galloped away between two hills and along a narrow winding valley. Her heart pounded, she felt reluctant to put Rosetta's advice to a test. She admitted to herself that she really was a little afraid of Jed. She just didn't understand men, him especially.

The winding valley she followed presently narrowed to a ravine. The scrub oak had thickened on its walls. The trickle of a small stream led between rust-colored rocks and the gravelly bed was the only passage. The steep banks on either side rose abruptly, brushy and rock-strewn, unless she faced about, she must follow the stream.

The mare paused, dropped her nose into a shallow pool and drank, sucking noisily. When she had her fill she traveled leisurely along the narrow stream and they followed its course through a deepening rock gorge for perhaps two hundred yards. There were bright, nodding flowers edging the waterway and low ferns grew luxuriantly fresh and green. The walling rocks rose higher, almost meeting above until only a blue bar of sky was visible directly overhead.

As Jane splashed along the stream it suddenly turned at a sharp angle and passed between towering rock pedestals so close together that the girl could have touched each side of the rock walls with outstretched hands. It was like a doorway and was, in truth, an entrance, for she found herself sitting her horse in a small box canyon. The walls were of the same rust-colored rock, rearing splinteredly high, perpendicular. Here and there smalls trees and bushes grew at improbable slants, their exposed roots frantically clutching the face of the rock.

There were dark streaks where water seeped through cracks, trickled down a ribboned trail to the stream, which had its source in the secret places of the craggy wall. The faint babble of water was the only sound in the dreaming quiet of the little hidden canyon. At the foot of the east wall the water pooled in a shallow rock basin; it was very clear, and surrounded by pebbly red sand. A tangle of scrub oak invaded much of the floor of the canyon, grass grew in clumps, and there were small red and yellow flowers.

A squirrel suddenly set up a rattle of indignant chatter. Melissa jumped nervously and then laughed aloud. The tiny animal sat impudently in full view on a rock, its tail twitching irritably the while it berated the intruder.

Jane dropped her nose into a clump of grass and Melissa dismounted, letting the reins drop. It was very hot in the unmoving air of the enclosure, her hair hung stickily on her neck. Kneeling on the sand by the little pool, Melissa scooped water in her hands to drink. It was cool and sweet and she splashed her face and neck gratefully.

She was still kneeling when she heard a sound, the click of horse's hoofs against the rocks of the stream bed. All at once she was alarmed. What if an Indian had seen her, was following? Jed had said that not seeing Indians didn't mean there were none around. What if it was one like the fierce savage that would have pulled her from Palouse? What if he came, got to her before Jed— *Could* Jed trail her? She'd come up the stream bed—would he know the way she'd taken?

The clicking was much louder now, near the oaks at the narrow mouth of the box canyon. Something, screened from her view was coming through the trees. And it was a box, this place—there was no other way out! Choking back the scream that panicked in her throat, Melissa crouched, terrified, on the sand, her eyes wide with fear—and saw Jed ride into view.

That was how Jed first glimpsed her: eyes wide and dark with genuine fear, her face flushed with heat and wet from her splashing. Her shining wealth of hair tumbling about her shoulders, the red mouth open and trembling. In the shadowy canyon her hair above the white blouse was like a golden flame.

The man sat his horse, his gaze on her long and serious. He seemed to loom so much bigger than life above the girl, his wide shoulders in the darkened buckskins, his silent stare shadowed by the wide brim of his hat. She noticed nervously that his mouth was set and unsmiling.

But then he was off Palouse and coming toward her with long purposeful strides. And she was flying to him in complete panic. They met in the center of the quiet little clearing. She halted uncertainly and looked up, her eyes met his hungry gaze and she knew of no need to speak. She hurled herself at him and was tight in his arms, hurtingly crushed against the hard chest, where she had longed to be.

Jed felt a jolting knot convulse inside him as the frightened little figure ran toward his arms. When she was there, close, her head burrowing under his shoulder, he had trouble not sobbing aloud, so exquisite was the relieving pain. He gathered her slightness up against him and carried her to the warm sand near the pool. Throwing off his hat, he pulled her close and kissed her, glorying in the instant, stormy response. She clung to him as though she would never let go.

For a long time there were no words and then, breathlessly, Melissa pulled back and looked up at him teasingly, in the old way. Jed's intent blue gaze met hers and they stared long and at the same instant began to laugh. Melissa's head went back and her teeth flashed white. They kissed between chuckles at the memory of their needless foolishness.

The shadows lengthened, the air became cooler. Jane and Palouse contentedly grazed, moving a slow step at a time. The outraged squirrel made an offended, complaining appearance from time to time, warily changing positions from tree to rock to make known his continuing resentment. Jed peeled out of his shirt to kneel by the pool and splash water over his face and chest. Melissa marked with wonder the whiteness of his skin below the sharply defined leather color of face and neck. She unbuttoned her slippers and put her feet in the water, dabbling at first and then splashing at the kneeling man. Jed grabbed at her foot and made as though to upset her into the pool. He stopped suddenly, staring at the little white foot in his grasp. Its ridiculously small size seemed to entrance him. Almost with wonder he placed the sole flat against his palm, which was wider and longer than her foot. Melissa stopped struggling and laughed at him indulgently, the dimples appearing in her cheeks.

He was kneeling on one knee, half facing her. The sleek line of neck muscle flowed down to band powerfully the wide chest, the brown sunburn line at the base of his throat emphasized his bareness. She had seen him like this once before: when he had stripped to fight Sol Ward. There was a tingling thrill as she remembered—he had seemed so slight before the bearded giant. And then with deadly efficiency he had whipped the bigger man, left him bleeding, unconscious. Her breathing quickened, remembering the almost unbearable excitement of it. Just after that fight Jed had really kissed her for the first time, causing her senses to reel, dizzily clamoring for more of the savage love-making. But he had been carefully withdrawn ever since. Meanwhile she had known a sweet, consuming interest; at times the surges of bewildering feeling frightened her and yet urged her on to tease, tantalize, whenever they were alone together. But always, irritatingly and yet comfortingly, Jed had withdrawn. Roughly, abruptly at times, he would limit their time together, he had guarded her well.

Jed's brown hand slid to the warm curve just below her knee and tightened. He raised his head, met a wide questioning stare. Her lips were parted, her breathing quickened at the hunger that flared in his eyes. "Lissy?" It was a whisper. Her mouth smiled, her eyes adored him, and their gaze did not falter as his hand unbuttoned her blouse and slid urgently inside.

The whole world swung dizzily for Melissa, and she pulled the blouse wide and, kneeling, thrust her soft whiteness against his bare, hard chest. His mouth came down on hers fiercely with complete and deliberate possession. His hands moved roughly the length of her arched and shaking slenderness.

The sun had set and the heavens were declaring their glory in a cathedral arched of long shafts of crimson cloud above the mountains as Jed and Melissa rode slowly back toward the meadows. They spoke but little; both were exquisitely at peace with themselves and each other. The man's eyes were on her constantly, marveling. He realized, thinking of the hours beside the pool, that there had been little of submission in her. She had been a joyous partner, exuberantly zestful for his love-making.

"Lissy," he said softly, "how about a trail wedding—like John and Rosetta?"

She was startled for a moment, and then her smile flashed, her eyes loved him. "While we're here, at Mountain Meadows?"

He nodded. "It's a pretty place for a weddin', let's see what David says——"

She tossed her head pertly. "It's not up to David," she said.

Jed laughed, everything was joy-filled this day. "Well," he said, "shall we wait till we get to Californy? It's a long ways yet." His glance coaxed her.

Melissa appeared to be seriously considering, but Jed did not miss the dimples in her cheeks. "All right!" she said, flushing suddenly, "tomorrow night—here at Mountain Meadows——"

David stood spraddle-legged by the fire, warming his behind, a wide grin on his face as he watched their leisurely approach. Rosetta had told him of the conniving that had brought the quarrel to an end and so he had unworriedly waited.

"Hello, David!" Melissa called gaily to her brother,

"are you starved for your supper? So are we!" She scrambled from Jane and ran to her brother, hugging him exuberantly. He looked down at her indulgently. "David," she rushed on, "Jed and I are going to be married—tomorrow night—a trail marriage." She looked up at him, her face glowing. "It's all right with you, isn't it?"

David looked over her head at Jed. The tall man had dismounted, had the reins of both horses in his hands; he looked anxiously at David. David smiled warmly, affectionate warmth in his voice. "Sure, it's fine with me. Tomorrow night will be just fine!"

## CHAPTER XVI

Melissa woke up slowly. She stretched and flexed deliciously, rolled over to snuggle deeper into her warm blankets. Then she realized it was morning although it was still dark inside the wagon, for she could hear morning and breakfast sounds, knew that the sun would be nearly up. Now she heard David's voice calling a cheery greeting to someone as he came in from the night herd. She hurriedly scrambled into her clothes and made an appearance as her brother got the cooking fire kindled. She shivered in the nippy cool of the earliness.

David laughed when he looked at his sister, she was like a drowsy kitten, stretching and yawning, her tawny eyes still vague from heavy sleep, her tumbling hair loose on her shoulders. "Slugabed," he teased, "wash your face and look around. It's going to be another hot day, not a cloud in the sky."

Melissa gasped as the cold water touched her face but she washed vigorously and it woke her up. She brushed her hair back, tied it with a ribbon, and surveyed the day, pleased that it was starting out bright—it was her wedding day. Her eyes glowed as she thought of the little secret canyon. She and Jed had planned to take along some food and spend all of the day in the lovely little retreat.

There was now no need for dawn rising but the whole camp was astir. Long trail habit had so accustomed them that few could sleep past first light.

Jed appeared promptly for breakfast with the Bollers, leading Jane and Palouse. Both horses had enjoyed many rolls in the deep meadow grass and all the trail dust was gone, their coats gleamed like satin. David grinned his approval of their plan to "explore" the surrounding country. The genial little man felt more than content to have their small circle complete again, with Melissa laughing and teasing, happy because of Jed's presence. And David smiled to see how the scout's intent gaze followed each quick, joyous movement the girl made.

David finished his breakfast, drained the last dregs of coffee, and stood to stretch, scratching sleepily. "I'd best get some sleep," he yawned, "though the herd was so quiet last night I dozed in the saddle, damn near fell off a coupla times."

He lifted the water bucket and drank, laughing at his own clumsiness when he spilled some chillingly down his shirt front. As he lowered the bucket his eye caught a movement on the hill to the east; his manner became so oddly intent that Jed turned to stare in the same direction.

Even as their eyes sought to pierce the shadows beneath the cedar trees there was a long, ululating shriek, followed by a fusillade of shots.

"INJUNS!" Jed's stentorian roar was heard by all in the stunned camp. "INJUNS! GET DOWN–GET DOWN–TAKE COVER—"

Swiftly he shoved Melissa down between two packing cases, drew his rifle from its saddle scabbard, and crouched, drawing a bead on an Indian who rode zigzag across the slanting face of the hill. He waited for him to come within range, and now many more, mounted and on foot, appeared, advancing from tree to bush in quick darting rushes.

There were shouts and yelling, combined with heavy firing on the meadows where the herds were. David had obeyed Jed's shout and wormed his way behind a wheel; rifle ready, he squatted waiting for the Indians to approach within range. But then the stocky little man heard a stallion's outraged, trumpeting whistle and started convulsively. "They're after the horses—" He choked, his eyes became frantic. "That was the King!" He ran crouchingly from the wagon and across the circle toward the herd ground.

"No! *No*—David—don't—" Jed's shout was lost in the noise. David had gone to see to his beloved horses.

Melissa, crouching between the cases, her head close to her knees, could see Jed where he knelt behind a barrel. He squinted, his head lowered until his cheek lay along the stock, he froze into rocklike stillness as he squeezed off his first shot. She heard a distant shriek that told he had not missed, and began to shake uncontrollably, shutting her eyes. But she could not bear to keep them shut and opened them just in time to see his jaw tighten as he fired again. The cry was much nearer, she heard a dull thud as a body struck the ground, the rattle of startled hoofs. Jed had knocked an Indian from a racing pony and not far away. Her eyes widened in horror; were they all that close? The weird yammering sounded as though there were thousands of savages, would they presently swarm over, engulf the train?

The two that Jed had brought down had plunged recklessly headlong in advance of the rest. He had used the two shots that his rifle held and now cocked his heavy Colt. He waited but there were no more who sought to risk a coup. Knowing that the two downed bodies would give them pause, Jed quickly reloaded his rifle.

His eyes surveyed the circled train. The women and children were all under some sort of cover. Most of the men lay flat on their bellies under the wagons, partly shielded by the thick wheel spokes. The firing was heaviest on the west arc of the uneven circle. They were pouring out shot as though they had an arsenal to fall back on. Jed frowned but reflected that they probably had more targets there, for it was clearly a raid on the herds. The Indians now skulking from tree to rock on the east hills did not appear too eager to advance under the range of the rifles.

The firing on the west side slackened, there was a thunder of hoofs, it sounded like the horse herd had stampeded toward the wagons. And then horses galloped into the enclosure. The huge shape of the King appeared, his big head forward, teeth bared as he drove his mares before him.

Jed's eyes searched the dusty melee for David, saw him astride Juno, a tall, gray mare, one hand clutching her silver mane. He rode oddly bent, leaning forward, and Jed saw that a dark stream ran from him, staining the shoulder of the mare. His hold slackened, he half slid, half fell to the ground.

Jed leaped across the dusty expanse, made his way through the milling horses, and gathered the smaller man up against him. Still crouching, he got the limp form under the wagon. Gently lowering the wounded man, Jed peered between the wheels to see if any of the savages had ventured nearer.

There was no movement among the trees and rocks on the east hill. That section of the attackers had either withdrawn or were discouraged, perhaps they had shifted to help with the raid on the cattle.

Jed turned back to David. His shirt front was soppingly red and the scout tore it gently back, disclosing a gaping wound in the chest. Blood oozed in a thick stream, the eyes were closed and the soggy bubbling of each breath told Jed that the heavy slug had smashed through his left lung.

Jed shot a glance at the packing cases, he could see the corner of Melissa's brown skirt. She was unaware of what had happened to David. Jed made a pad of his neckerchief and with David's belt bound it to cover the wound. The man's face was waxy, his eyes were sunken, there was a blue line around the gasping mouth and a red tinge to the foam on his lips. Jed knew that David was dying.

The scout hated what must follow. He wormed his way to Melissa's shelter and shielded her with his body as she scuttled between the wheels and under the wagon. As she knelt beside her brother, Jed crouched between the wheels, shielding the two of them.

David's eyelids flickered, opened. He stared up at his sister's tear-streaked face with surprise to see her so. One hand moved weakly, exploringly across his chest, found the sticky mass. There was unbelief, protest in the eyes that moved from Melissa's bowed head to Jed, whose jaw was clenched so that the muscles were painfully knotted. David's stare searched the scout's grim face. "Jed?" he whispered.

Melissa turned to see the slow shaking of Jed's head, his pain-filled eyes met David's steadily. The girl put her fist against her mouth to stem the deep sobs. David's eyes had closed, they lifted again, his glance beseeched. "The King?" he whispered faintly, "is he—" Jed nodded. "Inside—safe, with the mares. I'll see to him, David."

The whisper was almost inaudible. "The King—and Jane, and Juno—they're the finest—" He tried to lift a hand to Melissa's rumpled head but it sank limply. Melissa clutched it in both of hers, brought it to her wet cheek. There were several gasping, strangling breaths and then silence. Melissa leaned closer to stare with dilated eyes into her brother's face. There was a quivering of the muscles around the firm mouth and then they relaxed, the jaw dropped slowly, the teeth showing in the empty, involuntary grimace of death.

Jed's face had become hatchetlike, he reached and gathered the girl up against him, holding her with one arm while keeping a steely watch on the hills. She buried her face against his chest and cried wrenchingly.

Jed's roaming gaze caught a movement on the hillside where an almost impenetrable tangle of scrub oak made a line. In a low voice he warned the men in the next wagons, heard the word being passed on, the clicking back of hammers.

Jed put Melissa behind him, the girl sank against his back, put her arms around him and held close. She made no sound, but he could feel the shaking of her body.

A screaming mass of Indians charged from around a small hill to the north. They rode veering near the wagons to fire and angle away again. The ones on the hillsides opened fire at the same time. The besieged train answered with a steady hammer of shooting. Jed thought he accounted for one more who betrayed his location behind a bush. Once more the Indians pulled back.

Then followed long hours of relative quiet, laced by an occasional shot from the hillsides. There was little danger to those under cover except from splinters that flew from wagon boards and wheel spokes. The sun seemed caught directly overhead, its direct rays scorched. A shriveling wind swept across the meadows. Most of the horses had been caught up and were tethered to the wagons. Ebony King stomped restlessly by Melissa's wagon, Lady Jane and Juno flanked him. Jed had gotten the sorrel and Palouse inside during a quiet moment.

Leaving Lawson Mitchell on guard over Melissa and the blanket-shrouded form of David, Jed made his way to the west side of the train. He noted approvingly that cases and barrels had been drawn against the wheels, leaving only peepholes for shooting, as he had done at the Boller wagon. Jed and Captain Fancher and his council met for a short consultation.

There had been three deaths: David Boller, Rosetta Barker's ten-year-old son and the herder, Jared Hardy—the talkative young man who favored abandoning the train in favor of polygamy in Salt Lake City. Young Tommy had gone to the spring to fetch water and had been hit by the first fusillade. He had started at a staggering run for the wagons and Rosetta had dashed out to meet him. Although bullets kicked up dust around her flying feet, she had carried the boy to shelter. He died almost at once, only opened his eyes once to smile up at his mother.

Jared's body lay around the edge of the first hill to the north, where the cattle had been. Young McLean, who had been with him, told how the Indians had suddenly poured down the slope, firing as they came. He and Jared had returned the fire but they looked to be overwhelmed before they could reload. McLean had escaped by running through the milling herd. He heard Jared shrieking and got a glimpse as the man went down when two savages, hatchets raised, leaped upon him. From the sounds of it, McLean said, they chopped him up before he was dead. McLean had got a hold on a horse's mane and had been towed, running alongside, safely inside the wagon circle when David Boller recklessly rounded them up.

There were quite a few wounded casualties. Several of the Missouri faction had flesh wounds, the brunt of the attack had been near their western location. One man had a bullet in his groin. It was not thought he would live, they could not stop the bleeding. Joel Mitchell had a deep groove along the flesh of his upper left arm. Cintha Tackett's oldest girl, eight-year-old Sabina, had been hit by a large splinter, which pierced her thin little shoulder, narrowly missing bones. It was a jaggedly painful wound but it had stopped bleeding; the child would probably be all right.

Captain Fancher mentioned that he had sent a guard to the Tackett wagon, knowing that Cintha and Sairy Ward were without a rifleman. But the man returned and said that Sol Ward was looking out for his estranged wife and the Tacketts. Sol, at the first onslaught, had run recklessly across the wagon circle, gun in hand. The women were making much of the redbeard's heroism.

The attack had focused on the herds. The location of the horses—between the cattle and the train—had prevented the Indians from gaining many horses. David Boller's costly foray had saved most of his thoroughbreds.

The Indians had frustrated their own objective. They

had attacked first near the cattle herd and the animals had stampeded over the low incline, spooking the horses and mules, driving them near the train. Much of the livestock was now in a bowl-like declivity close to the train. There was plenty of grass and a small stream meandered across the near corner of it. It was possible they might retain the rest, for the Indians would have to come within rifle range to drive any more. By tallying the variously reported "sure" hits, Captain Fancher figured they must have accounted for perhaps eighteen or twenty Indians.

Jed nodded thoughtfully. "Unless I miss my guess," he offered, "likely they've near got a bellyful. These would be mostly Paiutes—and they ain't like Cheyennes or Utes —I expect they'll traipse off most any time now."

Jed was mistaken. The Indians had withdrawn but only to the higher ridges surrounding the meadow. They could be plainly seen, their bright feathers and painted horses moving among the trees. There was smoke from many cook fires, they had butchered some animals and were feasting.

As the afternoon waned, long cloud shadows stalked across the valley escorted by the hot wind. To the west thick clouds funneled like smoke from behind the mountains, were vomited up to boil and mount across the sky. Lightning ripped through the clouds and the mutter of thunder rolled and echoed like angry drums. Between gusts of wind, it was scorching to breathe.

The ridges were literally crawling with Indians. They rode across the slopes on their gaunt ponies, raising their rifles high, shrieking defiant insults at the train. They were stridently arrogant, seeming far from retreat.

Jed reconnoitered the encircling hills from inside the train, astonishing himself with the reluctant estimate that there were at least three hundred Indians in plain view. He reported this disquieting fact to Captain Fancher.

That stolid man was jarred. "*Three hundred!* For God's sweet sake—are you sure?"

Jed shrugged, "Give it a few, more or less," he said soberly, "with them movin' around all the time, it's hard to count but here's the thing—with that many showin', there's bound to be more. You never see them all."

Fancher's jaw set hard on the stem of his cold pipe. His eyes were grave as he stared around the train, heard the groaning of the dying man, the sobbing whimper of the wounded child, sighed at the sight of the blanketed form of David Boller. "How's our chances, agin that many?" he asked.

The two men were alone, kneeling among some barrels, staring at the swarming hillside. Jed was carefully honest. "Likely we'n make it if we can keep 'em out of the wagons. If that many once get in to where it's hand to hand, they'll take us—we ain't got a prayer!" He paused and then went on. "From the looks of things they're workin' themselves up to a big rush likely just about sundown, and we'll *have* to stop 'em. Best you pass the word for no man to pull his trigger without he's got a damn sure target. Tell 'em to let 'em get close. Best way to run them off is to scare the shit out of 'em by bringing down the front ones. If the men will hold their fire—alternate—so's one fires while the other reloads—make it continuous. Tell 'em, for God sake, to let 'em get close—the light will be bad for sightin' at sundown, and the bastards will attack heaviest to the west, where the sun will be in our eyes. They always pull that if they can. If we can keep them off, likely they'll pull out. I ain't seen many Injuns that wanted to try cases after dark."

Captain Fancher listened carefully, nodding his understanding and agreement. He assigned a few more men to the west half of the circle and passed the word along, was cheered by the steadiness of the acquiescence all around.

Presently they noticed that the Indians had vanished. Nothing stirred for a breathless time while the moving line of shadow reached the base of the east hills. The heat relented as the sun dipped lower. In the sky to the west dark streaks of red knifed through the restlessly billowing clouds.

Jed made a hurried scout of the circle to warn that

the heaviest attack would come fast from the declivities between the hills. Then he resumed his position beneath Melissa's wagon. The girl lay on her side against the barricade, her knees drawn up, one hand beneath her cheek. Her eyes were closed, but the occasional quiver of her mouth betrayed that she was not asleep. Jed knelt for an instant beside her, smoothed back her tousled hair. Her eyes opened and she caught his hand, held it against her cheek. "Are they—the Injuns—still out there?"

Jed nodded. "They're there." His voice was flat. "They'll be comin' again any time, now. Just you stay still, right where you are——" He saw the swift horror mount in her face. "Never you fear, we'll be all right. They'll likely make this one more try but soon's it's dark they'll pull out. They got no belly for night fightin'."

Even as he stroked her hair the weird, ominous shrilling began. And from the defiles, the mouths of the draws, and over the low ridges the Indians poured in a surging, bobbing stream, firing as they came. They rode wildly, superbly, many of them hanging from the off side of their lunging ponies, raising to fire and ducking down again. Some used bows, and arrows thudded into wagon boxes, tore shriekingly through the canvas tops.

The riflemen in the train sturdily obeyed instructions, holding their fire and then pouring a steady sheet of lead into the screaming mass of men and horses. They alternated grimly and the volleys took a terrible toll. And had the desired result. The attackers veered further and further away on each subsequent darting attack. They seemed loath to close with the smoking rifles that waited for them. They retreated to the ledges to ride hectically back and forth, seemed to be debating another attack.

Driven by a steady west wind, the mounting clouds had shrouded the meadows with gloom, shooting light was dissolving fast when Jed started up with a cursing exclamation.

Out there, among the milling, racing Indians, gaudy in their bright shirts and paint, was an alien figure. It was a huge, darkly hulking man, savagely riding a tall black horse. He wore black clothing and no decorations, he was black-bearded. And Jed knew him.

The dark-clad man appeared to be goading the Indians into another assault, his big black plunged in a rearing circle, the heavy rifle was flung high, he looked to be shouting something. A few warriors grouped about him and he kicked the black horse into a pounding run toward the train.

Jed crawled from under the wagon, stood up outside the barricade, rested his rifle, and led the approaching figure as though it were a running doe. He groaned at the distance for the shadows distorted, intruded on the dark outline. He waited until the rider neared what he estimated to be the apex of his slanting charge and then cursed under his breath. The light was too bad, he could not bring the rider to focus between his sights. He lowered his aim, drew a bead on his mount and squeezed the trigger.

The long-striding horse jerked as the bullet struck, gathered, plunged on a few ragged paces and crashed down. Jed saw the bearded man leap free, stagger clear as the horse rolled, and disappear behind a screen of trees. The Indians following him vanished also. As night enveloped the hillside Jed knew something infinitely worse about their situation. He had recognized Josh Wade—and cursed bitterly that he had been unable to kill the dangerous renegade.

He understood now a thing that had baffled him—well-planned attacks from Indians notorious for their listless lack of taste or talent for warfare. Wade led them, and the issue would not be done with because of nightfall. It would not end until Wade tired of it and dispersed the Indians. The hostiles had not pulled out, their fires leaped and glowed on the ridges encircling the train. They were boastingly high, advertising their continued presence. Dark figures leaped and contorted grotesquely around the flames; yammering, high-pitched singing came down into the silence of the shadowy meadows on the night wind.

Jed sought Captain Fancher, reported this last bit of discouraging news.

"Josh Wade!" Fancher remembered with dismay the grisly legends Eli Jacobs had told of this man. "But I thought he was a Mormon, how come—"

Jed shrugged. "Oh hell, he's been a renegade for years. I've known him to pull this sort of stuff any time he could get a few Injuns drunk and in a fightin' frame of mind—done it all the time with the Sioux and Cheyenne. The young bucks like to raid with him. He don't never care about loot, he just wants in on the killin'." Fancher's face turned a dirty gray, his mouth settled grimly as Jed continued.

"Wade ain't a Mormon except for his own damn convenience when he's in Mormon country. I doubt the Saints are ever glad to see him. He's trouble and there ain't a man can give him orders, less'n it'd be Rockwell. More'n like they don't even know he's in these parts, for he hangs out with the Injuns more'n he does the whites. And it's a damn cinch the Mormons wouldn't want him stirrin' up the tribes—it's too risky, few as they are hereabouts. They've always preached peace to the redskins."

Thus warned that their ordeal was not done, the night was taken over by preparation, they forted up the train. The wagons were laboriously manhandled into a tighter circle and chained together. Barrels, cases, furniture, anything that would stop or deflect a bullet were stacked into barriers. Rifle pits were dug beneath and between the wagons, the dirt from them was stacked high, pounded down to firmness. Mattresses and bedding were placed in the trenches for the women and children. The canvas covers were removed from the wagons as a precaution against fire arrows. Three milk cows were kept and the other cattle hazed out to join the herd. The horses were led out to drink by an alert guard and returned to be tethered to the wagons. A cautious bucket party made trips to the small stream, filling the few water barrels that were not still soaking by the spring. The water was none too clean, for the cattle drank from this stream, but none wanted to chance the distance to the spring.

When all was in readiness for a dawn attack they buried their dead. Three graves had been dug in the rifle pits between the wagons. It was in the last dark before dawn and the riflemen took their positions, so that it was mostly women and children who knelt to pray before consigning the bodies to the pits.

It had been a dark night, there had been only fleeting glimpses of the waning, lopsided moon sliding between the clouds that blotted out the stars. When the savages had ceased their yammering there had been the whimpering chorus of coyotes from the hills. And from far away, on the timbered high slopes, came the moaning call of timber wolves. Their fierce, pointed noses lifted to the wind had caught the reek of blood and death.

It was John Barker's deep voice which consigned the dead into the care of their Maker. He prayed simply, briefly and then repeated the Twenty-third Psalm. A few whispering, sobbing voices joined his and together they murmured the familiar beauty of these comforting words.

Melissa's tears were done now. It was with a white, drawn face, stiff with unbelief, that she stared at the quiet blanket-wrapped mound that was David.

"Yea, though I walk through the valley of the shadow of death . . ." John's reverent voice released the words slowly into the gloom and the girl raised her head. The valley of the shadow of death. So it was, indeed. A faintly grayish line of the sky indicated the high, ragged horizon. Slowly the summits of the impenetrable heights began to emerge, spectral through the curtain of fading night.

Melissa thought of how Mountain Meadows had appeared to them on Sunday—and now it neared the dawn of Wednesday. They had been so grateful to roll on to its friendly, green expanse. The surrounding beauty, the sparkling cool water. And only at breakfast this morning —yesterday, now, though none had slept—David had been so happy, laughing and teasing because it was their wedding day. But before that sunlit hour was done David was dead, his face contorted, his dear familiar body clotted with sticky blood.

Melissa felt a terrible bewilderment, it had happened so fast. In the space of minutes, from lilting happiness to sudden tragedy. She had never had death come close before. She had experienced no loss when her father failed to return. It had been a vague, unreal thing with little significance to the small child she was. He had been away so much that when David told her he would not return there had been no sorrow, no accompanying fear. Things were the same as always, for there was David. There had always been David, the sturdy foundation stone of her whole existence. And David was dead because he had tried to save his beloved horses from the vicious, yelping hordes of Indians.

The girl sat as though frozen while the soft dirt plumped down, covered her brother's body. She mechanically bowed her head for the benediction and when the others dispersed to their wagons she sought her own. Numbly she donned her pants and a dark calico shirt, tied a dark kerchief around her light head. Then she crawled into the pit beside Jed.

The scout had just finished checking his arsenal. His own and David's rifles stood ready, his supply of ammunition lay at hand, his heavy revolver was stuck in his belt. David's rifle was a single-shot Enfield, one that he had been able to wheedle from Eli Jacobs, having traded his carbine to Dick Washakie for the blue roan.

Jed's long arm reached for Melissa, drew her close. He was wordless, his thoughts had been somber while the burials took place. His big hand was tender on her hair, he pushed her head to its own place against his shoulder and cradled her. She lay still, taking comfort from his nearness, the strong male odor of his buckskins, the hard, dependable strength of him. He took her by the shoulders and peered down into her face, leaned and kissed her gently. "I love you, Lissy," he said, helpless to think of any other words.

Her eyes, shadowy deep in their sockets, were steady

and dry. Her voice, when she spoke, was very small. "I can load for you," she said, "I know how—"

And so they waited out the time of the graying dawn, waited for the savages to come again. The man's glance rested on her from time to time and he saw a difference in the small figure, the chiseled whiteness of her face. And he felt regret, recognizing what had changed. The artless child, Lissy, was forever gone. The gay, irresponsible little sister lay buried with David. This quiet, resilient shaft who waited beside him so quietly was a woman, with all of a woman's control and strength.

## CHAPTER XVII

Brigham Young was at his desk on Tuesday morning when his secretary announced that a special messenger had arrived from Dixie, urgently desired to speak with him. His nod was immediate, he smiled slightly at the coincidence for on his desk was a letter just signed which began "Dear Brother"—and was addressed to President Isaac Haight.

Hat in hand, young James Haslam entered, his spurs clinking musically over the carpet. The sweaty grime of fast travel was still on him, his eyes, peering through circles of dust, still squinted from the cutting wind.

He brought no written word; in careful quotes he made known the question posed by Isaac Haight and his council. As Brigham listened his shaggy brows met over the high-bridged nose and he exclaimed aloud. Haslam stopped his recital abruptly, confused by the expression on the other's face. Brigham shook his head, then motioned him to continue.

Having heard the express rider out, Brigham sat frowning, bewhiskered chin in hand. He waved Haslam to a chair, examined the man's drawn face. "When did you leave Cedar City?" he asked.

"Early Saturday afternoon," Haslam replied.

"You beat express time by quite a bit," Brigham observed commendingly. Haslam nodded. "I only slept a time or two while they changed horses for me."

Brigham studied him, concerned. "How long since you ate?"

"Well"—Haslam had to think about it—"not since yesterday, I guess. I figgered I'd best get to you first."

Brigham cleared his throat noisily. He was touched, as always, by the evidence of his people's endurance, their devoted confidence in him. He got up vigorously, went to the door, and ordered that food be brought to his office for Haslam. The young man flushed, immensely gratified at the leader's concern; worship was in the eyes that followed Young as he returned to his desk.

"I have just finished a letter to President Haight," Brigham said, "and it bears directly on the question." He paused and read aloud a paragraph from the letter: " 'In regards to the emigration trains passing through our settlements, we must not interfere with them until they are first notified to keep away. You must not meddle with them.' " Brigham raised his eyes to Haslam's still face and then read a further sentence from the letter. " 'The Indians, we expect, will do as they please but you should try and preserve good feelings with them.' "

During his recent visit, escorting the chiefs, Jacob Hamblin had been worried about the restlessness of the Indians. Brigham, too, realized that they might get out of hand. They had needed no further incentive after the news that rifles waited them in Dixie. They could hardly wait, they had left immediately for home. Jacob had been particularly disturbed about Kanosh, had reported that something was eating him, he'd had almost nothing to say the whole distance, had kept coldly to himself. It was a discouraging task, Brigham reflected, trying to civilize the savage Lamanites. Kanosh was intelligent, he'd been converted to the faith, lived in a brick house and aped many of the white man's ways. But let him smell blood and he took on the look of a kill-hungry cougar.

Brigham hoped his people would tread easy, he didn't want them—so few in number—antagonizing the likes of Kanosh and his horde of warriors. The trains would have to travel at their own risk, he wouldn't have his people chancing a rupture with the red men just to help Gentiles.

Brigham watched Haslam wolf down great chunks of bread, thick slices of meat. He drank glass after glass of cool thick buttermilk poured from a pitcher.

"The letter is ready, as it stands, Brother Haslam," Brigham said. He studied the rider's tired face. "I can send another express rider," he offered, "you look beat."

Haslam shook his head. "I can make it," he said. "President Haight is depending on me to bring the word, myself."

Brigham nodded, it was the answer he had expected. Steel, they were, his people. Bending at times under the weight of the elements and dangers of pioneering the wilderness, but never breaking. They remained stubbornly unconquerable. And because he knew their imponderable strength, their will to prevail, he dared pit his tattered, indignant hordes against the armed might of the United States. Thus far it was a battle of wills, only—a show of resistant power.

But if they were backed to the wall, Brigham Young knew that his people would fight to their last breath, shed the final drop of blood, if *he* gave the word. This realization had often, of late, slowed his angry hand.

"Does the letter," he asked Haslam, "make clear my decision about the Fancher Train, and any others?"

Haslam nodded uncertainly. "It ain't the answer they'll be expecting——"

Brigham nodded understandingly. "I know. I know all about this damned Fancher outfit and I don't doubt but that action might be justified against some of the people in it. But that train is headed for California—and we've got to consider the stories they'd tell the minute they hit there! Remember the damned outlaw rabble that poured through here?" Brigham's face became angry at the lawless, godless people they'd had to contend with. "The gold-rush trash—that's what is in California! Time the Fanchers got through babbling they'd be just as apt to jump our settlements on the coast!" Brigham took a restless turn about his desk, turned again to Haslam. "You be sure and tell that to Brother Isaac—make it very clear, what I say: *Word that Mormons are attacking Gentile trains must not be carried to California!*"

Haslam listened, his mouth partly open with the intensity of attention to the wording. His face was like a schoolboy's and Brigham wanted very much to smile; instead, his voice softened as he continued. "It would hurt our cause at this time, the situation is very touchy. Tell my people in Dixie that I pray for them constantly. Tell them that God, alone, provides a time of vengeance, in His own good time we will cut down our enemies!"

Haslam nodded, his face still puckered with the effort of memorizing the exact words. He placed the letter in his dispatch bag and Brigham shook his hand with vigorous warmth. A thought occurred to him. "Who did they have in mind to handle the Indians?" he asked interestedly, "Jacob Hamblin is still here in the city"—he chuckled then—"Brother John D. Lee isn't exactly cut to the pattern of a war chief——"

"I think," said Haslam, "they were countin' strong on Josh Wade."

Brigham was startled, he had forgotten that he had sent the bad-tempered man into isolated Dixie. He shook his head, that train was liable to see some action anyway, if Josh took a notion to lead the Indians against it. He placed a hand on Haslam's shoulder. "Can you make the same time back?" Concern was evident in his voice; he felt there should be no delay.

A quick smile lit Haslam's face, making it boyishly attractive. "I can better it, maybe. I'll try."

"God go with you, Brother Haslam," Brigham said, "keep you safe, you have my blessing." The leader moved to the window to watch as Haslam moved in his bowlegged, rider's gait down the walk, mounted the deep-chested restless horse in one easy, flowing step up and swing over. As his foot touched the stirrup, the horse broke into a canter, was galloping when he settled in the saddle. Brigham never tired of watching the picture his desert riders made—so beautifully co-ordinated in their movements, they seemed as one with the horse. He moved back to his desk, surveyed with distaste the amount of paper work to be done. The matter of the attack on the Fancher Train was a closed, dealt-with issue in his methodical mind.

But, even as he handed the letter into Haslam's keeping the guns were thundering on Mountain Meadows. The grass was already stained with the blood of some in the Fancher Train. And, outside the wagon circle, the bodies of the red men lay grotesquely still where they had fallen.

As Haslam galloped south from Salt Lake City, another messenger rode with equal haste from Mountain Meadows with word for Isaac Haight that the Indians had jumped the gun. They had attacked the Fancher Train at dawn that morning. John D. Lee had been unable to prevent it, he was ignored by the vengeance-hungry Josh Wade and the Pahvant chief, Kanosh, who had arrived with all of his warriors.

Lee, and the handful of troubled Mormons with him, took no active part in the initial onslaught. Josh Wade was the only white man who rode with the Indians. Had it not been for the bearded man's goading, the Paiutes would have deserted the battle to feast on the mules they captured.

The Indians were very angry at Lee, who had prophesied with tears flowing down his face that their efforts would be blessed, they would all come through the battle unharmed for the White God would hold a protecting hand over his Lamanites. They were displeased with this negligent God and His weeping spokesman, for they numbered nine dead and a score of wounded. Lee wished that someone else had charge of the boiling savages. He had had a very bad time with Kanosh, whose fury at the loss of three warriors was a terrible thing to see and he vented all his wrath on Lee, who had promised them safety. Josh Wade was a problem, too. The big man stalked about in a monumental rage because of the loss of his black horse.

It had been Josh who had goaded the listless Paiutes into taking part in the sundown attack. He had orated scornfully that his boy, Crazy Horse, had more guts for bloodshed than any three of the Paiute warriors. The boy, mounted on his sure-footed buckskin and armed only with a bow, had been Wade's shadow in every attack.

However they distrusted each other, the three leaders, Lee, Wade, and Kanosh, were agreed that the attacks must be continued. Lee, although sick of it, could not abandon the siege until it had been the success Isaac Haight expected. It was far from that; about half the cattle and mules remained near the train and the fine thoroughbreds were within the wagon circle.

Under Lee's direction the Mormons had dammed the stream which flowed down into the meadow. The train would have to drive the horses out, save the water for themselves. Most of their water barrels were by the spring, they could not have many for storing water.

It was decided that Kanosh would lead his Pahvants on a mounted foray at dawn while the Paiutes took positions closer to the wagons than they had thus far been able to attain.

The gray, fading curtain of night lifted reluctantly, the rugged mountain rims were bathed in delicate rosy light. The clouds had thinned during the night and those to the east were flame-lined. The air was chilly and Melissa shivered. Jed drew her close against him for warmth. Eyes in the train unceasingly searched the emerging hillsides, which seemed innocently quiet, empty of savages. But none was lulled by the peacefulness, the gaze of the waiting riflemen moved constantly to and fro, watching for movement.

Kanosh and Kasota led their band, mounted on painted ponies, circling away from the train to attack from the south. They would make the approach jointly and then split, encircle the train in a running fire, their ranks joining again at the north end of the meadow. Both chiefs wore full regalia, had painted their faces black. They had abandoned their plumed lances in favor of the new rifles.

The first rays of the cloud-hampered sun had just stretched across the meadows when high-pitched shrieks broke from the throats of Kanosh and Kasota. Their ponies, kicked into a headlong run, obeyed the pressure of muscular thighs and swept in two long arcs past the wagon train.

"HERE THEY COME!" The steady barking roar of the rifles commenced. The drumming of hoofs neared and now the wild riders thundered into the range of Jed's position. The searching black snout of his rifle led a hideously painted warrior and then he fired. When the smoke lifted he saw a riderless pony racing away. His gun spoke again and a rawboned white horse reared and went down, screaming and pawing, pinning his rider beneath him. Jed drew a bead on the man's head, waited only for the dust to clear, and fired. The man jerked convulsively and lay still beneath the white horse.

Jed handed the empty rifles to Melissa. Her small hands worked busily, as she reloaded she was grateful that they did not tremble.

But that one swift passage was to be all of the mounted attack. No other riders came within range and although they could hear the screeching and pounding of hoofs elsewhere, the attackers drew off. The dust began to settle stiflingly, the acrid stink of black powder lay over all. The people in the pits waited and presently became acquainted with what was to be the pattern of the day.

From the hillsides, from behind rocks, bushes, and trees a searching, irregular firing began. The Indians seemed to be as numerous as ants in a big anthill and they had concealed themselves with great skill. They alternated their fire and were changing position often, slithering on their bellies from cover to cover, giving the riflemen few sure targets.

The hours mounted drearily toward noon. It was hot, the same dust-laden blast of wind drove immense clouds across the brassy blue sky. As they sailed along on the wind, their cloud shadows moved enormously across the floor of the meadow bringing momentary gray relief from the pitiless sun.

Leaving Melissa with Joel Mitchell, Jed reconnoitered the train, held a conference with Captain Fancher. There were none dead and only two lightly wounded casualties from the dawn attack. But it had proved costly for the Pahvants—seven lay dead at various points outside the wagons.

It was not until in the afternoon that they realized what plan had been put into effect during the night. And with the realization came the knowledge that it was to be a lengthy siege. The animals in the meadow outside the train were moving away. They would approach the small stream and drop their heads—only to raise dry muzzles. There was no water. The stream had been diverted, their source of water had been cut off. Only a few barrels, part full, remained. It would have to be severely rationed immediately and the animals kept inside would have to go without. They were getting low in ammunition, now there remained but a few gallons of water.

Captain Fancher called his council together. They discussed the chances a small party might have of getting to Cedar City, where they would ask help from the territorial officials.

Jed was skeptical that help might be forthcoming from the Mormons but agreed that they might be willing to parley with the Indians, offer them a ransom to pull out. Captain Fancher was remembering his favorable impression of Isaac Haight.

"I know how you feel about Mormons, Jed," Fancher said, "but, hell, when you get right down to cases they won't sit still and let us be butchered! They're white and we're white—they'll come through when they know how it is with us here."

There were sober nods at this and John Barker said, "They can, at least, approach the Indians in a friendly fashion—we can't."

It was decided and the escape group was to consist of Jed, John Barker, and Lawson Mitchell. Joel, in spite of his wounded arm, was still able to use his rifle and he would take over Jed's post with Melissa. Captain Fancher began the composition of a letter to the local law authorities. Barker wrote one addressed to the heads of the Mormon Church in the area. A third letter was addressed to the commander of the Mormon militia.

It was then, learning of the plan, that the apostate, William Aden, spoke up and admitted that he had visited with an old friend in Cedar City—a man who was a member of the bishop's council. Quite pale with alarm at his own temerity, Aden volunteered to go, feeling that his friendship with Benjamin Aldrich would strengthen their chances of getting immediate help.

"Benjamin," he assured them solemnly, "is a good man. He will see to it himself even though I—am not in good standing."

It was decided that Aden would go in place of John Barker, for Jed insisted that the fighting strength of the train must not be diminished by too many.

Jed had a painful task to perform. He must tell Melissa that he was going. She clutched at him with desperate hands, "No—no, please, Jed, you can't leave me here——" He looked down at her helplessly. "I have to go, Lissy," he said, "we're goin' after dark. Ain't anybody in the train used to movin' through Injun country like I am, likely I'm the only one could get 'em through——"

"Then let me go with you."

"Honey"—his head was shaking, he was sick all through, he hated this—"you know I can't take you." He held her close, tried to comfort her with the assurance that he would be back soon and Joel Mitchell would be with her in the pit. She did not respond but neither did she rebel. The heedless, disobedient child was gone. She turned away, out of his arms. Her head was down, her shoulders slumped, she crept like a wounded thing into the pit beneath her wagon. Jed stared after her, deeply disturbed. He would have felt better if she had stormed at him but she had withdrawn, walked away as from sudden emptiness.

There was no sundown attack, only the potshooting from the hillsides and that ceased at twilight. Jed packed dry biscuits and jerked meat into his saddlebags. They were to set out at first dark. It was as he checked the things to take that he became aware that Melissa was not in the pit beneath the wagon. Jed scanned the shadowy wagon circle uneasily. Maybe she had crept over to Annie Fancher's wagon. And then he saw her, in the pit between her wagon and the next one.

She lay like a weary child, her arms circling her head, and one cheek was against the earth which covered her brother's body.

Jed began to hurt as though he had suffered a heavy blow. He was reminded of the bewildered young of the wild animals who would return time and again to the body of a dead mother, finding comfort and a feeling of security in the familiar scent. He crawled into the pit, lifted the girl into his arms, and sat cradling her like a baby. She sighed and buried her face against him, not speaking. He put a hand under her chin, lifted her face. Her mouth was tremulous, her eyes stayed lowered; when he gently kissed her lips he tasted salty tears. "Lissy," he whispered, "look at me." The heavy eyes raised, they were resigned, there was not even entreaty—only grief and weariness.

Jed was beaten, he could not stand for her to look at him so. "Lissy"—he held her to him with strangling urgency—"I know . . . I know . . ." He stammered, "You'd be safer . . . here, Lissy." He plunged recklessly on. "But I'm taking you—where I go, you go."

Melissa came as painfully alive as one who has suddenly been reprieved from an already knotted noose. She bit her lips to keep from sobbing aloud and put both arms around his neck in frantic thanksgiving.

Captain Fancher was shocked at Jed's terse announcement that Melissa was to be one of the night riders. "She can ride with any man." His tone forbade any argument. "If I go, she goes." Fancher's look searched the scout's set face and nodded.

At black dark the four set out. A passage through the barricade was opened and they filed out on foot, leading the horses. Jed, with the sorrel mare, Jane, went first. Next came Melissa and Palouse. Jed had decided to put her on the sure-footed roan, knowing the animal would stay near him whatever befell. Directly behind the girl came William Aden and the dependable Juno. Lawson Mitchell brought up the rear with his long-legged bay gelding.

The letters asking for help had been allotted with grim practicality—each man carried one. They were well aware that some—or all—of them might not get through alive. Jed and Joel carried those addressed to the military and civil authorities. Aden had the letter addressed to Isaac Haight. Each letter was officially signed by Captain Fancher and John Barker.

The night was cloudy, the waning, distorted moon rose, only to appear nervously and flee back into billowing concealment. The fires on the ridges burned boastfully high. As they inched along they could hear the yammering of the savage voices.

The circle of fires gapped in two places: near the spring, to the east, where there were several deep ravines, and directly west where a series of eroded draws wound away toward the foothills. The emigrant road was to the east, but they knew the spring would be heavily guarded so they moved to the west, slowly, like the grazing animals that were scattered here and there across the rolling meadows.

They must pass directly beneath the brow of a ridge on top of which a bright fire burned. The deepest draw opened along its base. Jed, muzzling Jane constantly with his hand, waited for the others to come close to him. "Now we've got to go like ghosts," he whispered, "keep hold on your horse's nose and stay close." He would go ahead, searching with his moccasined feet for rocks that would click if a hoof struck them. There was one more reminder.

"If we get jumped, remember, *separate and ride.* Don't locate yourself by shooting back—*just get the hell out!*" Jed waited for a moment, all had nodded their understanding, he led the way on.

The mouth of the draw loomed ahead of them, a V-shaped darker shadow, its narrow floor was inky black. They entered and crept along a winding course. Directly above them the glow of firelight reflected on trees and rocks. They could hear Indian voices plainly, some of it was drunken gobbling. Jed hoped they were all drinking, their savagely sharp senses dulled and sluggish.

After what seemed an eternity of time they were past the crucial bluff, could look back over their shoulders and see the fires burning between them and the meadow where lay the wagon train. Each drew a shaken breath to know that the most hazardous area had been covered.

The draw presently branched in two directions, they took the one that angled to the north. It widened as they proceeded and the floor began to rise until they stood once more on rolling ground. Mountain Meadows stretched behind them, hills and mountains to the east and north. In this direction, which they must take, all seemed dark, there were no fires. The Indians had apparently all camped in the circle about the train.

It was safe to mount and ride on from here. Vastly relieved at their progress, Jed made sure that everyone knew in what direction lay the emigrant road to Cedar City and then they rode quietly, at a slow gait, until they put several miles between themselves and the Indian fires. Jed reached over to squeeze Melissa's hand, his heart all but choking him with the relief he felt. They would be safe now, for across the end of this valley, near the foothills, was the emigrant road and a clear way to the Mormon town. Once on the road they could ride faster, they should reach the town before dawn.

In a draw near the emigrant road a small party gathered in a grove of trees. They had built a fire and were seated around it—all white men except for the Indian boy who stayed always with Josh Wade. The group included most of the interpreters who had come to the meadows to help John D. Lee handle the Indians.

Josh was in an ugly mood, the fighting now had become a monotonous sharpshooting contest. And, as always, the grave society of pious Mormons graveled him to excesses of obscenity; their submission to church authority had always aroused his scorn.

Bishop Phillip Klingensmith was delivering—in Isaac Haight's searing words—a denunciation of the way his well-laid plans had been distorted. The dour blacksmith had just returned from Cedar City and an interview with Haight. The stake president had completely lost his temper when he learned that the Indians had attacked ahead of time, disobeyed orders. He was enraged also at the mediocre results. But since they had gone ahead they must now finish it, get the thing done. The Indians were drifting away. They had taken to pilfering on the outlying Mormon farms—several women had been badly frightened. Another day or two, Haight had pointed out, and the redskins might neglect to distinguish between Mormons and just ordinary white people. He sent definite orders: Get more of the horses and cattle and then withdraw.

Josh listened, his glittering gaze roving the circle of compliant faces. He was revolted at their tame submission. Sit back and urge the Injuns on, he thought, not enough guts to lift a gun themselves and then raise hell because it wasn't pulled off to the letter of orders. *Orders* —Josh spat, grunted with disgust. He decided abruptly that he had had enough, he'd get on back to the Injuns. He grinned, thinking of the reception Kanosh and Kasota would give to the news that they must content their vengeance with a few cows, and then withdraw.

Josh reared up from his squatting position, reached for his rifle, and gestured to Crazy Horse. The men raised their heads at his movement, silence hung for a moment as they watched cautiously to learn his intent, none felt easy in Josh Wade's grim company. Crazy Horse trotted to his elbow and Josh told him to bring up their horses. As the boy turned to obey, a call from the darkness hailed those at the fire.

"Ho, there!" The heads of the Mormons swung, their eyes squinted into the gloom. Several mounted men could be discerned approaching. Their first thought was that it was a party from Isaac Haight. And then they tensed. These riders approached from the *west!*

"Ho, there." It was Jed's voice. Glimpsing the fire from a distance, he had realized it was on the emigrant road. And against the blackness of the night white canvas-topped wagons reflected the firelight. Wagons meant white men.

The wagons they saw were those Josh Wade had brought south, purchased, their loads intact, from Eli Jacobs, the border gun trader.

Klingensmith had been standing as he delivered Haight's rebuke, now he stepped back out of the firelight, narrowing his eyes to pierce the gloom. His heavy voice answered, "Name yourselves—"

The answering hail came clearly. "Jed Smith–from the wagon train at Mountain Meadows–the Fancher Party—"

The words were like a bolt of lightning, transfixing the Mormons motionless.

The mounted party moved closer. William Aden, nervously relieved at the sight of white men peacefully grouped around a fire, thrust his heels into Juno's flanks and the big mare leaped forward.

The confused silence at the fire was broken by the clicking of a rifle hammer. Josh Wade brought his rifle around, aimed from the hip. The heavy gun roared belchingly. Aden screamed as the slug tore through his chest. Juno reared and his body slid slowly and then thudded to the ground between her terrified hoofs. All was suddenly a pandemonium of pounding hoofs, screams, and rushing figures. Josh had pulled his revolver from his belt and leveled it at Jed. But Crazy Horse had heard the voice and the name "Jed Smith" and tensed joyfully that it was his friend who approached.

When Josh's shot struck Aden the boy's glance whipped to him incredulously. He was raising the revolver, aiming at Jed. Crazy Horse struck at the gun arm, deflecting the shot, which missed Jed and passed through Lawson Mitchell's body.

Lawson swayed, it had been like the blow of a heavy club. He clutched the saddle horn and, bent over, managed to keep his seat as the horse plunged away into the enveloping darkness.

Josh flung out his arm, caught the boy on the side of the head, knocked him yards away. Then he ran out into the darkness, cursing and firing again and again toward the sounds made by the horses.

Jed had recognized the heavy, ape-armed figure of Bishop Klingensmith and in the next instant had come the roar of the rifle. Jane screamed and reared back against Palouse, who went down on his haunches with the sudden weight of her. But the cat-footed gelding was up and away even as Jed hauled the mare down and around, sunk his heels into her quivering flanks, driving her behind Palouse, keeping himself a shield between Melissa and the guns. "*Ride, Lissy,* get the hell out—" Melissa, crouched like a burr in the saddle, heard him but she did not need to urge Palouse, who took his own way, swerving and bounding like a deer on the hillside.

The guns thundered behind them, Jed let out a grunting bellow, Melissa turned her head to see him drop his rifle and lean forward in the saddle. But he did not go down, he rode bent almost double, still driving Jane's terrified nose against the leaping Palouse.

The shots and shouting were fainter, they were out of range now. Jed shook his head to clear it of a reeling, drunken sensation. The two horses fled through the night shoulder to shoulder. Jed had caught a glimpse of Lawson's gelding headed west as they all spurted away from the fire. "Keep to the east, thataway." He motioned with his arm and almost fell from the saddle with the effort. Melissa reached out to him. "I'm all right," he gasped, "keep travelin'—"

The horses had steadied down from that first dangerously headlong pace. Jed was realizing with shock what this amounted to: they had been fired on by white men, Mormons, as soon as they identified themselves. He had also recognized Josh Wade in company with the Mormons, and he knew the whole of the thing to be the connivance of the settlers, not the Indians alone. Their only chance was back inside the circled train.

He must get Melissa back, warn the train. Maybe they could harness up, make a run for it. Within the waterless confines of the meadow lay nothing but death. He felt of himself exploringly, he had been hit in the right side just above the hip bone. It was numb, the pain had not started but it was bleeding a great deal. They would have to stop, bind it up. He had to hold out until he got Melissa back to the train.

"Hold up, Lissy," he managed, "we've got to fix me up a little."

Melissa pulled Palouse in and Jane slowed in unison. They dismounted in the shadow of some trees on a hillside. The girl's face showed waxen white in the gloom; her eyes were full of dark question, but Jed was relieved at her lack of hysteria. She whipped off her jacket, unbuttoned her shirt and folded it to make a pad for the wound. She bound the pad in place with Jed's belt as he directed. He wrapped his buckskin shirt tight around his body, shoving the long fringes inside his pants to further hold the dressing in place. Melissa donned her jacket again and peered anxiously up at him.

Jed reached an arm and unsteadily pulled her close for just a precious second, kissed her swiftly, found her lips warm, her white cheeks cool. And was amazed at the steadiness of her slender body. She was not shaking with fright, she was as controlled as a steel shaft.

"We've *got* to make it back," he said thickly, "got to warn them we're up agin' Mormons, too." He considered their present position, believing that if they angled slightly now, traveled south, they might be able to come across the narrow, winding ravine that led to the little box canyon. If they could locate that ravine, he told Melissa, they could creep down it, get through the line of Indian fires and be back with the train before dawn. Jed detailed carefully to the girl what they must do, grimly anticipating that she might have to follow the plan alone.

The fires still glowed on the ridges as they approached, pausing often in shadowy concealment to listen and watch. The night was silent, the only sound the soft, slow stepping of their horses and the small squeakings of saddle leather.

Jed's strength was ebbing, he was afraid he would not be able to sit the saddle much longer. And then they came suddenly to the edge of the ravine they sought and a little below, its slanting bank offered a way to descend. They dismounted, Melissa and Palouse went first, Jed clung desperately to the saddle horn, let Jane drag him down the incline. They splashed cautiously into the cool, gurgling water. The horses dropped their noses and drank. Melissa came around to Jed quickly, found him hanging limply against the mare's side, his eyes closed. He felt her anxious hands on him and whispered, "Lissy, I can't make it–you go–alone—"

Melissa paid no attention to this, it was beyond her furthest thought to leave him. She put her arms around him, bracing up against him with all her slender strength. The mare stood quietly, Jed was propped between them or he would have collapsed into the stream.

Melissa's head began to throb, aching with her terrible problem. She stood motionless for long moments and for each that passed the man's weight sagged more heavily on her. She couldn't get him back on the horse but they must move from where they were. She dared not try to get through the lines of Indian fires with Jed helpless. Not down the ravine, then— She made a decision.

"Hang on, tight, just a second, Jed." He heard her

urgent whisper and tightened his clutch on the saddle horn with the last of his ebbing strength. Long enough for her to whip off her leather belt, stand on tiptoe and bind his wrists to the horn. Then she took her position as a crutch, both arms around his body and gently clucked to the mare.

Jane was puzzled but she began to step slowly along the bottom of the little stream. Palouse raised his head, eyed the odd arrangement and then matter-of-factly joined the procession.

Melissa was at the very end of her strength when they reached the sharp turn between the rocks which was the doorway to the box canyon. Jed's weight had become mountainously sagging, but the sorrel mare, seeming to sense the emergency, towed him along unprotestingly. They reached the sand by the pool and halted. Jed hung so heavily in the belt when she took her arms away that she could not loosen his hands. Finally, murmuring soothingly to Jane, she loosened the cinches, letting his weight pull the saddle down, lowering him to the ground. Hastily, for fear Jane would spook at the weight settling between her nervous hoofs, Melissa tore away the belt and Jed collapsed. Jane waited quietly while she released her from the saddle and then ambled over to where Palouse cropped at a clump of grass.

Jed was so quiet that, filled with terror, Melissa leaned over him, turned his face up, ran her hands over his chest and neck. His skin felt cold but he was breathing, his heart beat strongly inside the hard chest, pulsed heavily in his neck. She pulled the shirt aside to check the bandage. It was still in place. She could not tell in the darkness but she thought the flow had ceased. If he rested for a while, maybe——

In the small, rock-walled canyon the air was still as a subterranean vault. Palouse and Jane remained together, nibbling at the grass. Melissa crept to the pool and drank from her cupped hands. Then she returned to Jed, propped herself against the saddle, and drew his head and shoulders across her lap, against her breast.

Exhausted, she lay listening to the dreamlike silence. Her eyes closed and she jerked them open, shook her head to keep awake. Her eyes felt scratchy, full of itching, heavy to painfulness. She closed them just for an instant's relief. Her head sagged forward, her cheek rested against Jed's wiry hair and she slept deeply.

## CHAPTER XVIII

Jed stirred and moaned. Melissa woke with a start, pulled herself to a sitting position. She looked, startled, around the little box canyon and realized with horror that she had slept—it was daylight.

Jed's lips moved murmuringly, his eyelids quivered. The girl looked around fearfully. Palouse and Jane dozed near the scrub oak which screened the entrance. The sky above the rock wall was tinged with rosy streaks. All was very quiet.

Melissa squirmed from under Jed and folded the saddle blanket, placed it under his head. Untying the canteen from his saddle she emptied it, wrinkling her nose at its smell. It was Indian make, fashioned from the bladder of some animal. She rinsed it at the pool and refilled it, returned to Jed and, using her neckerchief, gently washed his face. His eyes opened, he frowned, trying to focus his eyes. He became aware of an aching, burning sensation in his side. His attempt to raise a hand, brush away the fog that hampered him shocked him into consciousness, for the hand sagged weakly. His eyes flew wide. "Lissy?"

She nodded down at him, smiling tremulously in her relief that he was conscious. She leaned and pressed her mouth on his. "Sh," she whispered, "don't make any noise."

His face became alarmed as he remembered the night

before, stopping with his collapse in the ravine. His eyes lifted to the brightening sky, the circling walls of rock, and he knew to what precarious sanctuary Melissa had brought them in the night. And daylight had now trapped them.

They must remain here, these hills swarmed with hostile Indians. At any moment one of them might happen onto their tracks where they slanted down into the ravine. Any redskin would note at once that the horses were shod, indicating white riders. And would also know that their path had been the stream bed. They might as well have left a sign indicating their hiding place, it was only a matter of time.

Melissa saw the painful knotting of his brows, the whitening line around his mouth, his jaw set as he considered their predicament, but he did not voice his fear to her. She raised his head so he could drink and then undid his shirt and carefully inspected the stiff, blood-soaked pad. She told him with satisfaction that it had clotted, had not bled during the night. He whispered to her to drag the saddle nearer, help him turn so that he lay propped up over it, his face toward the entrance to the canyon.

"Bring me my rifle," he directed.

Melissa was surprised—he didn't remember. She got his revolver and placed it near his hand and his glance swiveled to her face. She shook her head. "You dropped the rifle back there when you were hit."

His reaction to this bad news was lost as each tensed at a sudden blast of sound. From the west, where lay the wagon train on Mountain Meadows, came the rattle of gunfire. Jed could distinguish between the sporadic bursts from the hillsides and the steadier, methodical firing from the train. He noted with satisfaction that the shots from the Indians were outnumbering ten to one those from the train—they were not panicky, then, were being careful with their supply of shot.

Jed lay quietly, facing the opening of the canyon, nursing his strength. His hand lay touching the butt of the revolver but he did not exert himself to hold it. Melissa crouched beside him, shredding dry biscuits and jerky which she fed alternately into his mouth and her own. Jed had difficulty chewing and swallowing the hard fare and needed many drinks of water to wash it down. But he persisted stubbornly, knowing that he must not lose further strength.

Suddenly his watchful eye noticed a difference in the stance of Palouse near the scrub oaks that screened the entrance. The stocky horse had raised his head, his sharply pricked ears were forward. He was listening to something, a sound that did not reach Jed's ears.

Cold sweat broke out on the scout's face, for now Palouse's head swung towards the hidden opening into tho canyon. There was still no sound other than the babbling murmur of the stream over the rocks but the gelding remained expectantly poised. Something—or someone—approached the entrance stealthily. Their trail had been found and followed.

Jed's grip fastened on the revolver; he brought it up to a position on the saddle, nearly against his cheek. He would aim it like a rifle. As he thumbed back the hammer his urgent whisper warned Melissa, "Get down, stretch out behind me—" Instantly she slid full length back of Jed and lay rigid, straining to hear, but there was no sound other than the water and Jed's rasping breaths. She shut her eyes, rejecting the sight of the blue expanse of merciless sky overhead.

Jed's line of vision included the spotted horse, which was still waiting interestedly, and the oaks covering the opening. He heard no sound but then there was a flicker of movement—a sliding glimpse and the impression of a brown thigh—an Indian moved behind the trees. Jed's trigger finger began its slow squeeze, he needed only a certain target. But there was no further movement. The hair on his neck began to rise; he knew the peculiar paralysis of being watched. Steady, piercing eyes were searching out their weakness, seeing the aimed revolver. Jed knew sickeningly that if the Indian had a rifle he could down him before Jed would even see a target!

The long silence began to have a nightmare quality and then Jed thought he must be out of his mind. For a sibilant cheeping came from the oaks, the call of a night bird which was a signal of the Plains Indians.

Again it sounded and then a slender, almost naked figure moved from the trees into full view, his hands open, empty of arms, extended palm upward. Jed nearly fainted with surprised shock. With concentrated care he slowly let the hammer down on the shell in the revolver chamber, amazed unbelief on his haggard face.

For the Indian standing there, a wide white smile on his high-boned face, was his friend, young Crazy Horse.

The boy greeted him in Sioux, in a guardedly low tone, and then came toward him, exuberance in every lithe line of him. Melissa heard the surprised, grunting intake of Jed's breath and then, unbelievably, incomprehensible syllables and his voice answering in the same way. Her eyes flew open to see the wild, brown face of an Indian beaming at the scout, who put down his revolver to reach up and clasp the brown paw. The Indian squatted now, his other hand affectionately on Jed's shoulder.

Jed's voice was half groan, half relieved chuckle as he murmured, "Lissy, this is my good friend, Crazy Horse!"

Melissa sat up and stared with amazement at the thin, wirily muscled boy. He was not yet tall, but the length of the narrow limbs indicated that he would be a big man. His bony shoulders had breadth and the gaunted rib cage already swelled wide above the narrow hips and flexible thighs. His body seemed oddly, flowingly constructed—a tensile skeleton over which lay whipcord muscle. Even kneeling there quietly he gave the feeling of a coiled steel spring. He seemed entirely self-sufficient. A heavy knife hung in a skin scabbard on the belt which circled a breechclout, his only clothing. A short curved hunting bow was slung over one shoulder, the quiver of arrows back of it. Melissa noticed that the skin of his lean body gleamed in the sunlight like creamy-gold satin.

The girl heard Jed speak her name in the incomprehensible talk they were making and Crazy Horse raised a pair of black, hawklike eyes to search her face with such an intentness that it was almost a shock to withstand and return the gaze. The glittering stare returned to Jed and the boy made a comment at which Jed smiled and nodded. Then Jed asked a question and the boy said with an odd accent, "Some—I talk some in the white man's way."

Melissa felt an enormous relief to hear him say words she could understand. She had felt a shrinking, he was so wild-looking and the strange speech had made it worse. She looked at his thin gauntness and reached in the saddlebag for a biscuit and shred of jerky, extended them somewhat hesitantly toward the boy.

He became as still as a rock, looking at the scanty offering of shared food and then into her narrow face with its sprinkling of freckles beneath the slanted eyes, his eyes dwelled long on the tumbled wealth of yellow hair. Her hand faltered, she thought perhaps he scorned the small offering. But he reached and accepted the food, his face breaking into a smile of wild sweetness, his eyes glowing with such brilliant warmth it all but stopped the breath in her throat. He bowed his head with an odd obeisance and rose in one lithe motion. "I go now," he said, his gaze lingering on her for a long moment. He turned and was swiftly gone through the trees, disappearing as soundlessly as he had appeared.

There was presently the sound of a horse moving up the gravel-bottomed stream. A black velvet nose pushed between the trees and the buckskin mare ambled contentedly into the clearing, surveyed the canyon calmly, moved to the water, and drank her fill. She turned to a clump of grass, then, and lowered her head contentedly. There had been no second sight of the boy, he had driven the little mare through the opening and slipped away again.

Jed remained propped against the saddle and Melissa crept close to him so he could whisper to her. He told her that the boy was the same youngster that Jed had helped recover the spotted war horse way back on the plains out of Fort Laramie. Jed was confused on just how he came to be in this area, for the boy had simply said he had traveled with a white hunter. But he had been at the Mormons' fire the night before and had trailed them here and—Jed grinned at this—the boy had spooked the Mormons' horses so there could be no quick pursuit and then covered their trail a good bit of the way. He had gone now to erase the telltale tracks leading down into the ravine and then he would mount guard just outside the entrance to the canyon. He would warn them of his own approach by sounding the lilting prattle of the meadow lark twice. If the lark sounded but once, it would signal the approach of an enemy.

Jed finished the strange story and closed his eyes in overwhelming relief. The arrival of the efficient young war hawk immeasurably eased his mind on Melissa's account. And the dangerous trail was being removed, they could not be surprised in the box canyon while Crazy Horse stood guard. They could remain, relatively safe, until dark—after which the boy could spirit Melissa down the ravine and to the wagon train. Jed had no fears about sending her in the boy's care, he knew the youngster to be more skillful at this sort of thing than he himself.

Melissa, too, felt more hopeful, seeing how reassured Jed was by the boy's appearance. They stayed very quiet, listening and waiting. There were only occasional shots now at long intervals and Jed knew them to be all from the Indians. The train was holding its fire.

A clear bird song lilted lazily into the waiting silence. So naturally it sounded that Melissa did not at first realize it was the signal. Jed cocked the revolver and motioned her down behind him. There was a very long silence. Jed's eyes remained glued on the curtain of trees before the entrance.

Then the meadow lark spoke again, a short trill, very close—and then the second time. Melissa heard Jed's grunt of surprise and raised herself to look. The boy came sliding from the trees, his eyes wild with triumph. Dangling from his hand was a stringy mess of black hair which ended in a wet-looking patch of skin. He held the grisly trophy aloft, his eyes glinting. "My first time to scalp," he said, "the yellow-hair is fine medicine."

Squatting on his haunches, he told Jed in swift Sioux how the man had come up the brook, seemed inclined to follow its course to the canyon. Crazy Horse had let him approach near and then let fly an arrow which passed through his throat. He had hidden the body in the ravine and was disgusted that the man carried only a poorly fashioned Paiute lance, not worth keeping. The boy fastened the dripping scalp to the rawhide rein on the buckskin and left to resume his guarding position.

"What did he mean about yellow hair?" Melissa asked.

Jed's glance was quizzical. "He was sayin' when he first looked at you that he'd heard yellow-haired women were powerful medicine—now he's convinced, seein' he took his first scalp for you."

Melissa was about to reject the honor and then her protest died, unvoiced. If Crazy Horse had not killed the Paiute so quietly, she realized, Jed would have had to use the revolver, and the noise might have brought a swarm of savages.

Jed watched as the conflicting expressions swiftly changed on her face and was pleased at the lack of squeamishness apparent in her final decision—signified only by the lift of her chin. She accepted her status in the killing.

"He'd likely give anythin' in the world for a lock of your hair," Jed informed her.

"Whatever for?"

"He'd put it in his medicine pouch. He's got one tucked away on him, for sure. It's to give him strength and luck—that's sorta the way they figger medicine." He paused and then added, "You done exactly the right thing, offerin' him food from your hand."

Melissa looked puzzled. "Well, it was just—he looks so nearly starved——"

Jed's look was tender on her. "You offer a Sioux food, honey, and it's the same as namin' him your good friend, makin' your lodge his. It had a power of meanin' to him. That kid would die to protect you, now."

Melissa sat silent, thinking this over. The boy had affected her strongly—that savage intensity coupled strangely with the peculiarly sweet, wild smile. He seemed so thinly young, almost frail until you noticed the sheath of wiry muscle. And he had just killed an enemy. She sighed deeply, her eyes shadowed and thoughtful. "I'll give him a lock of hair," she said, "any time at all."

Crazy Horse did not re-enter the canyon until the shadows were heavy, night closing in. They heard the double trill of bird song and he was suddenly there beside them. His face was drawn, he was very tired but his eyes glinted fiercely. He was obviously disappointed to report that no more Paiutes had tried the waterway. Before coming in, he had scouted down the ravine and mounted a hill. He brought news of unusual movement. There were white men going from camp to camp, talking to the Paiutes and Pahvants, but keeping carefully out of sight of the wagon train.

White men in this area meant Mormons and Jed hazarded the hope that Lawson had made it to Cedar City, maybe the Mormons were peace-talking the Indians. It was Mormons that fired on them, but they could have been a renegade outfit.

Crazy Horse stared at Jed, surprised at this interpretation. He lapsed into Sioux to make himself clear. The men *had* been Mormons but this was not cause for hope of peace. Did Little Ax not know that the Mormonies had planned the raid, right from the start, had called the warriors together? The Mormonies wanted the herds but they had no belly for fighting, so they furnished the guns and ammunition to the Indians. When the bug-eaters—the Paiutes—had gorged their big bellies with mule meat they would have crawled off to sleep but the Mormonies would not let them. They brought kegs of peppered whisky to rouse them again. The Mormonies wanted the raid continued until they got all the horses and cattle. The big leader—the Mormonie, Haight—sitting in his lodge in Cedar City, gave the orders. Almost hourly messengers rode to him and returned with his commands. He was truly a leader held in great esteem, the boy said, for he did not even lead his men into battle to ensure their obedience. It must be that he had proved himself greatly on other battlegrounds.

Jed was enraged at how smoothly Haight had deceived them with friendship and then planned a raid after lulling them into feeling secure. But he was also relieved, for the lack of water would force Captain Fancher to drive out the remaining animals and once they were in the hands of the attackers, the siege would end. It was a stiff price, but not too high for the lives of those in the train. So, feeling that it was now only a matter of time, Jed decided against the risk of sending Melissa and the boy out in an attempt to reach the train. The danger was not only from the Indians, someone in the train might take a shot at her before she could identify herself.

They were relatively safe here in the box canyon, with darkness all about them and the boy keeping his deadly efficient watch. They still had a small supply of biscuits and jerky, there was plenty of water. If Captain Fancher turned the animals out during the night, morning might find the hills empty of hostiles.

On that Thursday night Jed felt that the peril might resolve in a fashion much better than could have been hoped for at the outset. He and the boy took turns sleeping and keeping watch throughout the night. All was peacefully quiet, no person or sound intruded on their sanctuary.

During that afternoon, while Crazy Horse guarded those in the box canyon and the riflemen in the wagon train watched but seldom fired at the Indians on the hillsides, two riders approached Cedar City from opposite directions—each bearing urgent word for President Isaac Haight.

From the north, flogging his sweating horse, rode

James Haslam, reeling in the saddle. He had not paused to sleep for more than thirty-six hours and was near to collapse.

From the rim of Mountain Meadows, Bishop Phillip Klingensmith also rode to Isaac Haight and he was not eager to deliver his news. The dour blacksmith dreaded the wrath Haight would surely vent on him, for that imperious man could not tolerate blundering. And Klingensmith knew that they had fumbled miserably.

The bishop's gloomiest forebodings were entirely accurate. Haight, on learning of the escape group's visit to the night fire—and what followed—was incensed to a fury of foaming exasperation. In his dull monotone Klingensmith related how the riders had approached their fire the night before. How Jed Smith had hailed them, openly naming himself, and that they were from the Fancher Train.

"And 'fore I could think what to do, that goddamn Wade throwed down on them!" One man had been killed outright, he went on, but the three others had plunged off, gotten away in the darkness. They had separated, their tracks showed, one man traveled west, the other two went eastward. They had meant to follow them but there had been a delay. Their horses had been spooked and driven off by Wade's Indian boy, for some reason known only to himself—and the boy had also disappeared. At first light they had set Indian trackers on the trail. The tracks of the two who headed east were lost in the ravines above Mountain Meadows. Obviously they had regained the wagon train during the night, for the Indians had been drunken, were not guarding much. They knew for sure that the single rider had reached the train, for the stupid Paiutes had actually watched him ride across the meadow in the moonlight, seen him enter an opening in the barricade. The sluggish savages had not realized in time that the horse and rider moving so openly down a ravine and out onto the meadow had not been one of their own people.

Haight could not know that Lawson Mitchell was the

only one of the three to reach the Fancher Train—and that he had not been able to speak. Lawson had been dying in the saddle. He had managed to hold on to the saddle horn and they had had to pry his hands loose one finger at a time. The blood was still pouring from the gaping hole in his belly. When they hauled him tenderly down from his horse he sighed tiredly and did not open his eyes again.

Klingensmith finished his report and handed Haight the bloodstained letter they had taken from the body of William Aden. Some of it was illegible and Haight scanned it angrily. One sentence caught his attention, ". . . we believe the attackers to be led by a white renegade, one Josh Wade, who appears to be goading them on."

Haight's face grew thoughtful. So they had recognized Wade and named him renegade, but they apparently didn't connect him with the Mormons. But, wait! This letter had been written before the escape party had ridden out—they might have, by now, realized who were involved. He put the question and Klingensmith nodded unwillingly.

"I expect Smith could have recognized me," he conceded sourly, "I was standin' in the firelight, plain, when he hailed us. The others was all squattin' around." He chewed on the thing a moment, recalling just how it had been. "I seen *him* clear enough—he was leadin' the bunch until this other man's horse jumped ahead. And Smith seen *me* plain that day you and me talked to him and Fancher." The heavy voice paused and then added pessimistically, "I don't guess Smith is fooled, now, about who is mixed up in this mess."

Haight was displeased at his tone and ordered the bishop to go home and eat, rest until he was sent for. Haight would study the situation and work out a plan.

Klingensmith had just plodded away when Haslam rode up to Haight's doorway and all but fell from his horse. He staggered up the steps and entered. Haight poured a small glass of brandy, held it to the exhausted man's lips. The fiery sweet liquor revived him and he was able to repeat in a faint voice the exact words of the message, deliver the letter. As Haight listened, his black brows knotted in consternation, he sustained a terrible shock. When Haslam finished he helped the tired rider to a couch in another room and returned to his study to pace restlessly up and down. Isaac Haight found himself proddingly on the horns of a terrible dilemma.

"You must not meddle with the wagon trains." There could be no misunderstanding the clarity of the letter. Nor the other. *"Word that the Mormons are attacking Gentile trains must not be carried to California."*

For the rest of it Haslam's voice had been a rasping whisper, his eyes had been closed. "Tell my Saints in Dixie that God alone provides a time of vengeance—in His own good time we will cut down our enemies."

But the attack had already been made. It now neared the close of the third day of siege. Yesterday, Haight brooded, he could have obeyed the orders and no real damage done. The Mormons could have abandoned the thing. But now, due to the vicious, hair-trigger Wade and the senseless blundering delay which followed, the Fancher train was well aware that Mormons were among the hostiles. The word would inevitably be carried to California. Sweating with nervous dismay, Haight strode to and fro across his study. He paused, stared unseeingly out of the bleary-paned window. His long fingers twitched. There must be—there *had* to be some way to remedy the situation.

If he obeyed the first order now, called off the attack, he could still not secure the other. The forbidden word would be carried, wide spread. And if the Fanchers talked, violence could erupt against the small colonies of Mormons on the coast. And Isaac Haight and his council would be blamed for whatever disasters befell.

It would put an end to his dreams, cherished ambitions. Brigham Young could be utterly ruthless with those who fumbled, he had little patience with those whose mistakes in judgment proved costly. Haight would doubtless be removed from his high position. Brigham was completely without mercy to those who brought danger to the least of his flock. Haight wiped his face with a sweat-damp handkerchief. How could he extricate himself and prevent disaster from falling on the California missions? He returned to his desk and sat down, placed a shaking hand to his forehead. His head was beginning to throb, he was exhausted with the turmoil of conflicting emotions.

The sounds of his big household faintly intruded on his weary ears. He distinguished the bell-like tone of Caroline's lilting laugh. Caroline. His lovely, glowing jewel—how brilliant were her dark eyes, how luscious her teasing red mouth. How tempting she was—even to see her walk across a room with that swaying litheness, the tilt of her chin, the proud carriage of the imperious dark head.

How proudly would Caroline walk when he had been stripped of his position? If he had to labor, like a field hand, from dawn to dark to provide for his numerous family, could he hold Caroline's regard? Would she come so eagerly into his arms in the secret dark of the night if his hands were soil-roughened, if he stunk of toil, his hair and beard not silkenly groomed? If he could not provide her with the silks and jewels she cherished—and rightfully, he thought, for she was a queen among women, the austere rules were not for such as his Caroline. No more than they applied to himself. He had always been able to maneuver, plan—his brilliance had gained him much—could continue to forge his way upward if he played his cards right. But what were the cards now? What remedy was there that could deliver him safely, sustained in his position, from this predicament?

At sundown Phillip Klingensmith presented himself, as ordered, at Haight's, preparatory to continuing on to Mountain Meadows. The bishop was astonished to find the Mormon militia drawn up and waiting, with Major Higbee in command. Klingensmith's glance calculated that there were more than fifty men assembled. But Higbee was not in command. Isaac Haight now came from his house and mounted. He was going to the scene himself, take charge of a meeting to decide what they must do.

It was nearing midnight when Haight, Higbee, Klingensmith and the Mormon militia gathered with those already at Mountain Meadows. Josh Wade and several of the chiefs, among them Kanosh and Kasota, sat somewhat apart. Their restlessly glittering eyes were sardonic as the Saints bowed their heads while John D. Lee prayed.

Then Isaac Haight stood, advanced a step so that he was visible to all, a darkly stern figure in the firelight. He made known to them the message brought from Brigham Young—that they must not meddle with the wagon trains. He added, into the quiet after the horrified gasps had stilled, the reason for the directive: that word of Mormon action against Gentile trains must not be carried to California.

"It would have been possible," Haight said bitterly, "to have withdrawn with impunity but for the blundering which took place last night. Now the Fanchers know that there are white men involved." His somber gaze roamed the assemblage. "I see now no alternative to some sort of settlement with the wagon train—we must withdraw, anyway——"

He was interrupted, not by words, but by the approach of a menacing figure. Kanosh had risen, advanced to stand in the firelight, bringing his hawk face close to Haight's.

"Kanosh does not withdraw." His voice was a sullen growl. "Kanosh and Kasota have yet a vengeance to take!" Kasota, his ruined face horrible in the flickering light, came forward to stand beside his chief. The assemblage became taut with silence. And now Josh Wade rose, moved to hulk over Isaac Haight.

Haight's stare was appalled on the gory spectacle he presented: stripped to the waist, his bare chest was painted so that an oozing wound gaped between his ribs. One huge hand grasped a rifle, the other drew a knife, flipped it into the ground where it lit quivering, the silver trim of its handle glinting in the firelight. "I ride with

Kanosh," Wade said, his eyes watching Haight from under beetling brows. Haight's face had become pale under its sallowness. It became drawn as, silently, but none the less threateningly, Moquetas and Big Bill stepped forward to stare at him from the hostile line. Tutsegavitt moved with them, and two other war chiefs of the Paiutes.

Kanosh's glance on his cohorts was full of somber pride; he spoke again. "Our warriors fought at the bidding of the Mormonie chief, and many have died. No Mormonie has died—none has even fought! Does Kanosh" —significance was in the tone—"lead the red men into battle—and no Mormonies again? And then when we have done and return to our lodges there will be wailing of the women for the warriors who do not return. There will be no wailing from Mormonie lodges. Will Brother Isaac expect, then, to find the red man still his friend?"

Haight had become stiff with the shock of it. The faces around the fire showed great alarm. They stared at each other and then back at the menacing scene in the flickering light.

A man rose from where he sat and moved forward a little. His thin shoulders were hunched as though he felt chilled. "I ain't a fightin' man"—his voice seemed to come from far away, it was as if he urged the words out—"but I got a vengeance to take, myself, and there's others here"—his haunted eyes swept the circle—"that remembers Haun's Mill." He stood silently awkward for a moment, his gaze accusingly on Haight. "You wasn't hurt none in any of the persecutions, was you, Isaac? Nobody ever got raped or killed, and nobody in your family went hungry neither. Maybe"—his words were brooding, bitter—"you've always been a better manager." Resentment was in the feverish eyes and around the circle heads nodded in agreement. Several men rose as if they would speak and the thin man looked at them, his courage rose. "By God," he said, "I'm ridin' with Wade and the redskins!"

There was a confusion of voices: a growl of approval conflicted with exclamations of horror. Haight waved his arms for silence, "Do you realize," he said angrily, "that if we continue the battle that some of us will die? And if *any* of the Fancher Party survives, word will still be carried to California?"

A heavy voice spoke into the quiet that followed Haight's wrathful prediction, "There is one way—" The man's eyes met Isaac Haight's disturbed gaze with strange significance.

A separate council was held, consisting of some ten or twelve of the Mormon leaders. They withdrew, built a small fire, and their hushed voices continued until nearly dawn. They made a decision, a careful plan was evolved and each man assigned to his task. Then they bent their heads in prayer.

Isaac Haight rode alone back to Cedar City through a flaming dawn. A brisk breeze carried the pungent smell of sage and piñon, the air was clean and chill. It was a beautiful morning—Friday, September 11, 1857.

## CHAPTER XIX

Jed woke to a feeling of relief. His wound still throbbed painfully but he was not so weak and he was very hungry—a good sign of recovery.

Before daylight Crazy Horse had scouted the area around the ravine. At dawn the sporadic firing was listless, it was not returned from the wagon train. The boy came briefly into the canyon to report that the Indians seemed to be drifting off, very few remained on the hillsides. Jed and Melissa, crunching their biscuits and jerky, felt immeasurably cheered. They ate sparingly, however, washing the dry fare down with many drinks of water.

The day lengthened slowly, the air became hot, sultry; clouds surged up from the western horizon, their innards grumbling with thunder.

The meadow lark trilled twice and Crazy Horse came leaping excitedly into the canyon. He brought wonderful news—the Indians had left! They had gathered their motley gear from the nooks on the hillsides and trooped off in a straggling body toward the north. But this was not the most astounding thing. Crazy Horse had crept close to the meadow and from the top of a hill he had seen two white men approach the wagon train, waving a white flag. Men had come from the barricaded wagons to meet them, they had talked and then all gone inside the circle of wagons.

Crazy Horse, from the hilltop, could see the men plainly and he had recognized one of those who came with the white flag—it had been the Mormonie, John D. Lee.

Jed's expression was incredulous. "The *Mormons* called off the Injuns? After all their goddamned filthy tricks——?" He put it into Sioux so that the boy might understand easier. Crazy Horse lapsed into his own tongue to reply.

He agreed that this had been his own reaction, also. But that was before recalling the character of the man, Lee. Crazy Horse knew him well, had lived near him for many days, eaten of his food, saw how he was with all people—both red and white.

John D. Lee, the boy said, was good. He fed all who came to his door, be they red or white; he found clothing for those who went in rags; he bought the pitiful slave children from the Paiutes and cared for them with his own children. He was kind—too kind, perhaps—with his squaws, never lifting a hand to them though they shrilled and fought constantly.

In the night meetings, here at the meadow, Crazy Horse had seen that Lee was unhappy. He had not taken part in the attacks, had apparently been given orders which he obeyed, but he cried, Yaw-guts did, and prayed constantly. It was clear that Yaw-guts but obeyed the Mormonie leader, Haight, for his heart was not in it.

So it might be that Lee had finally persuaded the other Mormonies to call off the Indians, for Lee himself had come openly to the meadow. Perhaps to make peace terms.

Crazy Horse looked at the two while Jed translated this to Melissa, and his young face became stiff and stern. "I can now take the yellow-hair safely to your people," he offered, "and return to guard until help arrives for Little Ax." His eyes did not meet Jed's. "Then," he finished, "I shall go my way knowing that Little Ax and Yellow-hair are safe."

Jed's face was surprised for only an instant. Then he understood. Crazy Horse felt that, his usefulness now at an end, his welcome in the wagon train would be dubious. He would take himself off their hands.

Jed's answer was ceremonious, in dignified Sioux. "My people in the wagon train will welcome my brother Crazy Horse. They will listen with fast hearts to hear the great things he has done for their friends. And you are now the brother of Yellow-hair, for she is my woman and my brother is her brother. Where we go Crazy Horse goes. One day, all shall return to the lodge of your holy father."

The thin face had difficulty keeping its composure, the great dark eyes glowed. Crazy Horse swallowed but he found no words.

"I think," Jed murmured to Melissa, who, not understanding, was mystified by their solemnity, "you better give him that lock of hair."

Melissa had been disturbed at the seriousness of their voices, now her face was grave as she pointed to the knife the boy wore. He handed it to her. Matter-of-factly, the girl laid it in her lap and began to unbraid the heavy rope of hair which hung down her back. She shook the dull-gold mop, it tumbled in a waving shower about her shoulders. Crazy Horse's lips parted in wonder at the sight, his eyes became rapt as she took the knife and sawed a long tress from the back of her neck, held it out to him. She was smiling as she did so, her tilted eyes warm and sweet on his brown face. He accepted the hair with something very like reverence; his hand was unsteady as he received the knife, slid it into its scabbard. He looked into each of their faces in turn, but did not speak. He nodded, his eyes wide and solemn. Rising, he walked slowly behind the curtain of scrub oaks.

Melissa watched him. "Where's he going now?" she whispered. "He'll tuck it into his medicine pouch," Jed said, "but we mustn't see that—it's secret."

It was decided, a little later, that Crazy Horse and Melissa would go on foot to the train. There might yet be a lurking redskin or two and horses would attract attention. Jed tried to make them take the revolver but both refused to leave him both helpless and unarmed. Crazy Horse announced that, in any case, he was more efficient with his bow. Jed had no choice but to agree, and he felt, too, that the danger was past.

He pulled the girl down to him and kissed her. "It's been a bad time for you, Lissy," he whispered, "but it's mighty near over now—"

The two Mormons who had approached the Fancher Train were John D. Lee and young William Bateman, who carried a white flag fashioned from a ragged shirt hung on a willow branch.

John Barker and Rob Fancher met with them. Barker was now in command of the train, for Captain Fancher lay grievously wounded. That very morning, almost at the end of the desultory firing, a bullet had glanced off a rock and passed through his neck. He was propped up near a wagon. He could not lie down because of the bleeding in his throat, and was only able to breathe raggedly. He could not speak, for every movement of his throat brought great strangling gouts of blood into his mouth.

John D. Lee's open face was pasty under his sunburn. He dreaded this parley intensely. "My name is Lee," he said, "this is William Bateman—we have pulled the Indians off." He had announced this as soon as they came within speaking distance of those from the train.

Barker's bearded face worked with emotion. "Thank God!" he exclaimed joyfully. "Then they got through—Jed and his party—we were so terribly afraid when Mitchell rode back in, wounded——"

Lee blinked in confusion, trying to interpret the meaning of this. He had a carefully prepared explanation to meet the expected accusations concerning the firing on the escape party: he was to declare it to be the work of renegades, not Mormons.

"Mitchell?" He stalled, now, uneasily.

"Lawson Mitchell"—Barker nodded—"he was one of the party who rode out for help. He came back in so badly wounded that he was unable to tell us what happened. He died almost at once. We didn't know if the others had gotten through. Are they all right?"

Lee was drenched with relief. "I don't know," he said carefully, "but I would say so. I am following orders that were delivered by a messenger. All I saw was a letter that had been carried by a man named William Aden."

The haggard faces of Barker and Fancher were almost pitiable with relief. Together the four men entered the barricade. Barker's deep voice rang out joyfully. "We are saved!" he shouted and it was like a hosanna. "These good people have called off the Indians! All is well—Jed and Melissa and Aden got through!"

The people came surging out of the pits, their sweat-streaked dirty faces wore their joy oddly, their eyes were painfully relieved. Women clutched, wept over their children. Men who had remained stanch throughout were unashamed now of the tears that coursed through the dusty stubble on their cheeks. The children were bewildered, frightened at first, and then, as they began to understand, they capered about like bedraggled lambs.

John D. Lee stood stonily silent as they—the women and children—crowded around him, crying and laughing, reaching out to fondly touch their deliverer. The women with their tiny ones in their thin arms were like disheveled madonnas, their staggering small ones clutching their skirts. They smiled through their tears and asked God's blessing on their saviors.

Young William Bateman stood wordless and fidgeting,

uneasily embarrassed. But the tears came to Lee's eyes, poured down his face, and the people of the Fancher Train, seeing the sturdy Mormon weep, felt tender warmth for this good man who shared their emotion so completely.

Lee sternly reminded himself of his errand, cleared his throat, mopped off his face and, addressing the leaders, outlined how the Mormons would deliver the Fancher party from the hands of the savages. The Indians, he said, had been hard to deal with but they had finally agreed to leave, keeping what stock they now held, but on one condition. They must be guaranteed against reprisals from the riflemen in the train. They refused to lift the siege unless the Fancher party was disarmed before they left the barricade.

"Disarmed!" Barker was instantly aghast. "We cannot render ourselves helpless in the midst of hordes of Indians—"

Lee interrupted him, waving toward the hills to the north. "Mr. Barker," he said steadily, "over there, ready to come in and guard you are more than fifty well-armed men of the Mormon militia, commanded by Major John Higbee. You could not ask for safer conduct—believe me, the Indians know better than to challenge the militia."

Lee explained that they did not forfeit their arms. The guns would be concealed in a wagon, covered by bedding and always close at hand. Once they were clear of the surrounding Indians, the guns would be returned to them. It was the plan to take the people to Cedar City, bringing the wagons on later.

Rob Fancher did not approve of the plan. They would be fools to give up their guns, even for a short time, he said. And why should they leave part of the stock to the goddamned redskins? Reinforced by the militia, why didn't they jump the murderous devils and wipe them out—retrieve their cattle? There were many who agreed, clamoring to get their property back, punish the Indians.

But Lee was shaking his head, his eyes had become cold, his tone was peremptory. "Mr. Barker," he said, ignoring the fuming Rob Fancher, "we have come to your aid at considerable risk. We are outnumbered here, in our small settlements, by hundreds of Indians to every one of us. We have, thus far, managed to remain at peace with them—and we intend to preserve it! If we joined with you in such action as you suggest we would be wiped out by the tribes before you reached California! *We will not lift one finger against the Indians!* If you see fit to continue to fight them, we must withdraw at once. We can only guarantee your safety if you place yourselves completely in our hands. Remember, *we* are not in trouble with the Indians—we came in answer to your appeals for help. If you cannot accept it on our terms, we must leave here at once!"

A deep silence greeted this heated rebuttal. It was the women who spoke first, clamorously denouncing Rob Fancher and those who sought to fight again. The wives and mothers wanted no more of the siege, they wanted no more pitiful bodies lowered into the rifle pits. The babble of voices grew, everyone was having his say.

Lee raised a quieting hand. "We will leave you"—as protests began he quickly added—"to discuss it among yourselves. The militia will come to the edge of the meadow in one hour. If you have decided to fall in with our suggestion, wave us in."

In silence Lee and Bateman departed from the barricade. They walked faster and faster as they crossed the meadow, were almost running as they passed over a hill and out of sight. Lee collapsed onto his knees, his head bowed. "Almighty God," it was a broken, agonized whisper, "if Thou be willing, remove this cup from me—"

Appalled, Bateman stared at the huddled, sobbing figure. But with understanding, for there was a sickness in the pit of his own stomach. There had been so many women and children. He scanned the troubled sky, earnestly wishing that Brother Lee might be granted an answer from On High, have one of his revelations. But the heavens remained oblivious, obsessed with their own thunderous turmoil, indifferent to the petty affairs of men. There was a constant muttering which foretold a great storm advancing across the wind-swept barrens of the desert sprawling limitlessly just beyond the rim of the Great Basin.

When the hour had passed, Lee appeared with the militia and two wagons at the edge of the meadow. John Barker advanced to meet them, waving them in. The people of the Fancher Train had voted to place themselves in the hands of their Mormon saviors.

Lee suggested to Barker that the men place their money and small valuables, such as jewelry, inside their shirts, carry these precious items on their persons. He explained that, although the wagons would be guarded, they did not wish to assume responsibility for such.

It was when the two wagons that the Mormons brought were being loaded that John D. Lee suffered a terrible shock.

Captain Fancher's eyes opened dully as his litter was carried near the wagons which were drawn up at the opening in the barricade. His bearers put him down and went to bring up the other wounded. Fancher's pain-ridden gaze dwelt on the wagons the Mormons provided. They were sturdy, well-built vehicles, lighter than the prairie schooners in the train. He had seen their like before—they were border freighters. The canvas tops had been removed, leaving the bowed arches bare. That was why they looked strange, he thought vaguely. Strange, but familiar, too, the way the wheels were painted.

Suddenly the fog of pain receded before realization. Fancher had seen these very wagons before—and the impact of recognition bolted through his mind. These were Eli Jacobs' freighters, and their cargo had been destined for use against the enemies of the Mormons! Guns—and ammunition—Jacobs had said the Mormons were going to arm the Indians!

Captain Fancher knew, then. Not the whole, but he knew, and his eyes, desperately cognizant, turned on the face of John D. Lee. The Mormon started visibly, his face drained of every vestige of color, for Fancher laboriously raised on an elbow and pointed a shaking finger.

His gurgling, thickened voice was almost unintelligible, but Lee knew what he tried to say.

"No—*no—Barker—Rob*—no, God in Heaven, no——" A great gush of blood burst from his mouth and he fell forward on his face.

Annie Fancher ran to kneel beside her husband, lift him so that the blood would run out of his mouth, letting him breathe. When she gently lowered him again he was unconscious. Lee shook so inside that he could scarce keep his feet but he spoke to the woman. "You must not let him talk," he advised soberly, "that was what brought it on."

Annie looked up at the Mormon, her gaunt face deeply worried, "What did he say?"

"It wasn't very clear," Lee replied, "but he may have been trying to pray. He called on the Almighty." He peered searchingly at Fancher's corpselike face and helped to lift the still form onto the bed of the wagon.

All was now in readiness. The wagons carrying the babies and children too small to walk were loaded. The guns were covered by the quilts on which they rode. The driver of this wagon was Brother Samuel Knight, whose young wife carried her first baby in her arms at Hamblin's rock house at the north end of the meadow. Lee, his rifle across his arm, took a position near the tail gate of the second wagon, bracing himself against the narrow bow. He had allowed Annie Fancher to ride in this wagon with the wounded to tend her husband and the others.

Annie had placed her smallest, pretty little Tryphena, in the front wagon with the babies, assuring the child that her mother and father rode in the second wagon. She could wave back at them, she was not to be afraid, they were going for a ride in the sunshine.

The women and older children were grouped to walk together, the men of the Fancher Train were to bring up the rear. Pacing alongside were the members of the Mormon militia, rifles across arms, revolvers in belts. Many of the eyes of the militiamen roved searchingly among the Fancher men, seeking to identify two about whom they had special orders. They were there—had survived the siege—a huge red-bearded man and a fat man who carried a black bull whip folded into one hamlike hand.

Major Higbee, the only mounted member of the militia, now trotted his horse the length of the procession. Standing in his stirrups, he raised an arm, swept it forward. "Pull out—pull out!" His voice carried and rang, echoing to the hills as the drivers whipped up the teams and the walkers stepped out briskly.

Melissa and Crazy Horse had made their way down the ravine and reached the top of a hill overlooking the meadow. She realized, crouching behind a bush while the boy crept to the crest to reconnoiter, that this was the very hill from which she had watched Rosetta send Jed after her. So long ago. Astounded, she numbered the days on her fingers. They had reached Mountain Meadows on Sunday evening. Monday she and Jed had made up their quarrel and Tuesday was to have been their wedding day. But on Tuesday the trouble had begun and David—— On Wednesday night they had tried to escape through the Indians and had returned to the box canyon. On Thursday, Crazy Horse had found them. It was now Friday—and the siege was over. Just one week ago today they had bought garden greens and melons in Cedar City. The girl's mouth watered at the memory of the lusciousness of those melons.

She looked up at the boy where he peered from behind the thick trunk of a cedar tree. He was motioning her forward and she crept up to stand beside him. He placed a hand over her mouth and shook his head, she must be quiet. The two stared down onto the meadow just at the moment that Major Higbee waved the wagons ahead.

"Oh, look, they're leaving," Melissa whispered agitatedly, "we'll have to hurry——" She would have run from their concealment but the boy held her back, his narrow brown palm roughly across her mouth; he shook his head emphatically, his eyes wild with warning. He put his face close to her. "*Not speak!*" he hissed, "not speak—not move —*look*——" He pointed to a low ridge of hills that straggled away not far from their own position but closer to the floor of the meadow. The shallow declivities between their mounds were crowded with scrub oak. Melissa smothered her horrified gasp.

For concealed among the oaks and behind the ridges were many Indians. The path of the wagons and the walkers slanted to pass within a few yards of their ambush. Melissa's stare swung to the men of the train. Not one carried a weapon. Her eyes beseeched the boy whose grip held her motionless. "We must warn them," she whispered. "*Warn—tell them*—" Desperately she repeated the words, fearing he did not understand her.

Crazy Horse understood but he shook his head. "Too late," he whispered, "we die, too, if they see us."

The girl had not yet grasped the full meaning of the movement on the meadow but the Indian boy knew what spectacle was intended for the amphitheater of the green meadow. He looked at the girl's ashen face, they'd better get back to the canyon, they were in terrible danger here. But the decision came too late, for it had begun and then they stood paralyzed and watched. The boy's strong young arms held Melissa on her feet, his tight palm across her mouth kept her from screaming.

The file of women and children began to pass the oaks at the base of the hills. The wagons had drawn ahead of them quite a distance for the drivers had urged the teams into a fast running walk. The men, flanked on their right by the militia, were separated from the women and older children by about seventy-five yards.

A stentorian order rang clear. "*Halt! DO YOUR DUTY!*"

The black snouts of the rifles raised, Mormon fingers tightened, convulsively squeezed triggers. Almost as one, they fired, the volley thundering, rolled to the hills and re-echoed. Some of them fired twice, for they numbered just over fifty and there were more than sixty men in the Fancher party who could still walk after the siege. The range had been pointblank and, except for the designated two, every man of the Fancher Train went down.

The acrid smoke of the guns still drifted from their

barrels when the hordes of painted savages, brandishing axes and knives, swarmed from their cover and raced down on the women and children. Death would not be so quick, here, for the Mormons had distrusted the marksmanship of the red men and decreed that they must employ their primitive weapons.

John D. Lee started convulsively when the guns roared, he wanted to hold his ears, shut out the high-pitched yammering of the Indians, now mingled with the screams and groans of the women and children. But he could not, for he also had an assignment to perform. He must help dispatch the wounded in the second wagon—whereon he rode.

Annie Fancher had risen to her knees to look back when the signal was called. The driver pulled up his team and wound the reins around the hand brake. He drew his revolver and shot Annie between the shoulders while she looked away from him. She fell across her husband's unconscious body.

Lee nervously cocked his rifle but his shaking hands jerked the trigger prematurely and the slug ripped through the driver's clothes. The man screamed. "Christ, Lee," he protested, "watch what you're doing—you damn near hit me—"

Lee dropped the rifle from his nerveless hands, watched as the other man methodically cocked his revolver and fired into first one body and then another, taking first those who struggled to rise.

Lee swallowed convulsively, he closed his mind hypnotically and took a wood ax from its sling in the wagon box. He helped the driver make sure none of the wounded remained alive. Lee's mouth was open, he cried aloud in great, heaving moans like an injured child.

The wagon ahead had stopped. Sam Knight stood holding the reins, looking back. Some of the children were frightened, were crying loudly. Little Tryphena Fancher scrambled over the tail gate and dropped. She sprawled on the ground, picked herself up, and began to run back toward the wagon where her mother was.

An Indian came leaping towards the running child, his war ax raised—this would be a nice scalp, her long curling hair flew back of her head——

Lee saw what was about to happen to the little girl. "No!" he shouted, leaping from the wagon. He ran to meet the child, arms outstretched. The child dodged from the Indian, a glancing blow of the ax struck her shoulder. Lee threw himself on the Indian, wrenching the weapon from him, flung it away. "No!" he thundered, "not the children—the innocent little children——"

The surprised savage fell away from him, retreated from the furious assault. "Get away from here," Lee roared, "you murderous fiend——"

Lee gathered up the bleeding child and ran with her toward the wagon ahead. The Indian stared after him in confusion for a moment and then retrieved his ax, loped away.

Lee gained the other wagon, climbed in. "Drive on, Sam," he ordered. "For God's sake, hurry—we must save these babies——" Knight stared at him, stupefied and motionless. Lee knelt, drew the sobbing little ones to him. He still held Tryphena, his deep voice crooned soothingly, "Now, now," he coaxed, "everything is all right. Old Brother John is going to take care of you——"

Lee raised his head. Sam Knight was staring down at him blankly, for he had seen Lee at work in the other wagon, realizing what it was that he did. "Sam"—Lee's voice was sharp—"whip up that team. Get us out of here—drive to Hamblin's; your wife and Sister Hamblin will help us with these babies."

Sam Knight did as he was bidden, turned his back on the eighteen small occupants and the bloodstained man. These babies were the only survivors of the more than one hundred and sixty people in the Fancher Train, he recalled, and shuddered. He whipped the team into a gallop and drove out of the meadow.

When the volley roared over the meadow the women saw their men go down and they fought to protect their young. They turned and met the red men with tooth and nail, but it did not take long.

A tall woman with flowing red hair threw off her attacker and tried to shield her small son but she was caught by the shoulder and flung back, the Indian buried the blade of his ax in the white oval of face. Her body still twitched as he took the magnificent scalp.

Clara Barker, her infant against her breast, had tried to run, but a savage had drawn taut his bowstring, sent an arrow twanging after her. It drove between her shoulder blades, emerged through her breast, and pinned the baby to her.

Sairy Ward had shoved the Tackett baby into his mother's arms. "Run, Cinthy——" she cried and turned to cover her flight. But the Indians were upon them and they fell together, the tiny body of Jeremy between them.

Death was not swift for Sol Ward—nor for Jake Tibbetts. These two had been reserved for a special brand of vengeance and alone still stood when the rifles had done their chore and the Mormon militia stood back, revolvers ready to deliver a finish to any who stirred.

Josh Wade and Kanosh came leaping in before the smoke cleared from the volley. Jake lifted his unbelieving eyes from the bodies of his fellows and saw the hideously painted savage advancing on him. The fat man backed away, instinctively shaking out the length of the black whip.

Kanosh's mouth widened into a pleased grimace, his long teeth were bared like an animal's fangs. He advanced in a crouching manner, his slitted stare never leaving Jake's whip arm. The whip flicked back but it did not finish its forward stroke for the war ax flew from Kanosh's hand and buried itself the width of the blade in the shoulder socket. Jake went to his knees, a keening scream burst from him. The whip arm dropped, the whip dangled, and then its leaded stock thudded to the ground. Kanosh fitted an arrow into his bow and the feathered shaft quivered as its barbed head tore into Jake's belly. Jake fell sideways, his hand tearing at the shaft of the arrow. Kanosh leaped astride the floundering man, scalping knife in hand. But he did not scalp; in two strokes he hamstrung the fat man. Then he crouched and waited for a return of consciousness.

Jake's tortured eyes opened to meet the gaze of the savage only inches from his face. Incredibly, the Indian spoke to him. "I am Kanosh," the deep voice growled. *"It was my woman—and my son—who suffered your whip, white man!"*

Jake's face was a writhing mass. "No—no——" he sobbed, extending a shaking hand to ward off the savage, who only watched, grinning. Jake tried to struggle to his feet, but his legs did not answer, he crawled convulsively, inched horridly along. Kanosh let him crawl, smiling with complete enjoyment. He stood up and moved a pace away. His hands leisurely fitted an arrow into the bow and he moved to where Jake could see him. Deliberately he took aim but withheld the arrow until the man's eyes registered his intent. The drooling mouth opened to scream. "My son wears your scar on his face," Kanosh said and let fly the arrow through the sagging face. Then he waited again for the heaving mound to become aware again. He circled it slowly, the methodical arrows thudded one by one, precisely aimed, delicate care was taken that none reached a vital spot. It took Jake Tibbetts a long time to die. The war chief squatted on his haunches, his gaze never leaving his victim's face. When Jake's breathing stopped Kanosh rose and stood over him. Then he spat on the head and turned away, disdaining to take the scalp. The still body of Jake Tibbetts resembled a huge, bloody porcupine.

When the guns roared around him Sol Ward drew his knife, peered frantically about for an avenue of escape. A weight struck him from behind, sent him rolling. The redbeard regained his feet with desperate agility and faced a weird figure. It was the man who had leaped upon him and then away, and now waited.

Sol saw a gauntly tall man, naked from the hips, his wide chest painted as though a gaping wound bled between his ribs. His tangle of black hair and beard were so wildly matted that of his face only a hawk beak of nose and two gleaming eyes were recognizable. Now the shaggy head went back, a dark cavern of mouth split the beard, and he laughed mockingly. The man bore a war ax in one hand, a knife in the other.

The frightened redbeard suddenly seemed monstrously funny to Josh. He had not told the Mormons that the redbeard of Haun's Mill had been shot down in his own doorway nearly twenty years ago. He circled this redbeard now, laughing deep in his throat. Sol turned also, facing him, jerking with terror when he saw the still bodies on the grass and realized that he, alone, still stood, and armed with only a knife.

The man who baited him kept laughing but he was alert, for he saw Sol's knife hand move as the redbeard prepared to gamble on a throw. Josh's hairy arm went back, let fly with the hand ax. In a curving, end-over-end arc, the heavy blade approached Sol's face. He was too paralyzed to dodge. As in a nightmare he saw the ax approach, felt the thudding blow but soggily. As he went down the elkhorn knife with its silver trim slid from his hand.

The knife caught Josh's eyes. He swooped and picked it up, held it in his hand, staring in consternation. He reached and drew its twin from the scabbard on his rump. They were identical, could only have been fashioned by the same fine craftsman. And they had originally been carried by two red-bearded men—or was it one man? Had one man died on his doorstep and the other here? Or had the redbeard survived the shooting twenty years ago—to meet the same avenging hand at Mountain Meadows?

Josh flung back his shaggy head, his mouth wide; huge bellows of laughter roared insanely across the meadow.

Kasota, who had killed among the women and children like a seething scythe, now searched among the stripped bodies. But he did not find the small, yellow-haired one he sought. She was not there. Balked of his vengeance, his ruined face a mask of fury, Kasota hacked a mutilating path through the limp bodies. They lay like rag dolls, drenched in their own blood.

The bodies of the men had been stripped and carefully searched by the Mormons, the small valuables taken, and usable clothing prudently put in the wagons. And now they began a cataloguing of the contents of the wagons, a rounding up of the horses and stock.

Between the time that the people of the Fancher Train, numbering nearly a hundred and sixty, walked thankfully toward deliverance and the time that all lay unmoving in the grass of Mountain Meadows only minutes passed. The sun had emerged from a cloud, begun to cross an avenue of blue sky as their journey commenced. When the cloud shadow replaced the sun, stalked grayly across the meadows, the contorted bodies lay stripped and mutilated, left obscenely uncovered, abandoned to the unconcern of the heavens and the fouled earth.

## CHAPTER XX

Melissa moved blindly, like a sleepwalker. The boy almost carried her down the hill, urged her faltering steps up the brook through the ravine. Her face was chalk white, the freckles like small brown protrusions beneath her fixed eyes. From time to time deep shudders convulsed her slender frame.

Nothing penetrated her trauma of horror until they came through the trees and she saw Jed lying near the entrance, the revolver near his outspread fingers. His shirt dripped redly; the wound had reopened.

Waiting in the box canyon, Jed's thoughts had traveled the ravine with the two youngsters, calculating their progress. He glanced at the sun, figured that they must, about now, be approaching the train when he heard the thundering volley of many rifles.

"Lissy! Good God, *no*—Lissy——" He struggled to his knees, fought to his feet, began a staggering run toward the canyon opening, revolver in hand. His wound burst open from the violence of his movements and blood gushed out. He tottered a few steps and fell forward.

Melissa and Crazy Horse knelt beside the scout, gently turned him over. His face was waxen, his eyes closed, but he breathed and the pulse in his throat beat strongly. She stripped back his shirt, prepared another pad, and bound it with the other under his belt, not daring to remove the first because it was clotted stiffly to the wound. Cradling his head gently, she began to drop water between his parted lips.

Jed stirred, moved his hands, moaning protestingly, his head moved from side to side in a denying way. His eyes opened and in them was painful memory, his face set in bitter lines—he remembered the guns firing. But above him was the brown hawk face of Crazy Horse and Melissa, herself, was holding the canteen to his lips. He stared at them unbelievingly, all his love and terror stark in his eyes. "Lissy——?" His wondering whisper asked if he dreamed this. "But—I—heard—guns——"

She nodded. "They—the Mormons and Indians—killed them all, everybody in the train. Massacreed them, the women and little children"—there was sobbing in her voice—"none of our men had guns. They must have tricked them. We—got to the hill just in time to—see." Her voice became raw and hoarse. "The red men went at the women and children like a pack of mad dogs, they killed them with axes and knives, ran them down like beasts——" She put her head down against his and Jed felt the deep shudders that shook her. Jed closed his eyes for only a moment, trying to encompass the enormity of the thing. Everyone in the train dead—they, the three of them, were alone here now—they could not go back——

His eyes suddenly flew open, sought the boy's, sudden consternation in his face. "We've got to get out of here——"

But even as Crazy Horse nodded, Jed realized how impossible it was. He could not ride, neither of them could support him in the saddle. The two youngsters could make it, they could be miles out of the territory before any of the hostiles stumbled on the box canyon, none knew they were here. His chin jutted grimly, he began to frame the order sending them away without him.

But Crazy Horse watched his face, the black eyes oddly mature with understanding. He anticipated the decision Jed would seek to make and was shaking his head in denial. "No, Little Ax," he said softly in Sioux, "we do not go without my brother. He has said it himself, this day. We are brothers and the yellow-hair is my sister. She will flinch from nothing except leaving you. All will go, or none will go."

"I cannot ride," Jed replied helplessly, still in Sioux. He did not want Melissa to know of what they talked.

Crazy Horse had thought it out. "I will prepare a travois, while the yellow-hair makes the horses ready. We must leave soon, while they are still busy with—what they do, there on the meadow."

The boy went swiftly from the canyon and soon returned with a pair of strong, limber saplings. Using the heavy blanket from Jed's bedroll, he fashioned a travois. Melissa saddled Jane and Palouse, stowed their meager belongings in the saddlebags. The two youngsters got Jed's long length stretched on the travois, a strip of buckskin bound across his chest and under his arms to hold him in position on the slanting litter.

Jed had consulted his map while the preparations were being made. He reckoned if they could reach the channel of the Virgen River they might be able to follow its winding course to where it emptied into the Colorado. Then they could go north to the plains or south to California. It was, at best, a terrible gamble, for soon the surrounding country would be swarming with Indians returning to their villages. They were apt to stay this night in or near the meadows. Jed's heart sank as he thought of the trail the travois would make. Crazy Horse could not get them out fast and cover the trail, too. He could not take to the shale hillsides, the rock barrens to disguise their passing. The travois would have to be drawn over easier ground.

Jed raised his eyes to the sky; it would soon be sundown. The gray mass of clouds was sliced by crimson, thunder still rumbled. If it would only rain, the scout thought prayerfully, pour down in a torrential cloudburst, wash away the trail they would make.

Crazy Horse returned from a last reconnoitering of the area, reported that the Indians and Mormons were engrossed with their loot on the meadows, none seemed likely to leave there for a while. The boy took the buckskin's halter and led her, the travois dragging along behind her serene rump. Jed looked back at Melissa jerking at Jane's halter. The sorrel did not want to be led alongside Palouse until she expressed her disapproval.

There was awe in the gaze Jed leveled on Melissa. She appeared to be very calm, but her eyes were bleak. She —this small, tender one—had seen a massacre this day and God alone knew what horror might overtake them at any minute. And yet she gave no sign, did not panic; only the dead expression of her pointed face evidenced the terrible thoughts she must have.

Their pace was slow as the boy took them down a deep ravine which wound off toward the south. They followed its winding bed while the twilight deepened into the silence of a cloud-hung night. They traveled on through the night. Black masses of cloud hid the moon, flashes of lightning lit the southern horizon intermittently. There was the mourning of wolves from far away but here was only silence in a wilderness of gullies, rocks, and endless slanting hills. It did not rain that night.

At dawn they paused to rest the horses, eat and drink a little. Jed drank but he could eat nothing. His teeth had bitten through his lip to stifle the groans that sought to tear from his agonized body. The boy's mouth was set grimly, a bad thing had happened in the night, but after a searching glance at the pallor of Jed's pain-lined face, he did not speak of it.

The buckskin had slipped as they passed under an

overhang of rocks and Crazy Horse had leaped to steady the travois. He had done so, but his weight had thrust suddenly against a boulder and there had been a small cracking sound. His bow, slung over his shoulder, had a long crack in its slender length, it was as useless as a willow twig. Their only weapon—except for the knives—was now the revolver and it held but five shots. There were no reloads.

With foreboding the boy looked back at the track they left. Then he mounted the buckskin and led the way. Melissa now rode Jane. Palouse brought up the rear.

On the heels of the discovery that the body of the scout, Jed Smith, was not among the slain at Mountain Meadows, came information that a trail of shod horses led from a nearby ravine. He was an expert tracker, the Pahvant who saw the dragging marks of the travois, and he had noticed many details. There had been three people, he said, one wearing oddly fashioned moccasins and leading an unshod horse which left a slewed print. One of the three was very small and had long yellow hair—a wisp had clung to a branch. The third person was wounded—there had been blood in the canyon—and this one rode on the travois. They had left the ravine the day before, the Pahvant guessed, they were moving slowly. Josh Wade knew at once who they were, and sought out Kasota, who still seethed that he did not carry a yellow scalp.

Josh needed a strong horse to take the trail and he wanted a good mount for Kasota, who was going with him. The Mormons approved the Destroying Angel's mission. There must be no survivors of the massacre to carry the tale. Josh headed for the Mormons who were guarding the wagons to keep the Indians from looting. They waited nervously for the expected arrival of Isaac Haight and Colonel Dame. Mountain Meadows was not a pleasant sight that Saturday morning.

Some of the bodies had been thrown into the rifle pits, mostly those of the men, for they had fallen nearest the train. Nothing had been done about the corpses near the oaks, and wolves had come into the meadow after night fell. They could hear them snarling and fighting over their feast, it sounded like dozens of them. One wolf had sat on the sky line of a near hill and mourned all night, a terrible sobbing cry. There had been superstitious whispers that a woman had escaped and had gone mad. No wolf had ever been heard to sound like that. None ventured to put a bullet toward the sound, be it animal or human. They huddled near their large fires and shivered, avoiding each other's eyes.

Those guarding the thoroughbreds—at Bishop Klingensmith's order—looked up to see Josh Wade loping toward them, rifle in hand, Kasota at his shoulder.

Josh paid no attention to their covert stares. He walked up and laid his hand on the thick, arching neck of Ebony King. The stallion snorted his offense at the familiarity and tried to rear, his nostrils flaring. "I'm takin' this horse," Josh announced to Klingensmith. His eyes searched among the other horses, "and that gray mare for Kasota," he pointed to the sturdy Juno.

Klingensmith stiffened, his eyes were dull with exhaustion. "I got orders from President Isaac Haight," he said ploddingly, "these here horses is reserved for him."

Josh's face became ugly, the stare he laid on the obedient bishop was sardonic. "Them emigrators done fer my gelding," he said, "and Haight set safe on his ass at home. You just mention I said that—to *Brother Isaac!*" Suddenly his head lowered, he stared at Klingensmith. "*You* goin' to try to stop me?"

The bishop's heavily jowled face was set in an odd expression. He was thinking of the torrents of rage Haight would loose on him if the thoroughbreds were not delivered into his clean, aristocratic hands. Wade was right, Klingensmith thought painfully, Haight *had* stayed safely away; his hands were not stained with the actuality of Mountain Meadows.

Klingensmith's sloping shoulders straightened slightly. He loosened the King's rein, handed it to Josh Wade. "I'll saddle him for you," he said, his rebellion complete and satisfying.

Late in the afternoon Crazy Horse knew that he must find a place where they could hole up. Jed had been unconscious the last several hours, sagging against his binding, his face like that of a corpse. Melissa reeled in the saddle, her haunted, narrow face sunken with weariness.

They had come down into the sandy channel of the Virgen River and it was slow going, for the sand was soft, hindering the horses. Where it was wet they sunk deep, floundered. The stream was only a shallow trickle in the middle of its wide bed. High marks against the red walls of its gorge showed that there were seasons in which it became a torrential flood.

The boy found what he sought—a place where high rocks divided and a small ravine slashed the rock wall of the river gorge. The floor rose and widened out, a mass of scrub oak and cactus choked the ravine a few yards up its length. The red sandstone was eroded but it rose high, almost meeting above his head. And up a steeply slanted incline was a small cave. It stank of its last occupants, a coyote bitch had littered here and it was filthy with debris, gnawed bones and bits of trash. But it was shelter and the tenants long gone, the smell was stale and old.

The boy's reason for halting their flight was twofold; Jed could stand no more and the storm seemed about to burst upon them. They must be above the level of the river bed if it flooded and they should have shelter. Crazy Horse lifted his face to the angry heavens and besought his god to let the torrent loose—wipe out the traces of their passage.

They toiled up between the rocks and beyond to the bushy clearing. They urged the buckskin up and into the mouth of the cave. The patient little mare only whickered her disgust at the smell of it. Melissa bathed Jed's ashen face, tried to give him water. He swallowed weakly but his eyes did not open.

Crazy Horse unsaddled the horses, left them loose in the scraggly grass. Palouse grazed wearily for a moment and then lifted his head, turned it back over his shoulder, his pointed ears pricked. He was listening. The boy froze, watching the horse, and turned slowly to face the same direction, his face strained with listening. Then the sorrel turned her head, her ears flicked sharply and before the boy could leap to her she lifted her nose and her clarion neigh trumpeted through the ravine, echoing and re-echoing.

Melissa sprang down the incline to help, for the sorrel was excitedly plunging in evading circles. The boy could not lay a hand on her. And then both youngsters stopped, their eyes met in horrified significance. From a distance, but still distinct and clear, came a reply to the mare—a stallion's whistling, brassy blast!

"Ebony King!" Melissa's eyes mirrored the terror she felt. The King was in the hands of the Indians—or worse, the Mormons.

Crazy Horse understood that she recognized the stallion's call. Pursuers were almost upon them, and for only one reason. He ran for the cave with Melissa at his heels.

Jed was still unconscious. With a despairing, farewell look at his friend, the boy took the revolver from the scout's belt. He turned to Melissa, his face suddenly old and sad. He drew Jed's knife from its sheath, handed it to her. She accepted it numbly. He put a hand on her shoulder, looked into her face. "Sister," he said and tightened the hand lovingly, "if I—not stop them—you kill—"

Her face went sick. Crazy Horse nodded pleadingly. "Kill sister." He turned the blade toward her breast. "Crazy Horse go down—you kill, quick!" His narrow face twisted painfully. "They not kill squaw quick—*very bad way for squaw to die!*"

Then he was gone, leaping down the incline and toward the tall rocks near the stream bed, to meet the enemy from cover. He had five shots in the revolver and a knife in his belt.

The stallion's peremptory shriek sounded again, very close. The mare screamed in answer and rushed past the boy, heading for the opening between the rocks. She slipped on loose shale, fell and scrambled; regaining her feet she trumpeted her fury and hurled herself through the narrow passage. She plunged headlong across the path of Ebony King.

Josh had heard the mare and he had not tried to keep the stallion quiet, knowing the big horse would lead them directly to the quarry. The stallion was intent on the trail of one of his own mares. The King had been quiveringly restive, eager to travel much faster than the hazardous trail permitted.

That last call from the mare had been close and Josh reached toward the saddle scabbard for his rifle and turned to call to Kasota, who rode some yards to his rear.

It was then that Jane hurled from the opening. The King reared, blasted a startled roar of anger at her. She struck against him and he made a sideways plunge. Josh was flung from the saddle into the stream. His rifle splashed into the muddy water.

Juno, who had lunged forward as Kasota's heels dug into her, plowed past the opening in the rocks. At almost point-blank range Crazy Horse leveled the heavy revolver at the Pahvant and fired. The Indian flung up his arms, a torn, dark hole was in his chest. Juno bolted, carrying him away with tremendous strides. Some distance away he slid from her back, landing in the stream, lay unstirring.

Josh rolled behind the only shelter the stream afforded, a long, sandstone boulder which partly shielded his huge form. He peered around its edge, only to flatten hastily as a shot sent rock fragments whistling about his head. The boy's desperate aim was good. The next shot caught Josh high in the left shoulder.

Josh lay on his belly, cursing horribly. His rifle was lying uselessly in the muddy water, he drew his revolver, found it the same—coated with slimy mud. Now the bearded giant took stock of his situation.

The sharpshooter was the boy, Crazy Horse; he had caught a glimpse of him. Not Jed Smith, which meant that the scout was badly wounded or he would have been on his feet somehow, he would not have left the defense to the youngster. The Indian was holding a revolver, he knew that from the sound, which meant he had no rifle. He had fired three times, if he could be drawn to shoot twice more, Josh figured he could jump him before he had time to reload.

Josh gathered the muscles of his back and legs, lunged up and as swiftly down again. His ruse was rewarded, a hurried shot and the rock splinters whined. It had been very near. But Josh grinned through his beard, which dripped with muddy water. The kid was getting jumpy, he reasoned, that shot was too fast. One more bullet—and he'd best not give him time to think about it. But he heard a sound, and knew the boy was approaching, coming to take point-blank aim, he was too close already.

Josh flung himself back and to one side, hoping to dodge the shot. He heard the click as the hammer came down—the last cartridge did not fire, it was a dud.

Josh reared to his feet, dripping with mud, ready to leap and catch Crazy Horse before he had time to reload. But the boy stood at the stream's edge with the revolver clubbed in one hand as he drew the knife from his belt with the other.

Josh remained in a half crouch as he realized the boy's predicament. There were no reloads for the revolver, Crazy Horse intended to fight him hand to hand! The big man's beard parted in a fierce smile, he admired the wild courage, knew the youngster would fight with the viciousness of an enraged wildcat—but what wildcat ever downed a cougar?

Josh drew his knife, stepped slowly forward, watching intently to see if the boy would panic, or chance a throw with his knife. The boy stood rock still. His eyes were beady above the proud nose. He did not give an inch before the man's approach.

Melissa, the knife in her shaking hand, stayed in the cave for only a moment. How would she know when to —— Her mind blanked, she could not conceive of it. There was a scramble of sound, the King's angry blast, the slapping roar of the revolver.

She slid down the incline and crept along the ravine, neared the opening when the second shot sounded. And then a third and after a breathless silence the fourth. They had all been from a revolver, she realized, and from just outside the rock opening. There had been no return fire and the girl crept on. Palouse was there in the rocks, his ears pricked forward. She came up beside the stocky horse, peered over his shoulder. She saw the boy just to the left of the opening. He raised the revolver aiming at a rock in midstream. Then she saw the shoulder of a man behind the rock. And clearly heard the empty click from the revolver.

With stark terror Melissa saw the hulking form of Josh Wade rise from the stream, draw his knife, and begin his slow advance on the slender boy. Melissa faltered against Palouse, her shaking hand grasped a hold of his mane and she remembered the awful blow he had delivered, charging against the Indian in his path. She flung herself astride the gelding, urged him through the opening and out into the stream bed.

Josh's eyes widened with surprise as the girl rode out on the horse. Her face was ice white, her eyes blazed with terrified fury, her hands were clenched in the gelding's mane.

Josh laughed suddenly. "Ride, sister!" he shouted, "run off–hide–it won't do no good! I'll take care of this youngun and be after you–ride, now, dammit–make it a good try!"

Fear and hate erupted within Melissa and gave voice in a strangled shriek as she slammed her knees against Palouse's muscled barrel. She was almost unseated as the gelding hurled violently into the charge, launching himself straight at Josh.

The man was caught off balance. He tried to leap aside but his foot slipped, he went down on one knee as the gelding struck him, the broad, hard chest like an avalanche against his shouder. Josh went down, but his knife found the horse's belly and the gelding screamed.

Melissa was flung from his back as the horse swerved

and reared. She rolled in the water, dashed the mud from her eyes, to see Palouse attacking again. Screaming with tortured rage he was high on his hind legs, brought both front hoofs slashing down like cleavers.

The girl could only watch in horror, and presently, his sides heaving, nostrils flaring at the smell of blood, Palouse backed away from the motionless dark form. Crazy Horse came to him, placed his hand soothingly, lovingly on the thick neck, watched beside him, knife at the ready, to see if Josh Wade still lived. But the bearded man lay still, and the boy could see that the back of his head was crushed.

Jed's eyes opened slowly. He stared in dull bewilderment at the roof of the cave. There was an odd smell and a drumming, washing sound—there was also the woodsy aroma of smoke. The scout turned his head painfully, stared through gray gloom. Melissa squatted at the back of the cave, feeding twigs carefully into the sputtering flames of a small fire. Beyond the mouth of the cave silver rain slanted, struck splashingly on the rocks. It was a downpour, a cloudburst, and Jed closed his eyes with deep thanksgiving. The boy had found a place to hole up—and it was raining, their trail would be wiped out. But he suffered a shock when he opened his eyes again. Two long rifles were propped against the wall of the cave, one of them was smeared with mud.

Then he heard the pounding of hoofs and a stallion's snorting neigh. It was the King—it could only be Ebony King, that wrathful, brassy bellow. Jed rolled on his side, peered down the slant beyond the cave. Inexplicably the gray mare, Juno, plunged past, and the sorrel, and then the black stallion, his coat shining satin with the rain. Crazy Horse appeared, his brown hide a shining wet bronze. He had driven the horses into the little brushy clearing. Jed could see the buckskin and Palouse, also, now.

Crazy Horse came wearily up the incline, but his exhaustion-lined face was peaceful. He had concealed the two bodies under rocks, the rain would obliterate all trace of them. He had retrieved Josh's rifle from the stream; Juno still bore Kasota's in the saddle scabbard when he caught her. He had driven the horses into the ravine and rolled rocks, piled branches high, clogging the opening, penning them. There would be no tracks to indicate anyone had entered the wash.

The boy felt confidence now in their situation. They had five strong horses, two rifles, three revolvers, and a good supply of powder and shot in the saddlebags of Josh and Kasota. There had also been some food; he need not hunt immediately. Melissa had started a fire with the flint from Jed's gear, so they could dry out, stay warm, there was plenty of wood for the taking in the little gulch. The three of them would be safe here until Little Ax was able to ride. When the rain stopped, Crazy Horse would mount guard. Until then he could rest.

The boy shook the rain from his face, saw that Jed's eyes were open, cognizant and bewildered. Melissa turned her head and saw his consciousness at the same time. The two youngsters squatted on either side of him, she to lift his head and help him to drink. Jed swallowed, choked a little, put a protesting hand against the canteen. "For God's sake—tell me—what happened—"

The shadows deepened outside the cave, but the fire, now burning steadily, cast a rosy glow on the two tired young faces as they soberly told Jed of the day's events. The scout lay still when he knew the whole of it. He looked at first one thin face and then the other, unsteadily reached a hand to each, felt the quick grasp and warmth of their response.

Then he remembered, concern was in his voice. "Palouse?" he asked anxiously, "is he—?"

Melissa nodded reassuringly. "He took a gash in his belly. We plastered it with clay—it's stopped bleeding—he'll be all right."

The three ate a little, too exhausted to want to chew. Outside the cave was wet, black gloom, but inside, though it reeked of damp coyote stink, it was warm, peaceful. They spread the blanket from the travois over Jed, and the boy and Melissa crept beneath it on either side of him for warmth, for the wet of the fall night became cold.

Very soon the deep breathing told Jed that the two slept heavily, the sleep of complete exhaustion. But the scout did not sleep. His eyes were somberly on the rock roof of the cave, dim now in the dying glow from the fire.

In a few days he would be able to ride—his body healed fast, many times he had taken wounds greater than this. They would ride fast, at night for two or three days, put country between themselves and Mountain Meadows. But not south. Jed came to a quiet decision. He thought it out, how it must be, there in the quiet of the little cave.

They would circle and turn north, back to the plains and friends—Crazy Horse's people, the Sioux. They could lose themselves among the tribes, become Little Ax and his squaw, the yellow-hair. Perhaps they would go further north, into the Canadian Rockies—some of the Sioux had already gone, they were moving away from the troubles caused by the pushing inroads of the immigrant trains of demanding whites. And Jed knew he must remove himself and Melissa far beyond the reach of Mormon vengeance—and the stalking of the Mormon wolf pack—the Destroying Angels. No word must ever be voiced that he was Jed Smith, scout, and she Melissa Boller of the Fancher Train. It would be a death sentence, delayed, perhaps, but inevitable.

The bitterness of his thoughts faded before the memory of the country they would seek. Beyond the Powder River and the Wind—the fast-running white water of the snowy slopes, the good taste of fresh red meat. The clean, wilderness look of being untrod by man, uncluttered by his quarrelsome passage.

He remembered a blue, mirror-like lake high in the range of mountains that Meriwether Lewis had named for himself. The lake had no name, it was small, a sapphire jewel known only to the few who had seen it. Beautiful, of an evening, when the buck came stepping cautiously down to drink, the doe and fawn gentle in his track. Circled with tall pine and silver-white aspen on its rocky shore. And a sandy beach in one place, a good place for a cabin—a cabin, with Melissa cooking his vittles at the big fireplace he would put up for her. Maybe there she would lose the haunted look in her slanting eyes. After a while maybe the color and the dimples would return to her thin cheeks. She would learn to smile once again, forget, at times, what took place at Mountain Meadows.

His arm was around her, he pulled her gently closer to him. She was curled against him like a puppy, she whimpered in her sleep a little, nosing against him. He turned his head so he could have the warm smell of her hair in his nose and presently, he, too, slept deeply.

# AUTHOR'S NOTE

For the reader interested in historical accuracy I would like to say that the main events in this novel are true. The massacre at Haun's Mill occurred in October 1838; eighteen people were killed and as many wounded. The massacre at Mountain Meadows took place on or about September 11, 1857. About one hundred and fifty adults and older children were slaughtered; eighteen small children and babies were spared and taken into Mormon homes. Several years later the federal government assumed custody of these small survivors and returned most of them to relatives in the East.

Many of the lesser events in the book are also factual although some of them have been woven around fictitious characters. Little is known of the personnel of the Fancher Train, all that remains is an incomplete list of names and families of those who were from Arkansas. I have used some names from this list, others I have invented. There is no list of the Missouri-Illinois contingent although it is recorded fact that they joined the Fancher Train someplace on the overland trail.

With the exception of Josh Wade, who is a composite of Porter Rockwell and Bill Hickman, notorious Destroying Angels, I have not invented any of the Mormon characters in the book—all the people lived at that time where I placed them and were concerned in the events related. I have not invented any of the major happenings and, to the best of my knowledge, supported by years of study of history, autobiography and several unpublished journals of early Mormons, there is nothing contrary to the main historical truth of the incidents.

The Mormon pioneers were painstaking keepers of journals and a great many of these have survived. I have been fortunate in that a few of these uncensored diaries were made accessible to me. In an effort to suppress unfavorable publicity which would have aggravated their already precarious position the Mormon Church officially blamed the Indians for the massacre at Mountain Meadows. The leaders tried, without success, to keep it a secret and deleted from the Journal History of the Church most references which would have signified that Mormons were involved.

As to the pressures which finally pushed the Mormons in the southern settlements into a frame of mind in which massacre was possible, the sequence of events was exactly as I have told them: the army was approaching to deal with treason and rebellion, those in the isolated southern settlements believed implicitly that another army approached from California; the horror of the persecutions in Missouri and Illinois had been recalled to their minds by the crusading preachers Brigham Young had sent out to rouse them to the point of readiness to fight; the Beloved Apostle, Parley Pratt, had been murdered in Arkansas; and finally, there were troublemakers in the Fancher Train who had involved themselves continually in ugly incidents as they passed through the territory, finally focusing on themselves all the hate and fear of the enemy. Also, the first plan to raid the wagon train was actually in emulation of Brigham Young's tactics—he had sent a guerrilla force to raid and hamper the approaching army.

The speeches of Brigham Young and his leaders in which they incited the people to secession were taken literally from the *Journal of Discourses*, a Mormon publication. In only one instance have I knowingly distorted actual historical sequence of events—I placed the Morrisite Massacre as having happened in 1856, it took place, as told, but in 1862.

The character of Jed Smith is fictitious, although it is

recorded that Jim Bridger was at Fort Laramie in the summer of 1857 and supplied several trains with veteran mountain men as scouts. Young Crazy Horse, of later Little Big Horn fame, was actually about fifteen years old in 1857 and traveled with his people near the overland trail to the Great Council of the Teton Lakotas.

As to those who insist that there were no adult survivors of the Mountain Meadows Massacre, I would remind them of the escape group of which only one man, William Aden, was known to have been killed. Of the other two, or three, mystery shrouds their fate. That two of them were unable to rejoin the wagon train is known. The Paiutes, notoriously unwarlike and given to lying rather than exertion on occasions, were the only ones to assert they had been finished off but there is no actual evidence to support this claim.

I have been pleased to present John D. Lee in what was his actual role in the massacre—that of a man reluctantly obeying the orders of his military and religious superiors. For many years, possibly because he was the only man executed for the atrocity, he has suffered the stigma of being not only the leader but the instigator of the whole incident.

It is an established fact that the massacre, as such, was not planned until the night before it took place. It is also true that the Indians attacked ahead of their orders and that they were becoming hostile toward their Mormon neighbors. The Pahvants, Kanosh and Kasota, lived and were involved in the massacre. Kanosh's wife, Sally, actually was raised in Brigham Young's household. The incident concerning her is partly true, and there had been a situation which aroused Kanosh to a fury of vengeance. I believe that, at the time, the Mormons were so enmeshed that they could see no alternative, although it is a matter of record that the express rider, William Haslam, did make the long ride to Salt Lake City and returned with direct orders from Brigham Young expressly forbidding the attack on any emigrant train.

Because of the violence and bloodshed in this book

many readers may feel that I have sensationalized actual events. I would like to say that I have diminished rather than accented the ugliness of true details in several incidents. I gathered my facts concerning the massacres at Haun's Mill and Mountain Meadows from the writings of people who experienced them. Official records of the Missouri-Illinois persecutions are incontrovertible historical facts. Equally indisputable is evidence concerning the massacre of the Fancher wagon train—these people were betrayed, disarmed, and then slaughtered. Their bones still lie under a deep cairn of rocks at Mountain Meadows about one hundred miles from where I write this. Following the massacre the Mormons and Indians stripped and looted the bodies and, after a division of spoils was made, quit the scene as hastily as possible. It has long been debatable whether they buried the bodies. If so, admittedly the shallow graves were dug hurriedly, for wolves and coyotes desecrated the remains and scattered bones far about the meadows. Decent burial did not take place until 1859—nearly two years later—when Federal Judge John Cradlebaugh, with a military escort, arrived in the area bent on investigating the massacre. The dragoons gathered and buried the bones into one common grave and erected a twelve-foot cairn of rocks above it. An unknown soldier placed a rough cross at its summit on which was carved the words "Vengeance is mine and I will repay saith the Lord." A stone slab bore the inscription "Erected by Company K 1st Dragoons, May 1859."

Amelia Bean
*Kanab, Utah*
*December 6, 1957*

A
ace
A